Praise for *Love*

". . . a **sweeping historical epic** and a sensitively observed exploration of the passionate friendship between Colonna and Michelangelo . . . . the poet's story and her journey as a woman and a writer are dynamic and multilayered. . . . **A stirring and emotionally resonant portrait** of a pivotal relationship in the life of Michelangelo." – *Kirkus Reviews* (starred review)

"… **an intimate, rich, engrossing glimpse into the life of one of the most celebrated poets of the Renaissance and her extraordinary relationship with Michelangelo.** Anyone who loves being immersed in historical detail that's woven organically into a seamless narrative will love this beautifully researched and written novel." – Susanne Dunlap, author of *Émilie's Voice and Liszt's Kiss*

". . . an elegant portrayal of the friendship between the poet and the artist who stirred her from solitude. **Intimate and perspective-driven, it explores faith, love, and the lines where public and private life converge.**" – *Foreword* Clarion Reviews

"In this exquisite novel, Linda Cardillo brings the world of Renaissance Italy and this brilliant, heroic woman magnificently to life. **Brimming with action and passion**, *Love That Moves* the Sun grabbed hold of me and never let go." – Judith Arnold, *USA Today* bestselling author

". . . **absolutely absorbing**. . . *Love That Moves the Sun* will stay with the reader long after the last page is turned" – Parris Afton Bonds, *New York Times* bestselling author

". . . **a breathtaking novel, offering a magical blend of love story and Renaissance art and history.**" – Five-Star Amazon Review

LOVE THAT MOVES THE SUN

Vittoria Colonna and
Michelangelo Buonarroti

A Novel ·

LINDA CARDILLO

BELLASTORIA PRESS

Stories from the heart

ISBN: 978-1-942209-54-6
Love That Moves the Sun

Love That Moves the Sun is a work of fiction. Names, characters, places and incidents are the product of the author's imagination or are used fictitiously and are not to be construed as real. Any resemblance to actual events, locations, organizations or persons, living or dead, is entirely coincidental.

Cover art by Eliza Moser

BELLASTORIA PRESS
P.O. Box 60341
Longmeadow, Massachusetts 01116

For my family

"…but my desire and will were moved already…
by the Love that moves the sun and the other stars."

Dante Alighieri, Paradiso, Canto XXXIII

AUTHOR'S NOTE

As a writer of historical fiction, I am grateful for the scholarship and research of historians who have provided me with fundamental details of the lives of Vittoria Colonna and Michelangelo Buonarroti. I have attempted to remain faithful to the facts, but in instances where the record is either obscure, conflicted or missing because of lost or nonexistent documents, I have chosen—as writers of fiction are wont to do—to make things up.

What follows is not a biography but an imagined story of a relationship between two extraordinary artists. Based on their own words, in the remaining letters and poetry they shared with one another, I have created an inner life that reflects their mutual search for transcendence. To readers who may ask "What is true?" or "Did that actually happen?" I answer that I have followed the trajectory of what is known, with perhaps a slight adjustment of time now and then. But within the walls of the Castello d'Aragonese or the Convent of Santa Caterina or the house in the Macello dei Corvi, it is the heart that speaks the truth.

CONTENTS

LIST OF MAJOR CHARACTERS

Historical Figures

Michelangelo Buonarroti, the artist
Vittoria Colonna, the poet

The Colonna Family

Fabrizio Colonna, military leader and father of Vittoria

Agnese di Montefeltro, daughter of the Duke of Urbino and mother of Vittoria

Ascanio Colonna, brother of Vittoria

Federigo Colonna, brother of Vittoria

Pompeo Colonna, cousin of Fabrizio Colonna, military leader and cardinal

Prospero Colonna, cousin of Fabrizio and Pompeo, military leader

The d'Avalos Family

Ferrante Francesco d'Avalos, Vittoria's husband and a celebrated military leader

Costanza d'Avalos, chatelaine of Ischia, aunt of Ferrante

Alfonso d'Avalos del Vasto, nephew of Costanza, adopted son of Ferrante and Vittoria

Beatrice d'Avalos, sister-in-law of Costanza and aunt of Ferrante

Gian Giacomo Trivulzio, husband of Beatrice and uncle of Ferrante

The Popes and the Years They Reigned

Alexander VI (Rodrigo Borgia) 1492-1503

Pius III (Francesco Piccolomini) 1503

Julius II (Giuliano della Rovere) 1503-13

Leo X (Giovanni de' Medici) 1513-21

Adrian VI (Adrian Dedel) 1522-23

Clement VII (Giulio de' Medici) 1523-34
Paul III (Alessandro Farnese) 1534-49

The Monarchs and their Courts

Kingdom of Naples

King Federigo IV of Naples (1452-1504)

Queen Isabella, wife of King Federigo IV

Ferdinando d'Aragona y Guardato, brother of King Federigo

Castellana Cardona, wife of Ferdinando d'Aragona

Giovanna d'Aragona, daughter of Ferdinando d'Aragona and wife of Ascanio Colonna

Maria d'Aragona, daughter of Ferdinando d'Aragona and wife of Alfonso d'Avalos del Vasto

Ramón de Cardona, Spanish Viceroy of Naples and commander of the Holy League forces at the Battle of Ravenna

Isabella de Cardona, Spanish Vicereine of Naples

Spain

Ferdinand II (1452-1516), King of Spain, also known as Ferdinand III of Naples

Charles I (1500-1558), King of Spain and later Charles V, Emperor of the Holy Roman Empire

France

Louis XII (1462-1515), King of France

François I (1494-1547), King of France, cousin of Louis XII; rival of Charles V for leadership of the Holy Roman Empire; military leader in the Italian wars

Marguerite d'Angoulême (1492-1549), Queen of Navarre, sister of François I; poet, supporter of humanists and reformers, and friend of Vittoria

The Dukes and their Courts

Alfonso I d'Este, Duke of Ferrara, ally of France during the War of the League of Cambrai

Isabella d'Este, sister of Alfonso I and wife of Francesco II Gonzaga, Marquess of Mantua

Delia, lady-in-waiting to Isabella d'Este

Mario Equicola, secretary to Isabella d'Este

Ercole II d'Este, Duke of Ferrara, son of Alfonso I and husband of Renata di Francia

Renata di Francia (also known as Renée of France), Duchess of Ferrara, wife of Ercole II d'Este and daughter of King Louis XII of France

Lucia of Narni, mystic and spiritual advisor of Alfonso I

Military Leaders

Gaston de Foix, Duc de Nemours and commander of the French at the Battle of Ravenna

Pedro Navarro, commander of Spanish infantry and artillery at the Battle of Ravenna

Charles de Lannoy, leader with Ferrante d'Avalos at the Battle of Pavia

Charles III, Duke of Bourbon, leader with Ferrante d'Avalos at the Battle of Pavia

Poets, Writers and Vatican Emissaries

Pietro Bembo (1470-1547), secretary to Pope Leo X, scholar, poet and writer promoting Italian as a literary language; later instrumental in the dissemination of Vittoria's poetry

Giovanni Pietro Carafa, cardinal and founder of the Italian Inquisition

Ippolito de' Medici, cardinal and nephew of Pope Clement VII

Paolo Giovio (1483-1552), physician, historian and close friend of Vittoria

Tommaso Inghirami, Vatican librarian

Jacopo Sadoleto, secretary to Pope Leo X, humanist, poet and reformer

Jacopo Sannazzaro (1456-1530), court poet to the house of Aragon; author of *Arcadia*; frequent member of Costanza d'Avalos' salon

Reformist Religious Writers and Preachers

Bernardino Ochino (1487-1564), general of the Capuchin order of monks and itinerant preacher who gave voice to the reform movement in the Church and ultimately converted to Protestantism

Juan de Valdés (1509-1541, Spanish religious writer and preacher who influenced Ochino and Pietro Carnesecchi

The "Spirituali"—A Circle of Writers, Poets and Clerics Who Explored Questions of Faith

Cardinal Reginald Pole

Cardinal Gasparo Contarini

Pietro Carnesecchi

Marcantonio Flaminio

Vittoria's Friends

Caterina Cibo, Duchess of Camerino and supporter of the Capuchins

Giulia Gonzaga, Vittoria's cousin

Carlo Gualteruzzi, Vittoria's secretary and agent

Innocenza Gualteruzzi, daughter of Carlo Gualteruzzi

Michelangelo's Friends and Household

Baccio Rontini, Florentine physician

Urbino (Francesco d'Amadore, called "Urbino"), Michelanglo's assistant.

Fictional Characters
(in order of appearance)

Beata, Vittoria's childhood nurse

Nicolo and Salviata, Vittoria's servants

Arturo, chamberlain to Costanza d'Avalos

Alberto Moretti, singer and guest of Costanza d'Avalos

Giancarlo Brittonio, tutor to Alfonso d'Avalos del Vasto

Giacomo Porzio, Neapolitan baron

Suora Carita, gatekeeper of the Convent of San Silvestro

Suora Francesca, secretary and later Reverend Mother of the
Convent of San Silvestro

Suora Ursula, gatekeeper of the Convent of Santa Caterina

Clara and Barbara, members of Vittoria's traveling group of
women

Lady Alessandra, member of the court of Ercole II d' Este

Italy in the 16th Century

HISTORICAL NOTE

In the late 15th and 16th centuries, the Italian peninsula was home to widely divergent and unstable forms of government—small principalities, mainly in the north, led by powerful dynastic families; republics, such as Florence and Venice, ruled by equally powerful merchant families; the papal states, a vast temporal territory in the middle of the country controlled by the pope; and, to the south, the Kingdom of Naples, alternately held by Spain and France.

Between 1494 and 1559, Italy was in an almost constant state of war as Spain and France fought violently to establish and maintain control over the divided country. Territory was gained and lost; allegiances swung from one side to the next; and the condottieri, leaders of mercenary armies, moved from one battle to the next as treaties failed or changes in rulers set off yet another round of fighting.

During the same time period, the Roman Catholic Church was in a state of upheaval as the ideas of Martin Luther made their way south to Italy, threatening the power of the pope and introducing revolutionary ideas about individual spirituality.

1534

CHAPTER ONE

Having Seen Your Face

Michelangelo
1534
Florence

"Florence does not love you, Michelangelo, but Rome will."

Night visitors. Subdued voices. Despite the low murmurs, it is impossible to ignore the urgency, the warning in their message.

"His Holiness, Pope Clement, summons you. Not merely for his own pleasure, but for your safety. You have too many enemies in Florence. The Duke Alessandro de' Medici you know. His rancor toward you has only been held in check by his fear of his uncle on the papal throne. But there are others, hidden behind false smiles. The pope says, 'enough of hiding in the closets of your friends.' He can better protect you in Rome. You must leave now," they insist.

Michelangelo observes the faces of these papal messengers in the candlelight. They had not awakened him. When they made their stealthy entrance, he was bent over his worktable, sketching the staircase for the Medici library. Marble dust spills from his hair where it had settled earlier in the day, when he'd been at work on another project, an unfinished sculpture of Apollo.

He is almost sixty. Tired of being pursued to fulfill the demands of others. Weary of the complaints of his ungrateful relatives, currently asleep below. Bereft at the loss of his beloved younger brother. The words spoken by these midnight visitors strike a nerve.

Florence does not love you.

"Urbino!" He shouts for his assistant.

The young man rouses himself and enters the studio, his eyes widening at the presence of strangers.

"Prepare the horses and saddlebags for a journey. We leave tonight."

"Where are we going? What shall I bring? Shall I inform anyone of our departure?"

Michelangelo answers the last question first. "Leave no word at all. Pack only the drawings I have been working on for the pope's altar wall and enough money to get us to Rome. These gentlemen will accompany us."

He sees the visitors exchange glances. They must have been expecting a more difficult task in persuading him. When Julius was pope, his messengers had been chased back to Rome empty-handed by a much younger Michelangelo. Not tonight.

Urbino moves silently around the room, gathering the drawings Michelangelo requested and rolling them into a leather pouch. He finds Michelangelo's warmest cloak thrown in a heap by the door and presses it into his master's hands, along with fur-lined gloves and the battered felt hat he refuses to replace. Michelangelo takes the warm clothing as Urbino descends to the horses.

"Do not wake the rest of the household," he cautions.

The young man turns his head and nods.

The pope's men are pacing, casting anxious glances at the eastern sky for the first signs of dawn. Michelangelo observes them as he pulls on his boots. He has done this before, escaped one city or another ahead of enemies; fled through secret passageways; eluded those who would break down doors or pursue him over mountain passes. He vows to himself that this will be the last time.

He forces himself up from the bench as he hears Urbino's whistle. The horses are saddled. He grabs the satchel with the drawings, wraps the cloak around his shoulders and heads down the stairs.

Urbino waits in the courtyard with a lantern, stamping his feet in the cold. He hands Michelangelo a sack, weighty with coin.

"I had to climb over three snoring men to get to the strongbox, but I woke no one," he assures Michelangelo.

"Well done. Now to the road, before the whole city, let alone the household, realizes we're gone."

The artist, Urbino and their papal escort ride hard in the bitter cold and push beyond the boundaries of Florentine jurisdiction before they stop. Michelangelo never turns to look back.

When they finally arrive in Rome, the pope's men insist on bringing him to Pope Clement at once.

"Are you afraid I'll slip away from the pope as I have from his nephew?" But he goes with them. Clement is not the first pope he has served. He has learned to pick his battles, and this is not one of them.

As their small party charges through the Vatican corridors, he catches the shock of recognition on the faces of various men in the papal court. At least one, a bishop, moves quickly away.

"That one will have a messenger galloping to Alessandro de' Medici within the hour," he murmurs to his travelling companions.

"Did we not warn you truthfully?"

"I came, didn't I?"

They are halted outside the pope's audience chamber by two of the Swiss Guards installed by Pope Julius decades before.

"His Holiness is in conversation with two noblewomen from the south. We have been ordered to deny entry until they depart."

"Maestro, perhaps I should go on and open up the house and find us some dinner?"

Michelangelo sees the wisdom in Urbino's suggestion. There is no need for his young assistant to wait for Clement.

It is not Urbino the pope has summoned. Some of the weariness brought on by the journey is relieved by Urbino's mention of the house in the Macello dei Corvi. Michelangelo had purchased it with money secured when he'd renegotiated his contract with Pope Julius's heirs for the tomb that has burdened him for far too long. Clement had stepped in, found him a lawyer and made known his own interest in having Michelangelo freed from the overwhelming demands of Julius's original grand plans.

"I have waited long enough to have you for myself and *my* plans," the pope had shouted when he first took office.

The statues for the much-reduced tomb stand in the garden of Michelangelo's house. They are a reminder of the still-uncompleted work, but the house itself is a well-ordered refuge, not a hovel of a workshop and makeshift living space as he'd had when he was a younger man.

"Buy us some fish for tonight. And get the fires going. My body will need warmth before I can begin whatever it is Clement has as his heart's desire."

Michelangelo seeks out a bench and leans against the wall, the weariness that had been kept at bay by the urgency of their departure now creeping through his old man's bones. He closes his eyes but is granted only a brief respite as the door to the pope's chamber is thrust open.

He rises to his feet as two women emerge. One is dark-haired, severely dressed, agitated. The other, attired in a Spanish gown, moves serenely. But the haunted quality of her face suggests an intimacy with anguish. From beneath her veil, a wisp of gold curl is visible. She moves past without noticing him, her head bent as she listens to the high-pitched chatter of her companion.

"Who is that woman?" he asks the guards.

"The poet Vittoria Colonna, the Marchesa di Pescara. The widow of the hero of Pavia."

He knows the name. He knows the poems. *Of course*, he reflects. This is how he would have imagined her face, her presence. This is how he would have painted her.

He watches her move away, still attentive to the other woman, and is glad he has come to Rome.

Michelangelo has slept only fitfully since his arrival in Rome two days before. Despite his investment in a good bed, he has tossed uncomfortably, trying to find a position that eases his aging muscles, sore from the strenuous pace of the journey. If he were honest with himself, however, he would acknowledge that his lack of sleep has more of a mental than a physical cause.

Once again, he is at the mercy of yet another demanding pope. Giulio de' Medici, Pope Clement VII, is dying and wants a legacy. A fresco of Christ's Second Coming.

How many times must I tell them, he reflects, *that I am a sculptor, not a painter?*

He drags himself from the rumpled site of his nightly struggle, shrugs off the breakfast Urbino offers him and trudges in the direction of the Vatican, unable to avoid any longer the blank wall that awaits him in the Sistine Chapel.

When he arrives he is relieved to see that the altar end of the chapel is empty. He has successfully avoided the morning Mass, and most of the attendees have dispersed. He dislikes the drone of voices that reverberate off the walls and the ceiling. When the room is full, he can hear the din from several corridors away. Today, however, all is blessedly quiet.

He has brought neither measuring tools nor the preliminary sketches Urbino carefully packed when they made their escape from Florence. He wants no encumbrances on this first encounter with the wall. He needs to observe the expanse, to touch it, to grasp its dimensions so he can begin in his mind to fill it. Before he paints, he always imagines.

He paces, mainly to stretch his tightened muscles, still coiled from gripping the flanks of his horse. The pacing helps him concentrate, blocking out any distractions as people enter and leave the chapel. He has also noticed that it dissuades people from approaching him with intrusions.

His concentration is broken by a sudden squall of movement—the heavy footsteps of guards followed by a gust of white. Pope Clement's unmistakable voice calls out from the midst of this cloud of motion.

When they were boys in Lorenzo de' Medici's house—Michelangelo as a student in Lorenzo's art school and Giulio, the orphaned, bastard son of Lorenzo's brother Giuliano—Giulio had been the noisy, demanding one. As the youngest, Giulio had to work hard to be heard. When he flies into the chapel now, Michelangelo stops his pacing and faces him with folded arms, waiting for his explosive tirade to end.

"They told me I would find you here. I was about to march over to your house myself and drag you out of your bed or your workroom—wherever you have hidden yourself for the last two days. I told you. I do not have much time left, Michelangelo. God has already whispered twice in my ear that He was calling me home, and both times I answered Him that I still had more to do. This wall is what remains of my legacy. I *will* see you paint it before I die."

"Am I not here? Did I not promise you?" The artist continues to stand. He does not kneel to kiss the pope's ring.

"You are here. But where are the drawings, the scaffolding, the pigments? Have I not advanced you sufficient funds to undertake this endeavor?"

I cannot work if I am to be continually interrupted on his whim, Michelangelo broods. *Better to speak of my need for solitude now before he gets in the habit of stopping by for a visit every day.* He is not afraid to express himself frankly with the pope. He and Giulio understand each other.

"I have everything I need, Holy Father, except the solitude to implement what resides up here." Michelangelo taps his brain with a stained finger.

"Just see that those ideas start migrating to the wall. Soon."

With a flourish, the pope turns away from Michelangelo and leaves the chapel.

When the pope makes his departure as abruptly as he has burst in, Michelangelo resumes his solitary contemplation. But out of the corner of his eye he senses hurried movement, hears the rustle of silk sweeping across the marble floor and a woman's voice murmuring urgently, "Come, Vittoria."

The poet. Was she here again? Michelangelo follows the voice to see the serene woman from two days before trailing her companion. The other woman appears to be in a great hurry to pursue the pontiff, but Michelangelo detects in the poet almost a reluctance to leave the chapel.

When she reaches the doorway she stops and faces him. At first he assumes she's paused for a final glance at the ceiling. It is what people often do, although he himself never wishes to contemplate the fresco again after the years he spent painting it.

But the poet does not look up.

She regards *him*, with intention. Not accidently, as if her gaze is focused on something else and he happens to fall into her line of sight. No, she has deliberately altered her path to see him.

He studies her as purposefully and knowingly as she considers him. She intrigues him. Her poems have made their way to Florence and have certainly been a topic of discussion in his circle. But she is an enigma, despite the grief and deeply felt emotion revealed in her words. Her beauty, tinged with ineffable sadness, is remote, detached. That he sees all this, in the flash of time since she moved past him and then turned to face him, astonishes him.

With her glance alone she appears to be offering this insight into her. She is pursuing something, of that he is sure. And she seems to be seeking it in him.

He cannot avert his eyes. He has never before encountered a woman with such a direct and compelling gaze. She conveys a power and authority that both unnerves him and makes him hungry to be engulfed.

And then her spell is broken. The voice of the other woman beckons her. But before she leaves, the poet nods to him, acknowledging their wordless exchange.

As she departs, he notes the stiffness and formality of her Spanish gown in sharp contrast to the vulnerable beauty of her pale face. One of the ribbons on her sleeve has become undone, a sliver of black silk that ripples behind her when she turns away from him.

He casts a final, fleeting look at the wall and realizes he has no more room in his thoughts to consider the pope's commission this morning, even though the angel of death is hovering in Clement's shadow.

He leaves the Vatican and wanders slowly back to his house, aware of his yearning and his loneliness.

The next day he is in his garden, surrounded by the half-finished statues that remain to be completed for Pope Julius's tomb. But he ignores their hulking presence and sits sketching in the sunlight, taking advantage of the unseasonably warm fall day. Urbino insists on wrapping a cloak around his shoulders and brings him a heated cup of wine. The young man is good to him. Sensible, caring. Not a burden as some of the others have been, foisted upon him by misguided family members.

He dozes for a few minutes, warmed by the sun and the wine, when a commotion at the gate rouses him.

Urbino comes running back.

"Maestro, it's Cardinal Ippolito de' Medici with a beautiful woman."

Michelangelo groans. Now Giulio is sending his nephew to urge him along. Despite the very real dangers to Michelangelo in Florence, perhaps he should have stayed, rather than submit to being constantly watched and prodded. He rises to greet the cardinal and his companion. He wonders which of Ippolito's mistresses is with him. The cardinal's red cassock and broad hat obscure the woman as they approach. And then he sees the dress, unmistakable in its cut and fabric. The dress worn by the poet the day before.

He runs his hand over his hair and beard, smooths his jerkin and throws off the woolen cloak.

"Urbino, bring more wine and cups. And see if we have any cakes. If not, run to the baker."

The young man looks at him in astonishment, frozen.

"Go!" Michelangelo orders and Urbino scampers off.

"Maestro, good afternoon! I hope we are not disturbing your work or my uncle will not forgive me. May I present the Most Honorable Marchesa di Pescara, Vittoria Colonna? Lady Vittoria has expressed an interest in your current work and His Holiness asked me to arrange a meeting."

Like your uncle, you believe you can come unannounced whenever you please, Michelangelo reflects. *I am your servant, subject to your whims*. But the words he speaks out loud are quite different. He takes her hand and bends over it with a kiss. Her touch is delicate yet confident. He notes that despite exuding the fragrance of lavender in which they were probably bathed, her fingers still retain the tell-tale ink stains of a dedicated writer.

"My lady, you honor me with your visit."

"And you honor me by so graciously accepting our intrusion. Please forgive us for coming unannounced, but the cardinal assures me that you do not stand on ceremony."

"My house is always open to Rome, my lady. Especially to a Roman such as you."

Neither one of them mentions the striking encounter they had the day before, but the memory of it lingers in the look that passes between them.

"Come, come sit with me! Unless the air is too cool and you wish to go inside?"

"On the contrary, Maestro, I relish the outdoors and have missed the opportunity to be in the open air since my arrival in Rome."

"If I may ask, what brings you to Rome?"

"The same thing, I imagine, that calls you here. The pope." Her eyes twinkle as she speaks. She glances at the nephew, but he seems to be in agreement. All three of them obey Clement.

She launches into her own question. "I am eager to hear of your plans for the altar wall. I know that it's to depict the Last Judgment, a topic that transfixes me with its message. I can think of no subject more fitting for our times. Would you not agree?"

"We live in a world very different from the one that inspired my earlier work. And I am a different man. To be honest with you, my lady, I have only begun to envision how I might portray Christ's Second Coming."

He sees that Ippolito is already inattentive. Word is, the young cardinal is more interested in parties and plays than the theology of his uncle's wall.

"Shall we wander around the grounds to see the statues, Eminence?" he asks Ippolito. "My servant will be bringing refreshments shortly and we can sit then."

He hopes if they meander through the garden, Ippolito can more easily drift away from their conversation, relieving him of the pretense of courtesy and allowing Michelangelo to pursue his exchange with the poet. She rises enthusiastically in response to his suggestion.

"I have always enjoyed walking as I discuss the great questions that challenge my thoughts."

As Michelangelo anticipated, Ippolito soon finds another path and leaves them to their conversation. But even without him nearby and listening, Michelangelo refrains from bringing up the previous day. The poet avoids the topic, as well, keeping their dialogue focused on art.

"I am fascinated by the role art can play in devotion. Do you consider the uses to which your work will be put when you first set out to create it?"

"I am always mindful of my patron's intentions when a work is commissioned, but as it grows beneath my hands, it often takes on a life of its own. And how others respond after I complete it, well, I cannot control that. As much as I would prefer to...."

"It must be a great responsibility, knowing that all eyes will converge on your work and take meaning from it."

"But surely you've experienced the same terror when someone reads your poetry."

She stops and looks at him with the penetrating gaze that had stirred him in the Sistine Chapel.

"It *is* terrifying! In the beginning, I didn't write my poems for others' eyes and ears. They were my private grief. But now that moment is past. The words do not belong solely to me anymore."

"Is that why you've stayed away from society?"

He senses her closing down her openness. He has never been adept at courtly conversation. He prefers to delve beneath the surface of things or not at all. Clearly he has ventured too far in this first conversation, assuming a level of affinity between them because of their unspoken communication the day before. He is an old fool. Better to engage in these philosophical discussions with his intimate circle of friends, with whom he can bare his soul. No matter how intensely she has seen into him, no matter how eager she seems to be in her search for answers, she is still a noblewoman and a pious widow. The barriers between them are as impenetrable as the fortifications he once designed but never saw completed for Florence. He hopes he has not frightened her off.

At this moment Urbino arrives, breathless, with a carefully wrapped packet of cakes. Michelangelo and his guests return to the rough-hewn table where they began their visit.

His sketches are still lying about and he begins to roll them up. She stops him, placing her slender hand on one that he has not yet retrieved.

"Is this a preliminary sketch for the wall? May I?"

He nods.

She holds it out in front of her, examining the figures scattered haphazardly across the page. Her eyes flare with that same intensity she directed toward him in the chapel. She traces one of the figures with her finger, pausing on the countenance of a woman filled with undefined longing. He has drawn it from memory, his hand working swiftly to capture what he saw there.

She puts the sheet down and covers her face, stifling a barely audible sob that he senses only he has heard. The cardinal is too busy selecting a cake. But Urbino, observant young man that he is, grasps that something has happened.

"My lady, you have caught a fleck of dust in your eye. Please allow me to offer you this handkerchief and a glass of wine." Urbino leaps to her side, each hand offering a remedy.

She smiles at him, wipes her eyes and takes the wine. "To the artist," she proclaims, lifting her goblet in Michelangelo's direction, "who sees humanity's secrets and brings them to life on the page."

CHAPTER TWO

Pulled from Seclusion

Vittoria
1534
Rome

When I saw the face he'd sketched in red chalk on a corner of the page, I recognized both my image and my longing. Since the death of my husband, I live behind a mask, surrounded by the convent walls of San Silvestro here in Rome or atop the impregnable Castello d'Aragonese on Ischia. I allow no one—not my family, not my friends, not the literary world that passes my manuscripts from hand to hand—to breach the defenses that protect me from memory and loss.

And yet, this one sees me, pierces me with his perceptive insight. How long did the unspoken pass between us when I turned to him in the Sistine Chapel? Surely not more than a minute or two. I knew who *he* was, standing there before the blank wall, simmering after his sharp words with the pope.

But how does he know *me* to enable him to recognize my heart, to convey it in those brief, spare strokes?

I find myself terrified, challenged, awakened.

I retreat from Michelangelo's garden, from the frivolous but useful Cardinal Ippolito de' Medici and from the page of sketches, dropping it back onto the table as if it declared my secrets. I go back to my guest quarters at the Convent of San Silvestro and lose myself in my words, trying to recapture in poetry what he has revealed with a piece of chalk held in a lined and color-stained hand.

I am in Rome, pulled from my widow's seclusion at the request of my friend Caterina Cibo, the Duchessa of

Camerino, and a passionate advocate for the Capuchin monks.

Pope Clement has banned the Capuchin order—less for spiritual reasons than political ones, although that makes the ban all the more difficult to undo. Caterina helped fund the Capuchins when they broke off from an older order, the Observants. Despite her money and her influence, however, the Capuchins have been unable to defend themselves against the powerful allies of the Observants, who have convinced the pope to ban the new order. Caterina introduced me to the Capuchins in the hope of gaining my financial commitment. I am drawn to their simplicity, their return to the ideals of St. Francis of Assisi, and was happy to provide them with funds when she asked me. I assumed that was enough. But a few weeks ago, a monk sent by Caterina showed up at the citadel begging to see me, and I recognized a need beyond gold in his unwillingness to go away without speaking to me. I felt I could not deny him whatever words he had traveled here to say. And so, I left the solitude of my study, went to him and listened.

"My lady, I am more than grateful for your willingness to see me. I had nowhere else to turn." His face reflected a conflicting struggle of emotions—a core of anguish tinged with a thin veil of hope.

"I do not know what I can do for you, but I will listen to what you have come to ask."

"Her Grace, Duchessa Caterina of Camerino, assured me that you share her concerns for our order. We humbly beg you to accompany the duchessa to Rome to petition the Holy Father to rescind our banishment."

"I am happy to write to His Holiness on the order's behalf, Fra Matteo, but as you must realize, I have withdrawn from public life since my husband's death. It saddens me greatly that your desire to establish a spiritual path far removed from the excesses of the Church is now forcing you to beg for your very existence. But I do not have the strength of spirit to become entangled in papal politics, nor do I wish to resume the demands of a life at court, which my presence in Rome would surely entail."

"My lady, I appreciate your offer and respect your reluctance to return to Rome. But I beg you to reconsider. Your words of support are welcome and would serve our cause, but your personal appeal to His Holiness has far more power to effect change. In these few minutes, your words have imparted a deep compassion and warmth of heart. The Holy Father will be moved by such ardent eloquence. If you cannot give me an answer at this moment, I shall withdraw to the church I passed in the village beyond the gate. I will wait there in prayer as you consider my entreaty."

The monk departed in humility, leaving me to pace the room. I didn't want to go to Rome.

If anything could disrupt my retreat from the world, it would be a cause of such goodness as the Capuchins. And yet, I realized that once I opened that door, I'd then be vulnerable to all the others I've kept at a distance.

Pacing provided me with no answers, so I sought the wisdom of Costanza d'Avalos, the Principessa di Francavilla, ruler of Ischia and the woman who, after my mother, has had the most influence in shaping who I am.

I spent much of my life on the rock of Ischia, spewed from the mouth of Mount Epomeo in the midst of the Tyrrhenian Sea. Still, Michelangelo is correct in calling me a Roman. I am the daughter and granddaughter of warriors, a noblewoman of the ancient house of Colonna, whose strongholds ring the hills surrounding Rome—Marino, Paliano, Amelici, Rocca di Papa. It is my father, Fabrizio Colonna, whom Machiavelli named as the voice of experience and wisdom in *The Art of War*.

My childhood at Marino was idyllic, filled with the lyrical sound of my mother's learned voice opening a world of discovery to me in her library and the commanding but loving tones of my father's encouragement. But then, when I was ten, one of the many wars that embroiled our family in its tangles tore me away from all I had known.

1500

CHAPTER THREE

Exile

Vittoria
1500
Marino and Ischia

I heard the voices in the middle of the night. Not the imposing growl of my father when he discussed battle plans with his lieutenants, or the raucous shouts of his soldiers returning to the fortress after a hard-fought victory. I knew those voices, which had populated my childhood for as long as I could remember. No, these voices had a tone that my child's ears recognized as different. They were not the voices of war, but they spoke of something equally significant, although I couldn't distinguish the words or who was speaking them.

A glance at the bed of my nurse, Beata, revealed to me her stillness, her breathing as quiet as the example she tried to impart to me during our waking hours. Across the room my younger brothers, Ascanio and Federigo, sprawled open-mouthed in their own bed. Only I had been awakened by the voices. I crept out from under the covers and padded across the stone floor in my bare feet. Carefully, I eased the door open, enough to hear but not so much as to arouse the attention of the soldier my father had ordered to guard the nursery since the latest hostilities had flared between him and the Borgia pope.

The voices were no longer muted undercurrents; they had become distinct and recognizable. My mother, anguished. My father, adamant.

"I cannot fathom why she must go now. We agreed at the betrothal that she would marry Pescara when she turns twenty. She is *ten*."

"We are not sending her to be *married,* but to be fostered and protected by Pescara's aunt. Ischia is safe and too far for the Orsini to consider pursuing her as a hostage."

As young as I was, I knew the Orsini family had been Colonna enemies for generations, and the Orsini were allies of the pope. I shivered in the doorway, not from the cold air beyond the nursery or from fear of the age-old feud, but from the realization that I was the ten-year-old they were discussing.

"If it's for her safety you have concern, why not allow her to travel with me and the boys to my brother's fortress in Urbino? Do you not trust him to protect her as well as Costanza d'Avalos can?"

"It is more than her safety. By sending her to the duchessa now to raise alongside Pescara, we forge a far stronger link to the Spanish crown than if we wait until she becomes his wife. I've thrown in my lot with King Ferdinand, Agnese. Sending Vittoria to Ischia demonstrates my loyalty beyond a doubt."

"And expands your land holdings as a reward, I suppose."

"I am amassing that land for Ascanio and Federigo. Or would you prefer that I let the pope drive us out and take it all?"

"Fabrizio, I accept that the decisions you make are for the good of the family. I also recognize that a daughter's role is to strengthen the family through her marriage. If you recall, I made no objections five years ago when we agreed to the betrothal. And I have every confidence in Costanza d'Avalos as a guardian for Vittoria."

"Then why are you objecting?"

"I did not expect to lose my daughter so soon. That is all. It's breaking my heart. *You* are breaking my heart."

"Do you imagine I make this decision as if she were a unit of archers I'm sending to an ally? Yes, there are political implications, but she's my daughter, too. She will be treated well, Agnese. And she will be safe."

I knew that tone in my father's voice. It meant the discussion was over.

I closed the door and returned to my bed, but I could not sleep. My betrothal to Ferrante Francesco d'Avalos, the Marchese di Pescara, was no surprise. I even had a miniature of him, sent to me on my eighth birthday. He was the same age as I, a blessing according to Beata.

"Many girls are married off to much older men whose first or second wives have died. This is a good match for you, Vittoria," she had reassured me. It had been easy then to put it out of my mind. Marriage was a lifetime away, beyond imagining to my child's mind.

Now, it seemed, that lifetime was here.

I was a brave girl. My father's blood flowed in my veins. But for the first time, I resented that I was the oldest, that I was the girl, because those were the reasons I was being sent away. I didn't stamp my feet in protest or beg to go to Urbino instead of Ischia. My father responds to neither of those forms of resistance. To appeal to him, I summoned my logic and wrote my father a letter—in Latin, not Italian—as if I were petitioning him in a negotiation of peace.

I laid out my case—the help and support I could provide my mother in caring for my brothers and amusing and distracting her from the worries always engulfing the wife of a warrior.

My father read the letter (with some help from my mother, I believe, because his Latin was not so polished). Then he called me to him in the evening, after he'd dismissed his generals.

"Vittoria, you have composed an eloquent and sound argument, which brings me great pride as your father."

My heart lifted. His face in the candlelight was kind, the face of a father. I knew I had chosen my words well.

"I have no doubt that you could serve me and our family capably if you were to go to Urbino."

"Thank you, Papa!" I was about to clap my hands in joy, but he continued.

"However, there is a greater service you can do for me in Ischia. You know that your betrothal to the marchese was at the request of King Ferdinand of Spain. The success of your marriage is of great importance to our family's future.

"By going to Ischia now, you lay the groundwork for that future. For you to be accepted into the household of the duchessa and for you to form a childhood bond with your future husband—those things are of immeasurable worth to me.

"I am sending you with this responsibility because you are the only one I can trust to accomplish it. You may not ever be my warrior on the battlefield, but you are another kind of warrior. With your intellect and your instincts, you are my secret weapon at court."

With those words he obliterated my anger. Despite my fear, I swelled with a sense of myself. Let my brothers have their wooden swords and games in Urbino. My father had given me a mission.

But when the morning of my departure dawned and the horses were saddled and waiting with ten of my father's most trusted men, I found a hundred things to delay the moment when I finally had to take leave of my family. My azure-blue hair ribbons, a box of sketching chalk, even the gift I was to present to the duchessa—all had been forgotten in my room, not packed in my trunks. Beata, who was to accompany me to Ischia, scurried with mounting impatience to retrieve each suddenly remembered and irreplaceable object.

I waited in the great hall with my mother, clutching her slender fingers and willing myself not to cry for her sake. She squeezed my hand and pressed one of her embroidered handkerchiefs into it. Then she bent toward me, held my face and studied it for the longest time before kissing me on both cheeks.

"This will be the first of many of life's trials, Vittoria, but it can also be the first of your adventures, if you will permit it to be. You will find the duchessa most charming and welcoming. She loves Ferrante like her own son and will come to love you, too. I know you will represent the house of Colonna well. May God grant you a safe journey!"

I managed to utter my obedience to her and my father without tears. I kissed her as Beata flew into the hall with the retrieved articles, her head-covering askew and tiny drops of perspiration beading on the fine dark hairs of the mustache my mother had encouraged her to bleach before we left for the elegance of Costanza's court. I was sorry for the turmoil I'd caused Beata, but not for the extra moments it gave me in my mother's presence. Her handkerchief was infused with the scent of lavender, and I carried it with me throughout the journey to Ischia. It comforted me in my sleep in the strange beds along the route and soothed my homesickness. I wouldn't let Beata wash it for fear that I would lose this fragile remnant of my mother. It meant more to me than the miniature I wore around my neck, the image of my father in his battle armor on one side and my mother, her golden hair entwined with silk and lilies of the valley, on the other.

We traveled overland to the port of Ostia and then set sail for Ischia. Papa thought it too dangerous to go by road all the way to Napoli.

I was seasick. Beata held my head and wiped my face.

"Ischia is an island," I moaned. "To leave it, I'll have to endure this disgusting indignity again."

"Nonsense, Vittoria. You'll get used to travel by sea. Once you're the marchesa, you will most likely travel often—to the court at Napoli, to Rome. Now come, let's wash your face and comb your hair. You'll feel better if you freshen up."

"I'll feel better when this galley has docked and I can step on dry land."

To a sick child, it seemed like a journey of a thousand days, but in fact, it was barely three. The morning of our arrival, Beata took my rose-colored dress from the trunk and aired it while I still slept. She fussed with my hair after fastening the dress and tying the sash.

"You have your mother's hair," she mused as she pulled the brush through my curls. It was the same golden color as my mother's. When I was younger, she'd allowed me to play with her ringlets; I would wrap them around my fingers. Beata wasn't playing now.

She smoothed the strands that had been whipped into tangles by the wind and my own restless sleep. It wasn't easy. My hair was as unruly as my thoughts after such a miserable journey. Even the prospect that we'd soon be on solid ground was outweighed by my renewed fear of the strange household I was about to enter.

Despite the honor my father had bestowed upon me with my mission for the family—and my profession of obedience before I left Marino—as the rocky cliffs of Ischia grew taller with each ship's length of sea we traversed, I understood how unlike the Alban Hills this island was.

When Beata had tamed my hair into braids and wrapped them around my head, she secured them with a narrow garland of rose quartz and tiny pearls. I pressed my hands against it to make certain it was secure. I didn't want my first meeting with the duchessa to be remembered for my hairpiece slipping off my head and into the sea.

Beata had me twirl around so she could inspect all the details of my outfit. She seemed as concerned as I was that I make a good impression both in my clothing and my behavior.

She rehearsed with me for the fiftieth time how I was to greet the duchessa, although I'd been presented to noblewomen before at Marino.

"This occasion is different," Beata insisted. "The others were merely visitors in your parents' home. The duchessa will be a part of your life from this moment forward. She will be guiding you and protecting you, and one day, will be as a mother-in-law to you. I know you want to start your life here in the best of all possible ways. Now come, pick up your skirt. The moment has arrived to go up on deck for the landing."

On deck, my father's men were ready, standing at attention. I understood why Beata had insisted I change into a festive dress for my arrival. The duchessa was known for many things—her love of the arts and literature and music; the astuteness with which she governed Ischia, appointed by the king to fill her husband's role after his death; her devotion to her nephew Ferrante. But she was also known for her wardrobe, and my mother had instructed Beata that the Colonna didn't want to be embarrassed.

I was stunned by how quickly we had approached the harbor. I could already see the faces of those waiting to greet us. I took a deep breath and tried not to throw up as the galley lurched into port.

Beata saw my green face and swiftly turned me away from the dock, a towel in her hand. But I waved her off.

"I'll manage. Just get me off the ship as soon as it's safe...and seemly."

She spoke quietly to the captain of my father's guard, and suddenly the ship swarmed with activity. The sailors hustled to set down the gangplank. Half the soldiers descended first and lined my path. I walked alone down the sloping board, my eyes focused on the stones of the dock a few precious steps away.

When my feet finally felt the warmth and solidity of the earth, I lifted my head with a smile and faced the welcoming crowd with the duchessa at its center—elegant, smiling at me in return.

I made a deep curtsy as I greeted her. She placed her hands on my shoulders and kissed me as my mother had, in what seemed to me a lifetime ago.

"Welcome to Ischia, child. I haven't seen you since you were an infant in your mother's arms, but you've grown into her image. Come, let me introduce you to Ferrante."

She turned to a tall, dark-haired boy at her side, somberly dressed. Unlike me, still blessed with my parents, Ferrante was an orphan. I thought perhaps he was still in mourning for his parents. He had in his hand a small nosegay of roses and camellias. The roses were pink and I wondered how the duchessa had known the color of the dress I would be wearing. Ferrante bowed and held the flowers out to me. I reached for them and thanked him. He mumbled something in reply, but it wasn't intelligible.

"Vittoria doesn't speak Spanish yet, Ferrante. We will have to teach her."

I thought Ischia was still Italy, but for Ferrante, apparently not.

"Do you ride, Vittoria?" the duchessa asked.

It seemed an odd question, until I realized there was no carriage waiting for us at the quay.

I nodded. "I have a pony at Marino."

"Good! Then you can ride with Ferrante and me to the citadel. Come, the horses are at the end of the bridge."

She pointed to a long causeway paved with stone and stretching across the inner harbor from the dock to the Castello Aragonese, set apart on its own mountainous rock. At the top of the rough cliffs sat the fortress that guarded the duchessa's kingdom.

Beata fussed about how I might ruin my silk dress, but Costanza told her that the only other alternative was to walk with the mules that would carry our trunks, and Beata glumly acquiesced.

On a small piazza at the end of the bridge, several groomsmen stood with Costanza's horses. Their bridles were decorated with flowers. A flag-bearer on the lead horse carried Costanza's insignia—a round stone tower on a blue field, surrounded by alternating squares of red and white. If I craned my neck, I could see the actual towers at each corner of the fortress above us.

Once I was lifted into the saddle and everyone was mounted, we left the piazza. The sound of the waves slapping against the base of the footbridge receded as the sea that had been my companion and my enemy disappeared. The horses passed through a stone arch and turned toward a heavy wooden gate guarding a rough opening in the wall of stone that climbed straight up from the sea.

The gate was raised and we entered a tunnel. The sun, like the sea, was gone, and I shivered in my rose silk dress as my eyes strained to see the trail.

"The horse knows the way, Vittoria. Before long, you will as well."

The path rose in broad, shallow steps and the shod feet of the horses echoed against the stone walls deep within the mountain. Suddenly, the darkness was pierced by a shaft of light above us, and then another.

Costanza noted my upward glance. "Those openings provide us with light, but are also a means of defense should enemies breach the gate leading to the tunnel. Arrows and pitch can be launched through them." I nodded in understanding. I'd grown up in a fortress; defense was no mystery to me.

When we finally emerged from the tunnel into daylight, the path was steep, at times a mere dirt track and at others paved into broad steps with the same stones as the bridge. At first, it passed through a small village, where curious children ran alongside us and women watched from open windows. After leaving the village, the path wound through vineyards and then clung to the hillside on the edge of the sea.

I didn't look down, but kept my eyes on the fortress looming ahead on the top of the mountain. When we reached the piazza of the cathedral about halfway up the mountain, we stopped to rest the horses.

"Vittoria, this would be a good time to offer a prayer of thanksgiving for your safe journey," Costanza suggested.

While the horses watered at the fountain, we relinquished the warmth of the sunlight and stepped into the dimly lit church. A few old women were bent over their rosaries and a young monk was scrubbing the marble in front of the main altar.

Costanza moved swiftly toward the nave, and Ferrante and I raced to keep up with her. She stopped at a bank of candles fluttering in the draft caused by our arrival. Red wax overflowed the votive glasses and dripped like molten lava onto the floor. Above the candles hung a painting of St. Rocco staring down at the sinners and the suffering who came to the church seeking his intercession. The painting was dark from the smoke of the candles, obscuring the wound in his leg caused by the plague he had miraculously survived.

Kneeling, I crossed myself and squeezed my eyes shut. Images of saints sometimes gave me nightmares. As Costanza had directed me, I murmured a thank you to God, although He could have arranged a smoother passage. But I acknowledged that we had arrived safely, without drowning or being seized by pirates. I silently added a prayer of supplication to the Virgin.

"Holy Mother, I know your son has brought me here unharmed, and I don't mean to be ungrateful, but please intercede with him to make my stay blessedly short and bring me home to my family."

Amidst the blaze I found an unlit candle and lit it. I thought I saw my mother's face in the flames. I knew one was only supposed to have visions of the face of Jesus or Mary, but even if it was sinful, I didn't care. My mother had appeared to me and she was smiling. I stood, ready to continue the journey up the mountain.

We passed more churches as we wound our way along the narrow trail, although none as magnificent as the cathedral.

"If you're counting, Vittoria, we have thirteen churches within the protection of the Castello's fortifications. They serve the spiritual needs of the nearly two thousand families who live here. The priests and nuns worry about their souls and I worry that they have enough to eat and are safe from marauders."

If the immensity of the Castello had not already stunned me—the heights to which we were climbing, the vast sea surrounding us, the solidity of the impregnable walls—Costanza's words reinforced my sense that I was in a very different world from my home at Marino.

At last we reached the citadel, high above the churches and convents, the villages and vineyards. Bells were tolling when we approached the gates and a great commotion greeted us as we entered the courtyard.

My hands were stiff from clutching the reins. Riding my pony at Marino, even racing out on the plain with Papa, had never been so demanding. I was grateful for the strange, stalwart hands that lifted me off my horse and deposited me on the marble steps, surrounded by faces both unfamiliar and curious.

Thus began what my mother had rightly taught me to see as an adventure.

CHAPTER FOUR

Freedom and Sanctuary

Vittoria
1500
Castello Aragonese
Ischia

One of my favorite places on the island was a loggia at the top of the palace. Its stone arches framed the sea and the rocky crags that encircled my world from the day Costanza took me into her home.

I often sat there as a girl, distracted from my book or my sketching to search the horizon for a glimpse of my homeland—and, if not that, then the colors of my father's ship.

"What are you looking for? If you are afraid of pirates, our fleet and our army will protect you—as I hope to one day."

Ferrante had run quietly up the stone steps. He knew I frequently came to the loggia after our lessons, when the rest of the house was at siesta.

"I'm not afraid of pirates. I just don't like to be cooped up all day. And it reminds me of Marino, to be up here where I can see the whole world."

"Your Spanish is getting better."

"You could learn Italian, you know."

"I'm not as smart as you. Tia Costanza has already mentioned how quick you are. It's not so important for me. I need to excel at the language of the sword, not the language of the salon."

"Warriors need to understand their enemies—and their allies."

"Come away from your books and your observation tower and play with me for a while."

Ferrante was always in action, as a boy and as a man. He pulled me by the hand down the steps and onto the grass, gave me a stick and dared me to hit a ball farther than he could.

I had brothers. I was used to the bravado and challenges they threw at each other as simply and quickly as they threw a ball. I whacked Ferrante's ball over the tops of the duchessa's flowering shrubs and into the pond at the edge of the grounds.

"You'll have to retrieve it before the tortoise assumes it's one of her eggs." Another dare from Ferrante.

I was already knee-deep in the murky waters, my skirt hitched up like an apron and my shoes and stockings on a stone at the water's edge, before Beata saw me from a window and started shrieking. I could hear her as she raced through the citadel to get to the garden, probably waking the entire court from siesta.

By the time she reached the pond, I'd retrieved the ball and held it high as I waded back to the bank. I lobbed it at Ferrante just before Beata hustled me off to a bath.

"Your turn—and I'll be watching!" I shouted to him over my shoulder.

"From now on, limit your games with the marchese to chess and cards," Beata scolded as she scrubbed the scum from me and my dress.

"I'd beat him too easily if we only played board games, and that's no fun."

I stayed out of the pond after that to keep Beata happy. But Ferrante and I couldn't stop ourselves from competing like siblings—in the classroom, at the chess board and out of doors. We pushed and teased each other to feats of prowess. He was better with sticks and horses, but I could outrun him and outthink him. I always figured out where he was hiding when we played hide-and-seek and wasn't afraid to follow his trail, even when it meant crawling into dark places festooned with cobwebs and littered with the carcasses of dead insects. That, of course, continued to displease Beata.

But she stopped shrieking about the nettles in my hair and the dirt on my petticoats after the duchessa spoke to her one afternoon. They were walking along the sea path and I, instead of racing with Ferrante, had sought some quiet shade to read a letter from my mother that had been delivered that morning. These letters were my treasure, and I was willing to forgo anything that otherwise brought me pleasure—a game with Ferrante, sweet cakes the cook set aside for us—in order to savor every lovely word in a place apart.

Like me, my mother was the daughter of a warrior. Because she grew up in a house that honored learning as well as war, she came to her marriage with a dowry that surpassed the silver plates, tapestries and taffetas filling the trunks carved with amaranth and peacocks that accompanied her when she entered the house of Colonna. She came with an intellect sharply honed on the classics. She read Greek and Latin, could discourse on the poetry of Petrarch and Ovid and Dante, and composed sonnets in celebration of a saint's day or a battle. She cherished this learning and, in turn, was cherished by my father because of it. Everything I knew I'd learned from my mother, and with her letters she continued to instruct me.

The loggia in the air was not my only refuge. I also had a place on the ground where I could retreat. The low-sweeping branches of a giant pine tree at the far edge of the belvedere formed a bower, soft with fallen pine needles under the cascade of its dense and fragrant limbs. I never used it when Ferrante and I played our hiding games, because I didn't want to share the knowledge of it with him. The tree and the letters were tightly intertwined in my experience, and both were secrets that comforted me in my longing for home. I was afraid that sharing the refuge would break the thread that bound me to my family. I'd not bled yet; I wasn't ready to bind myself to Ferrante.

Which is why I sat alone under the tree undetected as Beata and the duchessa strolled along the path of crushed abalone shells to the belvedere.

"Beata, do you feel Vittoria is happy here?"

"Happy? She does not cry for home or beg to go back. But she was never a child given to such displays."

"Neither is she a docile child who keeps her true feelings masked, in my observation."

"She is exuberant, if that's what you mean. And as the eldest of my lady Agnese's children, she became accustomed to leading her little brothers rather than deferring to them. She loves them devotedly, but she takes no orders from them. I'm afraid it's the only way she knows how to be around boys."

"You needn't apologize!" The duchessa laughed as she laid a hand on Beata's arm. "I've seen—and heard—how Ferrante and Vittoria manage each other and dance around who holds the power."

"Oh, Vittoria is aware of her place. She would never…"

"Surely you don't believe that, Beata! You've spent your life in a warrior's household. You know Vittoria will need to be strong, will need to be in charge of her own sphere. I cannot imagine that Agnese would have taught her otherwise, especially by her own example."

"But Donna Agnese doesn't hold her husband's sword or wear his armor, and I worry that, even though it's child's play, Vittoria's crawling around in caves and swinging at balls with wooden spears is hardly preparing her for the life she'll lead as Ferrante's wife."

"No, Beata, it does precisely that. Ferrante is learning that Vittoria is resilient and unafraid as well as clever. When the time comes for him to take his place at the head of a legion, he will do so assured that the wife he leaves behind will not be paralyzed with indecision. She will run his household and manage their affairs with the same astuteness she applies to finding him in their games.

"There are those who assume I cannot speak wisely about how to rear children when I have borne none myself. But I have been mother to Ferrante since he was a babe, and I was also a child myself once. As a girl I was allowed the same freedom to play as my brothers. I also learned literature and art, and perhaps came to appreciate them more, in seeing their relationship to the world of nature, because I'd spent time exploring that world. Don't fret about Vittoria's mussed hair or muddy skirt. She'll be a young woman soon enough."

"It's not the condition of her clothing or her hairdo that concerns me, but that she'll lose sight of what it means to be a lady of nobility."

"Then I shall set an example for her. There is much more to being a lady than being able to follow the latest fashion, smile and nod at one's husband's wit and be able to read one's breviary."

And with that, the duchessa took Beata by the arm and steered her back to the villa.

After that conversation, Beata was less insistent on my engaging in what she called "ladylike" activities, although it was only after she'd written to my mother and received her endorsement of the duchessa's ideas that she was reluctantly prepared to accept them.

The duchessa was as willing to give me free run of the library as she was of the garden, however. She and her late husband had amassed a collection rivaled only by that of my mother's father, Federico da Montefeltro, the Duke of Urbino, who had employed thirty scribes to copy ancient texts.

As winter settled over the island, shrouding the view from the loggia, I took comfort in the library, not simply for the warmth of the fire in the hearth but also for the warmth of the duchessa's presence. Her kindness was even more welcoming to me than in my early months.in her household. Then, the pain of my homesickness had been acute, and yet I'd still held out hope that my father's war would be brief and

I would be called home to my family. But with the coming of winter and its rough seas, and no word of truce, I absorbed with a quiet despair that I would not be leaving Ischia.

The duchessa sensed my sadness before I had time to acknowledge it. She threw open the doors to a world that surpassed everything to which I'd already been introduced. As much freedom as Costanza had encouraged in the open air was doubled in the library. Names that my grandfather had uttered with reverence became my companions, the authors of works he had considered as valuable as the gold that built his city and paid his troops.

I can't say that the words in Costanza's library replaced the words from my mother's lips, but where hers had been a trilling stream, a lyrical accompaniment that washed over me to refresh my spirit and quench my thirst, the words in Costanza's books lit a fire, a conflagration that burns in me to this day.

1534

CHAPTER FIVE

Reawakening

Vittoria
1534
Castello Aragonese and Rome

Because of the profound influence she wielded in my young life, I know that when the Capuchin monk begs for my help, I can turn to Costanza and trust her to guide me.

"What shall I do? I believe in their cause, but going to Rome... They ask too much of me."

"My dear, may I ask if you intend to spend the rest of your life in mourning?"

Her question shatters me.

"You have always been intense and driven, Vittoria, even as a child. But you do not have to disappear inside yourself in order to honor Ferrante's memory. You have resurrected him—and his honor—with your poetry. Let those words speak to the world about your love and loyalty, but let them also free you now to resume your own life. No one, least of all me, expected your life to end when his did."

"For *me*, it did."

"Forgive me, Vittoria. It didn't. You are a vibrant, intelligent woman who still has much to offer this world. What I am about to say may appear cold and harsh, and I've withheld saying it out of love and concern for you. But today, you come to me and ask for my opinion. It is this: I believe that the Lord would look upon your voluntary solitude as an act of selfishness and pride, not one of self-abnegation. You are denying the gift of your person—your idealism, your compassion, your understanding—to a world desperately in need of you. The longer you stay away from the world, the more you will lose those gifts."

I tremble as I listen to her. She speaks softly, not accusingly. Rather than ripping away the veil behind which I had retreated, she is unraveling it, thread by painstakingly woven thread.

I protest. "I am mistress of my day. I write. I walk in the vineyard and appreciate God's creation. I read. I study. I pray. All when I choose to do so."

"Christ Himself withdrew for just forty days, Vittoria. He spent the rest of his life in the world, among the people He had come to save. There is only so much one can glean from the written word. You need to listen. You need to be heard. But most of all, *we* need *you.*

"I cannot imagine myself back in the world."

Costanza nods. "Nine years is too long," she says gently. "You are afraid."

I start to protest again, but she deftly places two fingers on my lips.

"Hear me out. You forget that I know the signs of your fear—as the child wrenched from her mother's arms and deposited on my shore. As the warrior's wife who had a premonition of her husband's fall on the battlefield. You were afraid. But on each occasion you overcame your fear. I implore you, Vittoria. Do not succumb to fear this time. Come out from hiding. God sent that monk today for a reason."

"I cannot hear any more of this." I choke out the words, my hands over my ears. "I am going to pray. Perhaps the Holy Ghost will give me a sign."

I leave her. But instead of climbing to the chapel within the citadel, as I intend, my feet make their way to the church outside the walls where Fra Matteo waits in prayer for my answer.

It is quiet along the path. A few sea birds hover over the water, squawking and circling in search of prey. When I slip out of the sunlight and into the cool darkness of the church, my eyes need a few seconds to adjust before I locate the monk kneeling close to the sanctuary. He does not turn around, but continues the low murmur of his *Pater Noster*.

I throw myself to my knees, breathless from the rapid pace that has brought me from my interview with Costanza to this holy place. No prayers emerge from my lips, only sobs. I do not know if I am any closer to an answer, but I accept that something has compelled me to seek out Fra Matteo.

My weeping alerts him to my presence and he hurries to my side.

"My lady! I didn't expect you to come yourself! Forgive me. . . . Are you unwell?"

He fumbles within the folds of his rough-spun robe for a handkerchief and offers it to me before stepping back. I press it against my face to dry my tears.

"No, Fra Matteo. Please forgive *me*. I should not have kept you waiting for an answer. Please accompany me back to the citadel. I am sure you are hungry, and while you eat you can tell me when the duchessa would like me to meet her in Rome."

"Then you will come and speak for us?"

"Yes, I will come."

The Rome to which I return after so many years is not the city I remember. As we enter, I see signs of the devastation left in the wake of the Sack in 1527, compounded by the plague that followed a few years later.

The Convent of San Silvestro has always been under the patronage of my family; it is where I originally retreated to mourn after the death of my husband and it's where I will reside while I'm here in Rome. Although I have been in communication with the sisters of San Silvestro since the Sack and helped them with funds for the convent's restoration after its destruction by an angry mob of mutinous imperial soldiers, I am unsure of what I will find when I arrive. There is only so much one is willing to reveal in a letter. A stranger answers my knock, not Suora Clarita, the porter I knew so many years ago.

"Welcome, Lady Pescara! We have been expecting you. The sisters are at prayer and Reverend Mother has asked me to show you to your quarters. She will greet you later."

I follow the suora to the guest quarters. Where once the walls had been hung with tapestries and the niches filled with the carved statues of saints, I see bare walls whitewashed to cover the epithets that had been scrawled in blood and excrement. The Reverend Mother shared with me some fragments of the convent's experience during the Sack. Through the colonnade I can see the cloister. Saplings tethered to posts are beginning to thrive, replacements for the chestnuts and fruit trees hacked down and burned by rampaging soldiers years before. All around me are signs of repair—a fresh coat of plaster, a door of plain wood with new hinges. The buildings, though lacking the artistry of the past, are whole again. I wonder, however, if I will find the nuns equally healed.

"Suora, may I ask if Suora Carita is still here? When I last stayed at San Silvestro, she was the gatekeeper."

The nun bows her head and makes the sign of the cross. "Sister Carita didn't survive the injuries she suffered during the Sack. She attempted to bar the way when Reverend Mother ordered the rest of us to hide in the crypt."

I can imagine the intrepid Suora Carita fiercely defending the convent, despite the futility. No one foresaw the horror that was visited upon Rome that day. Nothing in its past, the centuries of violent internal rivalries and foreign enemies, prepared the city for the brutality and rage of its invaders.

It is solely by God's grace that San Silvestro survived at all. So many of the city's convents, palaces and churches were gutted and burned.

We reach my quarters and the young nun selects a key from the iron ring she carries.

"Suora Ursula oversaw the preparation of your rooms yesterday. If there is anything you require, please call for me."

She nods and glides away, back to her post.

When the bells announce the end of prayers, I decide to walk in the quadrangle in hopes of seeing a familiar face. I surprise myself with that simple wish. All the years I withdrew from society, reluctant to engage even with old friends—and yet here I am, not an hour in Rome and seeking the company of others.

Drawing my cloak around my shoulders, I accept with bewilderment that something beyond my comprehension is at work and head outside. As I anticipated, the sisters are leaving the chapel and moving toward whatever occupations fill the hours they do not spend in prayer. I search among the faces of the women, but see only strangers until a voice behind me calls my name.

"Lady Pescara, you have arrived!" I turn. It is the Reverend Mother. We reach out to embrace each other and then step back. To assess. To acknowledge. We are approximately the same age, our early forties. Suora Francesca was not Reverend Mother when I first resided at San Silvestro. Her work then was as secretary for the convent, and she sought me out when she was translating some spiritual passages from Latin into Italian for some of the less educated sisters. We found a common bond in our love of language.

She was elected Reverend Mother four years ago. Rebuilding the convent's walls and population has consumed her. I suspect that she's found little time for the writing that so fulfilled her in the past. Her hands grasp mine. The ink stains that were once her identifying sign in the anonymity of the convent are gone.

"Come and have some wine with me. I would have had refreshments waiting for you in your rooms if I'd known when you were arriving."

I follow her to her study.

"The convent is excited to have you as a guest. The more literate sisters, especially those with brothers or cousins who move within the orbits of the poets Pietro Bembo or Jacopo Sadoleto, have been begging me to ask you to recite for us. I have tried to dampen their expectations, explaining that you are on a spiritual mission with your trip to Rome, not a literary tour."

"I hoped that by staying here, rather than with my brother, I could maintain the privacy that has been my solace. It never occurred to me that my work would have found its way into the convent." My face must reveal my dismay.

"But my lady, your poems could not be appreciated more than here! We do not close ourselves off to love when we take our vows, and your passionate portrayal of your husband and your devotion to him are an inspiration to us in our own relationship with Christ."

"I am touched and humbled by your interpretation, Suora. It is praise more meaningful to me than anything a courtier might proclaim in the midst of a salon. I have heard too many poets lavish words on a fellow writer's composition in the hopes of indebting him to return the favor."

"I assure you, I am not offering false praise, and I seek nothing in return, other than your willingness to grace one of our evenings with a recitation," she says. "Your poetry could be a blessing for the nuns of San Silvestro, my lady. Many of us remain fragile and without hope that good still resides in the hearts of men. Your words are a flame to rekindle broken spirits."

I cannot refuse her. I embrace her, and in doing so, embrace a new phase in my life.

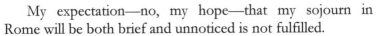

My expectation—no, my hope—that my sojourn in Rome will be both brief and unnoticed is not fulfilled.

As soon as I set foot in the Vatican with Caterina for our audience with Pope Clement, word begins to spread. One would suspect the members of the papal court have nothing to do except trade rumors as if they were currency.

I wonder how valuable a piece of information my presence in Rome is. I find out soon enough. Other than Suora Francesca and my sister-in-law, Giovanna, I told only two people about my plans—Paolo Giovio and Pietro Bembo.

Paolo Giovio has been a friend since my days as a young wife, when he was kind enough to assuage my anxiety by reporting back to me what he witnessed of Ferrante's actions on the battlefield. Because of that and because of his accomplishments as a historian, it was he whom I commissioned to write Ferrante's biography. He would have been deeply hurt if I had kept from him that I was coming to Rome.

Pietro Bembo has become a mentor, if not yet someone I can count as a friend. Knowing what I do of him and his position among the poets of our time, I believe he would take offense if I didn't write to tell him of my intentions to be in the city. I know he has been living in Venice for the last five years, after being appointed that city's historian and then librarian of St. Mark's Cathedral, so I do not expect him to come and visit me. My letter was merely a courtesy.

After Caterina and I present our petition to the Holy Father, we make our way back through the crowded corridors to the entrance hall of the Vatican. I am stunned to see Pietro in conversation with a bishop—no one I recognize. He breaks off when I enter the hall, bowing graciously but nonetheless abruptly to the purple-robed prelate. He crosses the floor to greet me.

Pietro Bembo is an imposing man when standing still, tall and broad-shouldered, with a body more fit for a suit of armor than a scholar's robes. In motion he is a stallion charging down a course, his black cloak billowing out behind him like a knight's colors. Caterina freezes at this giant approaching us. But I continue toward him, my hand extended in welcome. Despite his physical size, I know him from his letters to be a man of great courtesy and even greater sensibility.

"Lady Pescara! It is so good to see you at last. From the conversations I have had since arriving, Rome has missed you." He bows over my hand as he reaches us, all but enveloping me in the swaths of black that clothe his bulk.

"Signor Bembo, it is a delight to see you again after so many years and a wonderful surprise to find you in Rome. May I present my dear friend, Caterina Cibo, the Duchessa of Camerino."

After the introductions and inquiries about our journey, he invites us to a salon at the Farnese palazzo the following evening. I demur, words of my continued state of mourning about to emerge from my lips. But the memory of my last conversation with Costanza interrupts me.

In the lull, Pietro begins to list the names of others who will be in attendance. All men I either know or recognize, some dear to me for the kindness they showed me in the years of my loneliness or my widowhood. A tug of emotion pulls at me, an unfamiliar wish to be among my old friends.

I smile. "We would be delighted to join such an illustrious assembly. My thanks for including us."

Caterina stands gape-mouthed, her eyebrows raised in a silent question. I shrug in answer. I have no idea what is happening to me and can hardly explain it to her.

Pietro responds, "My dear lady, it is not simply that we are *including* you. You are the very reason we are gathering."

Now it's my turn to react with bewilderment. Pietro must see the shocked expression on my face.

"Surely you know how revered you are by this city, not only as a daughter of Rome, but as a poet whose luminous words both inspire and provoke us to follow your audacious lead."

I lower my eyes, attempting to deflect this unwanted praise with a humble demeanor. I can sense Caterina's confusion descending into disapproval. I need to end this conversation quickly.

"I am honored by your words, Signor, but they are undeserved. I write to assuage my inward grief, not to garner praise from poets who are far more accomplished than I. Once again I thank you for the invitation and look forward to seeing my friends tomorrow evening."

I nod to Pietro, gather my skirt and take Caterina's arm. We move away with as much alacrity as I can manage without appearing rude.

Our litter awaits us below the steps. I would have much preferred to ride, but Caterina is suffering in her joints and finds horseback too painful. I acquiesced to her need by joining her in the curtained conveyance, but now I regret it. It means we will be enclosed together in this stifling box for the trip up the Quirinal hill to San Silvestro. I won't be able to avoid her questions. She begins almost before we start to move.

"You were not yourself with Signor Bembo, Vittoria. At least not the reclusive, pious woman I have come to know."

"I don't recognize myself either, Caterina. Pietro Bembo caught me completely by surprise by even being in Rome, much less inviting us to his salon."

"When I consider of all I had to do to beg you to come here, and now you seem ready to leap into the very pit you quite diligently avoided all these years. I do not understand you." She sounds both angry and hurt, offended that I received Pietro so warmly.

"I do not understand *myself*, Caterina. Please, dearest friend, do not judge me harshly. I didn't ask for his praise."

"But you accepted his invitation."

"For both of us!"

"I have no desire to attend a Roman salon. It will likely descend into all the excesses against which we have been so fervently fighting, along with the Capuchins. Have you already forgotten the very reason we're in Rome?"

I am about to protest, to defend the circle of poets and writers Pietro named. But I hold myself in check. The cause of the Capuchins is a fire that burns ardently in Caterina's heart, and to her, Rome is the enemy. She will not recognize or admit to a distinction between the pope and the men named by Pietro.

"I have not forgotten," I tell her, "nor will I abandon the Capuchins if this attempt with His Holiness fails."

"It cannot fail!" Caterina grabs my hand. I need to shift her attention from her disapproval of Pietro's circle and, consequently, of me.

"It will not fail, but we must be prepared to take further steps to ensure the Capuchins' reinstatement. Come, let us plan and pray."

And so we spend the remainder of the journey with our heads together, first in supplication and then in strategy. By the time we arrive at the gates of San Silvestro she seems reassured of my commitment to her cause and doesn't mention again my willingness to participate in the salon.

She is traveling further, on to the convent her own family supports. I kiss her on both cheeks as we part.

"I will join you for Mass tomorrow morning at Santa Maria Maggiore," she says. The basilica lies between our two convents. "Perhaps God will answer our prayers quickly."

When I enter the convent, I go directly to the chapel. I have my own prayers, my own questions, that need answers.

I didn't dissemble when I told Caterina that I haven't absorbed what is happening to me. The quickening I felt at

Pietro's invitation was an experience I thought I'd lost long ago. But it was more than the anticipation of engaging in conversation with men whose words and ideas I follow so avidly. I can't deny that their opinion of my poetry matters to me. And that fills me with both excitement and apprehension.

The words of Suora Francesca and the meaning my poetry has given to the nuns of San Silvestro honored and humbled me. But to hear similar words from Pietro Bembo knots my stomach. I feel perched on a tightrope stretched across a chasm. Like a performer grasping a balancing pole as she takes one careful step after another on the wire, I feel the weight of my honor as a noblewoman pulling against my reputation as a poet. Caterina had implied that my willingness to take a place in Pietro's salon, not as an indulged guest but as an equal, is unseemly. She explicitly reminded me that my participation in the public dissemination of my poetry is at odds with my life as a pious widow.

Can I not be both? I implore God on my knees in the chapel. I remain there until the canonical hour of None, when the sisters arrive for the recitation of their Divine Office. I lose myself in the rhythm of their chant, the certainty of their faith reflected in the call-and-response of their prayers. I wish such certainty were mine, but do not find it that day.

The next morning, I receive a note from Paolo Giovio offering to accompany me to the salon. I suspect Pietro encouraged him, fearing I might make my excuses. I don't doubt that Pietro noticed Caterina's disapproval. Indeed, she informed me at Mass this morning that she would not join me. Shaking off the shadow of her reproach, I welcome Paolo's company on this first foray back into society.

The enthusiasm of his greeting helps dispel some of my uneasiness.

"Vittoria! What a void Rome has endured without you, and what joy it brings me to welcome you back."

"Paolo, I am equally happy to see you."

I'm not speaking mere courtesies. I truly am happy to bask in the warmth of his welcome. I'd forgotten how open, how filled with an inner energy Paolo is in the flesh. Certainly some of that comes through in the correspondence we have exchanged over the many years of our friendship. I hear Costanza's voice in my head once again. I admit that I'm experiencing what she so wisely counseled me to accept as a vital element in my life. I smile inwardly, cautiously venturing with a dear friend into a world I have denied myself.

We ride side by side to the Farnese palazzo, at first with Paolo pointing out to me the rebuilding of the city. But soon our conversation shifts to a more intimate topic.

"Vittoria, you're aware that Rome is ready to fall at your feet tonight, aren't you?"

"That's a rather potent image, Paolo. Have I really been away so long that my return is such a cause for celebration?"

"It isn't necessary for you to be reserved with me. I know that you feel compelled by your position to measure your words in society, but please, let's speak freely between ourselves. You are a star, Vittoria."

"And I suspect you had something to do with my ascendancy." I smile at him. Of course it can only have been him, taking my poems and discreetly passing them to those who would appreciate them, those with influence who could spread my words and my name beyond the isolation of Ischia.

"I was simply the conduit. Your own words propelled your reputation. But...you are troubled." He reins in his horse and I follow. Halted, we face each other. Perhaps this is the opportunity God is offering me to explore my dilemma with a trusted friend. I plunge in.

"I struggle with how to reconcile my life as a poet with my life as a pious widow. I cannot abandon either, and yet I fear I will be vilified because of the attention my poetry is receiving. I cannot pretend to you, of all people, that it doesn't thrill me to discover that my words have meaning for so many. But I feel constrained—by my position in society, by my very sex—to act as if that means nothing to me. To pretend that my poetry is the pastime of an idle lady, filling her quiet hours with words instead of stitches."

He laughs. "No one would believe you, Vittoria. You may have learned to ply needle and thread as a young girl, but the only instrument I've ever seen you wield as a woman is a pen."

"What am I to do, Paolo?"

He looks at me, no longer laughing. "You will continue to write. The poet I know you to be *cannot* stop writing. And the world would lose something precious if you were to abandon your poetry. God blessed you with an extraordinary gift. Don't deny us your truth."

"That's easy for you to say as a man. Society doesn't condemn you for flaunting your work. If I were a courtesan and not a devout woman, I would have the freedom to spread my truth, as you call it, beyond the circle of my friends. But I am no courtesan." *Perhaps if I'd been more like a courtesan, Ferrante might have continued to love me*, I reflect to myself. But I banish that thought.

"Vittoria, I would suggest that your poetry has more power and influence precisely because you *are* a woman of piety rather than a woman of the world. Your very modesty invites more praise. Because you've withdrawn from the world, the world seeks you in your poetry."

"So you believe my poetry and my piety are not incompatible?"

"On the contrary, I am convinced your spiritual life enhances the reception of your poetry. Your reputation as a poet has been established without your visible hand. Let me continue to be the means by which your work reaches others." He is earnest, and I hear in his voice his desire to be of service to me.

"Thank you, Paolo."

I might as well be a courtesan when I appear in the doorway of the reception room at the Palazzo Farnese, given the heads that turn and the murmurs that greet my entrance. I am the only woman. I resist the urge to adjust my head covering, stilling my hands by grasping Paolo's offered arm. I am thrust back into adolescence, when I first began to attend Costanza's salons, uneasy and ambivalent about the sudden focus of attention after so much silence and seclusion.

"Ready?" Paolo recognizes my hesitation from the rigidity of my posture and the unnecessary strength of my grip. I want to remain where we are, take my measure of the room and steel myself for the unknown. I also want to turn around and flee.

But I am Vittoria Colonna. I raise my head, release my hand from Paolo's protection and smile.

"My lady, we are grateful for your presence!" Pietro Bembo is the first to greet me. "Having read so much of your brilliant work, we've eagerly awaited the opportunity to discuss your ideas with you."

He leads me to a seat—as gilded and ornately cushioned as the throne of a minor potentate—and brings me a glass of wine. When I am settled, the guests approach in clusters of two or three to introduce themselves and display some familiarity with my writing. I can't tell how many of them memorized lines of my poetry because they learned I had accepted the invitation or whether they truly know my work. For some of them, strangers I've neither met before nor with whom I enjoy an epistolary friendship, I am sure that I'm an oddity and perhaps even a scandal. A woman who writes like a man, it's been said of me. Perhaps the phrase should be "who *dares* to write like a man." They converge around me with a mix of curiosity and animosity. I was not mistaken when I voiced my concerns to Paolo earlier about the risks I take in the dissemination of my writing.

When the stream of introductions wanes, Pietro Bembo gathers the guests and initiates the discussion. I am grateful that he doesn't focus specifically on my poetry, but poses a question about the role of poetry in modern life—is it to entertain, to inspire or to enlighten? I lean back against my elegant chair and allow the conversation to ebb and flow around me. The poems about my husband—what the critics insist on calling my "love" poems—I wrote with a specific intention that had nothing to do with inspiration or entertainment. They were written to redeem Ferrante, and in that I have succeeded.

With my poetry I raised a man from the dead, dragging him into the light to defy death and fate.

It was all I knew how to do when my husband was taken from me that last time. In life, he had abandoned my loving embrace for the arms of his mistress and the lure of glory on the battlefield. My love alone was not enough to bind him to me. But my words! The world calls the force of my words "a second sun." And so I wielded them like my husband's sword to restore him to the honor and the glory he craved. I bestowed upon him the sun, when all he'd offered me was shadow.

There is no need for the intellectuals drawn here tonight by my reputation to know the agonies that gave birth to my sonnets. Let them believe, as my words intend, that love resurrected him.

CHAPTER SIX

Fellow Travelers

Vittoria
1534
Rome

Caterina and I are summoned to an audience with Pope Clement two days after our petition.

"I have listened to your entreaties and given them thoughtful consideration. That two such noble and pious women as you have taken up the cause of the Capuchins speaks highly in their favor."

It is not only our nobility and our piety that speak to you, my cynicism interjects silently, *but also the power and wealth of our families.* I know the enemies of the Capuchins flaunted their financial strength, threatening to withhold funds from the Church if the ban was lifted. But Caterina and I let it be known, quietly, that we could more than match their threats. I am confident now that Clement will grant our petition and reinstate the Capuchins.

Caterina falls to her knees when the pope announces his decision.

"I have already signed the bull," he notes and gestures to the secretary on his right, who holds the document.

"We are most grateful, Your Holiness. The Capuchins will bring honor and simplicity to the worship of Our Lord." Although I remain standing, I bow my head in gratitude. And then, almost without forethought, I speak again.

"If I may ask, Holy Father, what is the commission you have bestowed upon Michelangelo in the Sistine Chapel?"

Clement raises his eyebrows. "Ah, yes, Lady Pescara. I have heard that you've developed a keen interest in religious art with your own commission from Titian, in addition to your devotion to our less extravagant brothers."

I shouldn't be surprised that the pope knows of my acquisition of Titian's painting of Mary Magdalene. It nevertheless rankles that how I conduct my life appears to be more public than I realized. Despite the intermediaries who conveyed my wishes and my gold to the artist, my name and my intentions for the painting have not escaped notice. The pope seems to be enjoying this opportunity to point out my inconsistencies.

"I do believe that religious imagery has a place in our contemplation of God," I answer forthrightly.

"Then you and I and Michelangelo are in agreement. I have commissioned a mural of the Last Judgment described in the Gospel of St. Matthew. But as to the nature of the images he intends to convey Christ's description of his Second Coming, you will have to ask Michelangelo himself. In fact, you may be able to get an answer from him sooner than I can."

He turns to a cardinal hovering nearby.

"Ippolito, please be so kind as to introduce the marchesa to our fellow Florentine. Perhaps she can encourage him to be more forthcoming about his vision for the Last Judgment."

"I thank you, Your Holiness, although I make no promises as to the outcome of my conversation with Michelangelo. I've heard that he can be…difficult."

"As are we all, my lady. In one way or another." He blesses us once again and gestures behind us to the next petitioners. We are dismissed.

As we leave, I speak to Cardinal Ippolito de' Medici. I know he's the pope's nephew. A young, unseasoned man, he does not strike me as the best go-between for my introduction to Michelangelo. He is too young to have been alive when Michelangelo lived with the Medicis. The relationship Pope Clement has with the artist was forged in their boyhood, under the roof and influence of Lorenzo the Magnificent. It would have been better if the pope himself had agreed to introduce me. I can't imagine Michelangelo affording much respect to this green young man playing at being a cardinal. But I have no choice.

"Cardinal, if I may ask your indulgence. The duchessa and I have much to do as a result of His Holiness's decision. I would appreciate if we could postpone the introduction to Michelangelo until another day."

"Of course, Lady Pescara. The wall, God knows, will not be finished today." He bows and leaves us.

Caterina looks after him, shaking her head.

"Whatever possessed you to ask about the commission? Your question has set in motion yet another demand on your time and energy."

Once more, I do not wish to explain myself. I realize that what I'm experiencing is not just curiosity, but longing. And that's something I don't expect Caterina to approve.

A few days later, when Cardinal Ippolito takes me to Michelangelo's garden and I discover the sketch, my longing ignites.

The purpose of my trip is completed. And yet, I linger. The serenity and simplicity of the convent of San Silvestro is a balm. I join the nuns at chapel for each of the holy offices and immerse myself in the rhythm of their prayers and songs. To be surrounded by their voices is an immense comfort to me, akin to the music of the sea washing over the stones of Ischia's shore. Their incantations pull me out of myself and into God.

When I am not at prayer, I write. And when I am not occupied with either the Word of God or my own words, I depart the convent in pursuit of something I am unable to identify. I dress simply, forgoing the formal and elaborate widow's gown in which I presented our petition to the pope. I do not wish to draw attention to myself, as I had when walking unannounced through the Vatican. Salviata and Nicolo, my servants, are nearby, unobtrusive, following me as if I were some merchant's wife on her way to market.

I am looking not for oranges, however, but for understanding.

Caterina has urged me to listen to the preaching of Fra Bernardino Ochino, one of the leaders of the Capuchins for whom we fought so passionately. The lifting of the ban gives him the opportunity to speak openly and he has lost no time in ascending the pulpit in the Basilica of Santa Maria Maggiore.

It is a Sunday afternoon in late September when I push open the heavy door of the church and enter the dim nave. Storm clouds have been gathering and are about to open up, presaged by brilliantly illuminated skies and shattering thunder. Salviata and Nicolo hurry in after me, relieved to be out of the bad weather.

The church is not crowded. A small group is clustered around the pulpit beneath its intricately carved railing. I recognize a few faces, but Fra Bernardino is a new voice in Rome, as yet unknown to those who might welcome his words.

I see Caterina, head uplifted, her determination reflected in the angle of her jaw, the rigidity of her posture. Her very pose speaks of defiance, "I will not be silenced."

She must have looked like that when she fought off attacks on Camerino after the death of her husband. She reminds me of Costanza, in that widowhood has empowered her rather than beaten her down. I had not been forced to take up the sword as they had when their husbands perished. I, instead, took up the pen.

I find a place on the periphery. I am curious, but not a devotee as Caterina is. Salviata blesses herself; Nicolo stands in the shadows, his hand resting on the hilt of his short sword.

Fra Bernardino is a provocative set of contradictions. I am sure that most of the feet that climbed to that pulpit before him were clad in supple leather; most of the arms raised in exhortation have been draped in silk, their fingers flashing gold rings inset with blood-red rubies or sapphires the color of the evening sky. Fra Bernardino is vested in a simple robe, his feet in sandals. His only adornment is a thin cross around his neck. In a crowd of clerics he would scarcely be noticed.

But the simplicity of his garb belies the profound clarity of his message. I am rapt, enveloped in his extraordinary words. God *chooses* us, and we must remain open to that grace. I feel the edges of my wounded heart start to knit back together this afternoon. Two hours pass under his voice as the rain competes unsuccessfully for our attention.

When he finishes, he descends the stairs and I approach him behind Caterina. As she had in following Pope Clement that day in the Sistine Chapel, she moves forcefully into his presence.

"Fra Bernardino, you have done it once more! Shed illuminating light on the questions that torment us."

"Your Grace, I am only the instrument. But you honor me with your grasp of these issues."

He turns to me. "Lady Pescara, I am most grateful to see you in attendance. I hope my words have offered you some insight into the nature of God's love."

"More than I can express at this moment. It is *I* who am grateful to you, Fra Bernardino."

We speak for a few minutes longer, at the center of the others who have heard him and are eager to question and to praise him. But during this spirited conversation the bells begin to toll and a priest emerges from the sacristy vested for mourning. Behind us, the church is filling, not with those desiring to hear a preacher or even seeking shelter from the downpour. *Someone of importance has died*, I reflect.

Nicolo, observant and protective as always, moves closer to me as the church becomes more crowded. The priest on the altar starts to intone the prayer for the dead and I pull my attention from Fra Bernardino to listen for the name. A few lines into the prayer I hear it.

The pope is dead.

Caterina and I exchange glances. She was right to appeal to me to with such urgency to visit Rome. The uncertainty and upheaval surrounding the election of a new pope could be a catastrophic setback for the Capuchins. Even with Pope Clement's reinstatement of the order, there is no guarantee that a new pope will not reverse his decision.

Caterina withdraws from the knot of followers around Fra Bernardino, takes me by the arm and leads me to a quiet corner.

"I knew he was ill, but didn't expect him to die so soon. He seemed strong when we met with him."

"Or perhaps just strong-willed, pushing death away whenever he had something he needed to finish." I remember his outburst with Michelangelo in the Sistine Chapel.

"I imagine the cardinals have been negotiating with one another for months, in anticipation of this day. We need to act, Vittoria, in order to protect the decision we won with so much effort."

I nod. "I'll write to the cardinals I know are sympathetic to the Capuchins' cause and entreat them, not just for Fra Bernardino and his monks, but for the entire church. Something has to change if the church is to survive its own excesses. I certainly have my opinion about who needs to lead at this moment in history."

"They will listen to you, Vittoria. They must."

She embraces me and we take our leave of each other.

As I emerge from the church I begin composing letters in my head. The transition to a new pope is always a fraught time, and I need to reach my friends in the Sacred College before they lock themselves away in conclave.

Lost in my thoughts, I do not see Michelangelo as I round the corner toward the Quirinal Hill. The rain has ceased but water is still rushing down the hill and I am carefully picking my way round puddles.

"Lady Pescara! I scarcely recognized you. What brings you out in such miserable weather?"

I look up, clutching my gathered skirts in my hand. He stands only a few feet from me, his felted hat and cloak drenched, beads of water glistening on his beard. Clearly he didn't seek the protection of a church during the downpour.

"Maestro Michelangelo! What a surprise to see you again so soon. I have just come from an inspiring sermon by Fra Bernardino Ochino, the general of the Capuchins. But I am returning to the convent with a heavy heart. Have you heard the news?"

"Of Pope Clement's death? Indeed I have."

"You knew him well, did you not? From a shared childhood, I've heard. I am very sorry for the loss of your friend."

"He may not have considered me a friend, but he protected me from members of his family who thought of me as the enemy of the Medici."

"Are you in danger now that he's gone?"

"I have always been in danger, from someone or other who imagines me to be their foe or rival. This time is no different, although I do not plan to return to Florence."

"What does Clement's death mean for the *Last Judgment*? Will you be able to continue?"

"It is too soon to tell. I imagine it depends on whom the cardinals choose to succeed him."

We stand all this time speaking on the street, oblivious to passersby, tolling bells and the onset of dusk. I suppose we arouse little attention, since we are both so simply dressed. I smile inwardly at the spectacle we might cause if anyone recognized us—Italy's greatest artist deep in conversation with the marchesa whose poetry is apparently spreading throughout the country like a rumor at court.

"Then we must do what we can to ensure that the right man is elected." I speak lightly, as if what I'm proposing is beyond our power. God, after all, directs the choice of the pope. I happen to believe that God needs a bit of assistance.

"It will be a tragedy if you are forced to abandon the *Last Judgment*." I surprise myself with my own fervency. I appear to surprise Michelangelo as well.

"Those are impassioned words, my lady."

"No one else but you could do the subject justice, Maestro. And as I told you when we met, the world is desperately in need of the *Last Judgment's* message. Pope Clement seemed to recognize that when he commissioned the work. With God's grace, so will his successor."

"With God's grace. This wall is perhaps my most formidable challenge."

"But surely the ceiling was more difficult!"

"In execution, yes. Even remembering the work makes my bones ache. But I'm speaking of the content—how am I to represent Christ's Second Coming? I'm an artist. Not a theologian."

"That is precisely why it should be *you* interpreting the church's teaching. I do not believe that God's message is so complicated that we always need intermediaries to tell us what it is."

"You sound as if you've reflected deeply on God's word." He speaks with a thoughtful acknowledgment, not with the disapproval I often hear from those who are either frightened or enraged by the ideas coming out of Germany, sparked by Martin Luther's defiance.

"You are far beyond me, my lady, when it comes to knowing God." He speaks with yearning.

I grab his hand, intending to comfort him, but also to thank him.

"On the contrary, Maestro. It is you who have led me on my journey, beginning with the Sistine ceiling. Your images speak to me far more eloquently than any sermon."

He does not let go of my hand at first. And then, suddenly aware of where and who we are, he brings it to his lips in a formal gesture and backs away.

"My lady, I have kept you for too long and from more important things than conversation with me. Shall I accompany you to your destination? It is growing dark."

I want to accept his offer, if only to continue talking with him. But I sense that he's uncomfortable with the direction our discussion has taken.

"Thank you, Maestro. But I am accompanied by my servants, and they'll see me safely home."

The relief I see in his face assures me I have judged correctly. But I am reluctant to end our encounter.

"I am delighted our paths crossed today, Maestro. I hope we meet again when your time and work permit—and not just in a random occurrence on the street."

"I am delighted as well, my lady. I bid you safe journey." And he turns the corner, heading away from me.

I am suddenly exhausted, not from the physical demands of a long day, but from the intensity of my conversation with Michelangelo. The man has a way of eliciting from me a profound emotional response. At least this time I do not dissolve into tears, as I did when I picked up the sketch on his garden table.

No layer of courteous formality impedes his exchanges with me. He seems impatient with any barrier to true expression. I have only rarely found that quality in the men I know, especially now that I seem to engender a curious mix of awe and incredulity in those who have read my poetry.

Michelangelo's conversational style is like that of a surgeon with a knife about to slit open my chest to observe my beating heart. I am both fascinated and terrified by his questions. A part of me cautions me to run in the other direction the next time I see him; the rest of me wants to pursue him, hungry for his insight and honesty.

The sight of the convent walls brings me back from my musing to the urgency with which I left Caterina and Fra Bernardino. I have responsibilities ahead—words to form into a persuasive entreaty that will foster the election of the right man to the papacy. In addition to ensuring the existence and legitimacy of the Capuchins, I now need to make sure the new pope is someone who will allow the *Last Judgment* to continue.

I do not know how significant my letters are in influencing the papal election. But Alessandro Farnese is the cardinal whom I urge my friends to support, and it is he whom the conclave chooses as pope less than three weeks after Clement's death. After more than one hundred years, we once again have a Roman pope. He takes the name Paul.

Winter is approaching. I do not wish to remain in Rome, despite the unexpected ease I have found here. I make plans to travel in late October, before the winter seas hold me back and after Caterina and I have secured the new pope's assurance that the Capuchins have his support.

I do not see Michelangelo again after our conversation on the street, but I receive a letter from him that answers my concern about the *Last Judgment*. He has met with Pope Paul, who has reaffirmed the commission for the Sistine wall. The *Last Judgment* will go forward. But in return, the pope is demanding a different project for his own legacy—as yet undefined. Michelangelo does not disguise his frustration in his letter. He also asks a favor of me.

"It would be a great service to me (and to the pope) if I might turn to you for advice on the imagery for the *Last Judgment*. Just as you can imagine no one better to paint it, I can identify no one better to be my guide in interpreting Christ's Second Coming."

The two warring parts of me concerning Michelangelo grapple with each other for supremacy in the decision. I want to retreat to the isolation and solitude of Ischia; at the same time, I want to explore the truths of the *Last Judgment* with a mind as inquisitive and hungry as my own. No defenses protect me from the compelling spirit who seems to know me as surely as he sees the shape of a limb or the anguish on a mother's face in a block of stone. I agree to meet him on a Sunday afternoon in the garden of the church of San Silvestro.

"What do you know of me that you would entrust me to be your guide?" I ask the moment I see him.

"I have read your poems. I have seen your face."

In the end, I agree to his request. But I am adamant that I will not to be the guide to his pilgrim. We are to make this journey together as equals, complete with debate and disagreement.

"I will not be your teacher," I say. "I am no expert, only a fellow traveler, seeking the same answers as you."

"But I don't know what questions to ask."

"You know more than you realize. You *see* things, Maestro, in ways that the rest of us cannot even imagine."

"You've worn me down, my lady. I accept this mutual partnership you are proposing. If we are to be partners, however, I must ask you not to call me Maestro, but Michelangelo."

I hesitate. We have moved very quickly to a level of intimacy in our conversation that I have not experienced with others—man or woman. But I consent to his request.

"Very well, Michelangelo. And I am Vittoria."

My preference is to leave Rome as quietly as I entered it, without fanfare. But my friends and family insist on a farewell dinner when they can't persuade me to stay through the winter. Even the nuns of San Silvestro plan an evening of entertainment, with a play and music. Suora Francesca has adapted some of my poems to be acted out, a startling surprise that brings tears to my eyes.

The night before I leave, my brother, Ascanio, and his wife, Giovanna, host the farewell celebration at the Palazzo Colonna. Giovanna is more than six months pregnant with her sixth child. I can see the exhaustion in her face when I arrive.

"I wish you'd listened to me when I told you and Ascanio that I didn't want so much attention. I worry that you've worn yourself out with the preparations for this party."

"Nonsense! I wanted to honor you. And the servants do most of the work. I just sit and direct."

"How are you feeling?" I refrain from adding that she looks unhealthy.

"Better now that the pregnancy has progressed. I will admit that this one is taxing me more than all the others. I am too old to be bearing children. But we don't need to dwell on my expanding waistline. I expect there'll be far more interesting topics to discuss with all the poets in attendance tonight. No one turned down the invitation."

She leads me into the reception room, where the eager and the curious surround me. As I smile and nod and listen and answer, I find myself scanning the corners for the one face I hoped to see but do not. Michelangelo.

I know it isn't the kind of event he is likely to attend. Better a conversation on a street corner than in a literary salon, he is apt to say. Still, I hope he might turn up for my sake.

When the hour for dinner arrives and he hasn't appeared, I shake off my disappointment and lead the way to the dining room.

As I look around I am reminded of how fortunate I am in my friendships. Genuine affection flows toward me—in the animated conversation, in the warm smiles. Costanza was right; I belong in the world. This visit to Rome has sustained me in unexpected ways.

The only shadow hovering over the evening is Giovanna. She sits at the opposite end of the table, which gives me an opportunity to observe her unobtrusively. Her pallor and exhaustion are unmistakable. At times, I see her staring blankly into space, not attending to her dinner partners. Has Ascanio noticed this dramatic change in his wife? Although I have always known Giovanna to be quiet, she was also gracious and perceptive. Tonight she appears to be neither.

I look at my brother. He is thoroughly engaged in a discussion with one of the papal secretaries. As far as I can tell, Ascanio never once glances at his wife.

Because I am traveling tomorrow, I'm able to prevail upon everyone to end the evening early. I hope for a moment alone with Ascanio but he extends his farewell in the company of several others and then retreats with a small knot of his friends. From the fragments of conversation I hear, it seems they're going out.

Giovanna, however, walks me to the door and waits with me for my carriage.

I stroke her hair, no longer the gleaming curls she once had.

"Take care of yourself. If you need anything at all, write to me." I hesitate to express my fears for her, comprehending that my worries will add to whatever burdens she's carrying along with her child. I do not believe that it is only pregnancy that has drained her of her spirit. Something else is consuming her energy and vitality.

She does not unburden herself, which troubles me. In the past, she always trusted me as a confidante. I cannot imagine what stands between us now. A small voice inside my head whispers, "Ascanio," but I shut it out.

The carriage rolls to the courtyard steps and Nicolo leaps down to open the door. Enfolding Giovanna in my arms one more time, I kiss her and descend the stairs. When I am settled in the carriage I lean out the window to wave goodbye, but she has already turned away.

Within the week I am home, spending the winter by the fire in Costanza's library or at the writing table in my apartment. In letters I carry on my discussion of the Second Coming with Michelangelo, and I begin to weave into my poetry the threads of my encounters in Rome—the sublime music of the nuns of San Silvestro, the prophetic brilliance of Fra Bernardino's preaching and the shattering emotion of Michelangelo's art. It is Costanza who recognizes the changes Rome has instigated in me.

"These poems of yours are breaking new ground," she tells me as she sets the pages on the table. I always give her my work to read, seeking her comments before all others. Her notes in the margins reveal the thoroughness and intensity she brings to the task.

"You've moved away from placing Ferrante at the center."

I start to defend the change, concerned that she will conclude I have forsaken my dead husband, but she holds up her hand to stop me.

"Vittoria, this is exactly what you should be doing. There's no need to explain or ask my permission. You have completed your encomium to your husband. Even Ludovico Ariosto praises you in *Orlando Furioso*, claiming that you've resurrected Ferrante with your poetry. You've taken a bold step with these new poems and I applaud you!"

I embrace her. "Thank you, Tia!"

Despite the success I became aware of in Rome, Costanza's opinion matters to me. Not only as my literary mentor and cultural beacon, but as one of the women who raised me.

1501 – 1509

CHAPTER SEVEN

A Father Returns

Vittoria
1501
Castello Aragonese
Ischia

My vigils from the loggia were rewarded the summer after I took up residence on Ischia.

I saw the ships even before the watch rang the bells that signaled a vessel approaching the harbor. The flag in the lead galley was unfamiliar to me, but I couldn't contain my excitement when I saw the fluttering Colonna colors on the ship following only a few hundred feet behind—a white column on a red field, capped by a golden crown.

I went flying down the steps. "He's come! Papa has come!"

I raced to the entry hall of the citadel, breathless and determined.

"Where do you think you're going, young lady?" The guard pulled me back as I tried to reach the latch of the great door that led to the courtyard.

"To the harbor, of course! To greet my father! I have to hurry. The wind is powerful today and the ships will be at the quay any moment."

By this time the bells were tolling and the citadel, normally barely stirring in the enervating heat of the July sirocco, was suddenly frantic with activity.

Someone called from a balcony. "It's the king!"

The guard kept a firm grip on my squirming shoulder.

"The harbor is no place for you right now, little one. If your father is indeed with the king, he'll make his way to our gates soon enough."

"Please! I must go." I felt my eyes fill with tears as I struggled to get away, pounding my fist on the guard's highly polished breast plate.

"Vittoria!"

Costanza was advancing across the marble floor of the hall, her footsteps unhurried. Behind her followed a cluster of her ladies, clearly interrupted from whatever embroidery or card games filled their afternoons.

"I beg you, Tia. Please let me go to the harbor to greet my father—the way you greeted me when I arrived."

"Vittoria, come here, child." She nodded to the guard to release me, held out her arms and knelt to be eye to eye with me.

Reluctantly, I stepped into her embrace.

"Vittoria, Napoli is at war with France. Your father is not coming here on a social visit. He is accompanying King Federigo, who is fleeing for his life and seeking refuge with us. My soldiers will greet the ship and accompany his majesty to the safety of the Castello. I cannot allow you to go down to the harbor because it isn't safe. For all we know, the French are pursuing the king. Your father is with him to protect him and he would judge me a very foolish chatelaine if I were to have a welcome party of little girls and ladies in fine dresses waiting at the quay. Do you understand?"

Pushing away my tears with the back of my hand, I nodded. I knew what it meant to flee to safety in time of war. I had not forgotten, despite the peaceful isolation of our existence on Ischia.

"Now, run and wash your face. You may find Guillermo and have him cut some blooms for you to give your father when he arrives. Right now, I need to give orders to my soldiers to protect the Castello, should the French be in pursuit."

I didn't want to leave for fear of missing my father's entrance and having him feel I didn't care enough to be waiting eagerly for him. In my excitement, I'd forgotten how long and challenging the journey was from the harbor to the palace. But I did as I was told, running back to my quarters as fast as I'd descended the steps from the loggia.

When I reached my room Beata was already there.

"Where have you been? Do you know that the ship approaching the harbor is carrying the King of Napoli? Come, wash your face, change your dress. And your hair! What have you been doing that it looks like a bird is building a nest there?"

"Beata! Did you not see the flag on the second ship? It is Papa accompanying the king." Of course, she hadn't seen either ship. Her knowledge came third- or fourth-hand as the news flew through the citadel. Did she even know about the war and why they were here?

"Dio! Your father here!"

"I only have time to clean my face and gather a bouquet for Papa."

I splashed my face with water and endured Beata's fussing as she dabbed a towel to dry me and attempted to smooth my unruly hair.

In the distance I heard a trumpet. "They must have landed. I have to go *now*. I must be there when Papa enters the citadel."

On my way back down to the reception hall, I dashed into the flower garden. Guillermo was nowhere to be found. Like the rest of the household, he had most likely been enlisted to prepare for the king's arrival.

Knowing exactly what I wanted to present to Papa, I headed toward a bed of gladioli. Guillermo called them "sword lilies." They were like sentinels, overseeing the entire garden. Strong, like Papa. I grabbed a trowel that had been left on the ground and used it to hack at the stalks of several of the blooms.

I cradled them in my arms, trying not to get sap all over my dress, and then hurried to the hall. I could hear the drone of hundreds of voices the closer I got. To my child's mind, the entire population of the Castello seemed to have gathered at the citadel to greet the king. What I didn't comprehend was that they were also there for protection.

When I stepped into the hall, I sought out Costanza by the entry to the courtyard. The doors were still sealed. I wasn't too late.

Ferrante was with her.

"Vittoria, did you hear? The king is seeking refuge with us."

Ferrante's excitement mirrored mine, but his was the eagerness of a boy caught up in the drama of war landing on his doorstep. Mine was quite simply the realization of a dream fulfilled—my father's return. I could not keep still and paced along the wall, wishing I was tall enough to see out the windows. It seemed an endless wait until we heard the cadence of drums and the rapid thump of boots on the stone path leading up the mountain, alerting us that the king and his escort were approaching with an urgency that was unfamiliar to our peaceful enclave.

Costanza brought her hand to her heart and bowed her head, eyes closed as if in prayer. When she lifted her head again, it was to signal to the guards at the entry, and they flung open the great iron doors. She glided through the doors onto the terrace overlooking the courtyard, followed by Ferrante and me and the senior members of her court. She led us all down the steps. Like the paths in the garden, the earthen yard was covered in several inches of crushed shells whose blindingly white color was a stark contrast to the deep burgundy of Costanza's gown. It was only then that I noticed the sword in a scabbard hanging from a belt encircling Costanza's waist and the breastplate etched with the d'Avalos coat of arms. A black lace veil covered her hair, and her hands were also gloved in black.

The buzz of voices behind us in the great hall had settled into a solemn hush as the drumming came to a halt just beyond the outer wall of the fortress. Slowly the gates were cranked open. Shifting my unwieldy bouquet into the crook of my elbow, I raised my free hand to shield my eyes from the sun as the king's party was framed in the arch. I stood on tiptoe, straining for a glimpse of my father, but I didn't see him.

A cold prickle of fear crept up my spine. What if *he* wasn't with the king? What if he'd sent a garrison of his men, but had not accompanied them? Was he still on the battlefield? I felt I could not bear it if my father hadn't come. I held my breath as the party moved through the tunnel under the thick walls of the fortress and onto the grounds of the courtyard. The king was still in battle dress on his horse, not the gleaming ceremonial armor of a monarch on parade, but dust-covered and blood-smeared. His face was haggard, lost. Behind him, also mounted, was a woman whom I took to be Queen Isabella. She held a baby in front of her on the saddle. Two other children, a boy of about twelve and a girl around eight, rode beside their mother on their own horses. Another younger child, also a baby like their sister, was being carried by a nurse. They were all surrounded by soldiers. Behind them, other members of the king's court filed in, appearing as exhausted and confused as the royal family.

Costanza sank into a deep curtsy as the king led his horse in front of us all, arrayed as we were in a wide semicircle below the terrace. We followed her example. I held the curtsy for as long as I thought I must, biting my lip with hope that the king would dismount quickly so that I could stand upright again and search for my father.

He finally eased himself from the saddle and spoke quietly to Costanza. He took her hand to lift her from her curtsy, then led her to his wife. The queen handed the baby to her husband and was helped from her horse. As soon as she was on the ground, she embraced Costanza and the two women held each other as if they were sisters reunited after a lengthy separation.

When they released their hold, I could see that the queen's face was streaked with tears.

Costanza turned to Ferrante and me.

"Your Majesties, may I present my nephew, Ferrante Ferdinand d'Avalos, Marchese di Pescara, and his betrothed, Vittoria Colonna, the daughter of your commander, Fabrizio Colonna."

Once again I curtsied. Ferrante made a great show of his sweeping bow.

The king nodded absently at us. The queen took back the baby, who whimpered and buried her head against her mother's breast. The queen didn't look to me at all like a queen. Her gown was wrinkled and the hem was caked with dried mud. One of her earrings was missing and her hair, not bound and pinned like Costanza's, was loose under her veil, as if there hadn't been time for her lady's maid to prepare her coiffure before she fled. She looked frightened, which I'd never seen in a grown woman before.

Before I had a chance to realize what I was doing, I raised the bouquet of gladioli in my arms and took a step toward the queen.

"Your Majesty, we welcome you to Ischia. The gladioli, because they are sword lilies, guard all the other flowers in our park and now they will watch over you and your children."

A sliver of a smile briefly made its appearance on her pale and weary face as she accepted the flowers from me.

"Thank you, Vittoria."

Costanza, realizing I'd given away the flowers I meant for my father, bent to whisper in my ear.

"You've done a great kindness to her Majesty, Vittoria. I am sure your father is very proud of you at this moment."

At her mention of Papa, my eyes sought out his familiar face from among the throng of armed men and relatives who'd made their escape from Napoli with King Federigo, but I still couldn't see him.

Costanza spoke again to the king and queen. "I know you and your family must be weary beyond imagining. Come, I've had apartments prepared for you—food, wine and a hot bath await you." She led them up the stairs and the welcome party dispersed.

I didn't follow everyone inside, but stopped on the terrace. I thought I might have a better chance of spotting Papa from a higher vantage point. Once again, I scanned the gathering and once again I couldn't find him. Wouldn't he be seeking me out as well, as eager to see my face as I was to see his?

I felt the resurgence of my fear that he hadn't come to Ischia with the king at all, and I swallowed my disappointment. But then a single rider appeared in the archway and I recognized the unmistakable shape of Fabrizio Colonna. I leaped from the steps and across the courtyard, pushing my way through the throng of soldiers.

He saw me coming and instead of dismounting to greet me, reached down and pulled me up onto his horse, encircling me with his powerful arms.

"My girl! How you have grown!"

He smelled of leather and earth and onions and gunpowder. He smelled like Papa. I leaned back against his chest, closed my eyes to shut out everything that was my life now and reveled in memories of his many homecomings at Marino.

We rode together through the courtyard and around to the stables, away from the ceremonial entrance where Costanza had greeted the king and queen. After handing off his horse to one of the stable boys, he put his arm around me.

"Come, let's take a walk and you can tell me about your life. There will be time enough later for me to hear about you from the duchessa."

To have him all to myself after enduring the formalities of the king's arrival and the excruciating tension of not knowing whether he was even there was an unexpected and most welcome gift. He had never been one to stand on ceremony. He played the courtier only when it suited his purposes. He was, first and foremost, a warrior.

"Papa, why didn't you ride in with the king and queen? I looked and looked for you, and when I didn't see you, I thought you hadn't come."

"I stayed behind at the ships with some of my men to guard against a possible landing by the French, who are in pursuit. Until the king was safely inside the walls of the Castello, I could not be at ease."

"And now that he is Tia Costanza's guest, what will you do? Is the war over?"

"For a time, little mouse, for a time. Napoli is once again in the hands of the French, thanks to the Borgia pope and his intrigues."

He spat on the path as we walked toward the belvedere. There was no love lost between my father and Pope Alexander, and that meant Alexander was my enemy, too. It was the pope who had taken our land, who had ordered the destruction of Marino, who was the reason we had fled our home and I'd been sent to Ischia.

"Ferdinand of Spain betrayed Federigo. He was supposed to be our ally. But Alexander offered him spoils to be shared with France, and Ferdinand abandoned Federigo in exchange for power. Whatever the two kings agreed to, it won't last. And I'll be back on the battlefield. But for now, I'm here with you and ready to hear what my daughter thinks of her new life."

And with that, he scooped me up and carried me on his back, galloping down the path as if he were my pony and not a weary general who had just rescued a king.

King Federigo and Queen Isabella stayed with us on Ischia through the summer, and because of that I reveled in the luxury of my father's presence. I discovered, however, that I had to share him with Ferrante as well as the king. Papa was more than happy to escape the stifling confines of meetings in the council room Costanza had prepared for Federigo. He much preferred to play war games with Ferrante and the king's son on the drill ground while I watched from an upper terrace. It was beyond Papa's reasoning that I should join them in their sword play, even though Costanza herself had once taken up arms to defend the Castello.

"Try not to begrudge Ferrante these moments with your father, Vittoria. Remember that Ferrante has been without his own father since he was younger than the king's baby daughter. And some day, he'll fight in earnest under your father's command. It may seem like only play right now— play from which you are excluded. But they're learning something vital. How to trust each other." Costanza had joined me. She seemed to read my thoughts.

"Papa says it was a breach of trust that caused Napoli to fall to the French again."

"Indeed it was. So you can appreciate why it is so important for those two to build *their* trust." She gestured to Papa and Ferrante sparring with wooden swords, Papa clearly relishing the game and Ferrante intent on countering every blow and seeking an opening to thrust.

"What you may not grasp yet is what their bond will mean for you, Vittoria."

I looked at her skeptically. I certainly didn't see how my exclusion from my father's playfulness could ever benefit me. I'd hungered so long for contact with my family. Now to have my father here at last, but distracted and preoccupied, seemed particularly cruel.

Costanza reached out and held my chin in her hand.

"I hated it as a girl when my mother would say to me 'you'll understand when you are a woman.' You'll be a woman soon, Vittoria. One day, Ferrante will be a man and your husband. The friendship and trust those games are engendering should, God willing, mean that you'll never be placed in an untenable position between your father and your husband."

"I cannot imagine ever choosing Ferrante over my father."

"I know you cannot imagine it, child. That's why this summer will be one of the most important in assuring your future."

I shrugged. Costanza's words had done nothing to ease my resentment. She seemed to realize that. She kissed the top of my head and retreated inside.

In early September, King Federigo and his family left Ischia. The queen seemed no less frightened than the day she'd arrived.

"Where are they going?" I asked my father.

"To France."

"But why, when France is the enemy of Napoli?" The decisions of adults made no sense to me.

"Federigo is a king without a kingdom. King Louis of France attacked him, but he didn't betray him, as King Ferdinand of Spain did. Federigo will never trust Ferdinand again. He's a broken man. All he can do now is beg for the safety of his family, which Louis seems prepared to give."

"Will you go with him?" I was afraid of the answer.

"No, Vittoria. My role protecting Federigo ends when he sets foot on the ship. My allegiance is to Spain. It was sealed the day you and Ferrante were betrothed."

"Am I a hostage?"

Papa looked at me with surprise. Overheard conversations in Costanza's drawing room had taught me what a hostage was and that a ransom could be paid with loyalty as well as gold.

"I told you when you left Marino what you are. My agent. My warrior."

He enveloped me in his vigorous embrace.

Even though Papa was not following King Federigo to France, he too left Ischia in the fall. I was allowed to ride with him from the citadel to the harbor.

"Where will you go now?" I believed if I could follow him in my mind or on a map of Italy, that would ease my loneliness.

"North, for now. Sooner or later, the truce between France and Spain to divide the spoils of Napoli will not hold, and we will be back on the battlefield. When that time comes, I'll be in Napoli again."

I didn't cry until he could no longer see me from the ship as it sailed away.

He was right about the truce. Two years later Spain and France fought over the Kingdom of Napoli once more. Papa bore arms at the side of Don Gonsalvo de Cordova. They succeeded in finally driving France from the Kingdom and securing it for King Ferdinand of Spain.

1503 was also a good year for my father for another reason. The Borgia pope died, and with him the penalties he had exacted against my father. Pope Julius II restored the Colonna lands and lifted the excommunication that had hovered over my father.

As a child, I'd assumed that once my family's land was under Colonna rule once more and our strongholds were not threatened with destruction, I would be reunited with my parents and my brothers at Marino. But when Cordova captured Napoli for Spain with my father's cavalry and Spain rewarded Fabrizio Colonna with even more land than the Borgias had seized from him, I was no longer a child. And I knew that Marino was no longer my home.

I belonged on the Rock. I belonged *to* the Rock.

CHAPTER EIGHT

The Feast of St. John

Vittoria
1506
Castello Aragonese
Ischia

By the time I was sixteen, I was a woman cast in Costanza's mold. Although noble families typically hid their daughters from society until they took their marriage vows, Ischia's court under Costanza's rule practiced no such custom. In the same way that she had given me free rein in both garden and library from the moment she welcomed me, Costanza also introduced me to her salon when I was old enough to share in the conversation and entertainment. Her ideas regarding my education had at their heart inquiry and experimentation, even when the lessons learned might be painful.

The Castello was a refuge for more than a young girl isolated from her family or a king defeated in war. In some ways, Costanza collected poets and artists as she collected books. She nurtured and protected them, gave them a place to write and paint, buffered their jealousies with her praise and advanced her own spirited challenges to their ideas.

She delighted in bringing together poets and philosophers, musicians and members of the Neapolitan court, to generate creativity as well as demonstrate the beauty and artistic richness of her kingdom. It was at one of these gatherings, during the celebration of the feast of St. John the Baptist, that I learned a vital lesson in the power women can hold with their words.

"Gather around, my friends! With this last toast I send you off, not to sleep or lovemaking or prayer, but to create." Costanza raised her wineglass.

It was past eleven in the evening. The last of the travelers had landed and been served a simple supper of a green potage and lamb stew. The crossing had been rough, and many guests seemed grateful for both the solid earth under their feet and Costanza's calling the evening to an early end. On the next night, the eve of St. John's feast, the bonfires and the Ndrezzata, Ischia's traditional dance, performed with clashing swords and sticks, would mean little sleep for most of us.

"First, special thanks to my illustrious and generous friend, Jacopo Sannazarro, who delivered the wine in your glasses from his Marcellino vineyard. In addition, he's graced us with a crate filled with the latest edition of his poetry, a copy of which you will find on your pillows when you return to your rooms."

A round of applause greeted Sannazarro, who beamed at Costanza's attention as she kissed his cheek. Costanza herself had suggested he bring the books. Her guests would carry them back across Italy and spread his fame.

"But don't believe for a minute that I'm going to let any of you off easily and not require you to compose as well as read poetry."

Murmurs accompanied her announcement. Most of the guests had enjoyed Costanza's hospitality before. They knew what was coming.

"Tomorrow's topic." She paused for effect and nodded to her chamberlain, Arturo, who stood behind her with a small drum. He took his cue and beat out a short but rousing drum roll.

"First love, first loss."

Another burst of applause and knowing glances passed among the guests.

"Recitation tomorrow morning after breakfast. Be ready!"

And with that, Costanza drained her glass and bid each guest a personal good night. Ferrante and I left when Costanza did. He accompanied me to my rooms.

"Will you write a poem tonight?"

"I might. But not for recitation. My knowledge of love and loss would barely fill one line. With so many accomplished poets under Costanza's roof tonight, the competition will be boisterous. No one will be interested in the scratchings of a mere girl who's only read about great love but not experienced it herself."

"You wound me, Vittoria! Am I not your great love?"

Ferrante made a fierce show of pain, as if I'd released an arrow or plunged a dagger into his heart. But a smile played on his lips.

I pushed him hard. "You mock me. I'll love you when I have to, and not a minute before. Besides, how can I describe you as a romantic hero for whom I long when I see you every day?"

"You take me for granted, as if you'll never lose me."

"Of course I do. And you do the same with me."

"I could become sick and die. I could fall from my horse and break my neck, or drown aboard a capsized ship."

"Don't say those things!"

"I'm just feeding you suggestions for your poem. I'm your muse. Imagine something driving us apart."

"I don't want to. That feels too much like tempting fate. I'll make up a lover entirely rather than pretend it's you I've loved and lost."

"Then I'll make one up, too, and we can see who wins."

"I told you, I don't intend to recite. I'm not ready to bare my soul to half the Neapolitan literati."

"Very well. We'll just recite to each other."

"And who will be the judge of our little contest?"

"You decide who it'll be. Tia Costanza? Sannazarro? The cook?"

"Go write your poem. I have to dream of my imaginary lover."

I hurried through the door. I already had someone in mind.

Beata was snoring in the adjoining room. Rather than hovering at the edge of the activities, she had excused herself early. She'd never grown comfortable with what she considered the excesses of the Neapolitans. Life at Marino had been far more subdued, she told me. It was a fortress, not a palace that attracted dilettantes in outrageous silks.

Although my memories of Marino were dim, I agreed with her that the colorful flock attending Costanza's festa this week would have been sorely out of place in the Alban Hills.

I moved quietly to my writing table and lit the lamp. I felt quite grown-up to have been included in Costanza's entertainment. Although I wasn't going to recite in front of the guests and only intended the poem for her ears and Ferrante's, I didn't want to disappoint her with a mediocre poem or no poem at all. I dipped my pen in the inkwell and made a brief sketch for inspiration.

The face I drew was that of the musician Alberto Moretti. He'd been at the Castello before, so I knew the contours well—brown eyes thickly lashed, prominent cheekbones, full lips from which emerged angelic sounds. He had made his entrance early in the day and had spent the afternoon in the park with Costanza and other guests. It had not taken much to persuade him to sing.

Because everyone was watching and listening to him with rapt attention, I wasn't conspicuous in the trance that overtook me. The spell of a fascinating story in Costanza's library had often captivated me, but this was the first time I'd been overwhelmed by beauty in the flesh. Being within the circle created by his music and his striking presence enveloped me in an unfamiliar but strangely pleasurable solitude. I imagined that the rest of the group disappeared and I alone was the object toward whom Moretti directed his extraordinary voice.

The spell was broken when the bells heralded the arrival of yet another boat full of guests and the gathered circle dispersed to greet the latecomers. As he ended his musical reverie, Moretti settled his gaze on me and nodded in a gentle bow. I felt the heat rise in my face as if I'd been discovered in a sin. He smiled and turned to join the others.

I put the afternoon's distraction behind me for the rest of the day, which was quite busy with so many illustrious and talented people thronging to our island.

But later, sitting at my table in the lamplight, pen poised, I knew what the subject of my poem would be. A young girl, condemned to deafness by an evil witch, is restored to hearing by the love of a beautiful singer whose music she cannot hear.

The loss that Costanza had stipulated in her directions for the topic of the poem still eluded me. Some losses I was not willing to write about—the loss of my family, the loss of my childhood memories. But then I realized that the poem need not follow the order of Costanza's command, just the theme.

Loss would come first! Then love to assuage the emptiness. My heroine had lost her hearing and love recovered it. I filled the page, recalling as I did Moretti's voice and form and power.

When I finished, I crawled into bed with a smile on my face. Perhaps I would recite, after all.

The next morning, I could hear voices below my window. Some of the guests were already awake and apparently eager to work up an appetite with a vigorous walk.

"Lorenzo, Michele, come join us. Elisabetta and I've heard there is a wonderful view of the sea from the cliffs at the end of the path."

"Ursula, Michele and I decided to settle ourselves under this almond tree and discuss the meaning of life while we nurse our throbbing heads. Either we drank too much wine last night or worked entirely too hard on our poems, but whichever we did, our brains are rebelling."

"Don't pout, Elisabetta. We'll be much better company later in the day."

"Very well, but you are missing our sparkling company as well as the sparkling sea."

Another man's voice, neither Lorenzo's nor Michele's, joined the conversation.

"I will be happy to accompany you, my ladies." It was Moretti! When he spoke, his voice had the same enthralling effect on me as his singing. I eased myself to the window, hiding behind the drapery so I could see but not be seen. I watched the tall and graceful singer place himself between the energetic Ursula and petulant Elisabetta, offering each of them an arm. The three set off down the path, laughing at some private joke as Ursula turned to look back at Michele and Lorenzo, who had lost their chance.

There was no sign of Ursula and Elisabetta's husbands. Perhaps they were walking with other men's wives in a different part of the grounds.

I promised myself that the next morning I would get up earlier and be the first one outside.

The morning seemed to drag on interminably as guests drifted into breakfast from their early-morning walks or late sleep. The sideboard was heavy with dishes for every appetite—oat cakes, sausages, stewed fruits spiced with cinnamon and studded with almonds and cloves, mutton stew, potages of greens or fowl, salted cod with olives and capers, cheeses both hard and soft.

I filled my plate and ate slowly, watching the parade of noble ladies and courtiers, poets and artists as if it were theater. I was anxious for the poetry recitation to begin, but had to content myself with the scenes being acted out at the breakfast table. It was all a revelation to me, the words whispered into a bejeweled ear, the light touch of hands reaching for the same pear, the silent glance that telegraphed longing across the room.

"What are you so puzzled about, Vittoria? Your face is as puckered as it used to be when you were trying to solve a mathematics problem." Ferrante pulled out the chair next to mine and set an overfull platter on the table. Cook always complained that she could predict when Ferrante was about to have a growth spurt by the increase in his appetite. If her predictions were accurate, he was going to add several more inches to his already tall frame.

"I'm observing the species homo nobilis. I confess that I do not understand their amatory behavior," I replied.

"Amatory? Do you surmise that love affairs are materializing under our roof?"

"Perhaps they're only playing at love, the way you play at swords—enough to prick, but not enough to wound."

"I no longer play at swords."

I looked at him in surprise and asked, "Since when have you given up the sword?"

After I started to bleed, I stopped playing with Ferrante out of doors. I didn't know that he had made such a radical change in his interests. It seemed impossible to imagine him without a blade in his hand.

"I haven't given up the sword. I've only given up *playing* at swords. I'm training now with Augusto and Ignatio."

The names he mentioned were the captains of Constanza's garrison. He was quite full of himself. I searched for the equivalent level of advancement in my girl's life, but was at a loss to find anything that could match or outdo his passage beyond our childhood games. Bleeding every month was not something I considered boasting about.

I went back to eating my breakfast and watching the guests exchange coy and witty remarks.

I didn't have long after breakfast, however, to demonstrate that I too no longer "played" at childish things.

Costanza invited the guests to gather at the garden pavilion for the poetry.

"The shade will protect us from the sun and the fountain will provide us with a gentle accompaniment to the music of your poems."

The pavilion stood on a promontory overlooking the outer harbor. It was a vividly clear day, and the late-morning sun had tossed thousands of sparkling beams upon the waves.

As a modest hostess, I waited while several guests recited their poetic compositions. Some were clever; some were amusing; many were explicit in declaring unrequited love for an unattainable goddess. Whispers and knowing looks seemed to multiply among the group as laughter, applause and sometimes more raucous outbursts from the men set off guessing games about the unidentified objects of the burning passion expressed in the poems.

I felt somewhat overwhelmed by the energy in the circle, and was ready to abandon my idea of reciting. I had no desire for the assembled company to start a guessing game about my poem. Costanza leaned over to me.

"It's just entertainment, Vittoria. It may not sound like that to your young ears, but it's quite under control. A ritual with rules and boundaries. They are far more interested in a turn of phrase than a turn in someone's bed."

I blushed.

"Did you compose a poem?"

I almost denied that I had, but I didn't want to disappoint Costanza. I nodded with a tentative smile on my face.

Ferrante was watching from across the pavilion. I could see that he was curious about my exchange with Costanza. He didn't have to wait long to know what Costanza had asked me.

"My friends, Vittoria is about to make her poetic debut," Costanza announced.

Ferrante looked up in surprise, then folded his arms as if to defy me to perform well while he judged.

Rising from my place, I glanced around the assembly to gather my thoughts and take my focus away from Ferrante. I was keenly aware of Moretti leaning against one of the pavilion's pillars and kept my eyes on him for a second longer than the others as I swept the circle. Swallowing my apprehension, I began.

The silence when I finished was crushing. I sat down, numb and as oblivious to any sound as my sonnet's heroine. And then applause and a "Brava!" resounded across the marble terrace of the pavilion. It was Ferrante. I was astonished by his praise and grateful that he had rescued me from humiliation. The others took up the applause.

"Well done, my dear. Well done!" Costanza squeezed my hand and kissed me.

Moretti still leaned against the pillar. He was not clapping, but when I met his eyes he nodded with a knowing smile.

I had joined the game.

After the remaining poets had graced us with their words, I'd hoped to walk back from the pavilion with Moretti, but Ferrante intercepted me.

"Thank you for your applause. You saved me."

"I thought you weren't going to recite."

"Costanza asked me. I didn't want her to conclude I'd ignored her request or been lazy."

"You did a good job." His tone was grudging, but his words rang true. "I could feel what it must have been like not to hear a sound, and then suddenly be surrounded by the voice of an angel. A brilliant metaphor for love."

It was rare to hear Ferrante speak of anything literary, and I'd certainly never heard him say anything as complimentary as he had just uttered.

"You surprise me, Ferrante."

"You surprise me as well, Vittoria."

"Did you write a poem?"

He shrugged. "It's not my forte. I'm more comfortable with a blade in my hand than a pen."

"I think you did write one. Why didn't you offer to recite it?"

"Costanza didn't ask me. Besides, I thought we were going to recite our poems to each other, not to the crowd."

I felt chastised. Not only because I'd given my recitation to all and not exclusively to Ferrante, but also because my intention in writing the poem was solely to attract Moretti's attention. Had Ferrante understood that? I wished I could hide the blush creeping up my neck and into my cheeks.

"I'm sorry," I whispered.

I'm not sure he heard me, because he was already taking his leave.

"I'm off to train for an hour or so. I'll see you at dinner."

And he was gone.

"Your marchese seemed in quite a hurry to be away. If I were he, I would not have passed up the opportunity to spend more time in such talented and delightful company."

I whirled around. It was Moretti, of course, smiling enigmatically. He held out his arm.

"I'm told the duchessa's sculpture garden is rivaled only by that of your grandfather in Urbino," he said. "I'd love a tour, if you would be so gracious as to lead me there."

The heat I'd felt from Ferrante's rebuke and my own guilty conscience was compounded by Moretti's arrival and request. I watched Ferrante disappear toward the stable and wished I could follow him. A younger Vittoria would have done so, picking up her skirts and running to catch him. But I was sixteen. And Costanza's surrogate as a host. Part of me felt trapped in a role; still, I had to acknowledge to myself that a walk in the garden with Moretti was what I'd dreamed my poem would elicit, and here it was...

But the excitement I felt was tempered by a fleeting stab of apprehension.

I hadn't stood so close to Moretti until that moment. The beauty and simmering passion observed from a distance were still present. But the eyes that held me in their gaze revealed no tenderness, only an intensity that heightened my sense of disquiet. Hesitantly, I took his arm and led him toward the sculpture garden.

The sun was lower, filtering through the pines and cedars that cast long shadows on the path. We passed a few guests gathered around a statue of Ares, but ahead of us was quite deserted.

Pointing out Costanza's treasures, I kept up a nervous monologue describing the subject, the artist, where Costanza had discovered the piece or why she'd commissioned it. I knew the stories about all of them.

Moretti hardly seemed to be paying attention. Occasionally he glanced at a statue, but most of the time he simply watched my face. I'd never been so closely examined or so aware of a man's presence. His fragrance was unfamiliar, a heavy sweetness masking the more masculine odors I was accustomed to with Ferrante and the other men of our household. Although the cut and fabric of his doublet and hose were elegant and brilliantly dyed, I saw that they were not cared for, with frayed edges and soiled sleeves.

I'd let go of his arm to gesture at a small goddess on a pedestal and took the opportunity to move some steps away from him, placing the statue between us. He laughed.

"You know a great deal about art, but not much about men, I see. I could teach you."

"What should I know about men?"

"A man's kiss, a man's touch, a man's song expressing his love as lyrically as you put into words your own passion in your poem this morning."

I was trying to mimic the playful banter I'd overheard at breakfast, but this encounter didn't feel like the lighthearted game whose rules Costanza assured me were well-defined and observed by her guests. Either Moretti had never learned the rules or he'd chosen to toss them aside.

I moved away from the goddess and toward the path to return to the house. But as I did, Moretti took my hand and tucked it into his silk- and velvet-covered arm.

I pulled away.

"I don't need you to find my way back."

"Ah, but you do need me to find your way through the maze of love. I watched you yesterday listening to my song. I heard you this morning with your poem that could not have been a more direct entreaty. You asked for this."

"I didn't! I was describing something pure and mystical. True love. Not this!"

I wanted to run away, but he held my hand, caressing it. The glimmer of apprehension I'd felt when Moretti had first come toward me was now full-blown fear. My skin was cold and prickled with gooseflesh beneath my gown. The sun had dipped well below the trees and dusk had settled on the garden. In the distance I heard the bells announcing that the dinner hour was near, which meant that anyone who might have seen us was moving toward the citadel to dress.

I was a stupid, stupid girl and I was alone. Moretti was right. I didn't know men.

But I did know Ferrante. And although it had been awhile since we'd played outside, I hadn't forgotten how to beat him, even though he was stronger.

I relaxed the hand Moretti was stroking.

"Ah, that's better, my little lady. Rather than fight your curiosity and longing, allow yourself to savor it."

"I realize I have much to learn, Signor Moretti. But there's very little time before I must appear at dinner to join the duchessa in hosting her guests. I will be missed if I'm late and it could cause needless worry—and some embarrassment. Could we arrange a time later this evening for you to continue my lessons?" I smiled sweetly and earnestly, looking up at him as if he were a learned master and I his student.

His face bore the barely concealed expression of a man who believes he has his opponent's king in check in a game of chess.

"I would be both honored and delighted, my lady. Where and when shall we meet?"

"There is a loggia at the top of the citadel with a spectacular view of the sea—a most beautiful setting, especially with a full moon. I'll wait for you at midnight, after the bonfires have been lit. But right now I must hurry to change my gown. I will hardly be able to contain my anticipation during dinner."

I drew my hand away, but not before he bent over it with a kiss.

"Until later then," he said, releasing me.

Then I picked up my skirts and ran as if I were racing Ferrante in the garden.

I was breathless when I arrived at the citadel.

"Vittoria!"

"Ferrante!" I reached for him with a sob.

"What is wrong? Costanza sent me to look for you. The guests are drifting in to dinner. Are you ill? You're so pale."

"No, not ill. But my nerves have been put to the test by my own foolishness."

"You, foolish? That's the last word I would use to describe you."

"I am admitting it with great difficulty, but it's true. My stupid poem has created a misunderstanding."

"Ah, your poem. That you hadn't intended to recite. But did. And now you regret it."

I didn't imagine the tone of satisfaction in his voice.

"Please don't berate me. I've done enough of that myself. I truly feel I've put myself in danger with my stupidity."

"Danger?"

I was surprised. He was genuinely concerned, rather than mocking.

"Has someone tried to hurt you?" His hand moved to his sword in a smooth, unhurried motion.

"Not physically. Emotionally." I hesitated for a moment, but realized that I didn't want to lie—couldn't lie—to Ferrante. "I believe that Moretti is trying to seduce me, not out of any true feeling but only to add me to his conquests." I'd said it. I closed my eyes to stop the tears that were overwhelming me, a temporary gesture at best. Ferrante was silent for too long. Then he let out a lengthy, pent-up breath.

"I'll kill him."

I had to hold him back from charging off to find Moretti.

"I doubt Costanza would appreciate a murder during her party."

"She wouldn't want a rape, either."

"I said he was *trying* to seduce me, not that he succeeded. I managed to escape by claiming my duties as hostess and pretending to agree to meet him later. Although I don't want you to kill him, I do want to find some way to put an end to his inappropriate overtures and...and false affections."

"What is it that you want?"

"I want to humiliate him, but I don't know how."

"Tia Costanza will know. We should go to her."

"Ferrante? Before we find Tia Costanza, I need to ask you... I haven't lost your love by being so foolish, have I?"

"You are not a foolish girl at all, Vittoria, but as clever as you ever were. I will always love you and protect you."

"How do you anticipate Tia Costanza will react?"

"I believe she'll want to be the first to confront Moretti. I wouldn't want to be him when the Duchessa di Francavilla accuses him."

"You would never be him, Ferrante. You're an honorable man."

He smiled. And with his thumb he wiped away the tears that were fresh on my cheeks.

"Hurry now and dress. I'll let Tia Costanza know I found you and that we need to speak with her."

I grabbed his fingers, still wet with my tears, and kissed them lightly before moving toward the stairs.

By the time I returned, the salon was buzzing with conversation. Costanza was surrounded by several men, including Sannazarro and Moretti.

"Ah, Vittoria, there you are! Come, join us."

She took my hand and kissed me on both cheeks. "Signor Moretti has been regaling us with your expertise as a guide in the sculpture garden. He was quite impressed with your knowledge and your poise."

Yet again that day, my cheeks were inflamed, but from the reaction around me, my discomfort seemed to signify to the others that I was embarrassed by the praise, rather than angry with Moretti. I addressed the circle of Costanza's admirers. "On both counts, I am indebted to the duchessa, who has taught me to appreciate art and to share my appreciation."

"Then you have had an excellent teacher, indeed. But I'm hardly surprised that the duchessa has trained you so well." Sannazarro had graciously turned the conversation away from me.

"And if you gentlemen will excuse us, Vittoria and I will steal away to continue that tutoring you've all admired." With a subtle nod of her head and a flourish of her skirts, she took my arm and steered me away with a smile.

"Ferrante tells me you have something urgent to discuss. Does it have anything to do with your absence?" She maintained the smile but her tone was firm.

"I made a serious mistake today. I thought I could imitate the amusing banter of your guests and play at their love games, but my words were misinterpreted as asking for more than attention and recognition of my literary cleverness."

"You mean your poem this morning."

"Yes."

"So it was Moretti who 'misinterpreted' its meaning?"

"Yes. It was he who asked me to accompany him. I was flattered, and a little giddy. I was foolish." I felt close to tears again.

Costanza lifted my chin with a delicate touch. "First, keep smiling as if you and I are discussing Signora Manzi's outrageous hairdo. Second, Moretti chooses to 'misinterpret' the words of far too many women. This is not to excuse your foolishness, but certainly to temper your sense of singular responsibility. Now, tell me exactly what happened that so upset you."

I swallowed and forced a smile. "He led me further into the garden, away from the others. He told me that although I knew much about art, I knew nothing about men. And that he would teach me. At that moment I realized how compromised I was and decided to return to the citadel. But he was insistent that I wanted what he had to offer and began to caress my hand. I was genuinely frightened."

"But you wisely left him."

I nodded. "I devised a ruse to convince him to let me go. But I want to make sure he doesn't persist in trying to seduce me. I need your help, Tia."

"Of course, Vittoria. I can send him away tonight and banish him from Ischia entirely. He is fortunate he didn't do anything more than take your hand. If he had, Ferrante would have every right to treat him far more brutally than banishment, and I would not stand in his way."

"May I suggest something between banishment and brutality?"

"What might that be?"

"Humiliation."

The artificial smile Costanza had maintained during our very public conversation broadened into one of actual delight.

"In order to escape him earlier, I convinced him I'd meet him later, after the bonfires were lit. What if I keep the assignation, but instead of meeting him alone, I'm joined by you and Ferrante, and perhaps other women he may have attempted to seduce? If I reflect back on the last two days, it seems to me that I've seen him hovering around more than one. Would they have the same desire to make him answer for his behavior? I am not trying to excuse my own imprudence," I added.

"But you are right in thinking you're not alone in your opinion of Signor Moretti. I know several women here who would enjoy the opportunity to shower him with unwanted attention. I shall recruit them with pleasure—and plan a little surprise for him.

"One other thing, Vittoria. Our foolish mistakes are the rough path that leads us to wisdom. Don't regret your foolishness. Learn from it."

"Thank you, Tia." I curtsied and left to find Ferrante, my heart lifted from the oppressive burden of my shame.

But I was intercepted by Moretti.

"I trust you were not too severely chastised by the duchessa for disappearing this afternoon."

"All is forgiven." I offered nothing more.

"And you were discreet about our plans for later this evening?"

"Not to worry, Signor. I may be naïve in the ways of men, but I know how to choose my words carefully with my guardian. Till later, then."

And I flew off, not trusting myself to sustain the deception through dinner, but also not wishing to give Ferrante any reason to doubt my fidelity to him.

Shortly before midnight I climbed to the loggia. Bonfires were burning all down the hillside below the citadel. Strains of music and the clacking of knives against wood from the Ndrezzata dance drowned out the normal drone of the night insects. After my eyes adjusted to the darkness, I recognized the shapes of Costanza and six other women in the shadows.

"Brilliant idea, Vittoria. We are only sorry we didn't conceive of it sooner and thereby protect you from this predator."

"He just sees us as fodder for his songs—and his would-be seductions."

"We relish the opportunity to make a fool of him."

"And now, everyone to your places as we rehearsed. Veils over your faces," Costanza commanded, and the others retreated to the shadowed recesses on the inner wall of the loggia.

Ferrante arrived at that moment, his expression one of a warrior about to face an archenemy. I was grateful that Costanza was there, because I feared that otherwise, Ferrante would have killed Moretti.

"Ferrante, take up a position near the foot of the stairs, to prevent Moretti from running away." Costanza was as efficient as a general with a battle plan. She whispered to me, "I'm rather enjoying this. Now, I know from others, he's an extraordinarily superstitious man. Use that richly developed imagination of yours to embellish the legends of the fortress." She faded back against the wall and I was alone, my heart beating along with the pounding of the surf hundreds of feet below. To calm myself, I stared out to sea, almost iridescent in the moonlight. I jumped when I felt the heat of his breath on my neck.

"Ah, you didn't disappoint me! I hoped you would be brave enough to come."

I stepped away quickly to avoid his embrace.

"You are brave as well, Signor."

"It doesn't take much courage to want to be with you, Vittoria. There is little I would allow to stand in my way, and much that I would be willing to overcome, especially to be the first."

My mind travelled to Ferrante, listening beneath the stairs. *It's playacting*, I wanted to reassure him.

"Even the ghosts?"

"What ghosts?"

I detected the slightest hesitation in his voice. Good. Costanza's knowledge about him seemed to be accurate.

"Of the lovers who have flung themselves over the balustrade, tortured by the lies of their seducers. Sometimes when I sit up here, I hear them, pacing back and forth, reciting the words that were used to ruin them."

A soft moan drifted out of the shadows.

"Did you hear that?" he asked, looking over his shoulder.

"It was probably the wind," I told him, knowing that the night air was exceptionally still and hardly able to generate such a human sound.

"You know nothing of men," another corner of darkness whispered. "But I can teach you."

"That was no wind." He whirled around to the voice.

"Don't fight your longing. Savor it," a second voice hissed.

And then there was a third... "Let me guide you through the maze of love."

The words began to bombard him from all corners of the loggia. The revelation to me was that these were the same phrases Moretti had spoken earlier in the day, but I hadn't given them to the other women as a script. They were speaking from their own experience.

The words continued, reverberating across the expanse of the loggia. In the moonlight I could see beads of sweat on his forehead. He paced from one sound to the next, growing more agitated. At a signal as subtle as a cicada's song, the veiled figures moved out of the shadows.

"Dio mio!" Moretti crossed himself and ran, white-faced, from the loggia. The stones of the floor were slick with his urine.

At the base of the steps we heard a scuffle, the voice of Ferrante demanding that Moretti explain his presence, the voice of Moretti pleading to be allowed to pass.

I peered over the landing. The tip of Ferrante's sword was precipitously close to Moretti's neck and Ferrante seemed to be struggling with the urge to do more than frighten an already terrified man.

I spoke to him from above. "Is it the ghosts you are afraid of, Signor, or the words of your lies they reveal? You have taught me well, Signor. Never to trust you or men like you. Go clean yourself up. I ask Ferrante to spare you, only because you are too pathetic to kill."

Moretti was whimpering at this point.

"You disgust me," Ferrante said as he spat at Moretti. As he released him, he scratched him with the tip of his blade, drawing blood.

Moretti ran, clutching his neck as the blood trickled through his fingers.

I raced down the stairs and embraced Ferrante.

On the loggia, Costanza and the other ghosts removed their veils, laughing.

"Come, we all need a glass of wine to celebrate our performance."

In the morning, Moretti was gone.

And the poem I'd written lay in ashes in my bedroom hearth, set to flame by my own hand.

1535

CHAPTER NINE

A Mother's Flight

Vittoria
1535
Castello d'Aragonese
Ischia

My immersion in the new direction of my poetry is disrupted in mid-February. We have had few visitors since Christmas and the isolation brought on by a particularly stormy winter has lulled us into believing that we remain undisturbed by whatever political intrigue, disease or natural disaster is occurring across the sea.

We are fools.

It is Castellana, Giovanna's mother, who announces that our lives are about to change.

"Giovanna's baby was born two weeks ago. The messenger arrived this morning." She still holds the letter in her hand. My communication with Giovanna over the final months of her pregnancy has been sparse. Something in Castellana's tone warns me that the news of the baby's birth is not the only message contained in the letter.

"Is Giovanna well?" I fear Castellana's answer.

"She came through the birth without difficulty and the child is sturdy. Who knew my scholarly daughter would be such a successful breeder?"

I try not to react. Although Castellana's comment cuts me deeply, I know she means no harm. How can she guess that after so many years it still pains me that I have not borne children?

Costanza enters the conversation. "If Giovanna and the baby are well, why do you still clutch the letter with such anguish on your face?"

"Is it Ascanio?" I jump to my feet. As overbearing and belligerent as my brother has been at times in my life, the thought that I might lose him takes my breath away.

"He is safe, but he is the cause of my heavy heart. Giovanna has left him. She was waiting only until she and the infant were strong enough to travel. She is on her way here with all the children."

"You don't seem surprised, Vittoria." Costanza sees the look on my face as the fragments I glimpsed in Rome of Giovanna and Ascanio's marriage come together for me.

"Only now do I comprehend what I couldn't identify when I was in Rome. I was baffled that Giovanna wouldn't confide in me when she was so clearly unhappy. Now I realize why. She expected me to be loyal to Ascanio. I wish she had told me."

I pace the floor, troubled. How could my brother be so blind to his wife's distress? What egregious behavior of his drove her to this drastic step?

Castellana looks at me. "I, too, didn't know how you would react to this news, Vittoria."

"Castellana, I love Giovanna. I am more than aware of the difficulties my brother presents. I wish that whatever has occurred between them had not driven her to flee. But flee she has, and I will welcome her and care for her as the sister she is to me."

I cross the room and hold Castellana close, who at that moment looks as lost and depleted as Giovanna had on my last night in Rome.

Costanza, ever the general, rallies us both.

"Come, we are about to experience an invasion. A mother with six children and servants will need quarters, tutors and God knows what else. Is she bringing a wet nurse with her?"

Castellana shakes her head. "No, she decided to nurse this one herself so that she could leave as soon as possible with the baby. She told Ascanio that I was gravely ill and she was bringing the children to see me one last time."

"Is there any possibility Ascanio might follow her and bring her back to Rome? Who else knows of her plans?" I can see Costanza's realization that our preparations might require more than sweeping out closed-up rooms and stuffing featherbeds.

"I am the only one. Not even her father knows. Ferdinando would not approve. Has she put herself in danger?" Castellana's distress is escalating.

"It will be wiser if we plan for the worst. How is she traveling—over land to Napoli or by sea from Ostia?"

"By sea."

"I will send a ship to escort her. With any luck, Ascanio is too busy enjoying a few days of freedom from his role as husband and father and will not be contemplating why his wife undertook such a strenuous journey so soon after childbirth."

"If I know my brother, he hasn't given Giovanna's departure a second thought." I remember how eager he was to head off into the night with his friends after my farewell party. Rome has no dearth of entertainments for a man who has tired of his wife.

Costanza has both soldiers and chambermaids mobilized within a few hours. Her ship sails on the evening tide with Castellana watching from the belvedere wrapped in her cloak and fingering her rosary.

The next day I leave my quills and ink untouched and join Costanza in occupying Castellana with the preparation of an apartment for Giovanna and her children. As far as the Castello is aware, Giovanna is coming for a visit. Costanza is careful not to indicate any connection between the sudden departure of the ship and the impending visit, but she also takes the precaution of restricting the movement of any boats to and from Napoli for the next three days. We have no reason to suspect that someone might try to send word to Ascanio, but, as Costanza said, it is best to anticipate the worst.

I find myself torn by the situation into which we are all thrust by Giovanna's decision. Loyalty to family was one of the foundation stones of my childhood. My brothers and I were raised to fight for and protect one another. I struggle to fathom what Ascanio did so that I can turn my back on him. But it kills me to imagine that it might come to that.

Frankly, Giovanna's flight is something I might have expected of her sister Maria—impulsive, stubborn, and quick to jump to conclusions. Giovanna is the more thoughtful and deliberate of the two. I painfully acknowledge that she most likely gave her decision careful consideration, examining all the consequences before deciding that she was willing to accept them.

Alone in my quarters, I weep. I weep for Giovanna and her children. I weep for my brother. And I weep for myself, for I am losing something as well—my belief that my brother, despite his faults, is an honorable man.

On the third day the lookout bell tolls at the sight of a sail. Word soon comes that two ships have been sighted—Costanza's and another. Costanza orders horses to be saddled and mules to be prepared. Too impatient to wait at the citadel, we join the procession of animals to the harbor, reasoning that our extra hands can do more than embrace the weary travelers.

The tide is out and the ships are forced to wait in deeper water, but Costanza sends two rowboats to fetch Giovanna, the children and the servants. We watch from the dock as they are lowered into the smaller boats bobbing beneath the caravel.

Strong arms bring them swiftly to shore, the baby wailing and the two younger children clinging to their mother's skirts. Fabrizio, now a sturdy boy of eleven with my father's nose and unruly hair, sits in the prow with his two older sisters. The look on his face is that of a boy on an adventure, and I realize, of course, that Giovanna didn't tell the children the true purpose of their trip.

I search Giovanna's face for the answers I need. I see relief and determination. I see survival. I see a woman who has rescued herself and her children.

We reach out hands to help them onto the dock. Castellana takes the baby into the crook of her elbow and then extends her free arm to her daughter.

Fabrizio jumps out of the boat and turns to help his sisters, who lift the younger ones into waiting arms. For all the exhaustion and confinement of several days at sea, the children are remarkably well-behaved, a testament to Giovanna's mothering.

The dock throngs with activity and confusion as exclamations of welcome greet the travelers, and the children are eager to recount their journey to anyone who will listen. Giovanna stands in the middle of it all, the wind catching loosed strands of her hair and tears streaming down her sunburned cheeks.

I move across the stones, tears in my own eyes.

"Giovanna!" I reach out my arms to her.

For a moment she hesitates, and then steps into my embrace.

"I was afraid you would be angry with me, turn against me," she sobs into my shoulder.

"I may not be aware of why you are doing this, but I know you did not make this decision rashly. Whatever your reasons, you will always have my love."

I kiss her and then hear Costanza urging everyone to mount up.

"I want everyone inside the citadel before the tide comes in. The oarsmen will continue to bring the baggage ashore, but we will not wait for them."

Slowly, with guards at our back and the mountain gates secured behind us, we enter the tunnel and begin the climb to safety and home for Giovanna and her children.

It is hours before everything has been brought to shore, the trunks loaded on the mules and Giovanna and her children settled into their quarters. Castellana spends the night with them and I retreat to my own rooms. There will be time enough for Giovanna to tell her story, and only when she is ready.

Over the next few weeks the Castello adjusts to its new inhabitants while Costanza posts extra guards. She assigns the sharpest-eyed lookouts to scan the sea for ships flying the Colonna colors and holds her fastest caravel always at the ready to intercept them. But Ascanio never comes.

I don't press myself upon Giovanna but let her know she can ask me for anything. I play with the children, especially Fabrizio, who is my favorite, and I sit with Giovanna in the afternoons and read to her when she nurses the baby.

"I wish I had done this with the others," she tells me as he contentedly suckles, his tiny hand grasping her finger. "It has brought me a protected circle of peace in the midst of this upheaval."

I broach the subject carefully.

"Do you still feel immersed in chaos? If you do, how can I help you?"

"Oh, Vittoria, please don't feel that you must make amends for your brother by sacrificing your time for me."

"It is no sacrifice, Giovanna."

"These afternoons with you are more than enough. Your reading brings me back to a simpler time in my life—before marriage, before children. This hour is precious to me. It restores my faith in myself."

I long to know what pushed her to such despair in her marriage, but I fear I will disturb the healing that is slowly underway. Simple signs of her recovery are already emerging. Cook takes it upon herself to provide Giovanna with every dish that pleased her as a child, coaxing her failed appetite with small plates of delicate dishes. At first, the plates go back to the kitchen with only a bite or two missing. But in time, Giovanna finds the will to eat, especially after her mother challenges her by suggesting they should find a wet nurse.

"If you do not eat, you cannot feed your child! Am I to lose you both?"

The hollow places in her weary body begin to fill out. And as spring warms the island, she spends more time out of doors. We move our reading to the pavilion in the garden while the baby sleeps soundly in a basket, his plump cheeks and cherubic limbs signaling the success of Cook's strategy.

"He could be the model for a *putto*," I coo as his rosebud mouth purses in a dream.

Giovanna's physical changes are a welcome relief to us all. But just below the surface of her healthy glow lingers the shadows of the crisis she faced with my brother. She speaks to no one about it—not even her mother.

"I do not know what to do to unburden her," Castellana admits to Costanza and me one evening. "How can I advise her to stay or return to her husband if I am unaware of what drove her here in the first place?"

"It may be beyond us all to unravel what she has endured. Perhaps she would be open to a spiritual advisor? I only suggest it because Pietro Carnesecchi has written me that Bernardino Ochino has arrived in Napoli to preach." Costanza offers the news.

"Fra Bernardino?" I interject. "I heard him in Rome last fall with Caterina Cibo. In my opinion, there is no one better to reach Giovanna's heart."

"I am willing to try any means to help my daughter, although I am skeptical that Giovanna would be receptive to the words of any man right now, even a priest."

"Let us try, at least. From what Caterina reports, Fra Bernardino is attracting an enormous following."

I feel a sense of purpose in our decision and a relief that at last we have something concrete to offer Giovanna. I only hope that Fra Bernardino's words can offer her what she needs, because I cannot.

It takes some effort to persuade Giovanna to join us, but I prevailed upon Caterina to send me a copy of one of Fra

Bernardino's sermons and I read it to her one afternoon without introduction. I don't have his oratorical gift, but his words flow from my heart as well as my lips.

Giovanna looks up from the baby, rapt with attention and curiosity. "What is that?"

"A sermon from Bernardino Ochino. You remember, the Capuchin monk for whom Caterina and I petitioned Pope Clement.

"It's very... moving. I haven't heard anything like it before. The sermons at Santi Apostoli used to put me to sleep."

"He's coming to Napoli. I'm planning to go hear him again."

"You like him that much?"

"I do. I can't explain the effect he has on me. But it changed me when I was in Rome."

"I had noticed. You were different. You *are* different. More *alive*."

"Would you like to come with me?." I speak casually, as if it were a spontaneous idea.

She shakes her head. "It's too soon for me to venture out. I feel safe here, at home." She gestures to our surroundings. I know she never considered Marino or even the palazzo in Rome "home."

"Besides," she adds, "I am still nursing Tomasino. I can't very well carry him into the cathedral and bare my breast."

"What if we brought his nurse along and she kept him while we are at church? We can stay at the Convent of San Francesco, not far from the cathedral." I deal with the easier issue first. She is already spending a few hours away from the baby each day. But her fear for her safety is more complicated.

Giovanna shrugs. "I'm not ready. Not even for a holy man."

That evening I turn to Costanza for help.

"She is afraid to leave the safety of the island. I don't know what we can do to reassure her, apart from surrounding her with soldiers everywhere she goes."

"I would invite the monk to preach here, but the pope has stepped in to determine where he goes. Every city from Venice to Napoli is vying for him, and Paul now wants to control access to him."

Costanza paces, determination on her face. Then she stops.

"I'll move the court to Napoli for Easter. Everyone. We'll take over the Castel Nuovo. I'll arrange it with the viceroy."

As chatelaine, Costanza could command, and command she does. Giovanna has no choice but to go.

The day of our departure she stands impassively on the deck of the ship, resigned. As we head toward Napoli she turns back toward Ischia and watches the island until it disappears behind the cliffs of Procida.

Once in Napoli we move without delay to the Castel Nuovo, already prepared ahead for us. Giovanna retreats to her rooms and doesn't join us for dinner.

In the morning I visit her. It is Good Friday.

"Giovanna, Fra Bernardino is preaching this afternoon at San Giovanni Maggiore. Please come with me." I take her hand in mine, hoping to send my own strength and longing through my flesh and bone and blood.

I look her in the eye. "You need this. As I did."

She ducks away from my gaze, but I gently turn her face back toward mine.

"It's not about your physical safety, is it? All of Costanza's guards with swords drawn would not diminish your fear. Please believe me when I tell you that I understand. And listen to me. I don't know what Ascanio did, but don't allow him to hurt you further by making you cower from living your life. Why should he stand in your way of hearing words I know will speak to you in your deepest heart? Come with me. Please."

She falls into my arms, sobbing, and I am reassured that she'll come with me.

Our little procession makes its way through the streets, Costanza in the lead, Giovanna well-hidden in the middle, surrounded not only by her mother and me on either side, but by all the women of Costanza's court. We are joined along the way by Caterina Cibo. We all wear heavy veils obscuring our faces, and Costanza's guards keep a watchful eye.

When we arrive we find an open spot near the pulpit. Around us the low murmur of voices in prayer or gossip rises steadily in a crescendo as both the devout and the merely curious throng the cathedral. The press of bodies grows more intense as the crowd swells, and Costanza's guards form a tight circle around us. Beneath her veil I can see Giovanna's eyes darting about, anxious. I reach for her hand and hold it tightly.

Finally, Fra Bernardino emerges from the sacristy. He is a tall, gaunt figure in his threadbare monk's robe, but despite his humble appearance he commands immediate attention as he rises in the pulpit. The roar inside the cavernous church ceases as heads lift in anticipation. He bows his head in silent prayer, then lifts his eyes to the assembled multitude and begins to speak.

The power of his words hangs in the smoky, incense-choked air. Their very simplicity is a key that unlocks tightly sealed hearts that were closed off to the joy of the divine. Giovanna squeezes my hand whenever a particular phrase pierces her. For hours, we stand there listening to him. His grasp of the human longing to know God and his offering of a way in the darkness toward the eternal light brings murmurs of assent to the lips of the thousand souls gathered under his voice.

When, exhausted and hoarse, he lifts his arms in final supplication, Giovanna wraps her arms around me and whispers in my ear, "Thank you."

We return to Ischia the week after Easter. With the words of Fra Bernardino in our heads, we find ourselves in deep discussion during our afternoons together. The breach between Giovanna and me begins to be knit together as a result of our religious journey. I resume my poetry, which I put aside when Giovanna's crisis disrupted our lives, consuming us all with both the practical and the spiritual.

1509

CHAPTER TEN

"Marry Me"

Vittoria
1509
Castello d'Aragonese
Ischia

Ferrante didn't share his aunt's enthusiasm—or mine—for the life of the mind. When conversation after dinner revolved around a single verse of the *Divine Comedy*, he was apt to pace or focus his attention on peeling a piece of fruit. He was more willing to participate when one of Costanza's guests was a general rather than a philosopher. He was always eager for news of the battlefield, extracting whatever reports he could from the travelers who landed on Ischia's remote shore. It was a constant frustration to him that we escaped attack during the early years of the new century, depriving him of an experience he craved. So it was no surprise when he persuaded Costanza to let him spend the winter months of his nineteenth year on the mainland, training with a garrison of Spanish soldiers.

If anyone had suggested to him that he shouldn't take up the sword, he would have been outraged. His father, his grandfather and his uncle, Costanza's husband, had not died as old men in their beds.

Despite our differences of opinion about either the value or the pleasure of Costanza's salon, Ferrante and I had found common ground elsewhere. Our familiarity, bred of lives so closely woven together, gave us a knowledge of each other that was both tender and honest. We knew each other's faults and loved each other despite them. But until he left that winter, it was a childlike love, still innocent and untested.

The months passed more quickly than I'd expected. I was as engrossed in my studies as he in his military exercises. As ever, I wrote to him more often than he did to me. I missed my companion, the boy who had sailed away the day after Christmas with scarcely a glance back at the wharf.

But it was not a boy who returned.

"I am so bored. If I have to listen to His Excellency spout one more quotation from St. Augustine on lust and abstinence, I will sail back to Napoli this evening and find a brothel."

One of Costanza's guests was a bishop from Toledo, and I had to agree with Ferrante that listening to the cleric's after-dinner conversation was excruciating.

"If you think you can shock me into rescuing you from this evening's entertainment to save your soul, you are mistaken."

We were scrambling up a muddy shepherd's path to the summit of Mount Epomeo. It was the first warm day of spring, not a week since Ferrante had returned, and he had insisted that I venture out with him. He had felt stifled and cooped up in the citadel and needed activity, he claimed.

Because we had left the safety of the Castello, several of Costanza's house guards accompanied us, but it was Ferrante who was leading the way, with a wineskin and leather sack over his shoulder. He held a walking stick that he had carved over the winter to occupy his hands during the long nights in the barracks. The staff was oiled and burnished, with a solidity that was also sinuous. Like Ferrante himself. And, like his sword, the wooden rod was an extension of his arm. When he turned to offer me his other arm at a slippery point on the path, I felt the strength that was echoed by the pole, and I knew he would not allow me to fall.

As he pulled me up, the sun caught the specks of gold in his beard. The fine auburn hairs that had first graced his upper lip when we turned fourteen were now the tightly coiled and carefully trimmed beard of a young man. When we were younger, I'd teased him unceasingly about how red and silky his mustache was, as only a girl whose body is becoming equally unfamiliar can do.

I didn't consider myself a beauty. Ferrante, on the other hand, had emerged from his adolescence with the features of the Greek gods whose statues had lined the walkways in my grandfather's courtyard. Where my instinct as a girl had been to tug on the wispy tendrils that hung from Ferrante's chin, I now extended my hand to stroke his face as if it were the smooth marble of a work of art. He had changed in those months away from me.

He smiled and placed his hand over mine.

"Wait," he said. "When we get to the summit, I have something to share with you."

I suspected it wasn't the wine or the meat pastry tucked inside his bag.

For a quarter of an hour more we trudged up the path in a silence that was expectant and full of promise. My silence was born of curiosity as I attempted to solve the puzzle of Ferrante's words. I was usually adept at figuring out his intentions, but he had given me no clues. Ferrante's silence seemed to be one of simmering anticipation. His steps grew more urgent the closer we got to the summit.

The wind at the top of the mountain was scattering fragments of rock and sand and sheep dung that littered the barren, rough stone. The Ischians regarded Mount Epomeo, a volcano that had been dormant for centuries, as the mother of the island itself—the source of our hot springs.

Across from us, the Castello sat solidly on its promontory guarding the harbor. Beyond the citadel, the sea churned with intimations of a coming storm, although the skies were still clear and the sun warmed us.

Ferrante led me to a small overhang where we were sheltered from the wind. The guards took up positions around the perimeter of the mountaintop as Ferrante spread his cloak on the ground to protect us. He leaned back against the rock wall and stared silently out at the sea, all his urgency to reach the summit and reveal his secret suddenly drained from him like sand from an hourglass.

I waited. I knew Ferrante to choose his words carefully, to measure them out as a man planning a journey across a desert takes care to ration his supply of water. Words to me were lifeblood—the commands of my father, the wisdom of my mother, the learning of the duchessa. I craved words. But still, I waited, no longer a chattering, playful child who in the past would have sought to tease Ferrante out of his silence.

I closed my eyes. This annual trek to the mountaintop always excited my imagination. It was higher than the Alban hills and wilder. As a little girl I'd gasped in awe at how high we were, above the trees and in the realm of great soaring birds that could have been models for the griffins and gargoyles perched on the roofs of cathedrals. To me, the winds swirling the dust seemed to speak with the voices of angels because I believed we were so close to heaven.

The sun and the wind competed with each other up here—the one biting, whipping my skirts and my cloak, the other searing, unfiltered by the clouds and the mist, which were now below us. I entertained myself with these musings and memories while Ferrante gathered his words.

Finally, he turned to me.

"Vittoria, marry me."

"Ferrante, of course I will marry you! That was decided years ago when we were betrothed."

"I mean, marry me *now*. I don't want to wait two more years. I want to petition your father and my aunt. We aren't children anymore. Our destinies await us, and yet we are held like prisoners in these childish roles."

His eyes blazed with a fervency I'd only seen when he was sword-training with one of Costanza's guards. I hadn't expected to elicit the same passion in him, and it stirred a heat in me that had nothing to do with the sun. "Yes," I murmured.

We reached for each other at the same time and he pulled me onto his lap. We had kissed before—in front of the court, occasionally during evenings in the loggia after wine and sweets. But never like this. He covered my face, my throat, my fingertips with his kisses.

"I want you as my wife, not my playmate. I don't want to listen to Costanza's poets reciting love poems. I want to experience love myself in our marriage bed, not play at it as we are now."

"Then come, we'll write to Papa immediately. We can propose that we should hold the wedding soon, in this relative peace. It's an argument a warrior will endorse."

We reluctantly released ourselves from the embrace. Much longer and our resolve to enter our marriage in purity would have been compromised. We ate and drank the provisions Ferrante had carried with him and began the descent, hands intertwined. Along the way, whenever he lifted me over a swift-running stream or down from a precipice, he held me tight against his lean and hungry body. During the hours it took for us to return to the citadel an ache unfurled within me, not from the exertion of our mountain climb but from the longing Ferrante had awakened in me.

He was eager to speak to Costanza and send a dispatch to my father with the first ship. For a man who pondered each spoken word with agonizing care, his actions were the opposite—rash, impetuous, a product of instinct rather than considered thought. He was ready to bound into Costanza's studiolo and proclaim our mutual decision as if he were leading an attack of lances.

"Ferrante, I need a bath. And we both need to cool the heat from our faces. Any fool can see that something has changed between us, and your aunt is no fool. All she needs is one glance at us and she'll assume we consummated our marriage on Mount Epomeo without benefit of nuptials. I will be ruined and my father would sooner kill you than have you join him in battle against our enemies."

Ferrante stopped on the stone steps and turned to study me, perhaps recognizing for the first time that I shared his passion.

"If I were to stand with you before Costanza now, I couldn't stop myself from flying into your arms. I love you, not as a sister loves a brother, not as a dutiful daughter accepting her political duty to seal the alliance between our houses. I love you as a woman who yearns to be your wife as soon as possible. If we are to succeed in hastening our wedding, we should appear to Costanza as thoughtful and reasonable."

I kissed him hard in the dim light of the stairwell, leaning into him as he pressed his back against the wall and pulled me toward him.

A moment later, I took a step back.

"After dinner, we'll speak to her. I'll see you at table."

I ran lightly up the stairs before I changed my mind.

For all the love poetry I'd read in Costanza's library or heard recited by poets in her salon, I found myself assaulted by overwhelming emotion. Where before I'd felt a sweet tenderness for Ferrante and a comfortable acceptance of my future as his wife, that afternoon on the mountain had changed my perception of our lives together.

In my naive certainty, I believed I knew Ferrante well. His silence. His impetuosity. My familiarity had lulled me into contentment. But I was no longer content. I was agitated. Consumed. Astounded by how much I didn't know and had still to discover about Ferrante and about myself. The curiosity that had fueled my learning in Costanza's library had new objects on which to focus.

I sank into the bath I'd called for when I'd arrived breathless in my rooms. Usually orderly, I'd peeled off the layers of clothing and let them lie where they fell. I was practically thrashing in the water as I scrubbed the dust from my skin. Breasts, belly, thighs were like a stranger's body to me, not those of the girl who had started out in the morning with her sturdy legs and steady, watchful eyes. Whose body was this that now seemed to overrule any attempt at calm? I felt both confused and exhilarated. The safety of the future I'd imagined as Ferrante's wife had been obliterated by the longing I now felt. I loved him. Not out of duty. Out of passion. And that frightened me. I'd begun to grasp in these few hours since Ferrante's expression of desire and my own response, that my mind— honed and supple with centuries of learning—was no longer mistress.

At the same time that my intellect reeled in dismay, my body and my spirit were reveling in delicious discovery. Energy surged through me, causing me to feel invincible. What incredible power I possessed that could elicit such desire in Ferrante! *"But,"* my mind kept interrupting. That kind of intensity burns fast and demands increasingly more fuel to sustain it. Have you ever observed a marriage with such a foundation, or is it only in tales of lovers whose passion flares and is then extinguished—by tragedy or betrayal? How does one base a life of partnership on passion?

Everything that I'd ever believed about marriage had been sent into disarray.

My ability to temper Ferrante's recklessness earlier on the steps had been achieved by sheer force of will and my own apprehension that I had to get away and catch my breath.

The warmth of the bath and the lavender I'd tossed into the water by the handfuls finally began to soothe me.

So many questions filled my head, and I needed someone in whom I could confide. Certainly not Beata, who, as far as I could gather, had never felt the touch of a man. Perhaps my mother, who was cherished and respected by my father, but who, in my childhood memories, had never appeared in the thrall of anything as powerful as I was experiencing. It may be that I couldn't have recognized it as a child. But there were other things I didn't miss with my child's perception—a sixth sense not dependent on words that nevertheless detected secrets the adults of my father's stronghold assumed they were keeping hidden. And even if my mother knew this kind of passion, it was not a question I could ask in a letter. That left me with Costanza, a widow for more than fifteen years. Unlike other noblewomen whose husbands had died untimely deaths, she had not retreated to a convent but had assumed the governance of Ischia at the king's command. Did her exercise of a man's power include the experience of a man's passion? The collection of poets and prelates and artists who had found refuge in Costanza's court leapt to mind. Had any of them also found their way into her bed? And would she tell me if they had?

I dressed carefully for dinner. We had no guests that I was aware of, unless someone had come unexpectedly while we were on the mountain. Composing my face in a calm mask, I hoped that the feverish tempo of my blood had slowed enough to assure Costanza that what Ferrante and I were about to request had not come out of anything other than honor.

When I entered Costanza's apartments I saw that only three places were set at the table. Not even the members of Costanza's household—the counselors and the ladies-in-waiting—were joining us.

"*Saludos querida!* As you see, we are having an intimate dinner this evening. Ferrante asked for my undivided attention, and I am delighted to have the exclusive company of my beloved children."

She deftly tucked a stray curl behind my ear. The earrings I wore had been a gift from her on my sixteenth birthday, opals in filigreed gold, and she lifted one with her slender fingers.

"They bring out the fire in your eyes tonight."

Those eyes darted to Ferrante who stood rigidly by the fire. At least he wasn't pacing. I understood that Costanza's choice of the word "children" to describe us could not have sat well with him.

"Tell me about your day on the mountain. It brings me such joy to know that you two are continuing the tradition. My beloved Federigo and I always welcomed spring with the climb. It was an opportunity for conversations that required the open air, not encroaching walls of thick stone and the presence of a hundred other ears."

My tension eased as the duchessa reminisced about her late husband. It was no mystery why the king had appointed her governor of Ischia at his death. Duke Federigo had shared all with her, and she had learned well on their mountain walks. But had they only talked about matters of state?

The duchessa waved her hand in front of her eyes to banish memories of a time long past. "Enough of the ramblings of a widow. Come, have a glass of wine and tell me about *your* conversation. It must have been important, no? It's not often that Ferrante seeks me out with such urgency."

I was grateful for the duchessa's acute observations and her directness. I turned to Ferrante, waiting for him to initiate the topic that was the burning center of our day.

"Tia Costanza, we come to you as our mother and our intercessor. I proposed to Vittoria today and she has accepted. We are no longer children playing games in your garden, but a man and a woman ready to pledge ourselves to each other as husband and wife. We beg you to agree to holding the wedding now, not in two years, and to intercede for us with Vittoria's father."

Those were more words than Ferrante had put together since his confirmation in the cathedral in Napoli.

"We are at peace right now, Duchessa," I continued, taking up where he'd left off. "My family would be able to travel. My father is not occupied elsewhere on the battlefield. Who has any insight into what state the world will be in two years hence? When we were betrothed as infants, perhaps you and my parents were cautious about setting the wedding date, not knowing who we would become and where allegiances would fall. But surely now you have no doubts? Ferrante and I do not."

Ferrante moved to my side and placed his arm around my waist. I almost flinched at his touch, not from pain but from the shock of pleasure that climbed up my spine. I managed to keep still, my eyes focused on the duchessa.

"Please see that we mean no dishonor to either house by moving up the wedding date. There is no reason other than our devotion to each other and our desire to fulfill the destiny our families defined for us."

Costanza studied us both in silence. She seemed unsurprised by our request. But she asked us frankly, without accusation, "And there is no other reason for this urgency to wed?" Her glance dropped to my belly. "No heir who will arrive a seven-months' babe?"

We protested simultaneously and vociferously. I even had the good fortune to blush.

"We swear it! I am still a maiden, although I yearn to be a wife."

The duchessa seemed convinced. She raised her glass to us. "Then you have my blessing, and my support in requesting the same from your parents. *Salud*!"

With the duchessa's blessing, it didn't take long for my parents to concur. Letters flew as swiftly as ships could carry them, and within a month a date was set for the wedding in late December. It seemed eons away compared to the flurry of activity that had surrounded our decision, but we accepted the date without complaint. My father was still in the field; my mother wrote of needing time to prepare. She'd thought she had two more years to commission my bride's trousseau from the nuns of San Silvestro and to amass the silver plates and candelabra and tapestries that would fill the painted *cassone* that had been constructed when I'd been betrothed to Ferrante as an infant. Costanza relieved my mother of the burden of the wedding feast itself. The wedding would take place at the Castello.

With our future secure, Ferrante and I were less frantic and anxious, but six months loomed ahead of us, fraught with longing and my unanswered questions about a marriage based on the fire of passion rather than the smooth and steady course of a wide river flowing through our lives.

The duchessa seemed confident that the years she'd invested in me had prepared me well for my role as Ferrante's wife. She had focused less of her concern on my embroidery stitches (a task she'd gladly turned over to Beata in my early years on the Rock) and more on my ability to reason. But she had spent scant time on the role of love in my education, and I approached her with uncertainty, although she was my only hope of gaining any knowledge of the path down which Ferrante and I were undeniably headed.

I sought her out one hot June morning under the pergola on the belvedere. She was reading. A pitcher of chilled wine filled with sliced peaches sat on the stone table and she welcomed me with the offer of a cup.

"Come sit, my dear, and take some shade. What brings you out this morning? I expected you to sleep in after the late hour of last evening's entertainment! I had serious doubts that Cariteo would ever end his ode, and I would have been more direct in bidding all an earlier good night, but didn't want to deny the others the pleasure of midsummer's eve. Did you and Ferrante stay till the bonfire had burned down?"

"We did. I planned to sleep later this morning as well but found myself too restless to stay in bed."

"And what prompted your restlessness? Surely not a desire to discuss our dear friend's poetry?"

"No." I smiled. I knew she felt that the poet Cariteo was sometimes too full of himself.

"But my restlessness does have to do with the subject of many poems."

She raised her eyebrows. "You're a very serious student if this is what fills your mind on a beautiful summer morning."

"It's not a scholarly question I'm pondering, but one of life. Married life, to be exact. I was hoping . . . that you could help me."

"Oh, child, I can try. But if it's answers you're seeking, each of us has to find those for herself in marriage. I have learned there are no truths, no hard and fast rules that will guarantee your success. What is it you're questioning? Are you having doubts now that the date is set? I can assure you you're not the first bride-to-be who's questioned the wisdom of her parents the closer the day looms." Her voice was kind.

"No, that's not it at all. I'm eagerly awaiting our wedding. In a manner I hadn't anticipated until that day on the mountain. And that's what keeps me awake. I am consumed with desire for Ferrante, and at the same time terrified about what that means for our marriage." I'd said it. Quickly, before I lost my courage.

"Fear and desire are two sides of the same coin, my dear. Every great passion has its price. You are wise beyond your years to have recognized the terror simmering beneath the heady pleasure of love."

My words spilled out like a torrent when I saw that Costanza understood me. I questioned her about my earlier sense of contentment and how my expectation that such contentment would strengthen our marriage had been dashed to pieces by our passion.

"What do you fear, Vittoria?"

"How can we sustain this passion and not be consumed by it? How can I be all I must be as a wife if I'm so driven by desire for my husband? I think of nothing else!"

"Do you know how fortunate you are to have found love with Ferrante, Vittoria? Most women resign themselves to the duties of marriage and turn their passion toward their children or their possessions. The love that has been ignited between you and Ferrante will nourish you both and give you the strength to weather the storms that will inevitably arrive on your shore. But you're right to expect sharper pain as well as sweeter pleasure because of your love. All I can say to you is anticipate that it will come, and like the new growth of skin that heals a flesh wound, you will find yourself the stronger for having survived it."

I believed her. She spoke as someone who had lived both the exquisite passion of love and the searing agony of loss. Perhaps with her husband, Federigo, but perhaps not. To the world of the court and her poets and artists, Costanza was the effervescent and learned patroness, the wise counsel and the just and astute governor. But her words to me that morning, woman to woman, revealed an understanding of the heart that could only have come from someone who knew, deeply and intensely, what it meant to love.

We finished our wine in silence. When it was time to return to the citadel, we walked arm in arm along the path. She kissed me gently on both cheeks as we separated.

"You will make a good wife to Ferrante, Vittoria. Of that I am certain."

CHAPTER ELEVEN

A Bride's Radiance

Vittoria
1509
Marino and Castello d'Aragonese

In October I left Ferrante and Ischia to join my mother at Marino for the final preparations for the wedding. In the nine years I'd been in exile from my home and family, she and I had enjoyed precious little time together. Our bond had been forged in her letters to me over the years—a bond even my close relationship with Costanza had not altered.

She was waiting for me in the great hall at Marino, the same spot from which she had relinquished me so many years before. Despite my weariness from the journey and my position as a grown woman about to be married, I felt simultaneously the eagerness and the trepidation of a child uncertain of what she'll find on the other side of a door that has been closed to her for so long.

I took a deep breath and entered my ancestral home. I thought I would be able to approach my mother with all the grace she had instilled in me both before my departure and through her missives. But my legs abandoned any semblance of decorum as soon as I saw her, and I broke into a run across the floor. She stretched out her arms to receive me and held me tight.

"Oh, my girl! My beautiful girl! What a joy to welcome you home. Let me look at you!" She released me and stepped back to survey me from head to toe, keeping our hands clasped the whole time.

Tears that I hadn't shed for many years, tears I'd willed away when I'd accepted the permanence of my place on Ischia, suddenly reappeared, liberated by the warmth of my mother's embrace.

She kissed my wet cheeks, linked her arm in mine and led me to her quarters.

"Come, have some wine and warm yourself by the fire while you tell me all your news. I have much to share with you about the wedding preparations, but that can wait while I simply delight in your presence."

She squeezed my hand. Through the blur of my tears I examined the face that I'd carried in my locket and my mind's eye. She was still beautiful, with only a few fine lines faintly etched around her luminous, intelligent eyes. Her voice still resonated with the same limpid tones that had soothed me when I was a child.

We passed the afternoon in blissful reunion, putting aside whatever duties awaited us. For a short time, the underlying purpose of my return to Marino shifted to the background as we indulged ourselves in the first flush of homecoming. Both of us were aware of what lay ahead—the lengthy list of tasks, the potential for disagreement, the short time we had to accomplish all that we needed for a December wedding. My mother wisely didn't greet me with one of her lists, but waited until I'd settled into my old room and had had a good night's rest.

By the next morning, however, she was ready to manage my wedding as if she were a general planning a major campaign.

"Vittoria, after breakfast be ready to travel. We are off to Rome."

This time, she did have her list: gowns to be fitted, the construction of a bed and the fabrication of its linens to supervise, the choice of fabrics for three cloaks that I was to present to Ferrante as gifts, and a visit to a jeweler to select a diamond cross for my husband-to-be.

My mother and father had duties as well, ones that I gladly left to them. Nightly, there were discussions that occasionally bordered on arguments over the guest list and the cost of transporting all those Roman nobles to Ischia. It was my mother who cautioned prudence, who was all too aware of the condition of the Colonna fortune, given my father's almost constant state of war and the need to outfit his army.

"She is our only daughter. Would you have me send her to the nuns at San Silvestro instead of back to Ischia?" My father saw things in black and white, win or lose, the veil or the marriage bed. If he was to marry me off to the Marchese di Pescara, it would be with all the pomp and ceremony and lengthy days of feasting that befitted the house of Colonna. And it would be witnessed by every noble family with whom he had ever been allied or needed to impress. My mother acquiesced and arranged for the boats to transport guests to Ischia.

For weeks the castle at Marino was awash in crimson and black brocades, white silk and purple velvet as a dozen seamstresses labored to finish Ferrante's cloaks. My wedding gown, fashioned of red and gold brocade, was in the Spanish style I requested, out of deference to Ferrante. My mother had raised her objections. She wanted me to carry on *her* tradition in my dress. But I reminded her that I'd been fostered by Costanza d'Avalos. The dress was as much a symbol of my embrace of my husband-to-be and his culture as my fluency in his language.

As the day approached for our departure, I was relieved to learn that we would travel overland to Napoli and make the voyage across the sea from there to Ischia. I'd never forgotten my tortured passage as a child and feared arriving as a bride too ill to stand and recite her vows. Over the years with Costanza, we had often journeyed to Napoli for pageants and celebrations, and I'd become accustomed to the sea on those shorter trips. But I'd never again ventured by sea for as long a voyage as the one that had first brought me to Ischia, and I had no desire to repeat it when I returned there as a bride.

Traveling across the water in a great convoy, several ships carried the wedding guests, the gifts, the household property that I brought to the marriage. The Colonna banners flew stiffly in the wind from the masts. Were it not a wedding, we would have appeared to be an invading navy. Cannons boomed as we approached the harbor. With my parents at my side, I stood on the deck, the heavy brocade of my dress scarcely stirring but the gold threads catching the winter sun. I looked up at the Castello first and the cap of Mount Epomeo in the distance. More than Marino, this was home to me now, the source of my happiness and my hope.

I shifted my eyes to the dock. Ferrante was waiting for me, no longer the somber boy in black holding a nosegay of pink roses for a strange and frightened little girl, but a tall and proud young man ready to embrace his future and his wife. Our months apart had not tempered my desire. If anything, I felt more vividly the surge of emotion as I watched with impatience as the ship was maneuvered into the slip. Fighting the urge to race down the gangplank and into Ferrante's arms, I restrained myself by holding fast to the arms of my mother and father. The nature of the ceremony was one I understood; I wasn't about to shame my parents or myself in front of hundreds of Colonna guests.

My father appeared to mistake my grip on his arm for fear. He patted my hand gently.

"Don't be afraid, little one. Ferrante is a noble young man and will treat you well. And if he does not, he will answer to me."

The ship lurched into the dock. Lines were thrown to waiting stevedores and the plank was thrust from the deck to the stones below. My father led the way. When we were all three on solid ground, my parents presented me to Ferrante and the duchessa. I made a deep curtsy, surrounded by the familiar faces of Costanza's court, who had witnessed my emergence from child to woman and who would that day witness my marriage to their marchese.

The next three days passed in a blur. The procession from the harbor to the cathedral took nearly two hours. We were mounted on my father's best horses, sent earlier in the month to make sure they were calm and had adapted to the stony terrain of the Castello. Along the route the folk of the island pressed to the center, hoping for a glimpse of us, tossing flowers and waving the colors of both houses.

"They love you!" my mother murmured in wonder, as cheers rose whenever I raised my hand to acknowledge the crowd.

"Why shouldn't they! She's a prize for Pescara and for Ischia," answered my father with pride. What he didn't say, but we all knew, was that this marriage was a prize for my father too. I thought back to the night so long ago when he charged me as his warrior as he sent me off to Costanza's court. In his eyes, I knew I'd done well. Ferrante's love, Costanza's joy, even the rejoicing in the streets, were the fruits of my years in exile.

Costanza was right when she described me as fortunate to have found passion in my marriage. Had I not— had Ferrante and I simply seen this marriage as a duty to our families, nothing more—it would still have proceeded, with the same pomp and ceremony. My father would still have satisfied the wishes of the king; the houses of d'Avalos and Colonna would still have been allied. The people would still have lined the streets, although probably more out of curiosity than genuine affection. But I'd done something more than fulfill the expected duty of any high-born daughter. I'd won their hearts, and to my father, that was as powerful as if I'd conquered them riding at the vanguard of his army.

When the horses reached the steps leading to the piazza where the cathedral commanded the harbor, we left them and proceeded on foot. The bishop was waiting for us, the tails of his mitered hat flapping in the December wind. My mother wrapped a crimson cloak lined with fur around my shoulders and fastened it with a pin of rubies, the Colonna gemstones, a gift from my parents on my sixteenth birthday. Again flanked by my parents, I began to move up the stairs, followed first by my brothers, Ascanio and Federigo, and then by the wedding guests. Ferrante had gone ahead and was waiting for me at the altar.

Fifty-four steps carved into the stone rose from the campo, where we left the horses, to the carved doors of the cathedral. Ferrante and I had once counted them as we raced to the top when we were too full of energy one day and our tutor had, in exasperation, assigned us the task. Whoever got the number correct first would win a sweet. We were both so determined and fierce to reach the top before the other. I'd won that day, out of breath but gleeful. Ferrante, in his zeal, had taken the steps two at a time. He wasn't as fast as I was, but he had longer legs and that was his strategy. Except that he'd missed a step in his count. I wondered, as I climbed in my heavy formal gown, if he had leapt up the stairs by twos this time to claim his ultimate prize.

The bishop swung the incense censer all the way to the cathedral, the smoke blowing out to sea on the swiftly moving wind. When we reached the piazza, the great doors swung open, the acolytes dipped the crucifix and I entered the dim stone cavern of the cathedral.

My parents and I entered a side chapel while the guests filled the nave. A choir of nuns from the cloister attached to the cathedral had begun to sing as soon as the doors had burst open, admitting the winter light as well as hundreds of murmuring, velvet-and-brocade-clad lords and ladies. My mother fussed with my hair and my head covering and smoothed the folds of my gown after she removed the cloak.

"With all these bodies and candles, you should be warm enough at the altar."

She took my face in her hands as she had so many years before when she released me from her care into the waiting and willing arms of the duchessa.

"You have become a beautiful woman, Vittoria. Don't deny it. So often we do not see in ourselves the beauty others recognize. You glow from within, with a radiance that lights up your face, and I have no doubt that Ferrante sees it as clearly as I do."

My mother's words have always wielded a special power over me. It was her voice in my head that comforted the lonely child thrust from all she had known and loved nine years before. Her letters, filled with news and advice and bits of poetry, had kept me connected to my distant family. Now, as I was about to step into another new life, embark on a journey as unknown as my first voyage to Ischia, she'd once again whispered words to me that were as powerful as an incantation.

I have no false modesty when I take stock of myself, but neither do I have illusions. My mind is sharp and, thanks to Costanza, had the privilege of a broad and deep education. I'd been taught to observe, to truly *see* the world, and been given gifts that I strove to perfect in all that I did. But I never felt at home among girls whose interests are focused on what they see in the mirror. Whenever one of Costanza's artists suggested that I sit for him, I found excuses to occupy myself elsewhere. I never considered my face as one of my gifts.

But my mother's words offered me another interpretation of beauty that had less to do with the shape of a chin or nose, the fullness of a mouth or the softness of a curl. She saw beauty in me that flowed from within, that had as its source my spirit. She gave me confidence that who I *was* shone through in how I appeared.

When the moment came for me to step forward and move toward Ferrante watching and waiting at the altar, I did so with a smile of secret knowledge. Whatever worldly gifts Ferrante and I would bestow upon each other that day, it was the gifts of ourselves, body and soul, that would seal this marriage. And thanks to my mother, I walked down the aisle with more to give him than when I'd started out that day.

As my father handed me to Ferrante, I felt his grip, as steady and protective as it had been the day we had climbed Mount Epomeo. His pulse throbbed next to my wrist and soon the rhythm of my own blood met the cadence of his.

The incense grew thick with no wind to waft it away. A hundred candles flanked the altar and swayed in great iron rings overhead. Mountain thyme had been strewn in the rushes on the stone floor and the thousand footsteps of our guests had released its fragrance to mingle with the odors of beeswax and myrrh. So close to Ferrante, I could also smell the familiar scent of the soap he used in his bath.

The nuns finished their Te Deum and receded into the shadows behind the grillwork on the other side of the altar. The bishop raised his voice so that even the last of the guests at the rear of the cathedral could hear him recite from the great book in his hands. I recognized it as an illuminated breviary from Costanza's own library. I'd once turned its pages, tracing the vines and fruits and angel's wings that brought to life the words of the psalms on its translucent pages, so thin that I could see a candle flame through the carefully executed letters.

He intoned the prayers in Latin, then lifted his head to Ferrante and me. I heard our names—the long list of ancestors and saints pronounced over our heads when we'd been baptized and again at our betrothal when we were five, but not spoken since. We had only been Vittoria and Ferrante through all these years together. Simple bonds, but forged in the shared experience of childhood. The formality and finality of this day required the long list again, the naming of our houses and parents lest we forget what this marriage meant to the wider circle beyond Vittoria and Ferrante. We spoke the vows. We bowed our heads for the blessing. We followed him to sign the marriage contract and then emerged from the vestry as husband and wife.

The viceroy of Napoli was in attendance, the representative of the king who had decreed that the houses of

Pescara and Colonna should be joined by the marriage of the two infants, their precious first-born. Ferrante and I paid our respects to him, I in a deep curtsy, my brocade gown cascading in a billow of crimson and gold around me, and Ferrante's velvet back muscular and lean as he bent in a bow.

We moved down the aisle, smiling and nodding to the murmured congratulations. My father beamed. My mother fought back tears. Costanza watched us with a fierce pride.

By the time we left the cathedral the sun was low on the horizon and shadows darkened the steps. When we reached the horses we would ride to the Citadel, Ferrante lifted me by the waist, his long fingers encircling me like a belt. Even through the layers of fabric, I could feel the strength and tenderness of his touch, a flicker of desire that in a few hours would finally be released—from the restrictions not only of brocade and velvet but also of abstinence.

Ferrante climbed onto his own horse and leaned across to kiss me, briefly and intensely. He traced my lips with his thumb after kissing me.

"Wife."

"Husband."

"Will anyone will notice if we skip the feast and bribe a ship's captain to spirit us away?"

"I can identify at least two. My father, who expects to relish this entire experience as an achievement as important to him as winning a battle; and your aunt, who has as much right as my father to see this day as her victory."

"Then we'll continue to fulfill our duties to our families. But tonight, we fulfill our pleasure with each other." He kissed me again and urged his horse to begin the parade to the citadel, brilliantly lit with torches and awaiting the celebration.

The guest hall was ablaze with fires in the two hearths that flanked the ends. Banks of candles lined the walls, illuminating the rich colors of earth and sea that filled the frescoes. Their light cast a honeyed glow on the wooden ceiling carved from the chestnut and hickory and walnut trees that covered the slopes of Mount Epomeo. Along one wall were trestle tables displayed with the wedding gifts—the clothing and furniture and jewelry Ferrante and I had given each other and the gifts that had been bestowed on us by our families and our guests.

We took our places at the head table, accepted the toasts of countless voices hoping to find favor with either my father or the duchessa, and watched as course after course was brought out—fish from the nets of the Tyrrhenian Sea, pork roasts, meat pies and sweet pies, figs and olives and preserved peaches from our orchards.

I couldn't eat a bite.

"You'll never make it through the evening if all you are taking in is wine," my mother cautioned me. Somehow she found a servant girt to fetch me something mild and located a pitcher of spring water to wash it down.

Lean as he was, Ferrante had a voracious appetite. It was as if he was satisfying with food what he couldn't satisfy at that moment with me.

Entertainments between the courses gave the guests time to digest and the servants time to clear the remnants before presenting the next delicacy. Music, a pageant, dancing all filled the hours.

When I thought I couldn't smile another minute or accept the congratulations of yet another nobleman whose words I'd heard fifty times already, my mother and Costanza nodded to each other across the din of music, voices, clattering plates and more than one shattered wine glass.

They approached our table from each side. Costanza whispered to Ferrante, who accepted her suggestion with relief and gratitude. Then she and my mother motioned for me to rise and go with them. Ferrante stayed behind.

Murmurs rose from those seated closest to us when they realized I was being led away. Ribald comments were flung at

Ferrante as I skimmed through the doorway and followed Costanza and my mother to the bridal chamber.

Costanza had given us an apartment at the top of the citadel, adjacent to the loggia, for our brief stay during the festivities. She knew how much I loved the heights.

"I thought you two would be more comfortable here than in a hut on Mount Epomeo," she teased. When the wedding feast was ended, Ferrante and I would take up residence outside Napoli, on the Pescara lands that had been his father's.

But for a few nights, we would sleep here. I'd asked Costanza and my mother to accompany me and prepare me for this night. It was more than the need for someone to help me out of my gown and unfasten my hair. Any number of the ladies at court would have been flattered to be chosen, and they had fluttered with anticipation in the summer when Costanza and my father had agreed to the early nuptials.

But I wanted my last hour as a maiden to be spent with the two women who had shaped me into the wife I was about to become.

My mother brushed my hair after Costanza floated the silk of my nightgown over my head. She tied the ribbons at the neckline loosely.

"I don't expect Ferrante to have any difficulty untying these, but no need to give him cause to fumble."

My mother blessed me and kissed me on the forehead.

"May this be the beginning of a long, fruitful and happy union, my daughter. You will be protected and loved if what I know of the duchessa and what I have seen today of the marchese is any indication of your future."

As she and Costanza left me, Costanza squeezed my hand.

"Enjoy your good fortune, Vittoria. Savor it in the moment."

And then they were gone. A crescent moon shone through the unshuttered window, and far below faint sounds of the continuing feast and the winter surf filtered up to the heights. I waited on the bed, my hair spread across the embroidered pillowcase that had been completed in time by the sisters of San Silvestro. The room was a combination of familiar and strange. A trunk that had come with me on the ship that morning held my clothing. On the walls hung tapestries that had surrounded me in the bedroom below, where I'd spent my girlhood. Costanza must have ordered them hung here to ease me. A new room to mark my passage to wife, but not so new that I would feel myself in a strange land. Costanza was a champion of change, but change that *evolved* in smooth rather than abrupt or violent ways.

The ewer and bowl for washing on the side table were brand-new, hammered and filigreed silver that had the look of one of Costanza's favorite artisans. Beside them, more handiwork from the nuns, my initials, "VC," in fine, pale blue silk stitched onto the immaculate linen.

I was still taking inventory, occupying my racing brain with this mundane catalog to keep from throwing open the door and seeking out Ferrante when a rap announced that he had finally arrived.

He was alone. My father and brothers and his uncle, the Marchese del Vasto, who had accompanied him to the chamber, had mercifully left him at the top of the stairs. I could hear them making their clattering descent, wine songs on their lips as they headed back to the feast.

Ferrante stepped into the room and stood for a moment at the door, absorbing what he could see as his eyes adjusted to the light. I don't believe he was paying attention to the tapestries, because he looked only at me.

"You are as beautiful as I imagined you would be."

The candlelight caught the fire in his eyes as he strode across the room to the bed. I reached up toward him as our hands worked feverishly to undo the lacings and fastenings of his wedding finery and my thin gown. We didn't seem to care if anything was torn or wound up in a crumpled heap on the floor. We wanted simply to touch bare skin, unhampered by the elegant and expensive drapery that our noble lives demanded, the camouflage that hid the pulsing, hungry flesh that had been waiting for this moment for months.

When I drew his shirt over his head I saw that his chest was covered with the same auburn hair as his beard. I buried my face in the tightly coiled, silken curls and breathed in the scent that had been hinted at earlier when he stood next to me in the cathedral. He leaned me back against the pillows and raised himself over me on his strong arms, then slid one hand under me to lift me as I wrapped my legs around him. I cried out with his first few strokes, but then felt myself soften and mold my body to his. Like the room in which we found ourselves, we were old and new to each other—enjoying both the thrill of discovery and the recognition of one cherished and known.

We didn't sleep much that night. In the morning Costanza and my mother woke us with fruit and wine, and then, following the Spanish custom, stripped the sheets from the bed and hung them from the balustrade of the loggia so that the bloodstain was visible.

Ferrante and I had fulfilled what was expected of us— Ferrante to consummate the marriage and I to enter it as a virgin. The families were satisfied, and my mother hauled in the sheets before the noon sun crossed the floor of the loggia.

Our obligations extended over two more days of feasting. On the second evening we floated from table to table, hand in hand, to express our gratitude to our guests. On the third, we led them all in a dance.

On the fourth day, as guests were transported to the harbor and the waiting ships, Ferrante hunted with my father and I supervised the packing of the household goods that had not already been sent to our villa in the shadow of Monte Sant'Eramo on the outskirts of Napoli. I was a wife now, with a ring of keys and lists like my mother had wielded in the months leading up to the wedding.

The last trunk I packed myself, precious things I didn't want to hand over to servants. Not silks or jewels, but books. Costanza had flung open the doors to the library for me.

"Choose what you wish, my dear. I doubt the villa has any books at all, so take a collection to entertain yourself, and when you tire of them, send them back to me and I'll choose another trunkful to send you. There will be plenty of society in Napoli, but I know you well enough to realize you'll want moments of repose and reflection. It won't hurt my nephew to read a bit, too, in between his sword-training and hunts."

On the fifth day we sailed, with trunks and furnishings, servants and ladies-in-waiting, and Costanza's books. I came to Ischia as my father's warrior and my mother's scholar, and I left it not only as Ferrante's bride but as Costanza's noblewoman—formed by her vision of what was both possible and necessary for a noblewoman in this world.

The next two years were a halcyon period. Peace spread over the land in a ripple like a smooth stone dropped in a pond. My father gently teased us that our marriage had been its source. "Our enemies made note of the alliance of Colonna and Pescara and kept to their own castles, so afraid were they of our combined strength." It didn't matter that Ferrante had never been to war. The fact that he *could* fight seemed to be sufficient. My father hadn't spent so much time with my mother since before I'd been sent to Ischia.

We were happy, Ferrante and I. The only cloud in the brilliant light of our marriage was my childlessness, but it was still early. I had not yet given up hope.

We rode. We read. We entertained in our little villa in the hills. We attended the weddings, pageants, parades and funerals that define the texture of life at court. At first, we played at being marchese and marchesa, compelled by our marriage into filling adult roles. But we'd been trained well by Costanza, and the words and gestures evolved from playacting into second nature. We thought we were master and mistress of our own lives.

And then, France once again asserted its dominance. The Italian peninsula, not a single country but a land fractured into several kingdoms with their own rivalries and split in half by the Papal States, had always been a ripe target for both France and Spain. Alliances shifted and soon the black smoke of the battlefield filled the sky. The French were marching forcefully through Romagna, taking one northern city after another, and Pope Julius summoned the armies of the Holy League to defend against them. As it was understood he would, my father took up arms with the Spanish, who formed the major force of the League. When news reached us that Colonna was raising his troops, I was not surprised by Ferrante's announcement that he would join my father. He told me in bed, holding me in his arms. At least he hadn't done it at the dinner table, surrounded by servants.

I'd always known the moment would come. It was what he had been raised to be. It was what I'd been raised to accept. I didn't weep or beg him to stay behind. We made love—I pliant, willing but acutely aware that his mind was already on the battlefield.

The next day he left. He didn't turn to raise a hand in farewell as he disappeared into the valley and I disappeared from his thoughts.

1536

CHAPTER TWELVE

Conversations

Vittoria
1536
Ischia and Fondi

"A mentor of Fra Bernardino Ochino has arrived in Napoli from Spain," Costanza announces to us one morning. "I have invited him to join us for dinner."

Juan de Valdés appears on our shore a haunted and hunted man. He sees visions; he is pursued by the Inquisition. We welcome him, feed him with almond cakes and our fervor for an unmediated connection with God, and follow him as he roams in a walled courtyard on Sunday mornings and speaks of what Christ's sacrifice means for each of us. He is ours. We are his—the women of Costanza's court.

While our experience of Fra Bernardino is awe-inspiring and powerful, and we are caught up like the thousands of others responding to him, our relationship with Juan de Valdés is intensely personal, a conversation in which we participate. Our voices are not murmured assent, but are questioning, probing, experimenting with new ideas. It never occurs to us, in the beginning, that what we are doing might be dangerous.

The conversations find a second life in my poetry as I turn prayer into image, molding and shaping idea into word like Hephaestus pounding molten metal. I am an armorer, forging a breastplate shaped to the human heart.

The words—both those of Juan de Valdés and my own—fill my life.

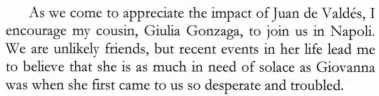

As we come to appreciate the impact of Juan de Valdés, I encourage my cousin, Giulia Gonzaga, to join us in Napoli. We are unlikely friends, but recent events in her life lead me to believe that she is as much in need of solace as Giovanna was when she first came to us so desperate and troubled.

Widowed within a few years of one another, Giulia and I were both wealthy enough to remain independent. But the trajectories of our lives after the deaths of our husbands took starkly different directions.

Giulia became Countess of Fondi at the age of thirteen when she married my cousin Vaspasiano, an aging and ailing widower more than twenty-five years her senior. His death two years after their marriage thrust Giulia, at the age of fifteen, into the role of head of the family and patroness of the arts. While I became a recluse after my husband's death, Giulia flourished under the responsibilities of her inheritance. The location of her palazzo in Fondi made it a stopping-off point for anyone traveling between Rome and Napoli, and she soon developed a reputation as a fascinating hostess, welcoming a glittering collection of artists, poets and philosophers. Her beauty as well as her generosity and hospitality added to her fame.

When my path and Giulia's first intersect, I am emerging from the shadows of my grief, basking in the light of my friendship with Michelangelo. When traveling between Rome and Ischia, I pause at Fondi and find myself in the midst of a vibrant salon populated by many who are familiar to me. I also encounter, once again, Ippolito de' Medici, the young cardinal who had been my introduction to Michelangelo.

The cardinal's infatuation with Giulia is unmistakable. Not one for subtlety or discretion, he proclaims his love in lavish sonnets. Giulia seems to enjoy the attention and the notoriety it gives her, although I sense genuine affection on her part. It isn't long after I arrive back in Ischia that Ippolito's poems follow, passed from hand to hand by the circle of artists and political leaders who make their way to Costanza's court. But within months, it is not the cardinal's poetry circulating; it is the news of his death in Fondi. August is rife with malaria and Fondi sits in the midst of marshes, but rumors abound that his death has been orchestrated by his cousin Alessandro, the ruler of Florence—Ippolito's known enemy.

I write to Giulia immediately. She responds, very much in need of understanding and compassion, and I am happy to offer what I know about coping with grief and loss. It is during this time of mourning for her that Costanza and I decide to invite her to become part of our circle with Juan de Valdés, recognizing the healing he could offer her. And, indeed, she finds in his teaching both respite and redemption. It is solely because of his decision to settle in Napoli that Giulia gives up her Fondi home and reestablishes her household at the convent of San Francesco in Napoli.

As a result, my friendship with Giulia deepens during our intense discussions of faith. Our small group, modeled after the simple gatherings of the early Church, leads us to expressions of spiritual renewal that fill us with hope.

And yet…A part of me remains empty. Untouched. I do not know why until a letter arrives from Michelangelo. It is time to return to Rome.

CHAPTER THIRTEEN

Revelations

Vittoria
1536
Rome

My decision to journey back to the city I so reluctantly entered two years before is one sign of the changes I am embracing. Another is a spontaneous invitation I extend to Giulia to accompany me for a brief visit. We have formed a bond in the months since she moved to Napoli and I'm reluctant to allow it to weaken with separation. We both appear to be on the cusp of transformation and are eager to nurture one another on our journey.

Shortly after we arrive at San Silvestro, we stroll in the garden, easing the sore muscles precipitated by our travels. I broach a subject that has been hovering at the periphery of my thoughts.

"May we speak honestly?"

"Of course, Vittoria! I have no secrets from you."

"You are a different woman from the gracious chatelaine of Fondi I remember. You are still gracious, but with a grace of a different sort."

"I scarcely recognize myself from the woman I once was. The life I led there now seems empty of meaning. I was hollow, trying to fill myself with the attention and acclaim of my famous guests."

"Cardinal Ippolito in particular?"

"He loved me. And I, understanding then only an incomplete form of love, thought I loved him, too. Did you know we were to marry?"

"I didn't know. How…?"

"He had requested to be released from Holy Orders."

"And then he died."

She nods. "In my arms. If you and Costanza hadn't invited me to Napoli, I might have succumbed to my grief. When Vaspasiano died, I felt no such despair."

"I saw something of myself in you. After Ferrante's death, I couldn't imagine my life without him. As distant as we had been in the last years of our marriage—separated not only by physical mountains, but also by an emotional desert—I clung to the only identity I had known. From the time I was a girl, I was connected irrevocably to Ferrante d'Avalos. First as his betrothed, then as his wife, and finally as his widow. Like you, I believed I loved him. But perhaps what I loved and what I sought to protect, was my own honor."

"We've both grown, haven't we?" She grasps my hand.

"The message of Juan de Valdés has resonated strongly with you."

"I am learning with him to confront my loneliness and my fears. When I was the mistress of Fondi, I lived my life solely on the surface—the charming muse, applauding and inspiring the poets and sitting for flattering portraits by the artists. All to appear pleasing in their eyes. I didn't reveal what was truly in my heart. With Juan, with you and our circle of women, I'm finding the words, finding the way to true happiness."

"We are all discovering a blessed freedom to know God on our own terms with Juan as our guide. But you, in particular, have formed a special bond."

"A special bond, yes, but not a comfortable one."

Her description skims close to the reason for my initiating this conversation. I know the discomfort she has named—not with Juan de Valdés but with Michelangelo. When I do not speak, she continues, perhaps recognizing something in my expression that conveys my need to explore this topic.

"He pushes me to confront my disquietude and seek the source of my fears. When I expect him to show me the way, because he has already made the journey to God, he wants me to struggle with my thoughts. He probes and questions and provokes me. He taunts me that I want to encounter the true path to the Divine without leaving my familiar world. I should be angry and exasperated with him—and often am—but he is so compelling that I am drawn to him in ways that strip me to my bare soul. It is both terrifying and enthralling."

"I know this soul-shattering emotion." I whisper, astounded and relieved by her honesty and its parallel in my emerging friendship with Michelangelo.

"This is why you have returned to Rome." She is not asking me, but stating what she suddenly apprehends. "It is the artist, Michelangelo."

"Yes."

"Don't run away from the fear, Vittoria. Open yourself to it, even when it causes you pain."

1512 – 1513

CHAPTER FOURTEEN

Waiting

Vittoria
1512
Pescara and Ischia

After Ferrante had gone to war, I wrote. The young bride, suddenly bereft, recalling the face and limbs of her husband in her poetry lest she forget his embrace while he was on the battlefield.

The words were a way to quell my anxiety and fill the hours. I was lonely. No child toddled into my waiting arms, fresh from his nap. After three years of marriage, we had hoped for at least the flutter of life inside my belly before Ferrante left for war.

As I wrote, my empty hand rested on that belly, my fingertips searching through the layers of brocade and silk for some sign, some impulse within my flesh. Did I hope to transmit through my outstretched hand the prayers I uttered each month before I bled, as if God was listening not only to my words but to my touch?

Three weeks after Ferrante departed, my prayers once again failed to elicit the compassion of the Lord. I awoke in the middle of a moonless night to bloody sheets and washed the stains out with my tears.

I didn't have the heart to convey the news to Ferrante in the field. A warrior's wife keeps her disappointments to herself.

When I'd been alone with my writing and my walks for a month, a messenger arrived with a letter. I was in the olive grove discussing the pruning with the ancient gardener who had probably planted the trees. He scarcely needed my direction, but he tolerated me and taught me a few things I would never have gleaned from Costanza's library. I saw the steward approaching us, picking his way carefully over the rock-strewn terrain as he balanced on his right hand the silver tray he used to deliver messages.

My hand flew to my breast. At first I was rooted to the spot where I stood, frozen, as if to delay the news I feared was contained in that letter. Was Ferrante injured? Captured? I refused to allow myself to anticipate the worst. I remembered my mother standing on the terrace at Marino every time a messenger appeared. Always still, her face a mask, waiting for the letter to be placed in her hand. I don't know how she did it, containing herself. I couldn't do it at that moment and found myself breaking away from the spot that had held me.

I lifted my skirts and ran toward the steward, meeting him on the hillside above the grove.

"My lady, a letter. I thought it best to bring it to you here rather than wait for your return to the villa."

"You acted wisely. Thank you. You may go back to the house. Give the messenger something to eat." I turned from him, my hand shaking until I saw the seal. It was neither Ferrante's nor my father's, but I recognized it immediately. Costanza's palm leaf.

A thousand questions rippled through my brain. Would she have been told first, to ease my pain and have the news come from her rather than the battlefield? I was so new at this, I didn't know what to expect.

I broke the seal and read the letter written in Costanza's hand as the old man leaned on his scythe and watched me. I'm sure he had seen little that had changed for women whose husbands were away at war. I shook my head to dispel the foolishness I felt after I read Costanza's words, for her message was an invitation.

"I see no reason for each of us to be deprived of company simply because Ferrante has taken up the sword," she wrote. "The villa will run itself in your absence, so I urge you to pack a trunk and come stay with me. You are missed."

I didn't need any further encouragement to accept her invitation. When I returned to the house, I wrote two letters for the messenger to carry. One to Costanza, telling her I would sail for Ischia as soon as I could arrange my affairs, and a second to Ferrante that, should he be seeking me, he would find me on the island.

A week later, I stepped once again onto the stones of Ischia and didn't leave the island the whole time Ferrante was at war.

Life with Costanza was the refuge it had always been for me and allowed me to lose myself for brief periods in her books and her company. But I never forgot I was the wife of a soldier. I resumed my post in the loggia at the top of the citadel, watching the sea as if I could read it for signs of Ferrante's well-being, but it told me nothing.

CHAPTER FIFTEEN

A Lonely and Frightened Child

Vittoria
1512
Ischia

Instead of news from or about my husband, what the sea delivered shortly after my arrival was a family tragedy that was to alter my life in unexpected ways. Costanza's brother, Inigo, and his wife, Laura, had perished in a shipwreck, leaving their young son, Alfonso, an orphan. In March, the boy disembarked on our shore and introduced chaos to the household.

I don't know if he had been indulged by his parents or if his grief precipitated his undisciplined behavior. Whatever the cause, he appeared to be beyond redemption, a danger to himself and anyone who stood in his path. He rewarded any attempt to control him with biting and kicking and screaming. At night, he either prowled the corridors or, when locked in his room to keep him from setting the citadel on fire or leaping from the loggia, he howled incessantly.

Costanza's experience of raising the somber Ferrante had not prepared her for this wild child. After only a week, she was ragged from worry and lack of sleep.

"If Ferrante were here, he could take the boy in hand—a mere wisp of a daydream," she said to me in despair. I suffered for her, but I suffered for the boy as well. I remembered the frightened girl who felt she'd been abandoned on this lonely rock, and thought of the times she had muffled her howls in a pillow in the dead of night, not expecting any sympathetic ears to hear her, any sympathetic voice to calm her.

One night when the howling began, I took a lantern and a book and traversed the corridor of the citadel leading to the boy's room. One of the stewards was assigned as sentinel should Alfonso break down the door. I asked him quietly to let me in and, despite his protests, succeeded in gaining entry into the chamber.

I lifted the lantern to the corner where Alfonso's screams had originated, although they'd stopped as soon as the key had turned in the lock and I'd slid quickly in.

"Go away!" He lunged at me but I stepped aside.

"Since I cannot sleep and apparently neither can you, I thought we could spend the night in each other's company."

"I don't want company. I want to go home!"

I didn't have the heart to tell the boy he no longer had a home.

"Did you know this was my room when I was sent here, away from my home? I was about your age."

"I don't believe you."

I ignored his distrust. He had no reason, after all, to believe me.

"There's a secret cupboard in the wall, where I kept my most precious things." It seemed cruel to tell him those things were my mother's letters, since he'd never have any of his own. "Would you like to see it?"

He started to nod his assent warily, but then pulled back, screaming at me. "This is a trick! You're going to lock me in the cupboard the way they've locked me in my room."

I could only imagine the nightmares that must be plaguing the boy. No wonder he howled all night. It was to prevent himself from falling asleep and into whatever terrors stalked him.

"It's far too small to hide a strapping boy like you. And I have no desire to lock you away. If you don't want to see it, it'll be my secret. Not even your Tia Costanza knows about it. When I was small, I wanted something that was wholly mine, where I could hold onto the memories I brought with me here from my home. Do you have memories you don't want to lose?"

I knew I was taking a risk, but it seemed to me that was all the boy believed he had now. If I could give him a means to protect those memories and keep them safe, perhaps he'd be able to lose the anger that appeared to be driving his unruly behavior.

Except for his one outburst, he'd been quiet since I'd entered his room. Despite his distrust, he'd listened to me. Whether he'd answer me, other than to spit out venom, was still a question in my mind. I truly had no plan when I took my lamp across the citadel, only a desire to comfort what I knew was a heart in pain.

I waited. I took a seat by the window, a padded alcove piled with tapestry pillows filled with down. It had been one of my favorite spots in the room for reading, and I now propped the lamp on the sill and opened the book I'd brought with me.

"What are you doing?"

"I'm reading, as you can see."

"But why? In the middle of the night?"

"I told you, I can't sleep. And since you don't want my company, I brought along a book to entertain me."

"Books don't entertain! Books are for schoolrooms and Papa's library." He choked on his father's name, as if invoking him was something he hadn't meant to do.

"Then you must've read the wrong books. Can you read?"

"Of course I can. I'm nine!"

"If you believe books can't entertain, you must not have read this one." And I put my head down in the book again, a smile on my lips that I hoped he didn't see.

He inched closer to me. "I don't believe you," he said again, but with less certainty than before.

"Shall I prove it to you?" I don't like to gamble, and I hardly wanted to encourage it in Alfonso, but I thought he might respond more willingly to me if I challenged him with a wager.

"I bet this book will entertain you," I said.

"Or what? What's the wager?"

"If it doesn't, what shall I forfeit?"

"If it doesn't entertain me, then you have to make up a story for me."

I couldn't have asked for more.

"Then come here and sit with me by the light. Do you want to read the book yourself, or shall I read aloud to you?"

He hesitated and pondered the choices. I suspected that although he clearly was a clever boy, he had no love of learning. His skill at reading was probably meager, and his father's library more than likely had not been his playroom.

"You read," he said gruffly, and clambered up onto the opposite end of the window seat.

I began the tale I'd chosen, one of my brothers' favorites, filled with daring exploits of knights, wild animals and grave dangers.

He listened with rapt attention, slashing at the air with an imaginary sword when the knights were battling their enemies and gasping when all appeared lost.

"Shall I continue?" I asked once the story had reached its peak and the knight must either slay the dragon or be slain.

"Keep going! Don't stop!"

As I finished, his eyes were heavy and he was struggling to stay awake. I dared not move him to his bed; I worried that disturbing him would start the cycle of howling again and reignite his fear of sleep and its attendant dark dreams. So I let him drift off on the window seat and remained there with him throughout the night.

I turned down the lamp, but left it to glimmer with a low flame. Because of the fear that he might set a fire during his nightly rages, he'd been denied any light, which must have fueled his panic and resistance to sleep. If he woke during the night, confused by his location and my presence, I wanted him at least to have the reassurance of light.

I settled in as comfortably as I could and threw a soft blanket over us both. I was exhausted. I hadn't gotten him to speak his memories aloud, but I'd succeeded in getting him to listen—if not to me, then to the story—and that was success enough for one night.

The window faced east, and all too soon I noticed the pink light of dawn easing across my face. Alfonso had had a tranquil night. For such a wild and energetic boy, I'd expected a sleep interrupted by thrashing and kicking. Perhaps my story had filled his dreams with fantasies of knights, replacing the reality of his parents' violent end. I watched his face in the sweet repose of sleep and ached. I would have gathered him up in my arms and held him close to protect him from the demons that haunted him in his inexplicable loss. But he was nine. He would have pushed away my solace as vigorously as he'd tried to push me out of his room the night before. No mother myself, I could not replace *his* mother.

As Costanza had admitted in her weariness, if Ferrante had been there, he would have taken Alfonso in hand. He understood what it meant to be orphaned as a boy and could have taught Alfonso how to look forward, not back. It would never serve the boy to allow his rages to continue. I had stilled them briefly, but I had no illusions that my persistence during the night had brought him and the rest of the household anything more than one night's rest.

I felt him stir against my feet and braced myself for the anger and confusion his waking might bring. He kicked off the blanket, arms and legs flailing as he turned on the narrow window seat. When he realized he wasn't in his bed and not alone, he rubbed his eyes.

"So it wasn't a dream."

"No. I'm real, and I'm here."

"When I was a little boy, my mother would sometimes send my nurse away and stay with me until I slept. But I don't need that anymore. I'm nine. Not a baby."

"No, you certainly are *not* a baby. But your howling makes us perceive you as one. Last night, however, you didn't act like a baby."

"Then why did you stay?"

"I saw no reason to disturb you after you'd fallen asleep, and I was so weary myself that I didn't want to trek across the citadel again in the cold and the dark. I'm grateful for your hospitality."

With that, I gathered my robe about me and got up to leave.

"What about our wager?"

"What about it? Were you entertained?"

"We had no books like that in my schoolroom."

"I have many more like that one. If you want to see how long I can entertain you, I can read to you again."

Alfonso struggled with his answer. He appeared to be a boy who was used to winning, but he also was a boy who thrilled to the kind of story I'd read to him the night before. In the end, the story won.

"They make me go to bed at eight. Can you come then?"

"Of course I can. Would you mind if I took supper with you this evening? If I come to read with you at eight, I will miss Costanza's meal." I might be pushing him too fast, but if the hours he was willing to spend with me were quiet ones that calmed him, then I wanted to spend as many as possible in his company.

"Cook is making pigeon pie and a baba. Do you like babas? I like them so sticky and sweet the syrup runs down my chin!"

It was the first time I'd seen him smile, and I promised myself that I would do everything in my power to give him cause to smile again.

When I joined Costanza for breakfast, she already knew from the steward the reason for the first quiet night in the citadel since Alfonso had joined us.

"How did you do it?"

"I was as stubborn as he was and refused to leave until I stumbled on the one thing that would quiet him."

"What was that?"

"Stories. I remembered how they'd held my brothers' attention when they were restless. I suspect Alfonso was never introduced to the pleasures of reading, only the discipline and the exercises."

"That would be Inigo's doing, God rest his soul. And Laura, sweet-tempered though she was, really wasn't very bright. I fear his education so far has been less than adequate."

"He's not a stupid boy. His mind is quick and clever, but untrained. I like him, Costanza. And I feel I'm beginning to understand him. In the right hands, he could become a fine young man."

"I'm too old to raise another of my brothers' sons. I despair what will become of him."

I wrote to Ferrante about my concerns for Alfonso and our need of his wisdom and experience in caring for the boy. I didn't know when I'd hear back from him—his correspondence was sporadic at best. But he was still at Marino and not on the march, and I received a reply from him sooner than I expected. What he wrote, however, was not something I expected at all.

"My beloved," he began, "I am about to ask of you a great service. With no children of our own to thrive in the gentle intelligence that you would bring to their upbringing, I beg you to take Alfonso as our adopted son and be the mother he has lost and that I know you long to be. I know he's not a babe to cradle and soothe with lullabies, but he needs the hand of a parent who loves him and wants to guide him. Were I home with you, I would share that role. But my place is here and I trust in who you are and all that you will bring to this task. Please do this for me and for Alfonso."

Of course I agreed. Not just because Ferrante had asked me, but because I'd already developed such affection and sympathy for this bitterly unhappy child. He'd made no friends in the household with his behavior and his tongue, and consequently, his loneliness only deepened his sense of abandonment. No one wanted to deal with him.

With Ferrante's request came the authority I needed to manage Alfonso and turn him from a biting, scratching gutter cat into a noble lion. This was infinitely more demanding— and more fulfilling—than supervising the pruning of olive groves and managing the Pescara lands. I embraced this unloved boy and hardened myself to his constant rejection. From that first night, when he allowed me to read to him, I knew that I would eventually find my way to his spirit.

The only difficult element for me in Ferrante's letter was the painful reminder that I would probably never have an infant of our own to comfort with my stories. Alfonso would be the child I'd never bear, and I was determined to make him a son Ferrante would be proud of.

It was not an easy task. The small victory I'd achieved the first night in his room formed the foundation for Alfonso's trust in me, but it was shattered after a few weeks, when Costanza and I made a brief visit to Napoli to attend a funeral. It was no place for a child, so I left Alfonso on Ischia in the care of one of Costanza's ladies-in-waiting.

We all paid a price for what Alfonso perceived as abandonment. For the two nights I was gone he screamed inconsolably, turned his dinner plates onto the floor and wouldn't let either Eleanora or one of the man servants near him. When I returned on the third morning, the household was once again in an uproar. This bout of his tantrums was more distressing than earlier incidents because of the contrast with the relative calm I'd managed to bring to Alfonso's behavior with my nightly stories.

I was stricken by the news of this setback and went to see him. He wasn't in his room and when I asked where he might be, no one had an answer. They had all found it easier to ignore the boy than to try to control him or even console him.

I spent most of the day searching for him in all the familiar corners I knew were his haunts. The cook, the only other person in the household for whom he had any appreciation and who at least tolerated the boy, hadn't seen him. She wasn't happy about the overturned dinner plates and was muttering about giving him bread and water for a few days instead of her baba that he loved so much.

I was frantic with worry. Costanza found me pacing the loggia, even peering over the balustrade, afraid I'd find his crumpled body dashed against the rocks.

She handed me a small glass of aqua vitae.

"Drink. It will brace you. I've sent four of my men to search the town, should he somehow have fled the citadel. Vittoria, I see what this is doing to you and I'm beginning to question Ferrante's judgment in burdening you with this responsibility."

I protested. "This is a setback, Costanza, but I refuse to believe that all is lost. I should have realized the bond of trust was too fragile. I shouldn't have left him."

"Oh, Vittoria! You mustn't blame yourself. Perhaps if Alfonso were younger, more tractable, a child more in need of a mother's comfort and affection, it would've made more sense for Ferrante to expect you to offer him your loving arms. Or if he were older, more like a younger brother to you, one with some comprehension of what was expected of him, a boy with whom you could reason."

"But he is neither, Costanza. He is who he is—a frightened, lonely boy who's likely never faced loss or been refused what he wanted. From the little he's told me about his parents, I can only assume that Inigo was solemn and distant, with no experience of a child's playfulness, and Laura spoiled him with sweets and free run of the house when he wasn't suffering in the classroom."

"Yet another confirmation that you shouldn't have to undo their mistakes. I intend to write to Spain. Laura has cousins who would be in a better position to educate Alfonso."

"But Alfonso is a del Vasto, not a Sanseverino! And I'm afraid of the effect another change, another unknown set of relatives, would have on his already damaged spirit. I am willing to continue. I *want* to continue."

"I worry for *you*, Vittoria. You are as much my child as Ferrante, and I see this uncontrollable boy draining you of your liveliness and your own spirit."

"Then you must realize how I feel about Alfonso. I'm aware it's only been a month, but to send him away now would feel as if you were ripping my child from my arms. Please, support me in this. I'm convinced I can reach him."

"When you find him. Surely he knows how much he's upset you by running away."

"On the contrary, I suspect he doesn't know that at all. My instinct tells me he's afraid that no one cares what happens to him now that his mother and father are gone. But you're right, before I can change him, I have to find him. I'm going to get a warm cloak. Now that the sun is lower, I feel a chill."

I hurried down the steps to my rooms, surprised at my own vehemence in response to Costanza's concern. I was aware that my affection for Alfonso was growing, but until Costanza suggested that we send him to Spain, I hadn't comprehended how much.

I hadn't been to my chamber at all that day. When we'd landed from Napoli in the morning and discovered that Alfonso had disappeared, I'd set out to search for him immediately.

I sensed something amiss as soon as I opened the door. Books were out of place on my bedside table. The bedclothes were rumpled as if someone had slept in them. *He has been here*, I thought, as my eyes scanned the corners and I listened for the sounds of breathing or the stirring of a boy I knew could not keep still for long. I was sure he was still in the room.

I busied myself, pretending to be unaware, but all the time monitoring my senses. I chastised myself for not looking here sooner. If my theory about Alfonso was correct, my rooms would have been the most likely place for him to hide. To touch my things and sleep in my bed were signs of his need for the familiar. Nothing had been destroyed. He had not ripped the books nor torn the bedding, which he might have done a few weeks before when all he did was lash out in anger.

I considered where in the room he might be hiding and began casually searching, opening a wardrobe to retrieve my merino wrap and parting the draperies that hung on the western windows. He was neither in the wardrobe nor behind the heavy folds of brocade. But as the late-afternoon sun poured into the room I caught a flicker of movement under the bed.

I got down on my knees and moved the skirting. Two deep blue eyes, swollen with tears and smudged from lack of sleep peered back at me.

"Now that you're found, will you come out on your own, or must I try to fit myself in there with you?"

"It's very dark and stuffy. You wouldn't like it."

"Do you? Is this where you'd prefer to sleep, and not in your own bed?"

"I couldn't sleep in my own bed without your story."

"Eleanora was supposed to read to you. Did she not?"

"I sent her away."

"By howling and throwing your dinner on the floor? I expect I wouldn't have stayed either."

"You heard?"

"Isn't that what you expected?"

"Are you angry with me?"

Was that what he wanted? To know, in the absence of his parents' love, that someone cared enough to be angry with him?

"I was disappointed in you when I learned how much you'd disrupted the household in my absence. But I was distraught when I couldn't find you today. I was afraid I'd lost you forever."

"I was afraid I'd lost *you*! You left in a ship. I watched from the loggia until I couldn't see the sail. I didn't watch when my parents left for Messina. Perhaps if I had, their ship would have been safe."

"Oh, my sweet boy, it was nothing you did or didn't do that brought harm to your parents. It was God's will that He brought them home to Him that day."

"Why didn't he take me, too!"

"Because God has another plan for you. And I've been thrust into your life to help you determine what that plan is."

"Do you know the plan? Did God tell you what is to become of me?"

"I don't know the whole plan. But I do know He's entrusted your care to me. And part of that care is to see that you come out of your hiding place, clean your face over there at my washbowl and dine with me and Tia Costanza— without getting a morsel of food on her beautiful carpet."

I reached out a hand to him. Our whole conversation had taken place with both of us lying prone on the floor facing each other. He slid out, dragging dust with him. His hair was matted with sweat and his doublet and hose were rumpled.

"How long have you been under there?"

"Since this morning, when I heard the steward tell one of the servant girls that your ship was docking. I thought you would come sooner."

He looked down at the floor. "I slept in your bed last night. I'm sorry."

"You have a great deal to be sorry for. I want you to apologize to everyone, individually. Starting with Tia

Costanza, who has been sick with worry for you. Then Eleanora, who didn't deserve to be treated so disrespectfully. And then Cook who, among this whole household, has been the kindest to you."

"You have been kindest of all."

"Then repay my kindness by listening to me. I want to bring happiness back into your life, Alfonso, but I cannot do it alone. If we are to fathom God's plan for you, which I truly believe will make you happy, you have to help me."

"It's hopeless. I can't be happy again."

"That's what I thought when I came here as a girl, alone and frightened, believing I would never see my home again. Will you trust me that the possibility for happiness in your life still exists?"

He shook his head. "Not for me."

I didn't push him. I wouldn't have had faith that happiness would find its way into my life either, had I been faced with the finality of my parents' deaths.

"Come, we'll both wash up and let Tia Costanza know that you are found. I may even be able to persuade Cook to bake you a baba after you apologize to her."

I suspect that Alfonso wasn't the only one in the citadel who was grateful that I'd returned from Napoli. As I escorted Alfonso first to his room to change his soiled clothing and then to Costanza's drawing room to make his apologies, I heard welcomes as if I'd been away for months.

"We are happier to see you than you can fathom, my lady!"

Oh, but I did grasp their collective relief.

I didn't tell Alfonso of Costanza's threat to write to his mother's cousins in Spain. I describe it as a threat because that's how Alfonso would have perceived it. I realize that Costanza spoke as she did out of her concerns for me. But for Alfonso, the knowledge that he was unwanted here would be disastrous—especially to the tentative progress I'd made even today in regaining if not his trust, at least his attention.

No, to tell the boy how precarious his future was as a result of his recent behavior would not have served as a deterrent. To be honest, I didn't know what kind of punishment would prevent him from future recklessness. I'd never been beaten as a child, neither at Marino nor in Ischia. I imagined that a day might come when Alfonso provoked others enough to deserve such a punishment, but at that moment, beating him would only drive him further away from the man I hoped to shape from this confused and bitter child.

With me observing and listening, he offered satisfactory apologies to all three of the people he had most severely offended. I didn't hear true remorse or empathy for what he'd made them endure, but I saw that he was trying his best to please me. It sufficed. For all I knew, he'd never had to apologize before in his life, and certainly not to a lady-in-waiting or a servant. I could tell that he struggled with the words, especially to the cook, but if he was to learn what it meant to be honest and just and noble, he needed to begin by addressing everyone, no matter their station, with respect. Had he treated his own mother with contempt? I suspected that the tolerance for his tantrums had begun with Laura. I had learned that she'd suffered many miscarriages and lost two babies to fevers before their first birthdays. Alfonso was her only surviving child, and I imagined that she'd acquiesced to his every whim out of gratitude that he was alive.

When Alfonso and I returned to Costanza for dinner, he ate every dish presented at table with relish. He was clearly famished. Cook, despite her threat of bread and water, was so taken by his apology that she outdid herself with the meal. I myself had forgotten to eat at midday, so consumed was I with the search for Alfonso. Making up for my missed meal, I savored the dinner as much as Alfonso appeared to. After a soup of lentils and spinach, we had fish stuffed with abalone and baked in parchment. The roast was lamb simmered with red wine, garlic and onions. Cook promised baba for the next day, since the cake needed to soak longer in the rum to be at its best. In its place for a sweet we had fig tarts and lemon poppy cake.

Alfonso's eyes were heavy when we finished the meal.

"It's been a long day for all of us. Alfonso, please bid Tia Costanza good night. We still have time for a quick story."

Sitting by his bedside, I read until he drifted off to sleep. I kissed him on the forehead—something I'd never done before—relieved to have him safe and finally acknowledging to myself how frantic I was at his disappearance and how important he was to my life.

"If I'd lost you, I would not be able to forgive myself," I whispered to the sleeping boy. "You are the plan God has for *me*."

My commitment to Alfonso was, indeed, a blessing. But despite how many of my hours and my thoughts he consumed, I still watched the sea.

On the Easter Vigil, I stood at the stone parapet wrapped in a heavy cloak as the wind howled around the promontory and churned the sea to furious waves that had stopped all the ships attempting to reach us. In all my days of watching I'd never seen a storm so fierce.

Steel-gray clouds filled with drenching rain turned day into night. Sharp fingers of lightning arced down from the clouds, piercing the sea and lighting fires all along the base of Mount Epomeo.

When I wouldn't come inside at the urging of the servant girl Costanza had sent to retrieve me, she came herself and stood with me a while before taking me by the arm and leading me to the warmth of the fire in her studiolo.

"It's an omen," I said, shivering not so much from the dampness as from my foreboding. "Something is wrong. I can feel it."

"Then you do not know your father and Ferrante as well I do. They put no stock in omens or the prayers of women. They trust their swords and their strategies, and in both I have faith, as well. Your father will not send his son-in-law into a hopeless fight. Wherever they are, they will prevail."

But she was wrong. They were at Ravenna, and Ravenna fell to the French. Word reached us at last after the storm subsided. The Spanish had been routed and the survivors fled, including the viceroy. But neither Ferrante nor my father was among them.

CHAPTER SIXTEEN

A Soldier Takes Command

Ferrante
1512
Ravenna

The horses were restless, disturbed by the torches and the clatter of armor in the hour before dawn. Hooves tapped out a cadence of agitation and warning, spreading from one stall to the next as squires dragged equipment from storage chambers and began to outfit the horses.

They were war horses, bred and trained for this moment, and as soon as the bits were placed in their mouths and the weight of the metal armor settled around their flanks, memory flared. Ferrante strode the length of the stable, inspecting the progress of the preparations, placing a hand against a heaving stallion to steady it or correcting a misplaced strap that caused the inexperienced squire to duck his head in shame.

The boy didn't know that Ferrante felt equally inexperienced. Despite the late-February chill in the stable that emanated from the ground and up through Ferrante's boots, he found himself sweating beneath the layers of wool and mail and leather. His heart throbbed with the same rhythm as the clamor generated by the excited horses.

Like the horses, he had trained for this moment. Waited for it with impatience. He was no diplomat, despite Costanza's efforts to mold him into someone who could negotiate with men and not simply lead them into battle. His hand gripped the hilt of his sword. It was his father's. When he'd attended Mass in the cathedral the morning before, he had prayed that he would honor the memory of Alfonso d'Avalos.

As the first streaks of light etched the outline of Vesuvio, all the steeds were saddled and the supply wagons packed. Ferrante gave the order and the horsemen of his lance rose as one to mount their chargers and set off for the north.

It took them over a week to reach the fortress of his father-in-law, massing with the other lance units as they wove through mountain passes. Each night, as the growing cohort settled into camp, Ferrante sensed the energy coursing through the trampled field. He listened. He watched. Unlike many of the other young soldiers, he didn't drink to excess or seek out any of the women following the camp. He didn't want to arrive at Fabrizio Colonna's gate with rumors of a lack of discipline or dissolute behavior reaching his father-in-law. But he also didn't want to miss any of this first experience of going to war. He had too much to learn, too much to savor, to be lost in a drunken stupor or the arms of a whore.

His intensity didn't go unnoticed.

"You remind me of your father," one of the older soldiers under his command said to him as they rode out on the third morning.

"I fought with him in '95 when we took Napoli back from the French. He was a thinker, your father. A strategist who observed and studied the enemy before he made his move. I see you doing the same. Sometimes, one needs to assess a situation quickly, react to changes that suddenly shift the focus of a battle. But if you haven't understood your enemy, those decisions can be reckless. Your father was never reckless."

Ferrante nodded. He'd overheard a lot of bravado among the younger men, an eagerness to engage that simmered just beneath the surface. The pace of the march north was a restraint that only increased the desire to burst into a charge. He struggled to manage that urge.

"I remember very little of my father, but your memories confirm what a small boy saw—a serious man, deliberate in his speech and his actions. He was the model I have held in my mind as the warrior I want to become."

Ferrante knew he'd set himself apart from the other young men-at-arms in the camp by his solemn nature and his intention to immerse himself as fully as possible in his role as a soldier. But he was also aware that something else separated him from the troops gathering under Fabrizio Colonna's command. He was Fabrizio Colonna's son-in-law, and everyone was waiting to see what that would mean, including Ferrante.

He didn't have long to wait once they rode into Marino. A messenger was waiting for him as soon as he dismounted.

"The commander has summoned you to his quarters, sir. He wants you to dine with him."

Ferrante had not seen his father-in-law since the wedding. Then, he had been a proud and expansive patriarch, wrapped in furs and confident of his position, skillfully maneuvering both his allies and his potential enemies.

When Ferrante strode into Fabrizio's hall, he saw none of the trappings of the celebratory host. Instead, he was greeted by Fabrizio the general, plainly outfitted and as intentional as Ferrante's own father had been. Surrounding him were his most trusted captains.

Fabrizio spread a map on the cleared table after a hearty meal.

"The Romagna," he said, pointing with a scarred finger to the northeast. "Most of it is now in French hands, and it's clear King Louis has no intention of stopping there. Pope Julius's papal army has been in disarray since June. It's no wonder he's come to us for help."

Ferrante watched the glances exchanged around the table, the unspoken acknowledgment of their sense of superiority over the warrior pope. Despite his reputation as a proudly vehement man, Julius was giving Spain an opportunity to establish itself as a power in Italy, and every man at the table knew it. Ramón de Cardona, the Spanish viceroy of Napoli, had taken control of the Spanish forces of the Holy League. Fabrizio and the men under him at his table were the commanders of the League's cavalry, the force that would lead the charge in taking back the Romagna.

"But we won't be able to stop the French if our forces aren't ready. That's why we're here now, not in the spring. You'll train your men as they'll be deployed. Padula, your forces will form the battle. Carvajal, yours will take the rear guard position. I'll lead my own men in the vanguard; and my son-in-law will command the light cavalry."

Ferrante felt both an exhilaration and a great weight pressing down on him. If any of the others at the table questioned Fabrizio's decision to put him in command, they held back their doubts for a more private confrontation. His own doubts he buried with a swift thought, and maintained an impassive demeanor as Fabrizio described the challenges facing them. He intended to show neither humility nor bravado, merely acceptance of the order. He was a soldier, not a boy being indulged by his wife's father. Fabrizio was too seasoned a warrior to risk a foolish assignment for the sake of family. His own sons, Ascanio and Federigo, were too young. Ferrante didn't allow himself to wonder if the command might have gone to one of them had they been old enough. But he had the command. He would take it without questioning why he'd been given it.

A month later the French, under the command of Gaston de Foix, Duc of Nemours, had Ravenna under siege. The Spanish forces, fully gathered and drilled, had traversed north through the Apennine valleys and were ready to confront them.

In training, Ferrante had always been in action, a mounted fury relentlessly battering away at straw targets. But as dawn emerged, he and his men sat and watched and listened to the tumult of the first forces of the battle engaging. When the light of day grew, Ferrante caught sight of what lay on the other side of their defenses—battalion after battalion of French infantry arrayed in a great semicircle curving around the Spanish camp within two hundred paces of the Spanish earthworks wall.

The smoke from the guns was dense, but it didn't block the sound of screams, drums and returning fire. Every few minutes an opening cleared in the billowing blackness and Ferrante saw a fragmented image of bodies fallen and falling under relentless bombardment.

The next few hours were not the battle he had envisioned as a young boy. He hadn't expected the confusion, the screams of wounded and dying men, the shuddering collapse of magnificent horses, weighted down with gleaming armor that didn't protect against the new century's weapons. But most of all, he hadn't expected his own rage at the incompetence of Ramón de Cardona, his superior commander. Cardona had not listened to the seasoned counsel of Fabrizio Colonna the night before the battle, when the commanders had met to plan the attack. Ignoring Colonna's advice, he had insisted on an ill-conceived strategy that resulted in the chaos in which Ferrante and his cavalry now found themselves.

He and his men fought as they had been required, answering vicious attack with equal brutality. But their mission had been thwarted by Cardona's weakness.

He fought his mounting sense that their cause was lost even as he pushed on, channeling his rage into the sword in his hand and urging his men to continue the fight. But he had only to look ahead at the continuing surge of French troops and behind at the straggling remains of his own forces to know they were beaten.

The only thing that heartened him was the sight of his father-in-law's powerful shape on a massive horse emerging with his forces and descending upon the French vanguard at the center of the field. But Colonna was alone with his men instead of presenting a shock of massed horses and men on foot.

Ferrante reeled to face another blow. Fabrizio could not contain the French vanguard on his own, and Ferrante, trapped by the Duke of Ferrara's powerful guns, could not ride to his aid.

He lost track of the time, lost sight of the other commanders, lost even the sound of the battle around him. He could no longer hear the guns or the screams or the drums. Sweat or blood—he didn't know which—poured down his face inside his visor. If he was wounded, he didn't feel it. He simply continued slashing with an arm that seemed detached from his body until he collapsed on the field, his horse dead beneath him and he abandoned for dead as well by the retreating Spanish troops.

CHAPTER SEVENTEEN

Prisoner

Ferrante
1512
Ferrara

He didn't know where he was, but he did know the face hovering at his bedside, his uncle's worry-creased brow easing into relief as Ferrante's eyes opened and signaled that he was conscious.

"Tio!"

"Nephew! The hours of vigil spent at your side and the prayers we have offered to our Lord and the Virgin have been rewarded."

"Where is Tia Beatrice?" He tried to lift his head, searching for his father's sister.

"Gone to rest, which you should also be doing."

"Where am I? The last thing I remember is the battlefield."

"You are in Ferrara, a prisoner of Alfonso d'Este."

Ferrante winced at the memory of the duke's artillery.

"Are you in pain?" His uncle's voice reacted with urgency; he was clearly ready to call for physicians. Gian Giacomo Trivulzio's fondness for his nephew had originated when Ferrante was only a toddler, and even though they'd fought on opposite sides in the conflict between France and the Holy League, family ties rose above political alliances.

Ferrante shook his head, registering the stiffness of neck, the thick bandages that impeded his movement.

"No, only the pain of memory. Alfonso d'Este caused unfathomable losses to my men."

"So we have heard. But I must assure you that he wishes you no harm now that you are under his protection."

"Am I in a dungeon? And how is it that you are here with me?"

Gian Giacomo smiled. "You are hardly in a dungeon, and you can thank your aunt for that. When we heard that you were the duke's prisoner, Beatrice took up her pen and implored his sister Isabella d'Este to intercede for you and your father-in-law. Your aunt's friendship with the Marchesa of Mantua has kept you safe."

"Fabrizio is here! Alive!"

"Indeed. Not quite so battered as you. More angry than wounded, I would venture to say. Giovanni de' Medici is here, too. When cardinals sojourn with armies, they are treated as soldiers."

"What will become of us?"

"It's too early to tell. The king of France is demanding that all three of you be released into his custody. He'd like nothing more than to have such prizes on his side of the Alps. But Alfonso is a man of honor, who has great respect for your father-in-law. So far, he has found excuses to keep you here. Your wounds are extensive and are reason enough not to subject you to the journey. As Alfonso told the king, a dead hostage is no hostage at all."

"Do you trust him?"

"I've known Alfonso all my life. He'll keep you as long as he can. It is, after all, in his best interests. The ransom being asked is not insignificant."

Ferrante leaned back against the pillows. It was all too much to absorb in these early moments of consciousness.

"My first foray on the battlefield and I have failed—my men, the League, the pope—and now my family as well with the burden of my ransom."

"Ferrante, judging by what I've learned from Fabrizio, the failure was not yours. If anything, your valor and leadership prevented far worse losses for the League. And as for the ransom—well, it's as much a part of war as your weapons and your training. You're alive, and for that we are all grateful.

Now, I can see I've taxed you far too much. Get some rest so I can assure your Tia Beatrice that you are on the path to recovery."

He did as his uncle bade him. He was too exhausted to protest. Of the many unanticipated consequences of battle, the excruciating process of recuperation became one of the most difficult for him to endure.

As his mind emerged from the fog caused by the severity of his injuries, his physical infirmities exacerbated his frustration. Despite his uncle's reassurances, his failure weighed on him. He relived the battle in his dreams, his body riven over and over with gunshots and ax and pike, the screams of his men echoing in his ears.

He woke from these troubled sleeps soaked in sweat and often blood, as his agitation loosened bandages and ripped open wounds that had only just begun to heal. Inaction was torture to him.

"You need some entertainment," his aunt proposed. "A book? A card game?"

He stared in disbelief at her suggestions and forced himself to be polite as he declined.

"Surely something other than contemplating blank walls and silence? Would you be up to a visit from the marchesa? She asks about you in her letters. It might lift your spirits to have her company." His aunt was optimistic, fluffing his pillows and smoothing the bedclothes.

He acquiesced. He knew he owed the marchesa the comfort and care with which he was being treated, thanks to her intercession with Alfonso d'Este on Ferrante's behalf.

A week later, Isabella d'Este swept into his room accompanied by three of her ladies-in-waiting.

"I hear from your aunt that you are not a very good patient. You may consider me ignorant of the afflictions that beset injured warriors, but I can assure that I am more than familiar, as the daughter, the wife and the sister of men who have been wounded in war. Have my brother's physicians been incompetent, or are you ignoring their advice out of some distrust of your captors?"

Ferrante was taken aback by the marchesa's frankness and command. But then he remembered that she was quite used to governing during her husband's long absences on the battlefield. He mumbled an incoherent response. He wasn't used to being addressed like a disobedient schoolboy.

The amusement on the faces of two of Isabella's ladies only increased his discomfort. He felt his disadvantage acutely—a man still too weak to leave his bed, his once-powerful body emaciated, his bedside table cluttered with medicine pots. What had he been thinking when he agreed to accept this visitation?

Isabella had taken a seat and was sniffing at the medications arrayed on the table.

"Your uncle and my brother are working tirelessly to negotiate your freedom. Despite the different sides on which you fought, you have a champion in General Trivulzio. But you need to do your part and heal if they are ever to release you. Are you able to sleep?"

He suspected she already knew the answer to that question and answered her truthfully.

"I'll speak to my own physician to prepare something for you," she promised him. "Don't protest as if it were unmanly to take a sleeping potion. If you do not sleep, you will not recover."

The third lady, the one who hadn't twittered at Isabella's earlier treatment of him, remained in the background, observing him silently. Ferrante thought she looked at him with understanding rather than pity. It was a small thing, but the distinction was oddly soothing.

"I suspect you need more than remedies for your physical ailments, however," Isabella continued. "What can I provide to comfort your soul? The music of Lorna here, who has the voice of an angel? A chess partner in Mariangela, who enjoys the competitiveness of the game? Or the poetry of Delia, who can recite in the language of your choice?" Isabella extended her hand to each one as she introduced them. Lorna and Mariangela curtsied and smiled with a tinge of mockery as she extolled their talents. Delia, however, nodded with at least the semblance of deference and grace.

He didn't want any of them, but could not refuse the marchesa's offer without offending, so he asked for Delia.

"Then we shall glide away to visit with your aunt Beatrice and leave Delia to entertain you with a few verses." And just as suddenly as they'd interrupted his solitude, Isabella and the two young women floated off.

Delia remained in the shadows after the door closed behind them. She didn't seem eager to approach him or to force her poetry on his unreceptive ears. Finally, she spoke.

"I can depart after a few minutes and say you fell asleep, lulled by my recitation."

"Is my reluctance and ingratitude that obvious?"

"You could not have sent a clearer message...I'm sure this isn't easy for you. No man wishes to be immobilized in his bed and told to endure it—especially not a warrior of your caliber."

"How would you know what kind of warrior I am?"

"You'd be surprised how much I know about you. Word travels when one distinguishes himself as you have."

He turned his head away. "I lost the battle. I lost hundreds of men. I am a prisoner. What is distinguished about any of those facts?"

"Your bravery in the face of extraordinary odds. Your rallying of discouraged troops who nonetheless followed you because you persevered. History will be kind to you."

He wanted to believe her, but decided she was merely spouting platitudes that brought false comfort.

"Please leave me. Tell the marchesa whatever you wish."

She bowed and started to move toward the door. But then she stopped and turned back. She approached his bed and knelt beside him.

"I may only be a woman who cannot possibly fathom your pain and loss, but I assure you that you also gained something at Ravenna. The respect of your enemies as well as your allies."

And then she left.

Her scent lingered around him as he drifted into an undisturbed sleep.

The days continued to stretch endlessly, but as promised, Isabella's physician sent a concoction—vile-tasting but effective—and he began to sleep. His appetite, sharply off since he'd been unable to digest anything except thin gruels, was rekindled.

"Your uncle and the duke were hunting yesterday. The cook has prepared a venison stew and I thought it might appeal to you."

His aunt herself carried the tray and set it on the table by the window. Although her role in his captivity had initially been as intercessor through her letters to influential friends, she had installed herself at Ferrara to oversee his recuperation.

"Do you want to try sitting at the table?" she asked.

He did. Anything to disrupt the monotony of his confinement, however painful or uncertain his steps might be. He pushed himself to his feet, grabbed the bedpost to steady himself and took his first faltering steps with Beatrice hovering at his side.

By the time he reached the table he was drenched, but the sutures binding his many wounds had held. He grasped the arms of the chair, carved with eagles, and settled himself with relief. Behind him, Beatrice let out her own breath.

In the following days he found the strength to dress and sit for a few hours. He was more willing to tolerate visitors now that he no longer had to greet them from his bed.

Mario Equicola, Isabella d'Este's secretary, was one of the first to come as his recovery quickened.

"I bring letters and books from the marchesa's library. She thought you might wish some amusement now that you are not totally consumed by pain. When you have finished with these, I'll collect them and bring you more."

He handed Ferrante a neat bundle of texts bound with a thin leather strap, histories considering what he could identify from the spines. Two letters lay atop the pile of books.

Equicola shared with him fragments of news from the world outside, but nothing of troop movements or political maneuvers. He confirmed that the Medici cardinal was still a prisoner, as was Fabrizio.

When he left, Ferrante took up the letters. The first was a simple note from Isabella d'Este accompanying the gift of the books. But the second caused him to catch his breath. It was from the Lady Delia.

"My lord, I hope this finds you in better spirits than when we first met. You have been on my mind and in my prayers since that day. As I told you then, I'd heard many reports about you before, but nothing had prepared me for the man himself. You remind me so of my dear brother, whom we lost at Agnadello. If you can bear my presence, it would bring me much joy to visit you again and perhaps lighten your confinement. Signor Equicola can convey your wishes to me if you are willing to see me again."

Putting the letter down with trembling hands, Ferrante reached instinctively for Vittoria's cross as if it were burning a brand into his chest. Then he remembered that Beatrice had told him it was taken from him when the surgeon had first stitched his wounds. Beatrice had it in safekeeping, rescued by her from the hands of victors who had considered it one of the spoils of war. So the cross was safe, but he was not. Without it, he felt all too vulnerable to Delia's suggestion.

He'd had no word at all from Vittoria herself. Was she aware he was alive? Was Ischia so isolated that word had not reached her?

"As comfortable as your captors have made you, Ferrante, you are still a prisoner," Tia Beatrice had told him. "They will not allow communication right now, to prevent any possibility of a plot to free you. You are too valuable to them, and it is taking all of Gian Giacomo's negotiating skill to keep you here and not turn you over to King Louis. Have patience. We have gotten word to Ischia that you and Fabrizio are alive. You and your bride will be reunited."

His aunt's reassurances did nothing to quell the temptation that presented itself in the possibility of Delia's companionship. He was isolated and lonely. His wife could not bring him even the simplest comfort. What harm, then, to accept Delia's offer of company and conversation? A week after the secretary had delivered Delia's letter, Ferrante asked for him, ostensibly to return the marchesa's books and request more. But with the books he put into Equicola's hand was a note for Delia, inviting her to visit.

And thus began a friendship that eased his captivity and restored his broken spirit. Delia had none of the intensity and studiousness of Vittoria, none of the drive for perfection that so characterized his wife. Her mood was lighter; she was adept at finding just the right words to assuage his bruised pride. Like him, she was separated by a great distance from her spouse, an emissary of the Duke of Mantua to the French court. She understood Ferrante's loneliness.

At first, Ferrante had concerns that Delia's attention would elicit disapproval. His uncle, after Delia had visited for the second time, simply said to him, "Be discreet. I hear Equicola can be trusted, so use only him in communicating with her." Tia Beatrice, who didn't welcome Delia but also didn't express any overt criticism, eventually seemed to accept that she was having a beneficial effect on his health and disposition.

Whatever guilt had prompted his original reluctance to let Delia into his life gradually receded. Her laughter elicited his laughter; her energy transformed his lethargic and dormant body to new vigor. And when her kiss whispered against his lips under the chestnut tree in the walled garden where he had been allowed to take his exercise as he grew stronger—well, he responded with gratitude that she had elicited more than his laughter.

From that moment, when the kiss pushed their Platonic bond across the line into passion, he abandoned the reserve that had kept him out of the arms of whores and courtesans during the campaign. Delia was neither. She was a willing mistress who had convinced him that after all he had endured, he deserved the happiness she brought him.

She'd persuaded him to take up his pen and write in the hours and days she wasn't with him.

"Write what?" he asked, as if turning to a muse.

"Hmm...You could record your memories of Ravenna, or thoughts of your homeland, or your longing for me when I'm absent." She smiled, and he knew he had his subject.

He called it "A Dialogue of Love." He intended to present it to her on All Saints, when she'd promised to visit him after her return from a journey to see her mother.

Six days before, as the October chills settled bleakly on the castle and he pulled a fur robe over his shoulders to ward off the cold that his still-recovering body found difficult to tolerate, Tio Gian Giacomo arrived.

"I have news, my boy! They have finally permitted a messenger from Ischia to deliver a letter from your wife for you, and 6,000 gold ducats for your captors. You're going home!"

He slapped Ferrante on the back and Ferrante hoped the shock registering on his face would be taken as elation rather than dismay.

"After so many months! How can I thank you, Tio, for your role in my release?" Ferrante stuttered through the words. Of course he wanted his release. He had simply not equated freedom with the loss of Delia. He had neatly confined his feelings for her as outside his experience of everything else that defined his life.

"We will make preparations at once for your departure. The duke is drafting documents of safe passage. Best for you to be on the way before the winter snows."

Ferrante nodded his assent. He understood the wisdom of his uncle's words. To delay for even a week in order to bid farewell to Delia would be both reckless and misunderstood.

He dared not leave the "Dialogue" for her, lest it fall into the wrong hands. In its place, he wrote her a brief note that he entrusted to Equicola, who had evolved into both a friend and a faithful confidant in his role as go-between with Delia.

"I promise to return. You have given me back my spirit, and I shall never forget you."

His departure was celebrated with a dinner two nights later. He toasted his gratitude to all, acknowledging the debt he owed them. Before he left the hall, his aunt approached him.

"It's time to put this back on," she said, and placed Vittoria's diamond cross in the center of his palm. She folded his fingers tightly around it. "Don't let anyone ever take it from you again."

In the early dawn of the next day, accompanied by a handful of his uncle's men, he set off for the south, retracing the steps that had initiated his life as a warrior so many months before. He turned his back on Ferrara and his sights toward Ischia.

That night on the road he opened Vittoria's letter, set aside in the tumult surrounding the announcement of his freedom. Its anguish and grief reflected his own state of mind months earlier when he'd first awakened from his ordeal, but he had long since put those emotions aside. Her words seemed alien to him. He had already forgotten how much he had yearned for her all those nights before he went into battle. Even if he hadn't been distracted by Delia, he believed he was a changed man. Vittoria wrote that as his wife, she shared his fate: "If he suffers trouble, she suffers; if he is happy, she is; if he dies, she dies. What happens to one happens to both."

He could not imagine a connection to her as intense as she described.

He could not imagine her at all.

1536

CHAPTER EIGHTEEN

A Stranger's Welcome

Vittoria Colonna
1536
Rome

The scaffolding is in place. Across the vast expanse at the top of the wall a vivid blue mimics the sky so completely that the wall seems to disappear. I crane my neck, searching for a living, breathing man among the figures taking form above me. I cannot see him, but I hear the slap of brush against wet plaster and feel the miniscule drops of pigment floating down like mist swirling through the loggia at the citadel.

"Michelangelo!" I call up to the sound. I hear a muffled curse in reply. A head, not his, pops up over the railing.

"Who calls the maestro?" the young apprentice asks. "He is too busy to interrupt his work. The plaster will set if he is called away before finishing this segment of the painting."

"Please tell Michelangelo that Vittoria Colonna is below."

The head disappears. More murmurs, but this time no curses. Then a clattering of metal and the thump of footsteps on wooden boards. Two paint-spattered hands grip the railing and Michelangelo leans out.

"Vittoria! You are here! Welcome, welcome!"

"I didn't mean to call you away from your work. Only to let you know that I've arrived."

"I am coming below. The painting can wait."

More thumping as he makes his way down. He wipes his hands on a rag as he emerges from the labyrinth of boards, trestles and ladders. The face he presents to me, as smeared with paint as his hands, grins with the delight of a child.

"I would take your hand, but as you can see, it is impossible for me to be both a courtier and a painter." He holds up his splayed fingers, his rough skin completely obscured by aquamarine.

"Come, come. I want to show you the sketches I wrote about in my letter."

He draws me to a corner under the scaffold draped in canvas and protected from the inquisitive eyes of visitors to the chapel. Spread out on a worktable are several drawings in red chalk. Some are individual figures, either writhing in agony or reaching out to be saved. At the center of the table is a large sheet. It is Michelangelo's original conception of a powerful yet serene Christ, His arm raised as a great circle of figures surges around Him.

I move slowly around the table, bending closely over the larger sheets of paper or picking up the more manageable smaller ones. Michelangelo stands in the corner, his arms folded, waiting.

"It is a great deal to absorb at once. Many thoughts are crowding my brain, many memories of the texts that underlie your conception. Let me go away and sort through these different threads. When can we meet to talk?"

I see what I suspect is a glimmer of disappointment cross his face. Was he assuming we would delve into the complexities right then and there? I only arrived in Rome the day before and came to the Vatican in the morning.

"I find these surroundings distracting," I add, waving my arms to encompass not just this private corner but the entire chapel. "In fact, to have any meaningful conversation in the whole of the Vatican is impossible."

He nods. "Too many eyes. Too many ears." At least he agrees.

"I'm a poet. I work in silence and solitude. This place encroaches upon me. I'm in awe that you can compose and create amidst the cacophony."

"In the heights I'm able to ignore the voices. From there, they are only babble, like a rushing river or the wind in the mountains. When I move lower, I'll require that the doors be sealed against the curious."

"How long will you work today? We could meet later."

"For you, I will stop before sunset. Come for dinner. Urbino has become quite a good cook. I'll send word with one of the urchins who hang around me, each of them hoping I'll take him under my wing and make him a great artist. He'll advise Urbino to prepare for a guest."

"Two guests, I'm afraid. May I bring my cousin Giulia? She's staying with me at the convent. It would be awkward for me to accept an invitation and exclude her." I do not add that it would also be awkward for me to dine with him alone.

Once again, he nods in understanding.

"Till later, then. I promise I will have my thoughts organized. But be prepared," I warn him with a smile. "I may be quite argumentative and opinionated."

"That is exactly why I asked for your help."

He holds open the curtain to allow me to pass through to the chapel.

"Vittoria." His voice is warm, grateful. "Thank you for coming. I have missed you."

"And I you." I smile and fight back the tears that spring without warning. *Why does this man always bring me to tears?* I ask myself. I'm a forty-six-year-old widow who has endured more than her share of sorrows and withstood them without dissolving into an emotional idiot.

I move briskly through the Vatican after I bid him farewell. I need to be alone for the rest of the day. Not only to sort through the meaning he is attempting to convey with his drawings but also to search my heart for the meaning his friendship is bringing to my life.

When I return to the convent I go to the chapel. It is empty, lit only by the sanctuary lamp and the sunlight casting pools of garnet and sapphire and emerald through the stained glass. I pray. Not the Pater Noster or a litany to the Virgin, which I learned as a girl. I open myself in meditation, a practice that my conversations with Juan de Valdés have taught me.

"Listen," he'd said. "Find the stillness within and God will fill it with his voice."

Michelangelo's images swirl behind my closed eyes, combined with fragments of Matthew's Gospel. But instead of focusing on the description of Christ coming in his glory to separate the blessed from the cursed, I hear a single phrase uttered by Christ in defining who will be saved: "I was a stranger and you made me welcome."

That is what Michelangelo has done for me. I am no actual stranger in Rome. I am a daughter of Rome, recognized and celebrated by a wide circle. But I am a wanderer, a stranger, in the spiritual landscape of God's truth, and that is where Michelangelo came upon me and welcomed me. I am surrounded by those who glimpse pieces of me—shards that glint in the light but do not comprise the vessel, whole and vibrant, that contains me. In the midst of so much society, I am achingly alone. Except with Michelangelo.

How did he find me? How did he know me? I remember someone at a salon many years ago describing him as "shrewd, wise and a great observer of men." An observer. Michelangelo *sees* me as no one else has. And in doing so, he forces me to see myself—the young bride who learned, with pain and patience, how to be wife to a warrior; the emerging poet who distilled her words in the alembic of her anguish; the pilgrim who carved out her path with those words.

MEDITATION

Resuming the Journey

Michelangelo
1536
Rome

When she returns to Rome from her isolated rock he realizes how much he has missed her. Like a young fool intoxicated by the elation of a newly discovered passion, he drops his brush, ignores the unforgiving plaster and clambers down the scaffolding to greet her. He is humbled by her willingness to come at his request. He is shattered by the mirror she holds up to his pain. He is terrified by his need for her.

She moves around the sketches, lifting them one by one, her face in concentration as still as the gaze of one of his Madonnas, hiding her first impressions and ignoring his impatient stance in the corner as he waits for her judgment. She takes a deep breath as she finishes her circumnavigation of his worktable and finally looks at him.

"I'm overwhelmed. Like Dante being led by Beatrice through Paradise—when she invites him to sit a while at her table. I need time to digest what I have seen."

Does she realize how deeply Dante informs his work? He smiles at the reference, another connection between their shared vision of art and their search for the Divine. He doesn't push her for answers now, only suggests that perhaps they, too, should sit together and explore how to interpret what he is trying to convey.

She agrees.

From that moment they resume the arduous journey they began months ago. Their starting point is the Second Coming of Christ and Michelangelo's struggles to translate Scripture into symbol. But their search ranges beyond the altar wall, boring into the questions that torment them both. How do I open myself to God? What does Christ's sacrifice mean? How do I move beyond the constraints and failures of my physical existence and find redemption?

She is unlike anyone he has ever known, able to see the world with eyes that penetrate the shadows of doubt and despair, and then to express in soul-piercing language what she has seen. He senses the shift she has caused in his own perception, daring him to follow her, the lines of his drawings echoing her impassioned vision.

He sketches for her—not out of obligation, not as the artist for his patron—but out of what he is coming to recognize as love. His subject is Christ at the well with the Samaritan woman. It is a topic they have plunged into many times. The woman, both a sinner and an alien, forbidden to associate with Jews, is asked by Christ for a drink of water. In her interaction with Him she comes to an acceptance of Him as the Messiah. But in Vittoria's eyes, the woman does more than understand Christ's redemptive power. She takes what she has learned and returns to her people to spread His message and lead them to Christ.

"As you are leading me." He smiles. "I am a blank page on which you write."

"On the contrary," she argues. "You are filling the page with your spiritual anguish, which then illuminates my own desolation and sheds the light that guides us as we take these halting steps together. Every stroke that emerges from your original conception of your questioning heart is a lifeline thrown in my direction, pulling me toward you."

"And do you come willingly?" He discovers he aches to know. He is on unfamiliar ground, this need to be in her presence, to immerse himself in her words that have so much power over him. He has not felt such joy or such terror as he does when he is with her.

She hesitates in answering him and he remains still and silent. It is too late to take back the question, so revealing of his vulnerability. But he realizes he's asking her to disclose her own secrets—and asking too soon. Once again he is the fool, imagining a connection where none exists. She lives on a plane so far beyond him that he cannot hope to reach her. Within the social and political tempests in which they navigate, everything about her places her apart from him— her wealth, her status, her ancient family, her literary fame, even her retreat to her lonely rock. And in the spiritual realm to which they both aspire, she surpasses his feeble, childlike attempts to grasp the truth of Christ's love. How dare he? And yet, and yet . . . . Something in her eyes speaks to him—a shared sadness, a generosity of spirit—that struggles to touch him, despite her reserve and her layers of protection.

And so he waits.

1512 – 1513

CHAPTER NINETEEN

A Warrior Returns

Vittoria
1512
Castello d'Aragonese
Ischia

The loneliness and disconnection brought about by Ferrante's departure for war nine months before was agonizing for me. I'd been so sure that in our separation we would still be able to sense each other's thoughts, even if we could no longer meld in the flesh and form the one being we became when we made love. Although my physical form sat watching and waiting on the rock, I thought that I'd be riding with him in spirit.

What I discovered, however, was that we were lost to each other. Words, so vital to my soul, were the only thing that could connect us without the touch that had warmed our bed since our wedding night. But after Ravenna, Ferrante's words didn't come.

It was weeks before we learned what had become of Ferrante and my father. Weeks during which I was ravaged by the struggle between hope and mourning, tortured by not knowing and unable to find any solace, either in prayer or poetry.

It was Ferrante's Tia Beatrice who informed us that the French had found him. The costliness of his equipment attracted their attention. When they saw he was still breathing despite the wreckage of his body, they realized they had a prize worth more than his magnificent armor. They wisely carried him as a prisoner back to the Ferrara castle of Alfonso d'Este, where my father, thank God, was also being held.

At least I knew Ferrante was alive, although gravely wounded.

The news released me from my emotional paralysis. Although I was prevented from communicating with him, I began that day to compose a letter I hoped would eventually reach him. When I finished it, I'd filled over one hundred lines with my ardor and my vision of his valor on the field. The words were a way for me to establish a link, however tenuous, across the emptiness that had separated us since he left for war.

Tia Beatrice kept us apprised of the unbearably slow progress of the negotiations that her husband and the Duke of Ferrara were attempting to forge with the French king. But the months dragged on, punctuated by missives from Beatrice reporting on Ferrante's improving health and the duke's failed diplomacy.

Finally, we received word that a ransom of 6,000 ducats would secure Ferrante's freedom.

With the gathering of the funds and the payment of the ransom, I began my education in the conduct of war in this age of shifting alliances and the struggle for control of the Italian peninsula. I learned what my mother had clearly understood as she oversaw the finances of the Colonna household. How many times did she have to sell chattel or borrow from her brother to rescue my father? It all came down to the money. How many horsemen and archers and foot soldiers could a nobleman sustain as a standing army? How many free lances could he hire when he had to raise a larger force? With how many weapons, especially the modern and more deadly ones, could he equip his soldiers?

Ferrante was released after the payment of the ransom. Protected by Alfonso d'Este's safe conduct, he set out for Ischia as soon as the documents were signed.

I didn't wait in the citadel when the bells announcing his ship resounded across the mountain, but called for a horse and rode as swiftly as I could in order to be on the quay when he stepped off the boat.

Despite the chill of that November morning, I felt a surge of heat as I saw my husband take his first breath of home. I dismounted and went to him, expectant, the loneliness of months without him spilling over into an urgency to take in as much of him as I could. In the public sphere of the harbor, I was limited to feeding on him with my eyes alone. While he stood on the deck I studied his face. He had closed his eyes and tipped his head back to the sun. I was stunned, not by the scar etched from the middle of his brow to the tip of his ear—Beatrice had warned me of this wound, which had faded from an angry slash to a silvery badge. His pallor and the translucence of his skin stretched taut against the bones of his face made me catch my breath. *This is what he will look like in death*, I thought to myself, and then quickly ordered that thought into oblivion. I called his name to bring the face to life.

"Ferrante!"

He opened his eyes and turned toward my voice. For a fraction of a second he showed no recognition, as if his months in captivity had been in a sunless dungeon and his eyes were now adjusting to the light and the world. But I knew that had not been the case at all.

And then he smiled.

"Vittoria!"

As the boat scraped against the stones of the dock, he held himself steady on the rigging, gripping the line with his gloved hand. The Ferrante I'd known before the war would have leapt from the boat and lifted me off my feet in his powerful arms. I smiled back and waited, holding my disappointment in check, but also hiding my concern that it was his injuries and not his lack of desire that kept him from jumping onto the quay.

At last he was on land, and he strode toward me. He took my hand and pressed it to his lips, cold and chapped from the voyage, but I didn't care. It was the touch of my husband. With my other hand I traced the river of his scar.

"Welcome home. Ride with me. Warmth and rest await you at the citadel."

He mounted, and I was boosted up in front of him by one of the Castello's men. We rode in silence, our breathing settling into a synchronized rhythm as the horse picked its careful way through the shadows of the tunnel and then up into the town. It was a somber crowd that lined the path as his people took stock of the same changes I'd noted.

"Welcome home, my lord."

"God bless you, sir."

He nodded to them. I knew he was exhausted, but he sat tall and straight in the saddle, ever the commander.

At last we reached the gates of the citadel. Costanza was waiting in the courtyard, her face rigid with the anxiety of the unknown. I had suffered as a wife, but she had endured the pain of a mother who cannot bear to see her child die before she does. Witnessing her expression, I realized how much she'd hidden in order to reassure me and keep me from plummeting into despair. Now that Ferrante was home and safe, she allowed herself a brief moment of release.

A groomsman helped me down and then Ferrante dismounted and bowed to his aunt.

"Tia."

Costanza took his face in her hands and kissed his cheeks and then the scar travelling diagonally across his brow.

"I have waited too long for this moment, but God must have known that I have lost too many of my men to bear another being taken." She relinquished her hold on him, and with it, her maternal emotions. Her tone shifted to that of governor and commander of her own troops.

"I see that my sister-in-law secured you a good surgeon in addition to a comfortable prison. The scar distinguishes you. It's a sign that you've been tested in battle and it will serve you well in commanding the respect of lesser men. Come meet Alfonso, who is as eager as any boy to hear your war stories." She turned to Alfonso, who had watched in curiosity as Ferrante made his entrance.

Alfonso bowed in the manner we had practiced during the days leading up to Ferrante's return.

"My lord, welcome home" he mumbled.

Ferrante tousled the boy's hair. "Cousin! It is I who should be welcoming you to our family! I'm grateful for another male—I was outnumbered until you arrived." I smiled at Ferrante's ease with the boy. He seemed to have accumulated some experience not only in warfare but in managing awe-struck young boys.

"If you are up to it, share some food and drink in an intimate dinner with the family alone and tell us at least a little." Costanza took his arm. I moved to his other side, and with my free arm encircled Alfonso. Together, the four of us climbed the steps and entered the citadel, where the household was assembled in the reception hall and greeted Ferrante with cheers and applause.

He acknowledged them with a smile and raised his arm. "It's good to be home."

Both Costanza and I could see that too much ceremony would exhaust him, and after the servants who'd been closest to Ferrante said a few words to him, we gently extracted him from the hall and retired to Costanza's private quarters.

After dinner, Costanza sent us to our own chambers. "I've taken enough of you for the evening, although it is not sufficient to make up for all the months you've been away. Go to bed with your wife."

I'd prepared Alfonso that I would not be reading him a story that night. Costanza had agreed to do the honors and shooed us away to our own bedtime rituals.

When we got to our apartment, we found Ferrante's trunk in the middle of the room, delivered from the ship.

"Shall I unpack it for you?" I asked, eager to perform even the simplest wifely task.

"It can wait until morning. I'm too weary to deal with it. Come to bed."

He reached for me and began to undo my gown. I felt like a maiden again, shy with this new man who resembled my husband but no longer was the man I recalled.

With more care than customary I undressed him, not knowing what I would find under his travelling clothes, how much pain he still experienced, or how I would react when I finally saw his wounds.

"Don't be afraid to touch me. I won't break apart." He took my hand and guided it to a ridge in his side. I could not hold back the image of the blow that had ripped his flesh. It was as I'd written in my poem to him—"If he suffers trouble, she suffers." I shook with the realization of what he had endured.

"You're cold," he murmured, misinterpreting my body's reaction. "Come, get under the covers."

We climbed into bed and he pulled me close. The leanness I'd seen in his face earlier was even more pronounced in his body. He began to caress me, but the strokes soon slowed. The fatigue of months on the march, a brutal battle and his extensive wounds overtook him. We would not be reigniting the fires of our earlier life tonight. He fell into a profound sleep, and I lay listening to his breathing, grateful that he was at least by my side. I willed away disappointment. It had no place in our bed or our marriage.

I slept finally, taking comfort in an embrace that had been only a phantom since he'd ridden off in the dark and cold of winter. When he stirred in the earliest hour of the morning, my body woke with him—like a sentinel who has drifted off into the thinnest slumber but is immediately alert when she senses she is no longer alone. A warrior's hands—hands that had wielded steel, that had spilled the blood of his enemies— now extended across the distance between us to my hopeful, waiting flesh. This time he didn't stop. I turned to meet him as his lips bent to my breast and he plunged inside me. He groaned with pleasure and I felt my body flood with the welcome it had waited so patiently to give him.

We moved rhythmically, as if in a pavane. A dance that began slowly, taking light steps across a once-familiar terrain that was being rediscovered. As memory reacquainted our flesh, the dance became more animated, more vigorous. Ferrante was focused, intent, eager—everything I'd hoped for in our reunion. The quickening of our breath was our music, our pulsating gasps for air mirroring the movement of our limbs as we sought the final notes. And then, peace.

He slid his hand under me and pulled me up to sit face-to-face with him. I wrapped my legs around him and pressed my forehead gently against his scar. We rocked, bathed in contentment, without words.

I felt the order of our lives returning. Altered, certainly. But not abandoned, as I'd feared in all the dark months without him.

"Welcome home, husband." I kissed him.

We took breakfast in our chambers. I wasn't ready to dispel the quiet intimacy that our lovemaking had initiated and begged off joining Costanza and Alfonso until later in the day. I thought we might linger by the fire or even return to bed, but when I suggested it with a shy smile, Ferrante demurred.

"I have spent far too many hours lying abed in the last months and am only now beginning to grasp the reality of my freedom. You know me well enough to appreciate how difficult I found my confinement and forced inactivity. I need to move today—and not just inside you." He gave me a look of appreciation that raised the heat in my cheeks and stirred once again the warmth in my belly.

"I'm going down to the barracks yard for a few hours. Both my physicians and my captors forbade me to hold a sword the whole time I was in Ferrara. My muscles are craving exercise as fervently as my body craved you this morning." He kissed the top of my head and then was gone. I heard his footsteps retreating down the steps, the pace energetic, a man exulting in his freedom the same way he'd rejoiced in a holiday from his lessons as a boy.

The room felt empty. During all the months without him, I'd gradually adapted to the solitude of our quarters. But now, when he had filled the space so completely with his presence in the last twelve hours, his sudden disappearance felt like abandonment, leaving me strikingly bereft. My eyes swept the room and rested on the trunk he had decided to ignore the previous night. I welcomed the opportunity to engage in a task still linked to him, since my mind was too full of the morning's pleasure and the sheer wonder of his return to do anything remotely intellectual.

I found the key to the trunk among the small items he had tossed on the table the night before. The lock was stiff. Months in the field in all kinds of elements had caused it to rust, and I made a mental note to arrange for it to be polished and oiled. There was no point in pretending that it wouldn't be on the road again. I lifted the heavy lid and was struck by Ferrante's scent. I breathed it in deeply as it filled the emptiness that had overwhelmed me when he'd raced away to his sword. I began to remove the clothing stacked on top, sorting into stacks on the floor what needed to be cleaned or repaired and what was beyond reclaiming.

Beneath the garments was a pair of boots and a leather document portfolio. His armor, of course, was gone—one of the spoils claimed by Ravenna's victors. We would need to go to Napoli to have him fitted for a new suit. Yet another expense I'd have to find the money to cover.

I pulled out the boots and the portfolio. As I did, a sheet of vellum floated to the floor. The portfolio had been carelessly bound, its ties dangling uselessly. I knelt to pick up the paper and replace it in the folder. I recognized Ferrante's handwriting and read the title at the top of the page. "A Dialogue of Love" it read in his familiar scrawl. I leaned back on my heels and could not stop myself from reading on.

It was an imagined conversation on paper, dated during his confinement as Alfonso d'Este's prisoner, not something he would've had time to compose during the campaign. Although it didn't have the polish or elegance of the poetry I was accustomed to hearing at Costanza's court, it conveyed Ferrante's spirit as clearly as if he were speaking. If only he'd been able to send this to me during the lonely months of our separation! My doubts would have been dispelled to realize that he shared the same sense of loss, the same longing, the same memories of past lovemaking.

When I finished reading the poem, I put it carefully back in the portfolio. I decided not to reveal that I'd discovered it, preferring to savor the moment when he presented it to me. Any lingering fears I had about the changes in my husband and their impact on our marriage were soothed by the "Dialogue." I went about the rest of the morning with a light heart.

It didn't last.

When Ferrante didn't return from the barracks for the midday meal, I chose to walk down in the afternoon to find him. From the terrace overlooking the exercise yard I saw him in the midst of a knot of Costanza's guards, at the center of an animated conversation. One of the guards noticed me and indicated my presence to Ferrante. He glanced up, distracted and distant. He nodded to acknowledge me and then returned to his discussion. In place of the ardent lover of the morning was a commander who apparently had just dismissed me.

Grasping my skirt, I whirled away. I was too agitated to retire to our apartment or spend time with Alfonso. Churning with frustration, I went for a walk to the belvedere, where the wind-tossed waves reflected my own emotional upheaval. I thought I'd prepared myself for Ferrante's return home, but I felt totally adrift. I was not a foolish, romantic girl who had expected all to be as it was before he left. I understood, as only the daughter of a soldier can, that war's effects go beyond the visible scars. Had I not held my disappointment in check when he was too exhausted to make love to me the night before? And then responded with passion when he did reach for me? What was the meaning of the "Dialogue" if he was too busy to break bread with me? Was it asking too much for him to spend time with me when he'd been home less than a day? I had much to learn if this was to be the pattern of our lives.

I had found no answers for my questions when I retraced my steps to the citadel. By the time I arrived at our apartment, Ferrante had returned.

He made no comment about my visit to the barracks. Rigid and accusing, he was standing by his empty trunk.

"Who unpacked my things?"

"I did. I've sent what could be salvaged to be cleaned."

"Where is my portfolio?" His voice had an edge to it.

"I put it on the table by the window."

He moved across the room and picked up the leather case, which I'd retied securely after replacing the "Dialogue."

"I'll need a desk and a locking cabinet. Perhaps I should ask Costanza for a study, separate from our living quarters."

He didn't seem to know what to do with the portfolio, and seemed reluctant to put it down. I thought he might be weighing whether this was the moment to give me the "Dialogue."

But he didn't.

We dressed for dinner. Various members of the court were joining us in Costanza's salon, unlike the intimate meal we had shared with her the night before. It was to be an evening of public welcome for Ferrante, and an unlikely time for him to present me with the poem. I accepted with resignation that I would have to wait.

Three days passed, similar to the first. We established a routine. I grew accustomed to Ferrante's daily excursions to the barracks and told myself they weren't intended as an escape from me. In addition to resuming his physical training, he began receiving messages from the mainland that needed his attention— from the viceroy of Napoli and from my father, safely returned to Marino after my mother's successful payment of his ransom. Ferrante was more than a commander in the field. Even before he'd returned, word of how he'd acquitted himself as a soldier and a leader had begun to drift across the sea. He was respected. He was revered. And I was proud of him.

The portfolio was out of sight, locked away in a cupboard. But it was not out of my mind. My intention to act surprised by the "Dialogue" had no opportunity to express itself, since the poem remained in the portfolio. At first, I thought he was holding it back because it was unfinished. But it had seemed quite complete when I'd read it that first morning.

Finally, when too many uncertainties were pricking me like a swarm of gnats, I decided to question Ferrante directly.

"May I ask you something?" I murmured one evening in bed. We had made love and were lying in each other's arms.

"Mmm. But speak quickly or I'll soon be snoring."

"The morning I unpacked your trunk, the portfolio was unfastened and a paper fell out."

He became very still. His face darkened to a look that hovered between anger and suspicion.

"That wasn't a question." He seemed to be challenging me. Whatever contentment we had achieved with our lovemaking I'd just dispelled with my mention of the portfolio. Did Ferrante have secrets from me? It only now occurred to me that he perceived my handling of the portfolio and its contents as a violation. I chose my next words carefully, words I'd rehearsed silently several times before opening the conversation.

"The paper was covered in your handwriting. It was a poem about your love for me. My question is why haven't you given it to me yet?"

A heartbeat of silence passed. Was he angry with me for finding the poem? Or for reproaching him about it?

"Ah, the 'Dialogue of Love.' You've stolen my surprise. I was waiting until Christmas."

It seemed a simple enough explanation. But why had he reacted with such suspicion when I'd introduced the topic? I'd never known him to be that fond of surprising me with gifts. But an inner voice reminded me that once a man goes to war, many things about him will remain unknown. I silenced my questions. His answer sufficed.

"Can you forgive my impatience? I'm quite content to wait until December to read it again."

"Of course I forgive you. Can you forgive me for keeping it a secret?"

I kissed him. Both of us appeared to be relieved, and we slept.

It was easy to put aside my doubts about the poem when I was confronted by a much more significant adjustment, the impact of which we felt within a week.

I'd heard in women's talk how the arrival of a child alters the character of a marriage. Alfonso was no babe suckling at my breast, but he was a presence to be reckoned with nonetheless. It certainly helped that he was in awe of his cousin, and it was clear that everything he saw in Ferrante was what he aspired to be.

"Do you understand now that all I'm trying to teach you is based on the model of nobleman and soldier embodied in Ferrante?" I asked him one morning as he was leaning on the wall overlooking the exercise yard. He had begged to watch the drills, and Ferrante had agreed. Ferrante was fiercer than I remembered, but fair. He knew that Alfonso was watching and sought to set an example for him.

"You've done a fine job with the boy," he told me that night. "I gather he was a wild and uncontrollable creature when he first came here. Costanza calls you a miracle worker."

It was a source of great satisfaction to me that Ferrante appreciated my role in "taming" Alfonso, as he described it. But despite Alfonso's admiration for Ferrante and Ferrante's pleasure in seeing Alfonso grow into a well-mannered and well-educated boy, each of them also saw the other as an interloper when it came to their relationship with me.

"Read another story with me tonight," Alfonso pleaded almost every evening, claiming that one story had been too short or he wasn't tired enough to sleep peacefully yet.

"Come with me to Napoli for a fortnight while I meet with the king's council," Ferrante said at dinner. "You would enjoy the company of society and a respite from the nursery." In the past he might have asked me in bed, languorously stroking my back or nibbling on my ear, and the enticement to join him would have been couched in terms of time with him rather than with society. But our pillow talk now was scant. More than once I was called from our bed by a knock on the door from the steward, letting me know that Alfonso had woken from a nightmare calling for me. The howling had long ceased, but I noted that since Ferrante's arrival, Alfonso's bad dreams had increased in frequency.

When I finally returned to him that night, the night of his invitation, Ferrante was asleep, his back turned away from my side of the bed. I warmed myself first by the fire to avoid waking him with my cold hands and feet, then climbed into bed and wrapped myself around him. He didn't stir.

Eventually, when it appeared that Ferrante would not be called away to fight, we found a new equilibrium in our triumvirate. Alfonso became accustomed to the hours I spent as wife and learned, although not willingly, that Ferrante had a claim on both my time and my heart. But I was also determined not to undo all the good I'd accomplished with Alfonso and convinced Ferrante to support me in my conviction that I needed to give Alfonso the attention that had wrought such a positive change in him.

Leaving Ischia with Ferrante was another matter, however. Alfonso was terrified still of the sea and could not be consoled when I decided Ferrante had waited long enough for me to join him in Napoli when he traveled there for one of his council meetings.

"Alfonso, you are old enough to know that the journey to Napoli is a short and safe one. In a week, we'll be back. The seas are calm; you've seen for yourself from the cliffs how many ships make the voyage unharmed."

In the end, I forced myself to be firm, despite his entreaties. I also told him that if I received word that he upset the household in my absence, I would only prolong my stay.

With that, he quieted his objections. I had arranged for two of the young squires attached to Ferrante's cavalry unit to stay at the citadel with him and gave him a holiday from his studies. According to Costanza, within hours of our departure the three boys were thoroughly engrossed in a game of hide-and-seek and Alfonso forgot to suffer.

CHAPTER TWENTY

Mothers

Vittoria
1513
Rome

After the death of Pope Julius in January, the cardinals elected as his successor Giovanni de' Medici, a fellow prisoner in Ferrara with my father and Ferrante after Ravenna. There was no question that we would go to Rome for his accession as Pope Leo.

My mother wrote, offering us accommodation in the Colonna palazzo in the city, but also subtly emphasizing how important it was that we attend.

"Every noble Roman family will be represented at the celebration. If you and Ferrante have not already made your decision, your father and I stress the wisdom of your presence in Rome at this time. Apart from the political prudence of a visit, I long to see you."

My mother's summons was to me as a Colonna, to represent our noble Roman family in that most Roman of events, the coronation of a pope. But I was not alone in answering my mother's call. Half of Costanza's court made the journey to see and be seen—Costanza herself, Ferrante and I with Alfonso, and Ferdinando d'Aragona y Guardato, the brother of the deposed King Federigo, who had sought shelter on our island twelve years before. When Federigo and his wife and children left for exile in France, Ferdinando had remained with his wife. Their daughters, Giovanna and Maria, had been born at the Castello. Now eleven and eight, the girls were as excited as Alfonso about attending the festivities in Rome.

"The new pope has an elephant and a dwarf!" Maria announced as we were gathering in the courtyard on a blustery March morning, preparing to descend to the wharf for the start of our journey.

"That's ridiculous. I don't believe you," countered Alfonso, ever the skeptic.

"It's true! Clothilda, my nurse, heard it from her cousin, who was in Rome and saw the elephant through the palace gate. He said the pope will ride the elephant in the coronation parade." Maria stomped her foot and stood her ground against Alfonso's mocking disbelief.

"That's even more ridiculous! Popes don't make silly spectacles of themselves, especially when they're being crowned. Crowning is very solemn."

I listened as the two children sparred. Alfonso reminded me in that moment of the serious and somber Ferrante who had met me on the dock when we were nearly as young as these two. I smiled at the memory and at the glimmer of similarity between Ferrante and Alfonso. Even though Alfonso wasn't his blood son, I sensed a kinship that I hoped would flourish.

I was also grateful that Maria's fascination with the pope's menagerie was distracting Alfonso from the trip ahead of us. Ferrante had neither patience nor understanding when it came to Alfonso's terror. "We live on an island. Unless the boy decides to become a hermit and live in a hut on Mount Epomeo, sooner or later he must conquer his fear," he had said to me when our plans to travel first began to take shape. "He's coming with us."

When we announced that we were planning to travel to Rome, Alfonso's fears of the sea resurfaced.

"You're leaving me again so soon?"

"We will not be leaving you, Alfonso. We are all going to Rome—Tia Costanza, Ferrante, you and I."

"It's hard enough to watch you sail away, but why must I go?" His face was white with apprehension and he was gripping the arms of his chair as if he feared being pulled away that very minute and hustled down to the harbor. "You torture me with this journey!"

"Alfonso!" Ferrante's voice silenced him. "We have a responsibility as the ruling family of Ischia to attend the coronation. You are a member of this family. And if you ever wish to lead and be a warrior, you must learn to conquer yourself before you can conquer your enemy. It is the first step toward bravery. Are you ready to take it?"

Ferrante's words met their mark. Alfonso made no more protestations. I knew how hard it was for him even to contemplate setting foot on a ship, but I also knew how intensely he wanted to emulate Ferrante.

"I can be brave," he nodded, his voice scarcely above a whisper.

Although he didn't throw himself into the preparations for the trip with enthusiasm, he at least took no extreme measures to avoid it, as he had that day in the summer when he had hidden from us all and launched the Castello into an uproar.

He was, in fact, just the opposite, scarcely saying a word at dinner, doing his lessons without any chattering. He seemed to be attempting to contain himself, to hold at bay whatever visions of his parents' death at sea still haunted him.

The day of our departure dawned clear. As we descended to the harbor, I could see tiny buds on the fig trees and shoots of wild flowers pushing up along the sides of the path. Hopeful signs that the earth was emerging from its winter sleep. It had been a year since Alfonso had joined us. This voyage was a fitting commemoration of that event—but also a way to mark the beginning of a new phase in his life. I didn't expect him ever to stop mourning his parents, but I saw this trip as an opportunity for him to see himself differently—a boy embracing the life he had been given.

When we got to the dock I said a silent prayer that Alfonso would not run away. Ferrante answered that prayer by clamping his arm around Alfonso. "Come, cousin. Let's fight this battle side by side." And with the boy firmly beside him, they climbed aboard before Alfonso had a chance to escape.

We were planning to sail all the way to Ostia. I hadn't taken this voyage in years. This time I had much to occupy me for the next three days—Alfonso, my husband and our traveling companions.

We set sail with the tide and rounded the Castello before heading north. The seas were calm, the sun was shining and Alfonso was still arguing with Maria over the existence of the pope's elephant.

We'd been underway about two hours when my body recalled its response to the journey I'd taken as a child thirteen years before. I barely had time to locate a bucket. Unfortunately, I never gained my bearings on the ship and suffered the entire three days. Once we finally docked, I was pale and weak.

My mother took one look at me when we arrived at the palazzo and greeted me with anguish. "Oh, Vittoria! What has happened to you?"

When I explained, she had some fennel tea prepared for me and sent me to rest. I protested.

"But our guests...Alfonso...I should be helping you."

"If you don't get some rest right now, you'll be no help at all in the coming week and you'll lose the very opportunity that brought you to Rome in the first place. Off with you! I'll take care of welcoming the others."

Listening to my mother, I collapsed into bed. Ferrante joined my father and conferred with him behind closed doors, eager to catch up on news of the skirmishes that still disrupted the north. Now that Julius was dead, it would be interesting to see what effect that would have on the political turmoil. Word had seeped out of the conclave that the cardinals were eager for a more peaceable pontiff, which was why they'd chosen Giovanni de' Medici. I must admit I was eager for peace, as well.

Alfonso discovered more playmates among the guests. In addition to our group from Ischia, my parents were hosting my mother's brother and his family.

Refreshed after sleep, I joined the company for dinner. Talk was of nothing but the elaborate preparations Rome was making for the coronation and the number of prominent families and clergy from throughout Italy who had chosen to be present.

"It's a sign of the city's resurgence that so many are here," my father boasted, as proud as any of the ancient Roman families to demonstrate what Rome had to offer.

"On our way through the city, the frenzy of building was like nothing I've seen before," my uncle remarked. "Even the arches and decorations erected during my father's triumphal processions pale by comparison."

The talk at the table of the displays of art and sculpture being created along the processional route led me to believe that Maria's insistence the pope's elephant would make an appearance was not so far-fetched.

One simply had to look out the window to see that Rome was teeming—with cardinals, bishops, abbots, knights and the inevitable courtesans. With just a few days before the coronation, activity both in the city and within my parents' palazzo was at a fever pitch.

My mother had managed to secure two seamstresses to help with any additions or alterations to our costumes. The women guests gathered in my mother's sitting room, followed by maids whose arms overflowed with voluminous brocades and velvets. I arrived somewhat later, as my body had not quite recovered from the voyage. I was still plagued by nausea and vomiting, despite nearly twenty-four hours on solid ground.

"Ah, there you are, Vittoria. What have you chosen to wear for the procession? Does it need any adjustments?"

I'd brought a green silk gown shot through with bronze threads, and matching sleeves with stripes of bronze and tied with bronze-colored ribbons. I hadn't had time to try it on before we left Ischia, so I slipped it on with my mother's deft assistance.

"When did you last wear this?" she asked. "It's quite snug."

"Oh, months ago. For Ferrante's welcome-home dinner, I recall."

"Well, your husband's presence has clearly made you a contented wife," she smiled. "If you are to be at all comfortable riding in the procession and lasting through the coronation, we need to let it out a bit."

I caught my mother assessing my body as the seamstress lifted the dress over my head and began to pick apart the side seams.

"Vittoria, come sit with me for a moment and help me choose my jewels." She led me to her dressing closet and closed the door.

I could see that she'd already laid out a ruby necklace and earrings.

"Were you delayed this morning because you were ill again?"

I nodded, ready to apologize. But she stopped me with two fingers pressed gently against my lips.

"When was the last time you bled?"

I looked at her, astounded by the question. She knew of my sorrow, unable to conceive after four years of marriage. How could she ask me such a question?

"I am not asking to hurt you, child. Just reflect and count."

I'd stopped my prayers for a child when Alfonso came into my life, because I accepted him as God's answer to my plea. I'd also stopped counting. I thought back. I'd bled at Christmas and then again around the end of January. But had I bled in February? I couldn't remember that I had, and now it was mid-March.

"January," I whispered. "Do you think...?" I placed my hands on my belly and she covered them with her own.

"It's possible. All the signs—the nausea, the tight dress. But it's still early. When you haven't bled for three cycles, then we can hope. Until then, we wait. Try to get as much rest as you can. I am now regretting that I urged you to come for the coronation. . ."

"I can use my slow recovery from the seasickness to excuse myself from some of the activities. I promise I'll be careful."

She took me in her arms. "Oh, my daughter. May this be the blessing you deserve."

My spirit floated between elation and apprehension. The possibility of my pregnancy had never before been so real, so palpable. But at the same time, the risk of loss seemed all the more heightened. It consumed my thoughts, my prayers.

Thankfully, the distractions of the coronation served to occupy me with more than worry. The morning of March 19, the feast of San Giuseppe, was clear and still. It appeared that no rain or wind would interfere with the pageantry. As in a hundred other houses throughout Rome, we assembled in the courtyard in our finery. The horses were draped in the colors of the four families under my parents' roof—Colonna, Montefeltro, d'Aragona and d'Avalos. Standard-bearers hoisted the insignia of each house. Knights and ladies-in-waiting surrounded us as we began our procession, my parents and brothers in the lead. The flags dipped as the standard bearers marched us through the arch of the palazzo's gate and we advanced into the street that led to the Via Triumphalis.

We joined a throng that included hundreds of cardinals, bishops and abbots. From the colors of the flags in front and behind, it seemed that every great family in Italy was represented. My mother had been right to insist that we come. With the reception that Rome was giving Giovanni de'

Medici and the power the Medicis wielded, Ferrante's absence would have been glaring.

Lining the streets were thousands of people jostling for a view of the spectacle and ultimately the blessing of the new pope, who rode at the very end of the procession. To Maria's profound disappointment, his steed was not an elephant but a white horse that sadly seemed too small for the pontiff's girth.

Along the route the wealthiest men in the city had outdone each other in erecting displays of honor for the new pope—decorated arches constructed for the procession, treasures hauled out of palazzos not only to welcome the pope with the art everyone knew he loved, but to proclaim the wealth and power of its owners. To some men, the acquisition of a painting or the discovery of an ancient sculpture was a sport, and the coronation was an extraordinary opportunity to show off their trophies. Madonnas hung next to nymphs in a riot of color and texture.

I rode between Ferrante and Alfonso at a pace that allowed me to absorb with all my senses the tumult and excitement of a city that seemed suddenly freed from the shadows and violence and neglect of its past. The election of Giovanni was recognized as a turning point, and the people marked it accordingly. The day was punctuated by roars of approval as a particular family or spectacular float came into view. The air, which had wafted so crisply in the morning, was redolent with the mingled odors of food vendors, burning incense and gun smoke from the cannons being fired from the hills in celebration. The bells of every church in the city pealed in sequence. It was exhausting; it was exhilarating. When we finally reached the Basilica of St. John Lateran, it had been hours since we'd left the palazzo.

We dismounted in the piazza and entered the Basilica, from which the sacred notes of the *Missa Pange Lingua* resounded. A place had been reserved for us by one of the Colonna coat of arms inlaid at intervals along the center aisle.

My father, who rarely paid attention to art, loved that floor. The Colonnas had paid for it almost a hundred years before, when the Colonna pope, Martin V, commissioned it. As a girl enduring interminable Lenten services, I'd amused myself by following with my eyes the intricate serpentine swirls or trying to count the different patterns on the floor. But, like my father, I felt my heart swell with pride at our crowned white column on a red field recurring up and down the nave.

I caught my mother eyeing me sharply, her maternal sense assessing my condition. I waved off her look of concern. I would not be treated as an invalid, not even a secret one. I was too absorbed in the whole experience—the vivid flamboyance and exuberance during this most holy and solemn rite.

As I had for much of the day, I watched Alfonso as he took it all in. Although he had grumbled at the formality of his clothing and fussed occasionally with his collar, he seemed to have forgotten his discomfort in the midst of his utter fascination with everything.

"Did you see the players on the float when we passed the Colosseo? They were acting out the story you read me the first night you came to me in the Castello," he whispered.

I was both stunned and touched that he'd made the connection and remembered so clearly. I squeezed his hand.

We didn't have long to wait before the procession of the cardinals led the new pope into the cathedral. A river of red silk, accompanied by the hum of Latin prayers, flowed in front of us. If there were those among the line of prelates who would rather have been pope, they masked it well.

Giovanni de' Medici moved slowly through the throng, smiling in genuine delight at his own spectacle, rather than in cunning at his accession to power.

"A very different man from Julius," my father commented to Ferrante, both of whom stood behind me.

"I don't expect we'll see him leading troops to amass more land for the Papal States," Ferrante said.

"But will he protect Italy from the French as fiercely as Julius did?"

My mother placed her hand on my father's arm, a subtle signal that to say any more in these surroundings might not be wise. He patted her hand and coughed loudly.

The air in the cathedral, already dense, became oppressive as the crush of thousands of bodies and the smoke from the candles and incense intensified. I could barely hear the prayers at the altar and out of the corner of my eye glimpsed a flash of gold from the papal crown before my body succumbed to fatigue. I felt myself crumple to the floor. The last thing I saw was my family's coat of arms underfoot. The last thing I heard was my mother's gasp.

When I opened my eyes again, I was in Ferrante's arms and we were moving through the crowd, which parted with curiosity as his commanding voice and warrior's body accepted no barrier. Despite his wounds, he forged ahead as if on the battlefield.

"Make way!" he shouted.

I leaned into his chest, the velvet of his doublet smooth against my cheek. He didn't stop until we were outside on the steps of the basilica.

"Alfonso, find our groomsman and have him bring my horse immediately."

The boy ran off. In his hand was one of my shoes. My mother was soon at my side, dabbing my forehead with her wet handkerchief.

"I dipped it in the holy water fount. God will understand."

It seemed an eternity before the horse arrived. While we waited, I fought off a wave of nausea and clung with rigid fingers to Ferrante, afraid that I might fall again.

"Suck this." My mother placed a candied plum in my mouth. The sweetness helped.

When the horse was finally at the steps, Ferrante gently lifted me into the saddle and climbed up behind me.

"We'll follow as quickly as we can," my mother said. "Get her into bed as soon as you return to the palazzo."

The ride back took less time than the procession as the throngs had dispersed along the route. Workmen were already dismantling the treasures that had been so prominently displayed in the morning. The road was littered with crushed flowers, the remnants of half-eaten pastries and torn banners with the papal insignia of crossed keys.

We arrived at the gates of the palazzo, and Ferrante shouted for the guard. Once inside the courtyard he dismounted and reached up to lift me from the horse. I sank again into his arms, unable to support myself or even think. I was unused to such weakness, and I could read in Ferrante's face his own concern and bewilderment. When I was finally in our bedroom he called for a maid to help me out of my gown and paced outside the door while she undressed me. Finally, unencumbered by the layers of my formal clothing, I sank back against the pillows and curled up with my knees against my chest.

"You're shivering." Ferrante was at my side, pulling the bedcovers up around me and wrapping me tightly. "I've never seen you so ill."

I debated telling him what had more than likely been the reason for my collapse, but I held back. If this pregnancy didn't last, I doubted I had the strength to console him as well as myself.

"It's an ague, nothing more," I told him. "The sea voyage was more difficult than I realized. I just need to rest."

I took his hand and kissed it. "Go get something to eat. You look as pale as I feel."

If he stayed with me, I feared that I'd tell him.

I slept.

When I woke, my mother was sitting in a chair close to the bed, a book open on her lap.

"How do you feel?"

"Drained. Frightened. Confused. Is this what it will always be like?"

"For some women in the early months. But today's event would put a strain on anyone, not just a pregnant woman. I should have kept you here."

"I feel as though I have no control. I don't recognize my own body."

My mother nodded. "In time it will become more familiar. Motherhood is meant to change us. Has there been any blood?"

I shook my head.

"Good. Now that you're awake, I'll call down for some soup for you."

"I'm keeping you from your guests."

"No guest is more important than you, Vittoria. Besides, they're family and will understand where a mother's priorities lie."

She took the tray herself when a servant girl brought it to the door.

"You don't need to feed me, Mama. I have enough strength to lift a spoon."

"It's not that. I just want to make sure you eat something. If the soup isn't appetizing, I can have Cook prepare something else."

"I'm famished. This is fine." I scooped up a spoonful of chicken and greens floating in a clear broth. "Mm. . . Nutmeg." I smiled and made a great show of enjoying the soup.

When I'd emptied the bowl without retching, I suspected we were both relieved.

"You don't need to watch over me, Mama. I'm only going to sleep again."

"Then I'll stay until you fall asleep. Call for me if anything changes."

Late that night, sounds from revelers in the street below woke me. Ferrante was asleep beside me, his arm draped protectively across my belly, as if he knew.

A week later, the Montefeltros returned to Urbino, and Costanza and the d'Aragonas made their preparations for the journey back to Ischia. But my mother, worried that it was still too early for me to travel, argued successfully, with my father's help, to keep Ferrante, Alfonso and me in Rome.

"I see little enough of my daughter," she said. "Indulge a mother's longing and stay another month."

"Ferrante, we could use the time well," my father added. "Many of the representatives of Julius's League of Cambrai are still in Rome. It wouldn't hurt to meet informally with them."

And so we stayed. At my mother's insistence, I rested. I thought it would be difficult to keep my condition a secret from Ferrante, but when he threw himself into the political life of the city, he was gone from the palazzo most of the day and had no idea I'd spent most of the time stretched out on a couch in my mother's studiolo, reading. On the evenings when he and my father were in for dinner, I was easily able to join them. My morning nausea had gradually lessened, but even when it attacked, Ferrante was such a heavy sleeper that he didn't notice.

The seeds of hope had been so fragile in March that I scarcely dared believe I was carrying our child. But by the end of April, those seeds had budded and were about to blossom.

The night of April 28, a violent storm swept down from the hills. I'd sat with Alfonso and read several stories as the rain drove against the windows and thunder seemed to explode directly over the palazzo.

"It was a storm just like this that killed my parents," he whispered as the candles by his bedside sputtered in the wind that slithered between the cracks of the shutters.

"But we're safely in the palazzo, Alfonso, not storm-tossed on the sea. By morning this will be a memory." I tucked him in.

"Stay with me."

Despite the great strides we'd made in the past year, I had to remind myself that he was still a boy.

"Of course!"

I read another story aloud and watched until he finally allowed sleep to overtake him.

As I left him and moved through the palazzo to my room, a thunderclap within seconds of a flash of lightning shook the skylight, and I heard a sharp snap. I flattened myself against the wall and looked up, expecting to see cracks in the glass, but it had apparently held.

Then I heard shouts from below on the far side of the palazzo overlooking the central courtyard. I ran to a window. A tree was burning, riven in two by the lightning strike. It was an old chestnut, an ancient tree. Servants swarmed around it, attempting to douse the fire before it spread to the house. The downpour helped, and soon it was nothing but a charred and smoldering skeleton. I drew my wrap around my shoulders as I stared at the blackened blossoms trampled under the tree.

I'd calmed Alfonso's fear of the storm, but ever since my premonition about Ravenna during the Easter storm the previous year, I found myself troubled by the power of nature and its reminder of the fragility of life. I went to bed, taking with me a warning not to be complacent about my pregnancy and resolving to share the news with Ferrante.

He returned to the palazzo after midnight when the storm had subsided. After the forced inertia of his imprisonment and his long recuperation from his wounds, these weeks in Rome had renewed his spirit. He was a man once again engaged with the world. He was absorbing the lessons my father offered him with far more zeal than he had ever applied to his studies.

I watched from the bed as he stripped off his courtier's clothing by the fire, his body once again sound and whole.

"I've missed you," I murmured as he climbed into bed.

"You're awake! Disturbed by the storm? I heard about the lightning strike."

"A fiery reminder of the power of nature. Did tonight's meeting go well?"

"Spies are reporting the French are on the move again. They seem to be emboldened by Julius's death and Leo's supposed docility. The Venetians have formed a treaty with King Louis to divide the north. They would never have dared while Julius was still alive."

"What will it mean for you?"

"It's not clear. But sooner or later I'll rejoin Cardona in the field."

"If you can hold off for even a few months, I have reason to want you near."

"More reason than you already seem to have?" He smiled and traced my lips with his thumb.

"Yes."

He looked at me. "What is it? Is your illness more serious than you realized?"

"Ferrante, I am with child."

The words hung over us. Then he took me in his arms. "I'd given up hope," he said.

"So had I."

"Are you sure? How long? Are you well?"

I smiled. "Slow down! Yes, nearly three months, and as well as can be expected. Since it took long enough for it to exist at all, this baby seems determined to make its presence felt."

"Why did you wait to tell me?"

"I was afraid to believe it at first. And I couldn't bear your pain in addition to my own if..."

"Don't say it. And don't ever try to protect me again. I've seen death, Vittoria. You shouldn't have to bear your sorrow alone. But, God willing, six months from now we will baptize this child."

"Then you'll stay?"

"That depends on the French. Last I heard, Louis didn't plan his battles around the lying-in dates of his enemies' wives. But if I can possibly be here when you deliver, I will be."

He bent to kiss my belly and drew me close.

Content in his arms and relieved to be unburdened of my secret, I ignored the unfamiliar fragrance that clung to him. Rome was rife with courtesans. It had been easier on Ischia to pretend that when a warrior was away from home, he remained true to his marital vows. The power and intrigue Ferrante was discovering in Rome had clearly been more intoxicating than I realized.

Romantic epics of true love do not dwell on the thousands of minute compromises one makes to sustain a marriage. I had my husband by my side, grateful for the life growing within me and cherishing me all the more for it. The steady drip of water from the palazzo's overflowing gutters lulled me to sleep.

We stayed in Rome another few weeks. By the middle of May, the rumors of French troop movements were confirmed. France had marched south over the Alps and its ally Venice had marched west, converging on Milan, the prize that had continued to elude King Louis until now. It was time for Ferrante to return home and raise his troops. It was time for me to prepare for the birth of our child.

My mother was reluctant to let me go.

"I wish you would stay here," she said.

"Mama, as much as I've reveled in your attention, Ischia is my home. Our child should be born on the rock."

"When your time draws near, send for me. You know I will come and care for you." She kissed me and finally released me. In some ways, I believe this was more difficult for her than when I'd left Marino as a child.

We traveled by sea directly from Rome to Ischia. Although I'd protested, my memories still raw because of my constant nausea aboard ship, my mother had overruled me.

"A journey overland on horseback is too risky at this stage. Better to spend the trip in bed in your cabin."

We reached the Castello in what I reckoned was my fourteenth week of pregnancy. My morning nausea had passed, and I'd managed the entire trip without vomiting. I was experiencing a burst of energy and vigor that my mother had predicted. As we crossed the causeway, I realized how eager I was to be home and prepare for my baby.

Costanza was waiting for us in the courtyard of the citadel.

"Welcome home! I am so relieved to see you thriving, Vittoria! The extra weeks in your mother's care have clearly done you good." She hugged me, holding me close longer than she did in her customary greeting. Although there'd never been any tension between Costanza and my mother, I understood that Costanza had taken a step back from our relationship the whole time I'd been in Rome.

"Come, you three, dine with me and regale me with your tales of Rome." She led us up the steps, her joy in our return filling the citadel with laughter, wine and the scent of roasted lamb. After Alfonso had gone to bed, Ferrante and I announced my pregnancy to her, and she cried.

The next day, after a frustrating morning trying to reestablish a routine with Alfonso in the classroom, I sent him down to the stables to make himself useful with the groomsmen.

"I have no patience with the boy today!" I sought some consolation from Costanza. "Even though we did some lessons in Rome, I must admit I was too exhausted to push him. And now I'm paying the price."

"Forgive yourself, Vittoria. You are with child. Most women would relish the opportunity to withdraw. You need not be all things to all people. If I might make a suggestion, now would be a good time to find Alfonso a tutor."

I started to protest. "I don't want him to feel that I'm abandoning him. He's experienced too much of that."

"He doesn't know yet that you're pregnant?"

I shook my head. "Not yet."

"When the baby arrives, you will have no choice but to divide your attention. Better to get him accustomed now. Castellana d'Aragona has mentioned to me that she wants to educate Giovanna and Maria. In spite of their little spats, the three are of a similar age and compatible. Let me contact the academy in Napoli."

"I know you speak wisely, Costanza. My emotions are so unpredictable right now. I don't feel like myself at all. After I sent Alfonso away this morning I cried, unable to stop my tears."

She reached out to take my hand.

"My dear girl, I do understand. Although I haven't borne any living child, I was pregnant once, long ago. I remember those few months vividly. For women like us, Vittoria, who place so much importance on the life of the mind, to be overtaken by the messiness and indignities of the body is a challenge few men would be able to survive." She smiled.

"Oh, Costanza, I had no idea you had lost a child."

"It is not something I speak of, nor dwell on. God gave me children to raise in you and Ferrante when He saw fit to take my own child. Come here."

She drew me into her arms.

"You will weather this pregnancy, Vittoria. You are strong and healthy, and I will be at your side."

I spent the afternoon walking in the garden, reveling in the sunlight and the explosion of color in the purples and deep pinks of the oleander, and in my own surge of energy.

That night, after reading with Alfonso, I joined Ferrante by the fire in our sitting room. A sack of mail had been awaiting him when we'd disembarked the day before and he was making his way through the messages. I told him about Costanza's offer to find a tutor for Alfonso, and he murmured a distracted assent, scarcely lifting his eyes from the letter in his hand. Although I was bursting with thoughts about the baby and its impact on our family, this was apparently not the time to share them. Now that we were home, it seemed we both had our preoccupations and they rarely overlapped. I turned to the bit of wool in my lap, a baby blanket I'd started in Rome with fumbling fingers. As a girl, I'd never been very good with the domestic arts and I despaired that motherhood alone was going to change that. I ripped out a row of stitches in frustration and decided to give up and go to bed.

I woke shortly before dawn. Ferrante was deeply asleep and I eased myself from the bed so as not to disturb him. Another change in my body was the need to empty my bladder more frequently than I'd been accustomed to. I lit a candle from the embers in the hearth and quietly dragged the chamber pot out from under the bed.

As I squatted, a sharp pain travelled across my belly and I gripped the edge of the bedside table. It passed, and I took a deep breath and stood up. But as I did, I felt something sticky glide down my thighs. I touched it with my hand and began to tremble when I pulled my fingers away covered in blood.

Every cell in my body screamed "No!" Not now, not when I felt so well, so vibrant. Not when I'd passed the most fragile early months, which held the greatest risk. Not when my hope had been nurtured and allowed to flourish.

"Ferrante!" I called out to him, crazed and frantic. He rolled over, disoriented, and then, jolted by what he must have recognized as the smell of fresh blood, sat up, alert and on guard.

"What is it? Are you injured?"

"Call for Costanza. I'm bleeding . . . I'm afraid I'm losing the baby."

"Lie down. Stay warm. I'll go for help."

He settled me back in our bed and wrapped me in the blankets before dressing and leaving me.

The pain returned in waves. I could not stop my body from shaking nor hold back the blood now sluicing out of me.

After what seemed an eternity Costanza was by my side, followed soon by the midwife. Ferrante hovered outside, but Costanza quietly sent him away.

After the midwife examined me, I saw her look across at Costanza and shake her head.

"No. No. No. It cannot be over! What did I do wrong?" I was sobbing.

"My lady, listen to me. We need to get you up to deliver the baby. You did nothing wrong. I see this many times. It is nature's way of correcting her mistakes. This is a child who would not have lived even if you carried it to term." The midwife had her arms under me and was lifting me with Costanza's help. My body was convulsed with pain, heightened by the knowledge that my labor would be fruitless.

If I'd thought the early weeks of my pregnancy had turned my body into unfamiliar terrain, the woman who delivered her dead son that morning was a total stranger to me. I screamed in an agony that went beyond the physical pain I felt. My body was out of my control, driven by forces all my learning had not prepared me to understand. My soul raged against the injustice of death. I was a wild woman and didn't know myself.

When it was over, the sun had already moved past noon. I begged for and was given the baby to hold. He was no bigger than my hand, with no signs of deformity that could provide me with the answers I sought.

My body, so full of promise, was now empty. I watched numbly as more women from the household entered my chamber to strip and burn the bed linens and wash the blood from the floor. I climbed into the tub and let them bathe me. I sipped the infusion the midwife prepared for me.

I had no more tears, no more words, as my tiny son, swaddled in a shroud, was taken from my arms and out the door.

Costanza decided to move me into her own quarters to look after me herself. Ferrante carried me, his face stricken, unable to find the words to comfort me. He sat with me for the rest of the day, but I could barely acknowledge his presence.

Costanza urged him to take care of himself. "Go get some air, Ferrante. There is nothing you can do here. You both need time to heal."

I lay curled up, conscious only of a dull ache in my belly, but unfeeling and uncaring of anything around me. When I refused the tray brought to me later in the day, Costanza propped me up and spoon-fed me sips of soup and wine.

"I know you can't contemplate anything right now except your loss. But do not slip away from us. We cannot lose you, too."

I don't know how long I stayed in a fog of emptiness. I no longer had the strength or will to rant in fury against the cruelty of fate.

And then one morning, Costanza took possession of my room as she always did and threw open the shutters to let in the light.

"Vittoria, it's time. Your body has healed, but your soul will not if you continue to smother it in your pain. You have a husband and a child who need you. You have a life full of promise to live. If you turn your back on the gifts God has given you, your spirit will die as completely as your baby. Today you are getting out of bed."

"I can't."

"You will. Even if it's only to take one step. I may seem cruel, but believe me, it would be far more cruel to allow you to remain in this state. Now come. Have a bath and get dressed."

She didn't accede to my protests. With the help of one of the maidservants, she lifted me from the bed and into the bath. The water, hot and sulfurous from the island's springs, soothed and calmed me.

When I was dressed, Costanza led me outside and we walked for a few minutes. It was a brilliant June morning, and the cultivated beds were bursting with life.

"The world has not stopped while you were in mourning, Vittoria. The cycle continues, just as we the living must continue. No one, least of all I, expects you to be the same as you were. But we long for you to rejoin us."

Waiting at the belvedere under the pavilion were Ferrante and Alfonso. As I approached, the boy ran to me, threw his arms around my waist and buried his face in my skirts. I kissed the top of his head and looked up at Ferrante, who took my hand, turned it palm up and kissed it.

"I am so sorry," I whispered.

That night I read to Alfonso and rejoined my husband in our bed.

CHAPTER TWENTY-ONE

Scholars, Poets, Historians and Artists

Vittoria
1513
Ischia and Rome

The summer I'd intended to prepare for the birth of my child became one of organizing the education of Alfonso instead. Costanza had so rightly reminded me that I had a child who was much in need of me.

I wrote letters; I interviewed tutors; and until we settled on a candidate I continued Alfonso's lessons myself, with Giovanna and Maria d'Aragona joining us. I had an ideal in mind during the search. I wanted someone who not only had an excellent grasp of the humanities, mathematics and science, but who could also appreciate a sometimes angry, clever boy whose energy needed to be channeled. The last thing we needed was some joyless scholar who had absorbed his own education as a docile sheep.

"Am I being unrealistic?" I asked Ferrante one evening as I sifted through the pile of letters and recommendations on my writing table.

He looked up from the latest military report of my father's, which had been delivered that morning.

"No. You are being Vittoria."

"Does that amuse you?"

"On the contrary. It is what I have always loved and admired about you. If you were a man, I'd have you at my right hand planning our next campaign."

"Well, the very least I can do is see that Alfonso is educated to be that right hand when the time comes."

"I know you will. Now come away from your frustrating search and sit with me by the fire for the rest of the evening.

I'm afraid it will be the last for a while. Your father is ordering me to sail with my men."

I set down my pen, crossed the room and climbed into his lap. I'd known this was coming from the moment we'd left Rome. The loss of the baby had put out of my mind the other losses one endures over and over as the wife of a soldier—the sudden departures, the uncertainties of where he was or even if he was alive. I knew Ferrante had stayed longer than he'd originally intended, claiming his men needed more training.

I'd recovered not only for Alfonso, but also for Ferrante. A wife who was resilient and unshaken by hardship freed a warrior to leave again and again and focus on the battle at hand, undistracted by concerns at home.

I kissed him. I didn't cry or beg him to stay. Later in the evening he carried me to bed and we made love for the first time since I'd miscarried.

The next day I bade him farewell.

"A knight should have a banner," I told him, and presented him with an embroidered token. I'd crafted it when I placed aside the baby blanket I'd been knitting. Creating the memento had given me a new way to occupy my hands and my thoughts.

"I shall carry it with me into battle."

"God keep you safe. I am at your right side in spirit."

And then he was gone.

I'd chosen not to accompany him to the harbor. The journey was still taxing on my recovering body, and this time I preferred to watch from the heights as his ship sailed away. The wind was brisk and soon carried the galley northward beyond the horizon.

I turned to my responsibilities. My mother had recommended a young scholar from Pisa and he was arriving that afternoon. If I liked him, I intended to give him a trial position.

About an hour after the bells announced the arrival of the packet boat from Napoli, Alfonso came bursting into my studiolo.

"Vittoria, have you heard? The boat brought a stranger! I was down at the barracks when he climbed up from the village. I knew he wasn't from these parts at all, so I questioned him. Now that Ferrante has left, I'm the man of the Castello." He put his hand on the wooden sword at his belt that he'd been wearing ever since we returned from Rome.

"That you are, Alfonso. And what did you learn?"

"His name is Giancarlo Brittonio, and he's a traveler and a scholar. He's been to Egypt and Constantinople and Greece and Hungary. He speaks five languages and he can juggle. He showed me, so I know it's true."

"He sounds quite accomplished. I take it you approve of him?" If Giancarlo was indeed as impressive as my mother had written and Alfonso believed, he appeared to have passed the most important test—that of holding Alfonso's attention and gaining his respect.

"I do. Can we invite him to stay? He promised to show me the skull of a giant wolf from the mountains of the Peloponnesus."

"I need to meet him first. Where is he?"

"In the reception hall. Shall I get him?"

"Thank you, Alfonso. But I will go myself to greet him. Please ask Cook to prepare some wine and cakes. He's probably hungry after his journey."

Alfonso ran off gladly on his assignment, pleased, I'm sure, at the prospect of one of Cook's sweets. I smoothed my hair and descended from my quarters to meet this paragon. He had his back to me, studying one of Costanza's tapestries. He was a tall man, not stooped as many who pore over books often are. And he was more flamboyantly dressed than the scholars I was accustomed to meeting. I understood Alfonso's immediate assessment that this man was not from here. His clothing was exotic, as was the jewel-handled dagger on his belt.

"Signor Brittonio?"

He turned, bowed and took my hand, hovering over it for a fraction of a second.

"My lady. Your mother described you well."

He was not as young as I expected, although it may have been that in his far-flung travels, his eyes had seen much that had aged him before his time. I saw wisdom and compassion staring out at me. More than the adventures that had made such an impression on Alfonso, I wondered if that was what had spoken so profoundly to the boy.

"I hear you've met Alfonso."

"The Marchese del Vasto, as he introduced himself to me. A spirited, intelligent boy."

"Have you tutored boys before, Signor?"

"The sons of the Crescenzi family in Rome, where I met your mother. Before that, the foster son of a merchant in Buda."

"You don't strike me as the typical tutor whose vita has crossed my desk."

He smiled. "If you're looking for a stern and sour taskmaster who has turned to teaching because he failed his doctor's exam, then I am not your man."

"I expect you'll find that the court at Ischia believes learning should be a source of wonder and delight, not a grim task to be endured."

"Then I may indeed be what you seek."

I liked him. I offered him a trial position until Michaelmas, assuming that three months would be ample time for him to prove himself. Less than that and Alfonso might still be captivated by his novelty. It was when the newness of any experience had worn off that I knew Alfonso could be difficult.

I discovered that Giancarlo Brittonio's expertise extended beyond the classroom. He understood the need of children to be engaged in vigorous physical activity. He often had Alfonso, Giovanna and Maria roaming the grounds of the Castello on treasure hunts or racing in the exercise yard now that Ferrante's soldiers were gone. He also didn't begrudge the time Alfonso devoted to sword-training. But when Alfonso protested about the number of hours he was required to spend in the classroom and appealed to me, Signor Brittonio stood his ground.

"I recognize, my lady, that the boy is being groomed to follow in his father's and your husband's military footsteps. His seat will be on a warhorse, not a bench of law. Nevertheless, a soldier who does not know his history, an officer who cannot carry out his commander's orders because he's unable to read them, will be as useless on the field as an untrained foot soldier."

"I could not agree more, Signor. You have my complete support. That was how the duchessa raised the marchese and me, and I know he would affirm my decision were he here."

Alfonso was sent back to study, and Giancarlo Brittonio and I became allies in his education. It was not unusual for us to spend an hour or two in the afternoon poring over a text one of us considered a favorite and discussing the best way to introduce it to the three pupils. Our conversations were often spirited, with one or the other of us seizing a passage and proclaiming it with either great drama or lively humor. I began to look forward to these respites from my melancholy. There were moments when Giancarlo even made me laugh.

"I don't know if you realize what a great pleasure it is to stretch my mind with someone of your intellect, my lady. The households where I've taught in the past appreciated the value of educating their children—their sons, mainly. But none of my patrons had a love of learning as you do. For them, it was a necessary element of their station in life. Useful, pragmatic. Their lack of passion for anything remotely literary was probably one of the reasons I changed positions so frequently. Now I have no desire to move on. Your joy in words is infectious!"

"I cannot imagine a life otherwise. My mother and the duchessa taught me to cherish learning—first as a refuge, then as an adventure. And the duchessa's court nurtures the pursuit of knowledge. Her salons are extraordinary, both for the minds they attract and the conversations they engender. You must come! I'll ask her to invite you. Forgive me for not considering it sooner. I know you'd be welcome."

I hadn't thought of including him because I hadn't attended one of Costanza's salons since the loss of my child. I still wasn't ready to be animated and charming in company. The afternoons with Giancarlo fed my soul in a quiet and undemanding manner that the salons decidedly didn't. That bit of personal revelation I kept to myself, but encouraged him to participate. He could certainly hold his own with no assistance from me in the company of the poets, philosophers and politicians who formed Costanza's circle.

Giancarlo's success with Alfonso in the classroom afforded me an unexpected surprise, in addition to the diversion and contentment I found in our afternoon conversations. I had time. Time I might have spent in brooding sorrow. Managing Alfonso's education had been a consuming distraction, but once Giancarlo was in place and in control, my daily role diminished.

I feared that the hour or two I enjoyed discussing books with Giancarlo wasn't enough to prevent me from slipping back into melancholy and mourning. I confided my concern to Costanza.

"Your little household is humming, Vittoria. Why not take advantage of your confidence in Signor Brittonio and use the opportunity to return to Rome? I am sure your mother is eager to see you, and it will bring you closer to Ferrante. If he has a chance to break away from the field for a few days, joining you in Rome is within the realm of possibility."

I wrote my mother, who was more than overjoyed to welcome me, and set out for Rome at the beginning of October, with assurances from both Giancarlo and Alfonso that they would continue diligently without me, although neither seemed particularly pleased that I was leaving.

When I arrived in Rome, my mother had as her goal my continued emotional recovery. As I'd realized when Giancarlo and Alfonso were well-settled in the classroom, it was too easy to become mired in despondency during the hours spent in contemplation rather than action. Mama was not about to allow me to retreat to my rooms in the palazzo as I had at Ischia. She was determined to turn my visit into an object lesson. When guests showed up to avail themselves of Colonna hospitality, I had to put aside my sadness, join them in the salon and follow my mother's advice.

"Listen well, Vittoria. Our visitors can bring you more than an account of Ferrante's bravery on the field; they can decipher for us the reasons he is fighting in the first place. Whatever you learn will help you bear the challenges of being a warrior's wife."

I listened and learned—not just about the war but also how to elicit information from men who were only too happy to display their importance. Paolo Giovio was one of them.

Giovio, who had been practicing medicine in Pavia, had left that city ahead of the plague and sought Pope Leo's patronage—not for medicine but for his literary pursuits as a historian of the war. My mother was happy to invite him to dinner and I greeted him warmly.

"Signor Giovio, you honor us with your presence. I beg you to humor a worried wife and share your insights about the progress of the campaign. Come, quench your thirst with our wine while you slake my hunger for news of my husband."

"I am most happy to bring you some solace, my lady, for I have nothing but magnificent things to report about the marchese. I was in his camp only a week ago."

"I turn to you to be my eyes and ears on the plain, Signor."

He sipped his wine delicately before beginning his observations. I caught Mama's eye over his head and her expression confirmed that I'd been successful. I tried to be forbearing as he gathered himself—as if he were about to deliver an oration at the university.

He recounted in great detail the shifting alliances, rivalries and power grabs among the French, the Spanish and the pope. At the heart of this season's conflict was control over Milano.

"And what was my husband's role?" I was trying to be patient, accepting that historians must be allowed to tell their stories, but I was eager for Ferrante to be the centerpiece of Giovio's story.

My mother smiled in amusement across the room, but she was not about to rescue me. It was her custom to sometimes let me flounder in order to find the means to rescue myself.

"Ah, my lady, all of what I am telling you is simply prologue to the great accomplishments of the marchese. The shifting fortunes on the battlefield are presaged by the impermanence of treaties and agreements. France's defeat in their latest attempt to seize Milano set the stage for your husband's next victory."

His *only* victory, I thought to myself, remembering the scarred prisoner who had returned from Ravenna. Giovio seemed either not to be aware that my husband had been defeated in his one other battle, or chose to ignore it in his attempt to flatter us by praising Ferrante. I checked my skepticism, however. He said that Ferrante had been victorious. That should've been enough. But I was impatient to know how.

"Please, Signor Giovio, do not keep me in suspense. Tell me all of it!"

He launched into an extended description of the latest battle, until at last, Ferrante made his appearance in Signor Giovio's chronicle!

"We were at dinner in the viceroy's tent when scouts brought the news that the Venetians had stolen away from the city and followed the Spanish troops. A heated discussion ensued and frustrations were high. The marchese kept his own counsel for several minutes and then offered his opinion, forged, he said, in his experience at Ravenna."

If I'd doubted Giovio's accuracy earlier, those doubts were dispelled by his perception of Ferrante. I'd always observed my husband to be deliberate in his speech, but never headstrong. And grasping how deeply the chaos at Ravenna had affected him, I wasn't surprised that he would use the lessons he'd gained in defeat to determine his strategy in the next battle.

"And did the viceroy listen?" I asked Giovio, remembering that at Ravenna he had *not* listened to my father.

"Absolutely and completely, my lady!"

"What was that counsel, Signor?"

"Communication and coordination, my lady. And most significantly, to attack rather than defend."

"And did his opinion prevail?"

"It did, my lady. The viceroy placed the marchese in command of the infantry, and the next morning he led them in a decisive attack at La Motta. In addition to his opinion, his actions prevailed. The Venetians suffered enormous casualties. I myself saw the battlefield in the aftermath. Thousands of Venetians lay dead or dying. The rest fled, scattered beyond the recall of their commander."

"And my husband?"

"Triumphant, my lady. His idea to attack first was brilliant."

"I am grateful to you for your account, Signor Giovio, and your confirmation of what I have never doubted about my husband's bravery. It's a great blessing that you found your way to Rome. Please know that you will always be welcome, not only in my parents' house, but also in mine on Ischia."

"I thank you, my lady, for your hospitality. My intention is to write all these things down to preserve them for the ages, as the ancients recorded their history. We have much to learn from the Romans and the Greeks. Perhaps future generations may learn from us."

"I could not agree more, Signor Giovio."

At that moment, Mama gently interrupted us and I took the opportunity to excuse myself from company and retreated to my chamber, where I wrote to my husband.

Rome was such a vibrant city that it wasn't difficult for me to follow my mother's prescription and engage with all that it had to offer. Pope Julius II had been more than the warrior whose ambitions had kept my husband on the battlefield; he'd also envisioned a new golden age for Rome. During the ten years he reigned, he had laid the cornerstone for a new St. Peter's Basilica, commissioned Michelangelo Buonarroti to fresco the vault of the Sistine Chapel and engaged Michelangelo's rival, Raffaello Sanzio, to transform the papal library and reception rooms with his own frescoes. Word of these wonders had been on the lips of every Roman visitor to Costanza's court.

Even more than when Julius had been pope, the city was a magnet for the poets and artists drawn there because Pope Leo was spending lavishly to employ them. The artists filled the churches and villas and public buildings with commissioned works; the poets filled manuscripts with illustrious sonnets; and all of them were vying for praise and fame. I wanted to see everything, especially the work on the walls of the Vatican, and with my mother's encouragement, prevailed upon my relationships as Costanza's niece, Ferrante's wife and Fabrizio Colonna's daughter to send a message to Pope Leo. The next day a letter arrived from

Jacopo Sadoleto, one of the Pope's secretaries and a close friend of Costanza's.

I ran to find Mama, waving the letter like a romantic girl who has received a message from her lover.

"Mama! My request has been granted! Leo will see us!"

On the day of our audience, we rode to the Vatican together. Mama was as accomplished a rider as I, so I was happy to be on horseback rather than traveling in a litter, curtained off from the sights and sounds of my native city. The Colonna household guards protected us as escorts and we traveled at a comfortable pace.

"The city is flourishing right now, Vittoria. It's a good time to be in Rome. A good time to be alive." She looked meaningfully at me. No doubt, Costanza had shared with her my despair after the miscarriage. The two women seemed to be conspiring to reawaken my spirit.

Freed of the familiar surroundings of the Castello and the memories contained within its ramparts, I laughed in the sunshine, absorbing the simple excitement of being out, beyond the walls of the palazzo and the confining texture of our women's lives.

We arrived at the gates of the Vatican in the midst of a tumult of supplicants. The Swiss Guards whom Pope Julius had engaged in his conquests now guarded the papal palace, their clothing even more colorful than Rome's courtesans. By contrast, Mama and I presented the modest image expected of us as noble matrons. We assumed our public face and abided by the rules.

It was Jacopo Sadoleto who greeted us and ushered us into an anteroom. While we were waiting, another man strode into the room—a tall, imposing figure whose presence dominated the confined space, not just because of his physical size but also because of a certain confidence and self-importance that emanated from him.

"My lady, Signora Colonna, may I present my colleague, Pietro Bembo, also secretary to His Holiness and instrumental in Pope Leo's promotion of the poetic arts."

I knew the name. His poetry had made its way to Ischia, but more than that, he'd written a dialogue on Platonic love that was in Costanza's library. Before I had a chance to utter a word, Bembo swooped with a flourish to kiss our hands and then addressed me with both condescension and curiosity.

"My lady, I have heard from my Neapolitan friends that you write poetry yourself from time to time. I would be most gratified to read your sonnets, if you would share them with me."

I blushed. I hadn't been aware that my attempts to put emotion to paper had circulated beyond our congenial circle on the rock. I tried to be graceful in answering him, but beneath my careful demeanor, I seethed as if a secret had been betrayed.

"I would be honored to receive your insights, my lord. However, I'm afraid they're only the scribbles of a woman who loves and longs for her husband."

"That is certainly not what I have heard, my lady. Your modesty becomes you, but I would nevertheless enjoy the opportunity to see your work. His Holiness is eager to encourage poets, and the importance of Italian as a literary language cannot be underestimated."

Mama squeezed my hand, and when Bembo and Sadoleto turned away to discuss something privately, she whispered to me. "Vittoria, you do realize what an honor it is to be recognized by Pietro Bembo? But I'm not surprised. Even if I *am* biased as your mother, your poetry is exceptional."

The attention made me uncomfortable. I'd written my poems as an escape from the emptiness left by Ferrante's absence, not for dissection by the man who was becoming Italy's authority on poetic expression.

I shook my head. "I fear I'll be ridiculed, or at the very least, misunderstood."

"I disagree! He wouldn't have asked for them if he thought they were drivel. Where is my brave and bold Vittoria?"

Her unabashed confidence cheered me and helped me regain my perspective on why we'd come. I calmed my agitation just as we were directed into the Pope's reception room and kept it in check even when Leo himself commented on my poems.

"Pietro tells me you are a poet, my dear. I look forward to reading your work one day, although Pietro insists that poems ought to be sung to be truly appreciated. I wholeheartedly agree that music is one of life's most wonderful pleasures. You must come again to one of our entertainments."

I found Leo congenial and cheerful during our conversation, and my apprehension about the mention of my poetry eased when he continued on to other subjects. The frescoes on the walls of the *Stanze,* in which he held his audiences, had been completed by Raffaello over the previous few years, and I could not keep my attention from wandering to the striking compositions. Leo noticed.

"Magnificent, aren't they? To be surrounded by such beauty is an exquisite privilege of the papacy. You must see the other rooms! I'll have the librarian take you for a tour, as I must proceed to my next appointment."

He turned to Jacopo Sadoleto. "Jacopo, please ask Inghirami to escort the marchesa and her mother on a tour of the Raffaello *Stanze.*"

And with that, he dismissed us, but not before we knelt for his blessing. Despite Leo's worldliness in pursuit of the arts, he had apparently not ignored his clerical role. He performed this priestly farewell with precision, if not a deep spirituality. By the time Mama and I had made the sign of the cross and risen from our knees, Sadoleto announced the next supplicants to the pope, and the librarian escorted us through the *Stanze.*

The tour of the private rooms beyond the reception hall was a rare glimpse into the genius of an artist whose reputation was a constant topic at Roman gatherings. I'd heard so much about the brilliant, charming and ambitious Raffaello in the weeks leading up to this papal visit that my appetite had been whetted and was eager to be satisfied.

I was not disappointed. Every aspect of the experience fulfilled my expectations. I was impressed by the subject matter, the scope of the composition, the lifelike quality of the figures, the colors Raffaello had chosen. Tommaso Inghirami was an effusive and eloquent tour guide, pointing out the meaning of various groupings of characters and even indulging in a bit of gossip in recounting the creation of these monumental works.

"Working with Raffaello was a pleasure—a man of great courtesy and refinement in addition to his talent. He was always open to my suggestions and, in fact, sought my knowledge in developing the ideas for his historical scenes. Although well-schooled as a painter, he of course had not had the classical education of someone like myself." The librarian seemed unaware of his preening.

"Raffaello wasn't at all like his rival on the other side of the wall," and Inghirami thrust his jaw in the direction of the Sistine Chapel. "That one was a stubborn, secretive recluse who kept his work hidden and had none of the grace and charm of Raffaello. I can assure you there were no screaming matches between Pope Julius and Raffaello, unlike the words that passed between His Holiness and the Florentine."

I wasn't sure how necessary grace and charm were to the creation of a masterpiece, but I was curious to compare the two painters. If Inghirami and half of Rome were to be believed, Michelangelo and Raffaello could not have been more different.

"Signor Inghirami, you have been so gracious yourself in guiding us." I smiled at him and watched the satisfaction spread across his face. "Would you be willing to show us the chapel? It would be fascinating to compare the work of the rivals. It must have been quite a feat to maintain harmony with them working in such proximity!"

He was more than happy to oblige and, keys in hand, led the way.

The chapel was empty. Later in the day the Pope would lead services, but for the moment, we three were alone in the immense, cavernous room. At first, I didn't know where to direct my eyes. The frescoes in the *Stanze* had been at eye level on the walls, and each presented a single, coherent scene that could be studied and absorbed as a whole. The chapel, on the other hand, was a complex puzzle that would take years to decipher—much as it had taken Michelangelo years to paint it.

I allowed myself a few moments to focus. Inghirami was prattling on about the portrait Raffaello had painted of him in thanks for his help, but soon enough my ears shut him out. As my vision swept over the ceiling I finally gained my bearings and began moving down the length of the chapel. I walked, head held back, totally engulfed by the narrative of the central images above me. Raffaello's paintings had been orderly, meticulous, lifelike. I'd felt that any one of his characters could have stepped off the wall and begun a conversation with me.

But what I saw in the Sistine Chapel was something else entirely. It was a dialogue with God, the Word made flesh via the artist's brush. I recognized familiar scenes from the Old Testament as I moved down the nave from the door to the altar—the Flood, Noah's Sacrifice, the Temptation and the Expulsion from the Garden—and felt the pain of God's wrath. Then, the Creation of Eve and Adam, the Separation of Sky and Water, the Creation of the Sun, Moon and Planets, and I trembled in awe at the power of the God who gave us light and life. I found and gazed upon a single face that spoke so eloquently to me of my own experience that it brought tears to my eyes. I wanted to reach up and stroke the face as if it were my own image, alone and searching deep in herself for the courage she knew she must find.

"Vittoria, are you ill?" Mama's voice broke through the spell the Sistine ceiling had cast over me. I turned to her.

"You're crying! Has something upset you?"

"On the contrary. I feel as if something has saved me."

I'd seen all I could digest that day. I vowed to myself not only to return to the chapel, but also to meet the man whose vision had touched me so profoundly.

1536

MEDITATION

Becoming Michelangelo

Vittoria
1536
Rome

My friendship with Michelangelo is an enigma. To the world that stumbles upon us poring over sketches in the shadows of the Sistine scaffolding, we are an incomprehensible pair—the pious, reclusive widow and the rough-hewn, obstinate thorn in every pontiff's side. But to me, our deepening connection staggers my imagination.

For over twenty years, Michelangelo resided dormant in my heart, a seed dropped on unintended—and untended—ground. Despite my vow in the Sistine Chapel as a young woman, I allowed the demands of my challenging marriage, my responsibilities to my adopted son and the tides of history to submerge a need I now recognize as profound.

Michelangelo believes I am leading him on this shared journey. I argue with him about this misconception, grasping on a visceral level the frustration Pope Clement often expressed when confronted by Michelangelo's immovable opinions. He sometimes appears to be willfully blind not only to his capacity to grasp what we're seeking together but also to his significant role in leading *me*. He, the observer with such acute powers, shuts his eyes when he's looking at himself.

Am I equally guilty of self-deception? Pain is no mystery to me. I transmute sorrow into a spiritual food, nourishing my poetry. What has been missing from my life is joy. Am I willing to embrace it now? Or will I retreat once again to a hollow piety defined by an outward restraint that denies and camouflages my inner turmoil?

Michelangelo has introduced me to exuberance, to the embrace of life in all its squalor and vitality. His images—not just the raw and perceptive sketches of me he throws down on the page and into my soul, but all the striving, reaching souls that populate his art—pull me away from my old self. St. Paul exhorts the Colossians, new in their relationship with Christ, to put on new garments and "clothe yourselves with compassion, kindness, humility, gentleness and patience."

For so long, I have held myself apart, too consumed with my own suffering to offer kindness and compassion to anyone else. Opening my heart to Michelangelo requires me to break into pieces, become a shattered vessel. I surprise myself with the violence of this choice of words. And then I rebuke my timidity. I am no stranger to the fierceness and ferocity of Christ's message to us. If I am to change, if I hope to come to Michelangelo, as well as Christ, as a new woman, I must demolish the old Vittoria. What astounds me in our relationship, what is so inexplicable to me, is that I actually welcome the loss of my old self.

The intimacy that binds us—intellectual, emotional and spiritual—has transformed me. The disruption Michelangelo has caused in my complacency forces me to see my life through his eyes, not mine.

I am becoming Michelangelo.

1513 – 1521

CHAPTER TWENTY-TWO

"You Rescue Me with Your Words"

Vittoria
1513 – 1516
Ischia and Rome

After visiting with my family in Rome, I returned to Ischia at the beginning of Advent. During my absence, our tutor, Giancarlo, had achieved great progress in Alfonso's education and had also become well-entrenched in Costanza's court.

"He holds his own in the salon when the poets descend on us from Napoli," Costanza reported with amusement. "It's not only Alfonso and the Aragona girls who find him captivating."

Costanza's approval wasn't easily won, so I was impressed by how quickly he'd made his mark.

"I knew Giancarlo was a storyteller from Alfonso's excitement the first day he arrived, but I took him for a learned adventurer, not a poet."

"Then you must judge for yourself this evening. Jacopo Sannazarro and Benedetto Cariteo are here and seem quite determined to compete with our scholar, whose reputation has apparently drifted across the water to Napoli and aroused some curiosity."

"I look forward to the entertainment." I was weary from travel, but felt I couldn't turn down Costanza's invitation.

That evening I dined in my apartment alone with Alfonso and then read to him.

"I missed you, Vittoria. I'm very busy during the day and don't think of you not being here, but the nights are empty without your stories."

"Did no one else read with you in the evenings?"

"Giovanna and Maria's mother did at first, but she doesn't love stories the way we do, so after the first week, I told her she needn't come anymore. She seemed relieved."

In addition to the two inches he appeared to have grown during the month I was away in Rome, he also struck me as remarkably grown up. I reminded myself that he was nearly twelve, but it was more than the years. The influence of Giancarlo was evident in the self-confident, thoughtful boy who had welcomed me home.

I bade him good-night only after we'd read several stories and I'd heard a full account of all his endeavors, both in the classroom and on the training ground.

By the time I arrived at Costanza's salon, the company was already engaged in spirited conversation. Scarcely anyone looked up to note my presence, so thoroughly engrossed were they in the evening's topic.

I took a goblet of wine from the tray offered by Arturo, Costanza's chamberlain.

"Welcome back, my lady. It is a pleasure to see you once again in company," he whispered to me, bowing with a gentle smile.

"Thank you, Arturo." I nodded in reply, with a brief touch on his arm. "It's a pleasure to be back."

He was referring not only to my sojourn in Rome but also to my absence from the salon in all the months since my miscarriage. I wasn't quite sure I was ready for this evening, despite how active I'd been in Rome. The discussions at the dinner table at the Colonna palazzo had been mainly political, and my role had primarily been one of listener, gleaning as much as I could of the currents that would determine Ferrante's future.

Although politics had its firm place in Costanza's court, this evening she was hosting a decidedly creative circle. I saw her favorite poet, Jacopo Sannazarro, intense as ever, leaning forward in his seat, ready to defend his position. A few feet away from him sat Giancarlo, listening with an expression that seemed to flit between awe and amusement, depending on who was speaking. I imagine in his travels he'd been a participant in many such discussions.

A corner seat away from the discussion beckoned me and I entered the room as unobtrusively as possible. I was in no mood, nor did I have the energy, to jump into the conversation. Only Giancarlo noted my arrival. He smiled and nodded, with a warmth that surprised me, but nevertheless made me feel welcome.

The conversation at times seemed the equivalent of a jousting match, with words instead of lances as weapons. Costanza had predicted that the Neapolitans had arrived not merely curious but competitive, and she seemed quite willing to let it play out.

The topic was whether daily life was a worthy subject for poetry. Some argued in the affirmative, referring to the ancient Latin poems that vividly described events. At his colleagues' urging, Sannazarro recited from his new poem "Arcadia," which he'd dedicated to Costanza, as an example of a realistic description of country life. Given how little I knew of peasant life on the Colonna and Pescara lands, Arcadia seemed an ideal and imagined life rather than a carefully observed reality. But I was too tired to voice my thoughts and join the fray. As the applause and murmurs of approval subsided, Sannazarro turned to his left and addressed Giancarlo.

"You've been unusually silent this evening, Signor Brittonio. I'm curious to learn whether, in your travels, the topic has surfaced and if it's been treated in verse."

"Such use of outward details to reflect the inner soul of humanity is still in its infancy north of the Alps. We Italians seem to have adapted the classical model and made it our own."

"And have you made it yours, Signor?" That came from one of Sannazarro's lesser acolytes. Costanza and I exchanged glances across the room. It appeared the competition was heating up. The Neapolitans were pushing Giancarlo to recite one of his own poems.

"If you mean, have I written sonnets that take as their subject the realities of our physical life as a way of expressing the joys and sorrows of the human soul, the answer is yes."

I smiled at our scholar's lack of humility in the presence of these learned and famous poets. He could have been addressing a schoolroom of unruly boys.

Costanza interjected at that moment. "Giancarlo, we would be honored to hear one of your sonnets."

It occurred to me that Costanza had warned Giancarlo that he might be called upon to recite. He stood, lowered his eyes for a moment and then raised them to look directly at me.

"This poem is dedicated to the marchesa, who accepted me into her household and trusted me with the education of her son."

I nodded in acknowledgment.

And with a flourish, he began his sonnet, immersing us in the life of the peasant, rooted in the changing of the seasons and the rhythm of the natural world. It was not the idealized simplicity of the country depicted by Sannazarro but one far more visceral, as if he had smelled the fecund earth and held the harvested fruit in his own hand. It was a celebration of the cycle of life, the dying vine in winter reemerging to hope and promise in the spring.

A hush greeted him when he finished. For a moment I could not believe that the others hadn't felt as I did, that they were denying the beauty of Giancarlo's poem out of jealousy. And then a voice rang out—the dynamic, sonorous voice of Sannazarro.

"Bravo!"

Having heard from the maestro himself, the others responded with equal acclaim. This time, Giancarlo displayed a joyful modesty as the company broke the circle and came up to him with congratulatory slaps on the back.

Costanza took the opportunity to call everyone to a midnight supper and we began to move to the dining hall.

Giancarlo held back from the throng and waited for me. "My lady, let me first welcome you home. You have been missed."

"So I heard from Alfonso. I hope my absence didn't interfere with the progress you'd been making."

"We had a few disruptive days. But when I understood the reason, we were able to find ways to overcome his agitation."

"So you took the time to determine why he was behaving badly?"

"Of course. It was fruitless not to get to the root of his misbehavior. I could've punished him, but I find that's often no solution, only a postponement."

"And what was the reason?"

"He has a secure attachment to you and has clearly learned to govern himself with your guidance. It's reasonable to expect at his age, with you away, that some of the self-control would falter. May I add, my lady, the bond between you and Alfonso is deep-rooted—stronger than many I've witnessed between mother and child in the households where I've taught."

"I love Alfonso, Signor. I make no excuses for how I'm raising him."

"Please, my lady, forgive me. I didn't mean to imply that you should do anything differently. I . . . I *admire* what you've accomplished, especially when I hear stories from the servants of what a wild child he was when he arrived."

"And I didn't mean to sound offended, Signor. Forgive *me* for my sensitivity. I'm tired after my journey. But let me congratulate you on your performance and thank you for your dedication. You made quite an impression on our Neapolitan luminaries."

"Thank you, my lady. I was less interested in winning their approval and more concerned with *your* assessment. What did you think of my sonnet?"

Suddenly the confident scholar was as hesitant as a schoolboy before a master. We had stopped walking with the others and he faced me, hungry for my opinion.

I paused for a moment, unsure how willing I was to give him my very personal and emotional response to his poem. But then I thought of how vulnerable a true poet had to be. A poet can't simply adhere to rules of structure or blindly follow the models established by Petrarch or Virgil. A true poet has to open a vein, spill blood. How could I deny him a sincere response out of some sense of decorum? I knew Giancarlo was not merely seeking academic literary criticism, and I felt a willingness to acknowledge the integrity and honesty of his poem. I spoke quietly.

"Your words brought me to the hillside your peasant was cultivating. I felt the earth yield to my hoe, the seed slide from my hand, the sun warm my back. I felt my own soul renew itself from death and loss as winter turned to spring."

"That's what I hoped," he whispered. "My lady, I wrote the poem specifically for you. I don't know what sadness preceded my arrival at the Castello—and you do not need to tell me. But I knew from watching you—your solitary walks along the ramparts, the absence of joy in your face—that something had touched you profoundly. Perhaps it was arrogant of me to assume I could rescue you with a poem. If I were a knight, I would have ridden to Jerusalem and back if I thought it would bring you happiness."

I was stunned. No one, not even Ferrante, had spoken such words to me. I was afraid I might unravel, standing in the torchlight of the corridor. Beyond us, I could hear the jovial murmurs of the others as they took their seats at table. In another minute we would be missed.

In the silence that followed his outpouring, a pained expression settled on Giancarlo's face.

"I've said too much!"

"No, no! I don't know how to respond, so I won't. We should join the others. The Neapolitans feed on gossip—it's like ripe figs to them. I don't want to give them any reason to imagine what we might be discussing. I'll go in first. Follow later and take a seat removed from me."

Struggling to gain control of myself, I attempted to resume the face of composure I knew I had to display to our guests. I remembered Costanza's lessons from my girlhood. No matter what agitation troubled my heart, I needed to present a calm exterior.

I turned from Giancarlo, lifted my skirts and climbed the marble steps to the dining hall. With relief, I saw that not everyone had taken a seat yet, so my delayed arrival was barely noticed. I avoided Castellana Aragona. Our conversation might have drifted to the children's education, and I didn't trust myself to discuss Giancarlo's role in the classroom with equanimity, lest an unguarded word reveal my disquiet. With relief, I found a seat next to one of the viceroy's cabinet ministers. Politics was a much safer topic than poetry for me at that moment. I made it through supper by being as animated and gracious as I could despite my fatigue and confusion.

Giancarlo was seated next to Sannazarro at Costanza's direction, and I was thankful that they were immersed in an animated dialogue. We didn't exchange a single glance. I was able to excuse myself after the meal, claiming the effects of my journey.

I thought I would collapse into bed, spent both emotionally and physically. But I couldn't sleep. To be touched by Giancarlo's poetry was one thing. Who among us, when hearing words of such beauty and truth, would *not* react with strong emotion? It was his admission later that had so upset me. His compassion, his ardor, his desire to bring me happiness—all spoke to me in ways that should not have moved me. I was a married woman who believed in her vows, I reminded myself, unlike many women of my generation and rank who flout the rules of courtly love as if they were heroines in some romantic epic, encountering "true" love in the arms of some forbidden gallant.

I'd found true love in my marriage, a privilege I knew was rare. But as fortunate as I was in the love between Ferrante and me, the physical and emotional distance created by his military campaigns had driven a wedge between us. My loneliness had made me weak.

In the morning, I resolved to put some distance between Giancarlo and me. But at breakfast, a letter was waiting for me that changed everything. It was written in an Italian as mellifluous as his sonnet.

Most illustrious lady, please forgive me for offending you with my honesty. My intention, as I expressed to you, was to bring you joy, not anger or discomfort or insult. As I have learned in reading and writing poetry, words must convey the truth of our existence, not some artificial, idealized representation that doesn't communicate the essence of what we experience. I was perhaps naïve to continue our conversation by speaking directly of my heart instead of couching my sentiments in the safety of a sonnet. I care deeply what you think of me—not just as your son's tutor or a fellow poet—but as a man. I never meant to dishonor you. I only know that in your presence I am aware of an inner beauty and luminous peace that has had more impact on my soul than any other encounter in all my travels.

I will understand if you send me away. But if you can find it in your heart to allow me to stay, I offer a deep and unshakable friendship that I swear will never compromise your virtue. Tell me what I must do, and I will abide by your decision.

Your humble and distraught servant,
Giancarlo Brittonio

I could not bear to send him away. But I was frightened of my own growing feelings if I let him stay. His ability to see into my soul and embrace what he found there surpassed anything I'd known in my relationships with others, including my husband. I folded the letter and considered burning it. I was halfway across the room, ready to toss it in the fire when I glanced out the window and caught sight of Giancarlo with the children in the garden. They were crouched over something on the ground, observing it with fascination. They were all so intent, so clearly enthralled by Giancarlo. That was when I acknowledged to myself that I would not cast him out, but would find a way to keep him in all our lives. Until I did, however, I stayed away from the classroom and excused myself from Costanza's salon. Only when I'd thought through my response to Giancarlo's entreaty would I be ready to face him.

Two days later, when Alfonso was released from the classroom for his sword training and Maria and Giovanna joined their mother for more domestic pursuits, I sent for Giancarlo.

He arrived in my studiolo, his arms full of books—books I recognized as ones I'd lent him from my library.

"Have you finished them all so soon?" I asked as I relieved him of several that were threatening to topple.

"Not all. But I wanted to return them before I leave, in case I mistakenly pack them with my own belongings."

Startled, I dropped the very books I'd just rescued.

"You're leaving?" I couldn't disguise the dismay in my voice.

"When I didn't hear back from you after my letter, I realized how much I'd upset you. I would rather leave than cause you pain. I assumed that's why you summoned me, and I want to spare you the questions that will inevitably follow if you're the one to send me away. I resign my position. You can tell everyone that I was wooed by the King of England to educate his children."

"King Henry has no children, the last I heard."

"He plans ahead."

"This is ridiculous." I was in turmoil, and knelt to pick up the scattered books. I'd resolved to keep Giancarlo with us, and now he wanted to leave.

He put the remainder of the books on the table and joined me on the floor.

"I didn't mean to be irreverent."

"Do you *want* to leave?"

"No. But it appears to be the only solution."

"For a poet, you have a remarkable lack of imagination. I only delayed my response in order to find a way to keep you *and* my sanity."

"You want me to stay?" His question was tinged with both hope and disbelief.

I could have tempered my answer with the requirements I was prepared to lay out—the boundaries of a friendship that I would not and could not allow to drift into physical passion. But there would be time enough to spell out my conditions. At that moment, I spoke only what was true. I wanted him to stay.

"Yes."

My assent hovered in the air between us. For a fleeting instant we acknowledged the unspoken—that in another lifetime, my "yes" would have had another meaning. But not here. Not now. Not for the Marchesa di Pescara and the scholar Giancarlo Brittonio.

He took my hand and lifted it to his lips, then lifted me from the floor.

"I will send my regrets to the King."

If I thought the decision to allow Giancarlo to stay had been difficult, living with the decision was alternately excruciating and exhilarating. Finding a balance in our daily communication, one that avoided both temptation and the appearance of temptation, was painful and not without its misunderstandings. Eventually, we grasped that we could reveal our souls to each other through our poetry, and use words in place of touch—not that his words were any less powerful or searing than his hands might have been on my body.

"You breathe life into me when I feel my sadness and loneliness like a great weight on my chest, suffocating me," I said to him. "You rescue me with your words."

I'd never felt so much in need of rescue.

"And you, in swallowing my words as if they were some elixir, heal the very one you call your healer."

It was not all that either one of us wanted. But it was enough. And as a result, Alfonso thrived, Giancarlo set down roots in the rocky soil of Ischia, and my soul, torn apart by loss and disillusionment, began to heal.

Alfonso was a robust, confident boy of twelve by the time Ferrante returned briefly to Ischia from Lombardy in March. We were strangers to each other. Ferrante was leaner, a man more accustomed to a camp bed on a windy plain than a feather mattress in a fortress high above the sea. His early nights were restless ones. Not even after our lovemaking could he find rest, when in the past we had both always sunk into a contented, sated sleep. This time he thrashed and tensed, half-intelligible words uttered in warning or command on his lips. He seemed to be reliving his battles in our bed.

In the dark I traced the new scars on his forearms, silvery ripples where a sword had grazed him. They were nothing, he told me. They hadn't even required stitching.

A woman's scars are more often than not invisible. Our wounds, whether the physical trauma caused by childbirth or the spiritual pains of despair or loss or loneliness, remain hidden. I had my husband home with me. That was all I asked for, nothing more. He could no more heal my wounds than I could his when he fell on the battlefield.

I was gay and pliant and grateful for every day we spent together, walking to the belvedere, discussing the next milestone in Alfonso's education, visiting with Costanza and her bevy of philosophers, politicians and artists. And at night, I welcomed every caress, returned every kiss.

But hovering over each cherished moment was the specter of duty. I had learned well the pattern of life in a warrior's family. A surfeit of pleasure, attention and even quiet moments of repose that one must salt away in memory to stave off the hunger pains when the moment comes, as it always does, and the warrior dons his armor, mounts his horse and rides away.

By the time Ferrante left me in April for the third time, I was a lifetime from the girl who had chafed with frustration at every minute that separated her from her beloved. I smiled to myself at how well I was learning to bear Ferrante's absences. In poems one can rage against the pain and describe with painterly words every thorn and lash and razor-sharp blade that pierces the soul when it longs for one distant and unattainable. But in life, to fasten oneself to such a teat is like sucking poison. At first, the tainted milk is a comfort, fueling the senses, offering a twisted kind of pleasure. But before long, it leads to paralysis. I can put those words on paper, but they are not a way to live. If I had only felt alive when Ferrante was with me, I would have had a very short life, indeed. But by the fifth year of my marriage, I had my own armor—Alfonso, Giancarlo, my writing and my awareness of the political turmoil and ever-shifting alliances that fueled the fighting.

Ferrante was as astute in the council chamber as he was on the battlefield, and I had listened well whenever he was at home. Perhaps I could not follow him with his camp or bind his wounds, but I was his ally and his lieutenant nevertheless. Costanza had introduced me to many of the men who wielded power as the century moved through its second decade. Bishops whose scholarship and discretion won them positions as secretaries to popes; historians and philosophers with powerful family connections; wealthy men to whom one could turn when a ransom was demanded or munitions were running low.

Costanza entertained them all and I joined her in offering hospitality and diversion that could someday be repaid. I am not a woman drawn to solitude, and I had learned, thanks to my mother and Costanza, that I could ease the loneliness of my marriage to a warrior not only through my friendship with Giancarlo, but also by engaging with the world that was drawn to the beacon of civility and culture Costanza had set ablaze on Ischia.

I traveled often to Rome to visit my family—sometimes with Ferrante, sometimes not. In 1516, it was not society but sadness that precipitated my journey. I went to my mother and gave her comfort following the horrific death of my brother Federigo, the baby of the family. When word came that he had succumbed, I was stunned from the blow dealt me by his inexplicable death. When I read the letter I howled as uncontrollably as Alfonso had when he first arrived at the Castello.

Like Ferrante, Federigo was a soldier, and had already distinguished himself, although not yet twenty. He had suffered no wounds. He was not even ill. When he did not appear one morning, a fellow officer went to find him, assuming he had perhaps had too much to drink. He was cold in his cot, his body already rigid. I rode to Marino and threw myself into my mother's arms, understanding as only a mother can, what it means to lose a child.

Federigo's death changed my mother. The indomitable strength that had sustained her during my father's absences on the battlefield or in prison and the political brilliance that helped to shape the world's perception of the house of Colonna began to flounder. In observing the trajectory of her life, I understood that my own could follow a similar path.

For the next few years that life had a steady tempo. When Ferrante was on the battlefield, I was the steward of our domestic life, a mother to Alfonso and secretary and supplicant for Ferrante's financial needs as a commander. When Ferrante returned intermittently, thanks to battles won or truces called, I kissed him, scrubbed his back myself in his bath, noted the white hairs already interspersed amid the auburn and rejoiced in our bed that he yet again returned whole to me. I never tired of his homecoming, each one like a ripe, sweet fruit in the middle of winter. A treasure. A wonder. A brief, bright shooting star that flashes cross the sky, searing itself into one's thoughts and then – gone.

CHAPTER TWENTY-THREE

A Hero's Homecoming
Ferrante
1516 – 1521
Ischia and Naples

As his ship rounded Procida and approached Ischia's harbor, Ferrante saw the bonfires strung out along the beaches and climbing up Mount Epomeo. He heard the faint tattoo of wood against steel as villagers danced the Ndrezzata in the piazzas of the Castello's borgos.

"We shall celebrate your homecoming with a hero's welcome!" Vittoria had written him when the treaty between François, the young French king, and Charles, the even younger king of Spain, was signed at Noyon in August 1516. Ferrante had been present. The deaths of King Louis of France and King Ferdinand of Spain a year apart in January 1515 and 1516 had stalled the momentum of the war and thrust the two young, inexperienced kings into the role of negotiators. At least for the moment, the deaths of the two old kings and the rise of the two young ones ushered in a respite from the wars, however temporary it might be.

Ferrante made his homage to Charles and departed Noyon for home.

Now that the citadel was in sight, with the ramparts ablaze with light, he stood at the prow of the ship acknowledging both pleasure and regret. The first time he'd returned home after war he'd been practically a cripple, drained by severe wounds and months of captivity, and separated from his mistress, Delia, with no expectation that he would ever see her again. The infrequent trips he'd made back to Ischia during the latest campaign had been without pomp—a few days snatched here and there from the constant and frustratingly indecisive skirmishes that had characterized the last three years.

This homecoming was different, as Vittoria had promised in her letter. Peace, however tentative or temporary, was formally at hand. In addition to the treaty at Noyon, he knew that negotiations were also underway between François and Maximillian, the Holy Roman Emperor.

He should be grateful. He *was* grateful. He was scarcely one to relish life in an army camp—the mud, the cold, the discontent of soldiers lacking payment or opportunities to loot. He was happy to be free of the long days of boredom that surrounded the intense hours of battle. He was happy to be relieved, even for a short time, of the burden of leading men to their inevitable deaths.

Costanza had raised him to be more than a warrior. But the prospect of settling down to life at court was as daunting now as it had been when he was sixteen and forced to suffer through evenings of philosophical discussions and poetry recitations. *God spare me,* he muttered, *if this homecoming involves poets.*

His regret also extended to Delia. The years away from Vittoria had allowed him the freedom to deepen his relationship with the woman he saw as the savior of his captivity. Her absence from his life had already left a hole in his heart that he didn't know how to fill.

The ship was making rapidly for the port. On the wharf waited the entire family, eager, expectant, overjoyed to welcome him. He let go of his discontent, at least for the ceremonies. He was their hero, after all, and this ritual was as much a part of being a warrior as lifting his sword and leading the charge against the enemy.

As the ship came alongside the dock and the harbor crew scrambled to secure it, he moved from the prow to the gangplank with his men lined up behind him.

On the wharf, drummers and trumpeters began their cadence and refrain. He scanned the waiting party.

Costanza, regal and elegant. He had half-expected her to show up in armor and girded with a sword, but she was dressed as the *principessa* she had been proclaimed during his absence. The tiara she wore was of diamonds and sapphires, reflecting the brilliance of the sea surrounding them. He had to look twice to identify the tall young man at her side, wearing a sword, hand casually resting on the hilt. How old was Alfonso now? Fourteen? How had he become almost a man in these intervening years? Next to him stood Vittoria, as beautiful and serene as ever. She lacked the lushness and fire and playfulness of Delia, but she was every man's model of a noble and honorable wife. He could not fault her devotion to him, nor the intelligence and eloquence that had already served him politically. Her inability to give him children was a tragedy he had struggled to overcome. But in every other way she had fulfilled his needs. He honored her. He never questioned that. And he imagined that as they resumed their domestic life, he would also desire her, with Delia beyond reach in Mantua.

The side of the ship scraped the wood of the wharf and was finally secured. Ferrante moved quickly to his waiting family.

He bowed deeply to his aunt and kissed her hand. "Tia!"

"Welcome home, my dear boy and our illustrious hero."

He turned to the eager face of Alfonso and clapped him on the shoulder. "You've become a man in my absence."

The boy beamed. "I can't wait to show you everything I've learned. Bruno says I'm the best trainee in swordsmanship he's ever had."

"Tomorrow. In the yard. You can demonstrate."

And then Vittoria. Waiting patiently. Beaming as widely as Alfonso at the praise and acknowledgment Ferrante had given the boy.

"Wife."

"Husband."

He took her in his arms, lifted her off the stones and spun her around.

Her surprise and relief assured him of a welcome in their bed that night. The last thing he wanted to cope with was a disaffected wife who felt estranged from her long-distant husband.

Costanza moved them toward the Castello.

"The horses await, as does the entire population of the Castello. Come, let's not disappoint them."

The reverberations of the Ndrezzata, the island's traditional dance with knives and sticks, intensified as they emerged from the tunnel, accompanied by the cheers of hundreds of townspeople when Ferrante came into sight. Unlike his arrival after Ravenna, when their march had been solemn and the people subdued with pity, this homecoming was a raucous celebration. He imagined that for some of the younger inhabitants of the island, it was more an excuse for Carneval-like revelry than any honor for him. He raised his hand in acknowledgment. Let them have their fun in his name.

The rest of the day and evening was spent on the formalities Costanza and Vittoria had devised. It appeared that half the Neapolitan court was in attendance at the banquet, in addition to the Ischians.

"It's no mere social nicety that they're here, Ferrante," Costanza answered him when he noted their presence. "You fought under Cardona for these nobles and they know you were at Noyon with the new king. They need you, probably more than they did when you were on the battlefield. You would be wise to pay attention to them and not scorn them, for you may need them, as well."

As expected, they were eager for his impressions of King Charles, but he kept his comments neutral. After his years away from the Neapolitan court, he didn't yet know whom he could trust. What he observed was a level of uncertainty and anxiety concerning the boy king and his reputedly insane mother with whom he shared the throne. Ferrante measured his words carefully.

"He's intelligent, if not yet wise. Well-educated and certainly an equal to the French king."

"For all his education, I heard he doesn't speak a word of Spanish!"

"His Spanish is limited. As I said, he's intelligent. Not only will he recognize the need to speak the language of the people he rules, but he has the capacity to learn."

"Does he have the will to fight?"

"I have no doubt that when the time comes, he will take up arms. Noyon was simply a temporary interlude, not a final destination. François may have seized an opportunity with Milan, but he can't hold it *and* take more territory. The truce is a chance for both sides to regroup."

The political talk came to a halt when the poets began their paeans to his accomplishments. Ferrante collected another goblet of wine and endured the recitations with glassy eyes until the last poet stood and raised her own glass. Vittoria.

He sat up. His wife had composed verses since they were children, but after her disastrous experience with that scum of a musician ten years before, she had refrained from any public displays of her literary prowess.

Discomfort crawled up his spine. A poem whispered in the privacy of their bed had been her accustomed greeting in the past. To have her proclaim these intimate expressions in front of hundreds of guests made him blanch. It was unseemly.

A hush had descended on the chamber, and all eyes were on Vittoria—expectant, curious. He knew that during his years away, she'd hardly spent her time doing embroidery locked away in her studiolo. She was Costanza's child as much as he was, and had flourished in Ischia's court. She was certainly better known than he was among those in the hall. She was in her element, and the guests familiar with her ideas and her poetry were waiting in anticipation to hear how she would welcome her husband home.

He clenched the stem of his goblet as she began to recite. His expectation that she would speak with intimacy was misplaced. Although the words revealed her profound love for her husband, they did so in a way that conferred only honor and nobility on him. His grip on the cup loosened as both relief and regret once again colored his mood, as they had earlier in the day. Vittoria and the myriad courtiers in the hall had no conception of his experience. If they did, they would shrink in disgust from the man who had both protected them and brought them more territory, more power, more riches. Let them have their delusions of heroic feats, fed by his wife's imagination.

When she finished, he drained his cup and rose as the hall resounded with applause and cries of "Brava!"

He turned and bowed to Vittoria, bringing her hand to his lips. Her eyes met his in a knowing glance, one that seemed to say to him, "I'm aware of what I'm doing with these words."

He bent to her ear and whispered, "Now that you've honored me with your poetry, will you honor me with your body?"

She responded with flushed cheeks and entwined her fingers with his.

He raised their hands high.

"My ladies and lords, I thank this goddess of mine for the eloquent praise I do not deserve, and I thank you all for this most extravagant welcome home. Enjoy the rest of the evening, but as we did on our wedding night, my bride and I will now take our leave."

To roars of approval, Ferrante led Vittoria through the hall. As they climbed to their quarters he unclasped their hands and slipped his arm around her waist, once again slender. She leaned into him.

"Welcome home," she murmured.

The night was satisfying. Unlike fellow officers' wives who fulfilled the letter of the marriage contract but not the spirit by submitting to their husbands' sexual needs only to produce the required heir, Vittoria truly relished their lovemaking, and this homecoming was no exception. His longing for and memories of Delia slipped into the further reaches of his mind as he took pleasure in his willing and welcoming wife.

Beneath him, Vittoria responded with a fluidity of movement and abandon, as wordless and uncalculated as her earlier performance had been controlled and intentional. She didn't appear to be seducing him, as she sometimes attempted when his interest in her was subdued. Her fervor was spontaneous from the moment he'd whispered in her ear in the hall.

If anything, Vittoria seemed even more passionate than he remembered, as if she had a surfeit of pent-up desire that needed expression. Whatever fueled her, he met with his own appetites, sinking into their passion. Like the instinct-driven heat of battle, sex for him was about losing himself in surging blood and gasping breath and yielding flesh.

When he was spent, he was not so senseless that he didn't recognize Vittoria's unsatisfied hunger.

"*Por favor*," she uttered, her voice on the edge of despair, a parched soul within sight but not reach of an abundant river. She grabbed his hand and placed it between her thighs, where his intimate knowledge of her body brought her at last to her own completion.

It was only later that he found himself observing his wife, when the night terrors that often disturbed his sleep reasserted themselves, even this far from the battlefield. She slept with an ease and contentment that he didn't remember seeing in her face since she'd lost their child. Her lips were parted in a half-smile, as if his kisses still rested there. She was a different Vittoria. Different from the composed and confident diva at the banquet. But also different from the wife who was acutely aware that she loved him more than he loved her. He and Vittoria had been raised by Costanza as intellectual equals. If anything, Vittoria had surpassed him in that sphere. But until this night, he had always assumed the dominance of the warrior. It was he who came and went at will, he who defined the character of their marriage.

He'd felt the balance shift when Vittoria had asked to be satisfied. It was a subtle change. And despite the unfettered pleasure of their tumultuous lovemaking that night, he could not quiet a sense of unease.

"This is the price you must pay for my passion," she seemed to be saying. And he didn't know if it was worth the cost.

When she reached for him in the morning, he demurred, despite his immediate arousal. He took the hand that was stroking him and kissed her fingertips.

"Later. I don't want to dispel the memory of last night with something that might be less spectacular and thus fall short."

If she was disappointed, she masked it well and smiled as if at a hazy memory.

"Till tonight, then. I have to remember that there will be many more 'tonights.' You are truly home, not just passing through on your way to the next battle."

Once again, the flicker of regret brushed his mind. Not simply for his nights with Delia, thoughts of whom Vittoria had quite successfully dispelled. But for the purpose and structure war had given his days.

What would he do here on this isolated rock?

In December, as Ferrante had expected, King François prevailed and Emperor Maximillian signed a treaty, accepting the French occupation of Milan and recognizing Venice's claims to the imperial territories in Lombardy. It was the final step in sealing the peace. After eight years of conflict, Italy was divided in exactly the same way it had been in 1508.

When word came in the mail pouch, he tossed the report on his desk with disgust and slammed his fist so forcefully that he knocked over his wine, the burgundy liquid seeping across the unwelcome document like the blood that had been spilled in pursuit of nothing.

Vittoria looked up from her writing table.

"Shall I call for Marta to mop up?"

"These papers can disintegrate for all I care."

"But you *do* care. Why else would you react with such drama?"

"I knew this was coming at Noyon and had accepted it—I thought—as a temporary halt. But the finality of this peace treaty at Brussels puts into question the value of everything I've done as a soldier. They've gone back to the '08 borders, as if nothing had been fought over or died for."

Vittoria left her seat and came to him, taking his face in her hands.

"Your one loss was at Ravenna, and you've told me yourself that despite the defeat, it was an invaluable lesson that has served you immeasurably in every campaign since then. Why have you lost faith in yourself? As much as I've longed for peace and your safe return, we both know this peace won't last. François's opportunism will not prevail over the long term. He took advantage of a favorable wind, but he has no strategy that will chart a successful course for the future."

Ferrante smiled thinly. "You've clearly listened carefully whenever I've ranted about the political realities. You do well to remind me of my more rational moments at times like this, when all I perceive is failure and defeat."

"It's only a defeat if you do not use this peace to prepare for the next war. And I do not mean drilling your troops."

"You're beginning to sound like Tia Costanza." He kissed her palm. "And exactly what kind of preparations did you have in mind?"

"It's not only poets who flock to Ischia's court, Ferrante. You saw how eager the Neapolitan barons were to hear your opinion of King Charles. Charles is our hope and our future, and Napoli sees you as the conduit to Charles."

"You dream, my darling."

"You're the most logical choice. The Aragonese don't trust the Italians, much as I disagree. Thanks to your reputation, your heritage, your proven leadership—they'll come calling."

"I'm a soldier, not a diplomat."

"Nonsense. I remember how quickly you absorbed my father's lessons in Rome. Do you ever listen to yourself? Your astute analysis certainly makes others listen."

"Anything else you'd like to foretell?"

But she had managed to dispel his morose reaction to the news of the treaty. As she advised, he would wait and see.

He didn't have to wait long.

In February, as Carneval approached, he was summoned to the Castel Nuovo, Napoli's military fortress and the seat of the Spanish viceroy, Ramón de Cardona. Both Costanza and Vittoria smiled knowingly when the message came. No longer on the battlefield, Cardona had resumed his duties ruling Napoli in the name of the Spanish king.

Ferrante sailed on a blustery day that nearly tore the sails as it pushed the galley forcefully across the eighteen-mile stretch of sea and into the Neapolitan harbor. A detail of royal guards was waiting at the wharf to accompany him to the fortress.

When they arrived, he forced himself to slow his pace. The sea voyage and the ride from the harbor had created an urgency that he felt the need to still. He wanted to appear neither too eager nor too indifferent to what awaited him in the viceroy's chamber, but the reality was that after only six months on Ischia, he was craving action and purpose.

His boots echoed in the marble hall as he followed the guards up the stairs to the chamber. It was late afternoon and the sun was setting, casting a vibrant glow through the tall windows facing the sea. His pulse raced, his blood in rhythm with the wind-blown waves reflecting the red of the sun.

He bowed with a deep flourish to Ramón de Cardona.

"Pescara, we are grateful to you for accepting our invitation. It's good to see you again."

"My pleasure, your Excellency. As always, I am at your service."

"As you have been valiantly throughout the war. But now that we are at peace, at least for the moment, the Royal House has another need for your talents. What say you to the role of Grand Chamberlain?"

He did not hesitate. "I accept, your Excellency, with honor and gratitude."

The power and access de Cardona was offering him as Grand Chamberlain was staggering. As the viceroy's minister, he'd control who was received into the chamber, whose petitions would be heard. Vittoria's comments had been prescient. The position would both strengthen his connection to the Spanish crown and heighten his value to the Neapolitan barons.

De Cardona clasped his hand. "You earned my respect and trust on the battlefield. I proposed you as a natural choice, and the King agreed. Come, my wife expects you as our guest for dinner. How is your own wife?" He led Ferrante through the fortress to his private quarters.

Dona Isabella awaited them in a frescoed salon overlooking the castle's immense central courtyard. Much younger than the viceroy, she had become his ward at the age of six when her father died, leaving her a wealthy heiress. As first her guardian and then her husband, Cardona had educated the young woman to become an astute surrogate who ruled Napoli in his absence during the campaigns.

Having never seen her before, even during his brief visits to the court in the past, Ferrante was astonished by her beauty, and found himself nearly speechless when introduced.

Cardona laughed as Ferrante stumbled over his greeting.

"My wife's beauty and charm often leave men quite defenseless."

"Ramón says I am his secret weapon." The beautiful vicereine smiled at her husband as she lifted her slender hand to Ferrante.

"Oh, it's more than your beauty that disarms them, my dear. They are no match for your combination of stunning appearance and brilliant wit."

"I shall have to watch myself, then, in case I fall victim to your power." Ferrante brushed the warm and lushly scented hand with his lips.

"You will find in me a strong ally, my lord, if you serve my husband and His Majesty well."

"As I intend to, your Excellency."

"Come, a toast to your future in the house of Charles of Spain."

She handed him a goblet of wine and the three entered into liaison to govern the Neapolitan kingdom.

As Grand Chamberlain, Ferrante's presence in Napoli would be essential. Cardona offered him an apartment in the Castel Nuovo not far from his own quarters. Vittoria's delight in his homecoming was tempered by the demands of his new position.

"I didn't expect peace to be a cause of our separation. Why can't you continue to live on Ischia and be in attendance in Napoli only when the viceroy holds court?"

"You know as well as I do that my ability to perform my duties lies in my access to information—the subtle reference dropped at a card game or observations culled from a hunting party or dinner. The isolation of Ischia would cut me off from what I need to hear and see on a daily basis. But since I must be in Napoli, come live with me there."

"As much as you need to be in the thick of the Neapolitan court, I need to be here. Alfonso's education, for one. I'm not made for the extravagance and frivolity and excesses of Neapolitan life. And such an environment would threaten what I've accomplished with Alfonso. I'm not willing to abandon him."

Ferrante wasn't going to push her. Their marriage had withstood the far more challenging separation of war. A mere eighteen miles of sea was a slight impediment, easily overcome when he wished to be welcomed to his wife's bed. If he needed her political acumen, letters and a fortnightly visit could serve just as well. And he respected her decision about the boy. At fourteen he was on the cusp of manhood. The distractions that abounded in Napoli, from the gaming to the women, could turn him from the right path. It was painfully apparent that Ferrante would have no other legacy than Alfonso. Best not to chance the boy's ruin with a move to Napoli.

"Very well. I see your point. But at least plan to come to court every now and then. I need you—your judgment and your warmth."

Resigned, she kissed him.

"I remember how bored you were by the inactivity and lack of purpose when you first came home. And this position is an extraordinary honor, Ferrante. You deserve it! I just wish it didn't take you away from us again."

"I know, my love. But I'm not far, nor am I in danger."

He plunged into his new duties with the fervor that had once served him on the battlefield. He reacquainted himself with the barons, an often unruly bunch who held their historical lands on the outskirts of the city with fierceness.

They had never been docile citizens eager to bow down to the Spanish king. As he had told Vittoria, his visibility in Napoli was a key to his ascent. He was seen in the right places, with the right people. For all his complaints and discomfort with Costanza's court in Ischia, he adapted quickly to the more flamboyant and raucous nature of Neapolitan social life. It wouldn't have suited Vittoria, of that he was certain.

He couldn't deny that he relished the constant swirl of activity required in his position. Although it didn't match the surge of power he felt in the midst of battle, he loved being on the move and representing the viceroy. He had realized soon enough that he wasn't a man content with the idle pastimes of society. Not even the hunt, with its predictable outcomes, held anything more than a fleeting sense of excitement. No, he was much happier in the saddle chasing a recalcitrant baron who was unwilling to bend the knee to a new king or pay his taxes, than he was chasing a boar in the wilds of Ischia. The barons were a far more dangerous prey, and gaining the upper hand with them became the driving force behind his actions over the next three years.

His advantages with the barons were two. First, they considered him one of them. Despite being raised on Ischia, his hereditary lands lay in Pescara, in the heart of the Kingdom of Napoli. And second, his ties to Spain, especially now as grand chamberlain to the viceroy, placed him in a position that indebted them to him.

It was no surprise to anyone when the barons elected him as their ambassador to Charles. In 1519 when Emperor Maximillian, Charles' paternal grandfather, died, a struggle to assume control of the Holy Roman Empire erupted among four candidates—Frederick of Saxony, François of France, Henry VIII of England and Charles. Charles won election as Emperor unanimously, but only with the help of the power and money of the Fugger banking family of Augsburg. He was nineteen.

"It's time we had our own eyes and ears in Charles's court," Giacomo Porzio, the spokesman for the Neapolitan barons, told Ferrante over dinner in Ischia. "He's not just King of Spain anymore, he's the Holy Roman Emperor. The barons have conferred, and we've agreed. We want you to be our ambassador."

Vittoria, sitting across from the baron, put down her goblet, her face a mask. Ferrante recognized the look and expected he'd hear her opinion about this latest opportunity for him to be away from her yet again. But for the moment, she kept her own counsel.

"I'm honored, Giacomo. Charles's ascendancy to the empire holds great meaning for us in Napoli and is no doubt rife with potential for our benefit—or our detriment. There's no substitute for having one of our own present, especially as power shifts. We need to be aware of what the losers in the election intend, as well as Charles."

"If I were the Emperor-elect, I'd watch my back around the French king."

"Precisely. And be assured, I have every intention of showing Charles I'm the best one to be doing that for him."

"How soon can you leave?"

"As soon as you give me my portfolio, I'll sail for Germany. Word has it Charles left Spain as soon as the news of his grandfather's death reached him."

Later that night he steeled himself for Vittoria's reaction. He had managed to muffle her complaints about his absences as chamberlain over the last three years by brief but intense visits to the Castello. He had found that by arriving unexpectedly and unannounced every few weeks, he created an element of excitement to his homecoming that was usually rewarded in his bed.

But as ambassador to the Holy Roman Emperor, he would no longer be a short sail away from his ever-patient wife.

"Did you know this was coming?" Her tone was neither plaintive nor explosive. Either he had lost the ability to read his wife's emotions or she had schooled herself to hide her innermost thoughts even from him.

"Murmurs in the corridors of the Castel Nuovo, but merely murmurs. No one had broached the subject to me before Giacomo did tonight."

"They must have been sure of your answer. They don't like to be turned down."

"Despite your isolation, you've become an astute political observer. The literary lights of Italy may consider you a poet, but I know you as quite something else."

"I was well taught by both Costanza and Mama. Your future is my future. Only a fool would ignore the shifting tides. I don't want your career to end like a ship run aground on the rocks of Santa Anna."

"So, no complaints, no long-suffering pouts that I am leaving?"

"As much as I enjoy your presence and yearn for you when you're away, this is a plum you must seize, Ferrante. The Emperor-elect is young and impressionable. He needs a man like you, and so does Napoli. And since when have I ever acted as the long-suffering neglected wife!?"

"Never, my love. Forgive me for assuming that I might have finally pushed you over the edge." He smiled and grabbed her around the waist, pulling her toward him. He detected the slightest resistance, just enough to convey that when she molded herself to him, she did so by choice, not compulsion.

When the time came for him to depart for the north, Vittoria traveled with him to the mainland and rode with him as far as Rome instead of retreating to her aerie at the top of the citadel to watch him sail away as she had so often in the past.

"It's an opportunity to visit with my family and immerse myself in the literary salons that have flourished under Leo's patronage," she told him. "Mama is also starting to talk about making a suitable marriage for Ascanio, and I've written to her to suggest Giovanna d'Aragona."

"A good match. The family's loyalty to us for giving them refuge will be strengthened by your brother taking one of the daughters as his wife."

"I won't deny that visiting with my family is also a way to banish my loneliness. I'll bring Alfonso and his tutor, as well. The boy hasn't been to Rome since Leo's coronation."

Ferrante could have traveled faster without the entourage, but he enjoyed Alfonso's unbridled enthusiasm for the journey.

"I love Ischia, cousin, but Giancarlo has filled my head with the wonders of Rome and I'm eager to explore them myself."

"It's a fascinating city, though also a savage one. Be on your guard. The Colonna still have enemies."

"Don't worry. I've learned well how to defend myself. I only wish I could come with you."

"Time enough for that, Alfonso. Once I assess the lay of the land at Charles's court, I'll consider sending for you."

"Do you promise? Sometimes I think Vittoria would like to keep me wrapped in a scholar's swaddling clothes and not let me experience anything outside of books."

"She's bringing you to Rome, is she not?"

"Probably to spend all my time in the Vatican library."

"I'll speak to her. I'm sure we can find you something exciting to do in Rome."

"Thank you, cousin!" The boy rode off with a whoop.

Ferrante took his leave of Vittoria on the morning after their arrival at the Colonna palazzo. His father-in-law, no longer the robust warrior, did not look well.

He reached Aachen in two weeks' time and presented himself to the Emperor-elect, now King of Germany as well as Spain. He was pleased to learn that Charles had acquired some Spanish in the intervening years.

"I remember you from Noyon, Marchese."

"I'm honored, your Majesty, that you remember me."

"When one has been thrust upon the world's stage at the age of fifteen, one notices everything."

"The empire is fortunate indeed to have a monarch who has such focus."

"I have learned a great deal in the last four years by paying attention, but I still have much to learn about this growing realm of mine. Now come, tell me what you know about Napoli that I must know to rule it with strength."

CHAPTER TWENTY-FOUR

Encroaching Loneliness

Vittoria
1520 – 1521
Ischia and Rome

Ferrante's diplomacy took him in ever-widening circles away from Italy and from me. After he left us in Rome, he traveled first to Germany, then Poland, and finally England, where he accompanied Charles to the court of King Henry VIII. I couldn't begrudge Ferrante the months he spent in the court of the Emperor-elect. Every moment they were together, every word they spoke with each other, could only build the trust so necessary in our unpredictable and uncertain times. Costanza had wisely pointed out to me the importance of trust when my father and Ferrante had first forged their bond with sword games so long ago. While I doubted that Ferrante was sparring with the Emperor, I imagined that he was rapidly becoming a voice of wisdom, an advisor on whom Charles could rely.

As always, I occupied myself in my husband's absence with responsibilities thrust upon me, as well as pleasures freely chosen. But there were also pleasures relinquished in those months of Ferrante's ambassadorship.

It was Costanza who steered our conversation in a direction I'd been trying to push away. We were walking along the southern path, sharing tidbits of the negotiations between my parents and the d'Aragonas over the proposed marriage between my brother, Ascanio, and Giovanna.

"She has grown up before our eyes! Eighteen already… What a wonderful companion she'll be as a sister-in-law to you. It seems such a short while ago that the d'Aragona girls and Alfonso were just beginning their education with Giancarlo, but it's been seven years! I must admit, I never expected Giancarlo to stay with us for so long. He struck me as quite the wanderer when he first arrived."

"I shared your reaction," I said. "I thought we might be too isolated and quiet a court to hold his attention for more than a year or two."

"Has he made any mention of moving on now that the children are grown? I imagine Alfonso has already told you about his readiness to put down his books."

I glanced at her. Over the years Giancarlo and I had taken great care to keep our friendship above reproach. But someone as attuned to nuance and the unspoken as Costanza could not have missed the profound level of affinity Giancarlo and I shared. She'd never confronted me, however, or even offered indirect cautionary words in the guise of counsel.

"Has Alfonso asked you to be an intermediary in bringing his studies to an end?" I tried to put a light tone in my voice, although I wished Alfonso had brought the request directly to me.

"It's just my own observation. He's nearly as old as you and Ferrante were at your marriage. The boy was never destined to sit for law or medicine. I would hate for him to develop a distaste for history or philosophy because you prolonged his time under a tutor."

"He's more like Ferrante than I care to admit." I smiled. "I know you're right. He's hardly the unruly boy who arrived so unexpectedly on our shore, but I suppose I'm reluctant to admit he's nearly a man."

"Change is coming, Vittoria, whether it's Alfonso saying farewell to childhood or departing from us for the wider world. Best to meet it head-on than be caught unprepared."

It was not only Alfonso's leaving that concerned me, but Giancarlo's. There would be nothing to keep him once Alfonso's studies were over. I attempted to conceal my sense of loss as Costanza and I continued our walk. But when I came back to the solitude of my quarters I couldn't contain the sadness that engulfed me.

Giancarlo's presence in my life throughout these lonely years had been a refuge. I didn't want to contemplate the emptiness that would once again be my companion. Surely I'd known that someday he would move on, whether by his own choice or the circumstance now facing us. I didn't want to accept that knowledge, and sobbed alone in the darkness.

When I'd steeled myself the next day, I sent for Giancarlo. I felt not unlike that day so many years before when he'd offered to go in order to spare me disgrace. This time I wouldn't be able to say, "Yes, stay with us. Stay with me."

"Vittoria, I was told that you wish to see me." He only called me by my given name when we weren't within hearing range of others. It was late afternoon in my studiolo. The other ladies of the court were busy elsewhere with their own pursuits.

"Thank you for coming, Giancarlo."

"Is something wrong? It's so unlike you to summon me. Have you heard from the marchese? Is he well?"

"Quite well. I rather imagine you'd envy him right now, traveling with the Emperor."

"I do envy him, but not for the time he spends away from you."

I cast my eyes down. Despite the years and the familiarity bred of our almost daily conversations, Giancarlo's feelings for me were never far from the surface. Nor was my reaction. I struggled to compose myself.

"Your presence has always been a great comfort to me," I said.

"You speak as if it were a thing of the past. Am I no longer a comfort to you?" I heard anguish in his voice and rushed to correct his misunderstanding of my words.

"You will always be a comfort to me. It is your presence I must learn to live without."

"Must? Has the marchese demanded my exile?"

"You speak as if you were a conquered leader banished from his home. No, my husband had no hand in this decision."

"Then who? After so many years and apparent success with Alfonso's education, why?"

"Precisely because of your success. Alfonso is no longer the impetuous but curious boy whose energy you directed. Giovanna is preparing to marry, and Maria may soon follow in her sister's footsteps. There are no more children in the citadel to educate, Giancarlo, much to my deep regret."

"And without children to tutor, there is no place for me in your life. No façade behind which I can hide to protect your good name."

He didn't sound resigned to the reality of our situation. Only bitter.

I nodded, because I couldn't find the words either to defuse his anger or assuage my grief. I reached out to gently touch his face.

But he flinched and moved away from me, pacing the length of the room as if to dissipate some terrible, explosive force inside him.

"I've loved you from the shadows for all these years, accepting the constraints you dictated so I could keep you close and be a part of your life. By banishing me, you take away even that!"

"I am not banishing you! You're welcome here for as long as you need to find another position. Or if you wish to start a school in Napoli, I could provide you with the funds. You're well-known to the Neapolitan circle. Your reputation would attract students from all over the kingdom."

"I've never doubted that I could easily secure patronage beyond Ischia. You needn't trouble yourself with trying to help me. But I have no desire to set myself up in Napoli. It would only cause me more agony to know that you were so close and yet totally beyond my reach."

"I could visit…"

"No, you couldn't. What possible reason could justify the Marchesa di Pescara visiting her son's former tutor? Imagine what the Neapolitan gossips could do with that! Don't compromise yourself for my sake."

"Do you think this is easy for me? Do you believe I *want* you to go? I always feared that *you* would be the one to make the decision to leave *me*—that the meager portion of my life I was able to offer you would ultimately not suffice."

"It has not sufficed."

"And yet, you stayed."

"And yet, I stayed. Because I knew you wanted me as much as I did you. I was willing to sacrifice, to accept less than a full measure of your love because I love you. But now I will go, since that's what you ask of me. I will depart as soon as a ship can take me."

"Where will you go?"

"I have no idea. The new world, perhaps. As far away as I can find."

He had stopped pacing and stood in front of me again.

"I will take my leave now, in private."

Rather than bowing over my hand, he took my head in his slender fingers, lacing them in my hair. His lips met mine, crushing them in a kiss full of hunger and want and despair. I reached out for him, both of us gasping for breath. He held me in a bone-crushing embrace.

Then he released me and was gone.

I didn't see him again before he left Ischia.

Because I could not bear the silence that replaced the lively philosophical arguments and deeply satisfying poetry recitations that had been the foundation of my relationship with Giancarlo, I left Ischia for Rome shortly after his departure.

"Your husband's absence is my blessing in disguise," my mother said as she welcomed me. She and my father were in residence at the palazzo, not at Marino, where I'd expected to find them.

"Papa is not well, Vittoria. We are closer to physicians here in Rome, and it's not so far for his friends to visit."

"I didn't realize how serious his illness was. What do the physicians say?"

Their prognosis was not good. The distractions of Rome's literary salons and musical performances at Pope Leo's Vatican apartments were put aside, and I spent my visit assisting my mother in nursing my father.

In the afternoons I read to him. His eyes, the shrewd, observant weapons of the powerful warrior and wily politician, were going blind. I hadn't witnessed the anger and frustration with which he flung reports from the north into the fire some weeks ago, unable to make sense of what to him was a blurred mass of hieroglyphics.

"That day was the beginning of the end," my mother told me. "Whatever spirit he'd mustered to fight injury and insult in the past was drained from him when he was confronted by this failure of his body."

He had refused my mother and Ascanio when they'd offered to read to him. But I managed to coax him, at first with my own poetry. He grudgingly agreed to listen.

"Pietro Bembo tells me you are becoming the voice of the Italian language."

"Perhaps he was looking for a favor by praising your daughter," I scoffed.

"It is Pietro Bembo who *bestows* favors in this city, not requests them. He seems quite taken with your poetry. So go ahead, amuse your proud papa with a few verses."

Gradually he allowed me to open and read to him the messages that continued to arrive, despite his withdrawal from active life. I wrote replies for him when he had the will to respond.

As the weeks passed, the parade of cronies visiting him dwindled as that of the physicians surged. My mother was haggard from lack of sleep and my father's rages at his approaching death.

Our cousin Pompeo Colonna, whom Pope Leo had elevated to cardinal, arrived to give him last rites. The air in his bed chamber was oppressive with the mingled aromas of the cardinal's incense, the physicians' useless medicine pots and my father's decaying breath.

After the cardinal left, I kept vigil with my mother and brother, numb from the realization that the man who had carried me on his shoulders and taught me to ride and sent me off as his warrior to Ischia would soon leave us for his last battle.

I knelt at his bedside and whispered into his ear the Advent canticles, the promise of light in the midst of darkness.

He died at dawn.

We buried him in the church of Santi Apostoli with a mass celebrated by three cardinals and attended by the half of Rome who were not his age-old enemies. Ferrante, still with the Emperor, didn't return to Rome for the funeral.

Afterward, my mother closed the palazzo and retreated to our fortress at Rocca. She had successfully arranged Ascanio's betrothal to Giovanna before my father's death. The families agreed to allow my mother a year of mourning before the marriage was consecrated.

I stayed with Mama a few months at Rocca and then returned to Ischia, where I immersed myself in assisting Giovanna and her mother with the wedding preparations. The anguish left by Giancarlo's departure from my life was still present, but by then it was only a dull ache instead of a sharp and piercing stab, joining the others that had accumulated in my soul with each loss.

By the time the wedding day arrived for Giovanna and Ascanio, Ferrante had returned from his diplomatic mission, my mother had regained her strength and Italy was once again on the verge of war.

1536

MEDITATION

A Sacred Meal

Vittoria
1536
Rome

My spiritual life is no longer my own. My contemplative and deeply personal practice of prayer has expanded beyond the words with which I once entreated God alone. When I acknowledge the power of my words to influence—indeed, alter—the world's perception of my husband, I recognize my writing as a formidable vehicle for communicating my growing understanding of the sacred.

In addition to my role as fellow traveler with Michelangelo on our spiritual journey, I am also the only woman in Rome participating in a circle of intellectuals, artists and clerics engaged in a vigorous exploration and discussion of scripture. It is not enough that I've come to know Christ for myself, hoarding the precious gift of grace so freely bestowed by the divine. As the Samaritan woman and Mary Magdalene did, I must give witness to the transcendent power of a personal relationship with God. In particular, I want to offer women an example they can recognize in their own lives.

Who better than the Virgin?

When I sit down to write, I see her with eyes that reflect the influence of Michelangelo, my now dearest and most magnificent friend. I *become* Mary, my words conveying her thoughts at the moment when her son is taken down from the cross and placed in her arms. As Mary, I know that His suffering and death are for the good of humanity; I have always known it would come to this. But I am a mother. His sacrifice is also my sacrifice, my agony. I trace his wounds, the body of my beautiful child mutilated by evil and ignorance.

The words pour out of me like tears, like blood. Memories of my own motherhood—of the lost son who never breathed the sun-warmed air of Ischia; of the frightened and unruly Alfonso whom I despaired of ever convincing that he was loved—inform my meditation. I remember the strength and wisdom imparted to me by both Costanza and Mama. Mary is no fragile, powerless vessel. She carries the Son of God in her womb, she holds Him and mourns Him in his death. She does not turn away from her grief and not only bears it, but lifts it up in intercession for us.

When I put down my pen, I expect to be exhausted, depleted by the descent into such tortured suffering. But I rise from my table as if nourished by a sacred meal.

1521 – 1522

CHAPTER TWENTY-FIVE

A Mother's Blessing

Vittoria
1521
Ischia

Italy, forever in the middle, was the spoils both the King of France and Emperor Charles of Spain wanted to claim. Ferrante was named to command the Imperial infantry, after Pope Leo placed Italy's future in Spanish hands. Ferrante was preparing to leave for what we both knew would be a many months' sojourn in Lombardy. We were together in the Castello's armory as he took stock of his equipment and I made note of what might need repair before he sailed. I recognized the set of his jaw, the shift in his posture, the tension in his neck. My courtier and consort was discarding his peacetime demeanor as starkly as if he were flinging off his velvets and silks for leather and steel. Even his breathing was different.

No matter how many times we'd been through these moments of departure, I'd never become inured to them.

We were so engrossed in our routine we didn't hear Alfonso's approach until he was at the top of the steps. But we were aware of him soon enough, his voice a crescendo of agitation and conviction.

"Cousin, word is all over town that we are at war. I beg you, take me with you! I am ready."

His words cut my heart in two. One side for the mother who wants to keep her child safe; the other for the warrior's woman who knows that the battlefield is the only honor for her men. Alfonso was eighteen. Old enough. Trained, thanks to Ferrante's commitment to the boy, a commitment as powerful as my own, to give him all that he needed to become a just and honorable man.

I observed him with new eyes. He was as tall and lean as Ferrante, but with his mother's fair coloring. His blond hair had caused the servants to describe him as a devil in angel's guise when he'd been the impossible boy turning our household on its head nine years before. Now it curled over his collar, still golden.

His earnest, eager request had been addressed to Ferrante, who would be his commander in the field and who was father to him at home. But then he looked at me, the woman who had raised him, who had brought him to the threshold of his adult life and must now watch him go.

I held back my tears. I restrained the words that would have voiced my objections, countered his assertions of readiness or pleaded with Ferrante to keep him with me as vociferously as Alfonso had begged to go.

I put down the gloves I'd been inspecting. They needed restitching, but I'd deal with them later. I wouldn't interfere. I wouldn't influence Ferrante's decision, either to stand in Alfonso's way or to champion his request. But I also couldn't bear to stay. Without a word, I left them. Alfonso may have believed himself ready, but I certainly was not.

An unbidden memory came to me of the day so long ago when Alfonso had disappeared and I'd felt physical pain at the thought that he was lost to me forever. This time he would not be hiding, safe beneath my bed.

Walking briskly out of the armory, I crossed the courtyard, scattering chickens and dogs; they must have sensed I wouldn't pause for them. I didn't know where I was headed, just that I needed to distance myself from Alfonso and Ferrante. Without deliberation, I began to climb the stone steps that led to the loggia. Had I been more intentional in my escape I might have left the citadel entirely and retreated to the cathedral, to pray and light a bank of candles. But my legs took no direction from my thoughts. I could only climb to the one place that still meant refuge. That still gave me solitude when the world pressed in on me.

When I reached it, I found a servant girl scrubbing the tiles of the floor, a mosaic in blues and greens of the god Neptune roaring up from the sea, surrounded by his creatures.

"Leave me," I said.

She glanced up fearfully and grabbed her bucket. What was it? My tone? My face? I was stunned by my own anger. Sadness at the end of Alfonso's childhood and fear for his safety had driven me to the heights, but my fury came from my powerlessness. I was as enraged as the god under my feet, brandishing his trident as he rose from the waves. What weapon did *I* wield? And who was *my* enemy?

Wrapping my arms tightly around my body, I paced the length of the loggia. I wasn't cold, despite the wind that always whirled through the arches, lifting the petals of the flowering vines that wound around the pillars supporting the roof. I felt as if I were holding myself together; that if I released my arms, I would spin out of control.

I'd learned, with time and with discipline, how to let go of Ferrante each time he went to war. I thought I knew how to do this. But I discovered that letting go of a child was entirely different. How had my mother done this? How had she gone on living after my brother Federigo had died?

I was physically ill. I leaned over the balustrade and retched, as if to expel the anger that I could not allow to fester. Alfonso would go, if not this time, then soon enough. To keep him would destroy his spirit. I could envision his future if I did, the slow creep of dissolution and softness, the loss of esteem that would attach itself to him because a woman had stood in his way and prevented him from taking his place in the long line of fighting men from the house of d'Avalos. I knew all this. I'd known it since the first night I went to Alfonso with my lamp and my book. I was not only creating a scholar. I was creating a soldier who could control his impulses and act with discipline and decisiveness. A man who would lead, not with arrogance or recklessness, but with reason and justice. I'd succeeded. He was all those things, and now I must not undo all my work, all my sacrifice, by denying him the future I'd made possible.

I knew the agony of childbirth. My body had once labored to deliver a child. That afternoon, as I struggled to accept Alfonso's destiny and push him out into the world, it was my soul that labored. I felt myself in the throes of an uncontrollable force I could not stop.

It was Alfonso himself who came to find me.

"It used to be that I was the one who was hiding and you the seeker."

"I am not hiding. Everyone knows, especially you, that this is where I'll be."

"You don't want me to go. I saw it in your face as soon as I said the words to Ferrante, even though you didn't utter a sound. You taught me that. To hear the unspoken."

"Then I taught you well."

"I thought that convincing Ferrante would be the more difficult task."

"You don't have to convince me."

"And yet, you do not want me to go."

"What I want and what you or I must do are not always the same."

"You taught me that, as well. So you won't stand in my way?"

I shook my head with sadness. My anger wasn't for him.

"You know, I believe if my mother were alive now, she would have done everything in her power to keep me from the war. She would have hidden me, if she couldn't persuade my father."

"A piece of me realizes that, Alfonso. But I am not your mother."

"No, Vittoria. You are more than my mother. I am who I am because of you. I would be someone else entirely had my mother lived. Someone I don't imagine I would have liked very much."

He had never spoken so frankly to me before.

"Don't dishonor your mother's memory, Alfonso. She loved you the best she knew how. She suffered many losses, many babies who died before she had you. I cannot fault her for wanting to protect you."

"You gave me a different kind of protection."

He knelt in front of me and bowed his head. "Give me a mother's blessing. I need it as much as my armor."

I placed my hand on his golden hair. A shaft of late-afternoon sun slipped through the curtain of flowers fluttering in the wind and I spoke a mother's words, a mother's wish.

"Godspeed, my son. May the Lord bless you in this undertaking, keep you safe and bring you home."

He grasped my fingers and kissed them. As he rose he put his arm around me.

"And now," he said, "Tia Costanza has commanded our presence for a feast. I'm to escort you and make sure that you do not go into hiding."

The feast was Costanza's way of bearing the anguish of seeing her men off to war. I'd never recognized that before. She had the best wine brought up from the cellars, ordered a suckling pig slaughtered and roasted whole with apples and sage, and asked Cook to prepare both Ferrante's and Alfonso's favorite sweets. The baba sat on a sideboard in a pool of rum, sprinkled with sugar, and I wished we could pack it for him to carry. The food in a war camp, while hearty, wasn't like home, and that was precisely why Costanza always made such a display.

"If nothing else, I can fill their bellies and their memories with the tastes of what they are defending," she commented to me as we observed the enthusiasm with which the men ate. There were courtiers and ladies present to wish them well, but the guests of honor were those about to leave—Ferrante's garrison and the soldiers who served Costanza herself.

The music was raucous, not the usually refined performances that entertained at Costanza's dinners. Toward the end of the evening, the tables were pushed to the edges of the room and the dancing began.

I didn't have the heart to join the dance. I'd barely eaten, afraid the bile that had risen earlier in the day had not settled.

Ferrante, observant, leaned in to speak to me quietly, with words only for me.

"You are not well." It was a statement, not a question.

I shook my head slightly. "It's nothing. It will pass."

"Alfonso tells me you gave him your blessing this afternoon."

I nodded.

"I told him this morning that I wouldn't take him without it. Did he tell you that?"

"He didn't."

"Would it have made a difference if you knew?"

"You mean, if I knew I had the power to hold him back, would I have denied him my blessing?"

"I thought I could spare you a few more years of the pain I saw in your eyes. You've already lost a brother. I didn't want to be the one who took your son."

"You're the one who gave me my son, Ferrante. And I've always known this day would come."

"But not so soon."

"No, not so soon."

"You haven't answered me. Would you have withheld your blessing?"

I looked at my husband and understood the sacrifice he was willing to make to keep Alfonso safe for my sake. I kissed him.

"I struggled all day with what Alfonso's request meant for me. I gave my blessing willingly, Ferrante. To keep him by my side would only have killed him in a different way than a sword on a battlefield. He would have considered himself a coward, and in time, so would others, including you. I would have destroyed everything I'd worked to achieve in raising Alfonso."

"You're wiser than I am, Vittoria. I saw too much of the hot-headed boy in his request, not the man he's destined to become."

"You'll take him?"

"I promised. He'll sail with me to Lombardy."

"Watch over him, Ferrante. He needs your guidance as well as my blessing."

"He's my son, too, Vittoria."

We left the feast early, accompanied by the strains of the music and the raised voices of men, heightened not only by Costanza's wine but by the prospect of war. Alfonso was in their midst, flushed and animated on the eve of his departure from childhood.

Ferrante and I made love tenderly that night. We had each sought to give the other something precious and more valuable than either of the diamond crosses that hung from our necks, the wedding gifts to each other that neither of us had ever removed except during Ferrante's imprisonment.

Alfonso and Ferrante left two days later. I'd repaired the frayed gloves and stitched a small handkerchief for Alfonso to carry with him. I didn't go to the docks, but bade farewell and then climbed to my aerie to watch their ship depart the safety and refuge of our rock. A steady wind blew that day and the sails billowed full and taut. Far too soon, they were gone from my sight and I retreated to my apartment. For the first time, I would take my evening meal without Alfonso to fill the emptiness left by Ferrante's departure.

Ferrante's imperial infantry captured Milan and Parma. They were victorious; they were safe. The death of another, however, stilled the battle cries. Pope Leo X was dead. For a few months, the war abated, a new pope was elected and once again Rome made its adjustments. Ferrante and Alfonso didn't return home, but stayed in the north. The future was too uncertain with the change in papal power.

Adrian VI was a considered a "barbarian" pope, a German who had never before set foot in Italy. He was a theologian and a philosopher, born of a humble family but chosen by the Emperor Maximilian to tutor his grandson, who was then six years old. That boy was now the Emperor Charles V, Ferrante's sovereign commander. Spain was ecstatic. France was threatening schism from the church. In the end, Adrian pleased no one. The heavy burdens of the papacy proved too severe for the scholarly, ascetic man, and Ferrante and our son once more found themselves in a muddy field, surrounded by the deafening sounds of cannon, clashing swords and dying men. But Ferrante kept the boy unharmed. I do not know how, whether it was at his elbow, where he could fend off any attack, or at the rear of the garrison, protected by a wall of imperial fighters. I knew only that Ferrante was victorious, both in winning and holding yet another patch of ground—and in keeping Alfonso alive.

CHAPTER TWENTY-SIX

A Rough Passion

Vittoria
1522
Ischia

It was a year before I saw either of them again. Their return was unheralded; no message preceded their homecoming. I'd become used to the need for secrecy. Messengers could be intercepted. News of the commander's departure from the field was a treasure in the hands of the enemy. They traveled with a small band of men and made most of the journey by sea, slipping into Ischia under cover of night.

Torches, horses, the clattering of heavily armored feet in the courtyard alerted me. A knock on the door by the house guard brought me the news.

"The marchese has arrived."

I'd been reading. I'd long before discovered that I could stave off the loneliness of an empty bed with a full book. I marked the page and prepared myself for my husband's presence.

When he entered the room I barely recognized him. Despite his victories, or perhaps because of their cost, he wore a hard and bitter face. He was only thirty-two, but the sun-weathered lines on his brow, the silver threads in his hair, suggested many more years. "A day on the field is a hundred in the comfort of home and peace," he had once told me. If that was true, I looked at a man old enough to be my father.

"Something has happened," I whispered. "Alfonso?"

"He's well and probably having a glass of wine with the others as we speak. I told him he could visit you in the morning. He deserves a night with his comrades."

His tone was weary, brusque. If Alfonso had come to see me, it would have delayed Ferrante from our bed.

"I need a bath."

He always needed a bath when he returned. I'd already ordered that the water be drawn and heated.

As ever, I washed him myself. The sinews in his arms were more pronounced, molded from wielding a heavy sword. The muscles in his back were knotted, as tight as the expression on his face. He leaned back and closed his eyes as I washed his hair. It was matted with sweat and the dust of the fields of Parma.

If only I could have washed away the strangeness in his face, but the healing waters of Ischia's hot springs didn't dispel the coldness that had fixed his features as rigidly as a freezing wind. Whatever had happened in this last campaign to change him, he was not going to tell me that night.

I brought him some warm spiced wine to help him sleep, and had ordered warm stones to be placed in the bed before he climbed into it, weary but clean.

I thought he might turn away from me in exhaustion. But he took me with a ferocity and hunger that was as distressing as if he had ignored me. He didn't speak endearments or kiss me or hold me in his arms when he had spent himself inside me. He rolled off me, heavy and unthinking. Within minutes, his breathing was loud and rhythmic, the sleep of the warrior who must take his rest when he finds it.

I pulled the blankets over my nakedness and stared at the night beyond the windows.

In the morning, a fierce wind howled outside the shutters, silencing the birds that usually announced the dawn. I have always been an early riser. It's the time my pen seems most fluid, silent words flowing from thought to page before the noise of the day drowns them out. I considered quietly leaving the bed and sitting close by with my paper and quill, but Ferrante's body was wrapped around me, his right arm and leg a heavy, possessive weight. To stir would wake him, and I wasn't ready for whatever that might bring, especially if it meant a reprise of his falling upon me as he had in the night.

I resigned myself to staying in bed and concentrated on matching the rhythm of my breathing to his. I'm no believer in the powers of those who claim to read minds or foresee the future in the dregs of a teacup or the remains of a burnt offering. That was for the ancients, not the cinquecento. But I couldn't suppress the desire to understand whatever dreams haunted my husband. Within the circle of his body, breathing with him, absorbing the river of sweat that coated my skin, I listened.

Ferrante spoke in his sleep. The words were no more than a code to be deciphered, fragments of dreams, past not prophecy. But often enough, I could tease meaning out of his incoherence. I combined what I heard from him in sleep with the spare reports he had sent me in letters or the news I'd learned from travelers.

The words that morning were spat out bitterly. "Como," "sack," "not mine." His last battle had been fought at Bicocca on the Lago di Como. The victory had been decidedly Ferrante's. But why it had brought such darkness to him was a mystery to me until after his departure. We never spoke of it, but I mark that day as a turning point in Ferrante's ascendant and, until then, luminous life.

He spent most of that first day in the leaden, unresponsive sleep of a man in need of shutting out the world. When he lifted himself off me and turned to huddle alone, I slid from the bed, washing and dressing in a silent pantomime. It was too late by then to write, and I was too restless to sit and wait for him to wake.

My life didn't stop when Ferrante flew back into it, disturbing the air with the beat and flap of his warrior wings. I left the apartment, closing the heavy door silently behind me and sending a servant to wait in the hall until Ferrante awoke and asked for me.

I found Alfonso at breakfast with Costanza, showing considerably more vigor and good humor than my husband. I appraised him from the end of the room before he had a chance to notice my arrival. His once clean-shaven face was covered now in a full beard, as golden as his hair. The hands that broke bread were no longer the smooth ones of a scholar and a courtier. Fine scars traced a map across one; a finger of the other was bent, as if a break had healed badly. I wondered how many other scars he bore, covered by the plain soldier's garment he was wearing. Wiping any hint of worry from my face, I strode into the room to greet him with a smile. A warrior does not need his mother to hover over him, inspecting every scratch as if it were a mortal wound. Scars were his badges.

"Welcome home, Alfonso!" He rose as soon as he saw me and embraced me, lifting me off the floor in a powerful hug that demonstrated quite effectively that a year on the battlefield had given him more than scarred hands. From the strength in his arms, I could only surmise that the sword he had lifted with them had caused a few scars, as well.

However, he was still my eager boy, full of tales that rivaled the stories we used to read at his bedside. I searched his face for the changes that had been so pronounced in Ferrante with each successive tour of war. But Alfonso was in that first stage of a soldier's life, when the thrill of the fight fuels him and slakes his thirst as effectively as wine. He had not yet had to make the kinds of decisions that were the warp and weft of Ferrante's life as a commander. And if my trust in Ferrante was as well-placed as I believed it was, he had protected the boy from the most severe horrors of the battlefield.

Alfonso was glad to be with us, eager to hear news and to entertain us with his exploits. But I could sense that this was merely a visit, a taste of what we could expect from him in years to come. His home was elsewhere now, in the company of his fellow soldiers, and defined by his sword, his armor and his horse.

When Ferrante woke, I brought his food and wine myself. It was clear he had no desire to be among company. The meal included some of his favorite dishes—mussels simmered in white wine and garlic; a duckling with crisp skin, glazed with honey; pears and cheese that spread like butter on a fragrant bread studded with rosemary. But he ate without relish, as if the meal were the salted dried beef and hard biscuits of the battlefield. As if it were his soldier's duty, part of his regimen, like sword training.

The wine he drank in great quantity, and I thought I would be faced with yet another night of a husband deadened in heavy sleep, this time bred of drunkenness instead of exhaustion.

When he finished, he rose abruptly.

"I need to walk in the air. These walls are crowding in on me."

"Shall I join you?"

"If you wish." His indifference sent a message that his need was purely for exercise, not for conversation with me. Despite his lack of interest, I went with him. His arrival had only brought oppression, and I needed the air as much as he did. If, in the course of our excursion, the wind loosened his tongue, I wanted to be within listening range.

I knew enough not to chatter. It had never been our custom. I ached to discover what troubled him, but coaxing him to reveal his thoughts required patience, and I didn't know how much time I had. I walked silently beside him toward the belvedere. At least he gave me his arm. To anyone watching from a distance, we were the warrior and his wife, enjoying a welcome respite from war. As we traversed the winter path, I noticed no limp, no favoring of one side or the other, no flinching to indicate he had sustained a physical injury. I would have seen evidence the night before anyway as I bathed him.

Nevertheless, my husband was a bruised man. I couldn't comprehend why, since by all reports he was a hero. After Ravenna, he had never lost a battle. His men followed him fearlessly because of the model of courage he was to them.

I could not bring myself to ask Alfonso. If Ferrante didn't wish to share with me what had affected him so profoundly, I didn't want to place Alfonso in the position of betraying his trust. I would not use the son to spy on the father.

I asked no questions, not even "How long can you stay?" I made no demands on his beleaguered brain. Whatever matters of the estate or family demanded his attention, I'd already dispatched and reported to him in letters.

This time together should have been one of pleasure and recuperation for him, renewal for us. We should've been celebrating his victory and acknowledging the apparent success of Alfonso's initiation into soldiering. But my husband's temperament was as unpredictable and fluid as the outcomes of even the most carefully planned battles. His brooding and silence on this visit were no strangers to me, but deeper and more profound than I'd seen in the past.

I suspected that he had failed at something. But without his willingness to speak, I would not be able to pry it from him, as much as I believed that by expressing it in words he could free himself of the burden it had so clearly placed on him.

We continued to walk in silence, the weather matching his mood—a cold wind, glowering skies and a churning sea.

Later in the evening he consented to dinner with Costanza and Alfonso.

"I hope she doesn't have any guests I have to put on a show for," he grumbled as we dressed.

"Have no worries. We're eating alone. You will not be asked to perform as the conquering hero. Still, there was a time when you enjoyed that role," I reminded him. I was treading on unstable ground, but I thought it was an opportunity, when so few had presented themselves during the day.

He gave me a sour smile. "Glory can be fleeting, snatched away more quickly than the arduous route required to achieve it."

I looked at him with a question about to form on my lips, but he was standing with the door open.

"Costanza awaits, and I don't want to be the reason my aunt's dinner turns cold."

Despite his protestation that he didn't want to play a part at dinner, he put aside his glumness for the duration of the meal and entertained his aunt with his old grace. Alfonso had trimmed his beard, probably at Costanza's request. We were a congenial family group, with little talk of warfare and more of the music and art that were the essence of Costanza's existence. She'd managed to preserve her vibrant corner of culture here on Ischia, despite the shriveling of the artistic flower that had bloomed in Rome during Leo's reign. Pope Adrian had neither the means nor the love of the arts to sustain the boom that had brought the city to life only a few short years before.

"At times I feel like the last bastion of arts and letters in all of Italy," Costanza said. "The poets whose work was in such demand in Leo's Vatican come flocking to my roost like some great migration. Some of them have true talent and some simply hovered around Leo, who loved them all, no matter how unoriginal and flat their work."

"I'm sure you're far more discerning and demanding of your poets, Tia. You certainly wouldn't let any work of mine get by you without an expectation that it would 'sparkle.' I believe that was the word you used. Like the sun dancing on the sea or the jewels hanging at your throat, you wanted our words to gleam."

I smiled at Ferrante's recollection, because I shared it. Costanza's influence had affected both of us in so many ways.

After a sojourn of three difficult days, Ferrante and Alfonso took off once again for the battlefield. I rode across the causeway with him to the harbor. The hood of my cloak protected me from the wind but it also shielded my face from Ferrante's gaze. I struggled to maintain the composure that had always been expected of me when my husband departed for war.

Too much had been left unsaid during this visit. I couldn't even call it a homecoming, because I no longer believed that Ferrante considered Ischia, or me, "home."

The sun had barely risen when we reached the dock. The sea was rough and waves were cresting over the stones of the quay, making the horses skittish. The galley was rolling in the turbulent sea, its decks reverberating with the boots of Ferrante's men leading their nervous horses on board.

Ferrante dismounted, his attention already focused on the ship. The courtier who had reminisced about composing poetry in his youth during Costanza's dinner the night before was gone, replaced by the commander about to step into a scene of tumult and restore order. I loved both of them, courtier and commander.

I followed him in dismounting, ignoring the water and mud swirling around my skirts. I placed my hand on his arm and felt him flinch. He had already left me and whatever safety I might represent. To a warrior, a touch on the arm from behind is the touch of an enemy.

But he turned, recovering himself, remembering that until he boarded the ship, he was husband as well as soldier.

"Farewell. God be with you," I said.

I traced the sign of the cross on his forehead. I'd done the same to Alfonso the previous night, when he'd bade me his own farewell.

Ferrante grabbed my hand and raised it to his lips. It was no courtly gesture, delicate and refined, the kiss hovering in the air. Instead it was the equivalent of his taking me on the night of his return. Rough, hungry, his lips chapped and dry scraping my skin, his hand gripping mine like an iron claw.

And then he turned back to the ship and strode up the gangplank shouting orders. I stood in the gray cold, oblivious to the dampness wicking up my dress and my cloak, unable to take my eyes off Ferrante. He was constantly in motion, driven by some unseen mechanism that dragged him from one corner of chaos to another.

The voice of one of the household guards who had accompanied us from the castle interrupted my watch.

"My lady, if you wish to remain until the ship sails, it might be safer if you were mounted. The tide is still rising and the water will only get higher."

I looked down and saw that he was right, and allowed him to lift me to my saddle. I ignored the barely disguised impatience of the guards and calmed my horse by moving back from the water's edge. But I didn't leave. My body was on the horse, my hands firmly on the reins. My soul was on board the ship, shadowing Ferrante, unwilling to let him out of my sight.

The shouts and grunts, the whinnying of anxious animals and the thud of wooden crates landing on the deck soon gave way to a flurry of another kind as the loading came to an end. The tide was receding. Orders were shouted, ropes unbound, the gangplank hauled on board. The rasping sound of wood dragged across wood was almost obliterated by the snap of canvas as the sails were unfurled and hauled aloft, filling immediately with the wind that had been roiling the sea all night.

Perhaps it was the tensing of my body, straining, aching as I realized the ship was about to sail—but my horse reacted as if I'd prodded him. He began to canter away from the harbor. It took all my strength, already drained by the past three days, to pull him up and turn him back to the sea. By the time we returned, the ship was heading out in the brisk wind. If Ferrante had been at the rail to bid me farewell, he would have seen me riding away, not waiting as I'd been all morning to raise my hand in a gesture of love and recognition.

I couldn't tell if he was still on deck. But I pulled out my handkerchief and waved it, a small signal thrown across the water in hopes that it would be caught and cherished.

When the sails were no more than a speck on the horizon, I turned once again for the Castello and began the lonely trek across the causeway, followed by my band of muttering guards, probably relieved I wasn't their wife.

CHAPTER TWENTY-SEVEN

Love's Imbalance

Vittoria
1522
Castello Aragonese
Ischia

In the weeks that followed Ferrante's departure, I could not find any release from my sense that his visit had been unfinished. I wandered the grounds of the Castello despite abysmal weather, searching for answers—but this time as abandoned wife, not as the playmate seeking Ferrante in his hiding place. I felt old and empty, weary of being denied his trust in addition to his embrace.

Costanza, realizing that she could not rescue me, refrained from false gaiety and somber lectures. She left me alone after I rebuffed her first invitation. I retreated to my apartment and took up my pen. It was the only way I knew to exorcise the foreboding and darkness that had permeated Ferrante's stay.

There were times I felt as if the nib was carving the lines on my skin, the ink my blood. On those days, I took the paper and held its edge to the candle flame, as though to banish the heartache it contained by turning it to ash.

I collected these fragments of blackened anguish in a small copper bowl on my writing desk. I crumbled them between my fingers, a reminder of the mortality of all that is human—not just our skin and bone that disintegrates in the grave, but our hopes and dreams, as well. Like the bishop on Ash Wednesday, mashing the remnants of burned palm leaves with chrism to form the paste that marked us all at the beginning of Lent, I blended the ashes with my tears and smeared them on my body.

Anyone who found me might have feared I was delirious with fever, not in my right mind. Vittoria, the rational, thoughtful one, would never do something so impulsive, so wild and incomprehensible.

But my act was neither impulsive nor wild. I lived and breathed the paradox of Christianity. To live one must die— put aside the old ways, the old garments, and put on the new.

Covered with the burned poems, I plunged into my bath and watched them float away on the water. Had it been summer, I might have walked into the sea. But that would have attracted attention, and I was doing this not for its drama but for its peace.

I scrubbed my flesh and sluiced the last of the ashes away with a sponge squeezed over my body. I rose from the tub, wrapped myself in a new bed gown, braided my hair, said my prayers and slept peacefully for the first time since Ferrante had left.

The next day I called upon Costanza and resumed the rhythm of our women's lives on the rock. I no longer waited for Ferrante to return.

The answers I'd been seeking about Ferrante's despair and detachment began to drift onto the island like the flotsam thrown up on the beach after a storm. The first was news of the aftermath of Ferrante's last battle at Bicocca. Word had seeped out of the city, raw sewage fouling Ferrante's name. It was claimed that he had allowed his troops to savagely sack Como and Genoa. More than six hundred of its inhabitants had been killed in the rampage.

I wanted to cover my ears against the rumors. I could not imagine Ferrante condoning such brutality. But I also couldn't put out of my mind the garbled words of his restless sleep and his cryptic comments about lost honor.

"Do you believe these vile reports?" I sought Costanza's counsel and reassurance. Surely she would wipe away my doubts.

"War is an unpredictable and uncontrollable act once set in motion, Vittoria. You must know strategies may be fashioned, but in the end it's only men who are carrying them out."

She spoke with regret and sadness. Ferrante was more a son than a nephew. How could she bear these rumors if they were true?

I could not. I swallowed my doubts, refusing to entertain the thought that my husband had lost control of his men and stood by as they murdered innocents. That was not the man I knew. Not the man I loved.

The next blow was harder to refute.

I was writing on the loggia on an afternoon that had been unexpectedly warm, the sun burning through the morning fog to warm the tiles. I'd spent too long inside and decided to have my writing table brought up. I still needed a wool wrap, but the sunshine and cloudless sky were a welcome respite from stuffy rooms and dim light.

As my pen flew across the page I heard the footsteps of my maid approaching, taking the steps at a pace too rapid to be bringing me a pitcher of wine. Breathless, she reached the loggia in a state of excitement that was familiar to me. A ship had made anchor in the harbor, no doubt bringing someone or something to the Castello.

For a fleeting moment, I let myself believe it was Ferrante, and I dropped my pen, spattering ink across the page. But then I noticed that Gemma's hands were carrying a carved wooden box. *Something*, not *someone*, had arrived.

"My lady, this chest and a letter were delivered by the *Paloma*. It came from Napoli."

"Put it here on the table, Gemma. And ask Cook to warm a jug of wine for me. The sun is strong, but I'm feeling a chill."

She reluctantly left the box and departed, obviously curious about its contents and disappointed not to witness its opening. But, after the distressing and unwelcome words that had reached us so recently about Ferrante, I was wary of this unexpected delivery and in no mood to open it either quickly or in the presence of anyone else.

Its appearance was disruptive nonetheless, and I found myself unable to continue writing. When Gemma returned with the wine, I sat and sipped it, staring out to sea as I had when I was a forlorn child waiting for my father to return and rescue me.

But there was very little Fabrizio Colonna could do for his daughter, then or now. This life, this marriage—they were my burdens.

I gathered together my unfinished poems, picked up the mysterious box and retreated to my apartment.

The box was surprisingly light. In happier times I might have played a guessing game with myself. Who had sent it? Was it a gift? What could it be? Certainly over the years I'd frequently been the recipient of the generosity of others. Miniatures crafted by one or another of the artists who had shared our table and our home. Songs and poems commemorating festive times on Ischia or heroic moments on the many battlefields of the last decade. Jewelry from Ferrante himself, sometimes marking an occasion but often simply a bauble he'd seen in a distant city and chosen to send me as a token of his love.

I had no illusions that this box was from Ferrante. The handwriting on the accompanying letter was not his and totally unfamiliar to me. However, it was almost certainly the hand of a woman. I could tell that much.

I set down the box and unfastened its bindings. Inside was a velvet bag cushioned by a satin pillow. Something fragile. I loosened the ribbons securing the bag and poured its contents into my hand. A string of exquisite pearls with an intricate diamond clasp. The pearls were large, luminous and perfectly matched. The clasp was a unique design incorporating my initials. I recognized the necklace immediately as I let it fall from my hand and back into the box. Because it was mine. Ferrante had given it to me. One of those precious tokens from years past.

I hadn't worn it since the wedding of Bona Maria Sforza in Napoli. The occasions on which one displayed such finery were infrequent. I hadn't known it was gone from my possession. Had the thief repented and returned it out of a guilty conscience? Or had someone discovered it and, realizing it was mine, sent it back to me?

My curiosity, stilled until I opened the box, was now inflamed. I ripped open the letter and began to read.

When I finished I wanted to tear it to shreds. But I didn't. The writer was indeed a sinner hoping to atone, but no thief. And her words, in seeking peace in the eyes of God, served only to cause harm.

In lieu of destroying the letter I grabbed the pearls and slit the silk on which they were strung, scattering those perfect orbs across the stones of the floor. One landed near my foot and I smashed it with the paperweight from my desk. I had no intention of ever wearing the necklace again. Not after it had touched *her* neck.

I didn't know what to do next. I'd learned a great deal from Costanza and my mother about how to be a good wife. I'd added my own lessons over the years, coping with solitude and responding to the needs of a man returning from war.

But I had not learned how one faces betrayal.

My husband had a lover. To whom he had given my necklace. I tried to comprehend what I'd just read, to fathom the actions of a man whom I loved and whom I believed I knew. The writer of the letter, Isabella de Cardona, the wife of the viceroy, had apparently had second thoughts about accepting the gift when she realized it was mine. But she had taken it when it was first offered. She couldn't have worn it in public, not with the diamond initials proclaiming that it was mine. Not when hundreds of people had seen me wearing it. She could only have worn it alone with Ferrante, naked in his arms except for the pearls.

I couldn't free myself of that image. Why had she returned the pearls to me? Because the gift was "inappropriate"? But could she return my husband to me?

I paced the floor, the sweep of my skirts flinging the pearls into the corners of the room. I could not cry. My despair, rather than releasing my anguish in tears, had shriveled my emotions. I felt desiccated—a hollow, brittle shell. A milkweed pod whose silk has burst out of the husk and been dissipated on the wind.

I didn't join Costanza for dinner. I sent Gemma away for the night and locked the door because I would not have her see the disarray in my room and therefore the disarray in my mind. I didn't sleep. Several times I attempted a letter to Ferrante and several times threw the crumpled sheets into the fire. I prayed, clutching the crucifix around my neck and wishing like a child that Ferrante would feel the heat in his own crucifix and hear the words I was sending heavenward, begging for answers, for guidance.

I must have fallen asleep at my prie-dieux, because as the dawn began to trickle through the shutters I stirred, aching, my face pressed against my prayer book and the crucifix still in my hand, its imprint deep in the flesh of my palm.

I pulled myself up off my knees and stretched, massaging the stiffness in my neck and my back before gathering a heavy wool wrap around my shoulders to ward off the chill in the room. The fire had receded to a few glimmers among the ashes without Gemma to feed it during the night. I threw some twigs onto the remaining embers and fanned them until they caught. Within moments I had a warming fire that also illuminated the chamber, revealing the scattered pearls.

I was still angry. If I'd had the opportunity, I would have ripped apart the strand again. But I knew I couldn't leave the pearls loose. Their discovery would have been swift enough and the gossip mill in the Castello would have seized upon the story soon thereafter. I am not a woman who cares overmuch about others' opinions of me. But I do care what they say about Ferrante. I could not bear to have his achievements overshadowed by more rumors and innuendo.

Back down on my knees, this time on the stones of the floor, I retrieved every pearl. I stuffed them all into the velvet sack and replaced the sack in the chest. In my dressing chamber is a niche carved into the stone, disguised by a false façade. I placed the box there, along with my other precious jewels.

I fit the box in among the other packets—embroidered envelopes of silk, brocade-covered boxes, even a small bundle wrapped in fur. It occurred to me to take inventory of what was there. Were the pearls the only thing of mine he had given away, or had he plucked other gems to distribute to Isabella or other lovers? I didn't want to know.

I replaced the façade, brushed into the hearth the pearl dust from the one pearl I'd destroyed the night before and washed my hands.

Only then did I sit at my writing table, finally ready to pick up my pen and form the words I needed to express to my husband. The distraction and distance I'd witnessed during his last sojourn at home revisited my thoughts, explained now by my knowledge of the pearls.

The catastrophe of the sack at Bicocca may have contributed to his dark mood, but more than likely it was his passion for Isabella that had consumed him with such draining effect. I questioned whether the haste with which he left me on that most recent visit had truly been precipitated by the call to return to the battlefield or the entreaty of his lover.

I'd become accustomed to being second in Ferrante's life. As a man who wielded power both on the battlefield and in the political sphere, he had always put his professional life ahead of his personal. Like my father. Like his father, and generations before them. I understood that; I had embraced and fostered it, had muffled the disappointments I experienced in my marriage because they were to be expected. Although in retrospect I should have, I had not expected this, had not foreseen that I would be displaced in my husband's heart. The place I occupied there was scant enough. The pearls mattered little to me if I didn't have Ferrante's love.

My pen moved across the page as if guided by a hand that was not my own, reporting to Ferrante the return of the pearls, the revelations of Isabella. I offered no forgiveness, since none had been sought. I made no demands. Wrenched from the complacency of our thirteen years together, my soul screamed in entreaty, but I didn't transcribe those words onto the page.

I sealed the letter. Some of the wax dripped onto my finger, hot and fragrant. I sucked at the tiny dot of pain, wishing it was this simple to banish the aching in my heart.

When I joined Costanza for breakfast, I slipped the letter into the pouch in which the Castello's outgoing correspondence was collected before the letters were carried by messenger to their final destinations. Anyone observing me would have seen a familiar act—the marchesa sending one of her weekly epistles to her beloved husband.

Costanza, on the other hand, noted that my behavior and demeanor were not at all characteristic of me.

"Vittoria, are you ill? When you excused yourself from dinner last night, I thought you were just tired. But you do not look well."

She gently lifted her hand to my forehead and studied my face.

"Did you not sleep? Shall I call for a physician?"

Her concern seemed too dramatic. Was my despair so palpable? Was what I could not express in words manifesting itself in hollow eyes and feverish skin?

I couldn't bring myself to reveal to Costanza what I hadn't yet fully absorbed. But more than my own distress kept me from speaking out loud the devastating contents of Isabella's letter. Ferrante was Costanza's son in all but name. As worldly and astute as she was in her political and artistic spheres, she was still a mother who adored her child. And even though she recognized his faults and chided him for his moodiness, I didn't believe she could accept that he'd betrayed me.

Perhaps I feared the news would cause a rift between Costanza and me. At that moment I couldn't risk another loss.

To protect us both, I brushed off her suspicions that something was quite wrong.

"Merely some indigestion. I overindulged in sweets yesterday and should have taken a brisk walk instead of languishing in my apartment. I'm already feeling better. I didn't mean to alarm you with my appearance!"

She accepted my explanation with a skeptical shrug.

"Very well. But don't suffer silently if you are ill."

"I won't. I promise. I'm going out right now to dispel my pallor and fatigue with some sunshine."

I needed to be alone, away from Costanza's far-too-perceptive gaze and the curious eyes of Gemma and the other servants who, if they hadn't seen the package delivered yesterday, were certainly aware of it now.

I forced a smile and feigned renewed energy as I gathered my cloak around me and swept out of the dining room. I strode purposefully to the garden, determined not only to deflect any suspicion that I was suffering but also to begin to free myself from the crushing burden this unwelcome knowledge had brought me.

The natural world has always been a refuge for me from the time I was a girl reading my mother's letters in the sweet shelter of the pine grove. Living on Ischia had heightened my awareness of the minutiae of the plants and birds that share this island with us. I sought to distract myself and spent the morning mentally cataloging the signs of our emerging spring.

The fragile shoots and tight buds reaffirmed for me the perpetual cycle of life reasserting itself after winter's death. If these tiny plants could push up through dense layers of earth year after year, surely I'd be able to break through the hardening shell of despair forming around me.

By the end of the day I'd recovered some of my vitality and forced myself to join Costanza for dinner. I couldn't hide in my apartment indefinitely. As much as I wanted to withdraw from all social exchange, I saw that doing so would only feed the maw of curiosity and maudlin innuendo that nourishes a closed society like the Castello, especially after the dark months of winter, when fewer guests arrive to entertain and distract us.

Costanza required no false gaiety, and eased my re-entry by steering the conversation to a folio of poetry she had received from one of her former guests. The delight and arguments precipitated by her unexpected gift drew attention away from any probing questions about my mysterious package, and I was grateful.

I discovered over the next weeks that maintaining a façade of composure becomes an accustomed practice. One doesn't have to reflect or make choices. It's like a nun's habit that hangs on a hook in one's wardrobe, waiting to be donned every morning, fastened securely and then forgotten. Only alone at night in my chamber, when I loosened the pins that held this false garment together, did I remember that I was a woman betrayed.

Ferrante didn't respond to my letter for several months. I learned that by the time my message reached his headquarters, he had left for Spain. When he returned to Italy, he was enmeshed in the intensity of his military life. The domestic concerns of his distant wife fell further from his attention. His response was not something he could easily dictate to a secretary.

When I wrote to him I hadn't considered what I'd receive in reply. A confession? A denial? An apology? An expectation that I should accept, like many noble wives, that these amorous affairs were ordinary and insignificant occurrences for men charged with such dangerous responsibilities far from home?

In the end, he gave me neither confession nor denial. He dismissed the act as a "lapse." He had lent Isabella the necklace for an important event at court, and I'd been traveling at the time and not available to discuss the loan. He had meant it merely as a kindness to the wife of his viceroy. Of course, he was fond of her, and perhaps she had misconstrued his intentions.

Accompanying Ferrante's letter was a brooch, an extravagantly fashioned, expensive piece that I might have cherished and worn with delight in the earlier years of our marriage. But in the current state of our relationship, the bauble saddened rather than excited me. I put it away and never put it on. I'm sure Ferrante believed that he'd dispatched with the unpleasantness created by Isabella's revelations. His next letter returned to the topics that customarily filled our exchanges—the state of negotiations or conflict, his own political and economic future when the war came to an end, reports on Alfonso's activities and well-being. I was still his trusted confidante despite the sweet words he had whispered in Isabella's ears.

I came to acknowledge that the dreams of romantic passion that had fueled me as a young bride and sustained me in the long intervals when Ferrante was away at war were simply that—dreams and illusions. The reality of my marriage to Ferrante had evolved over the many years we'd been together, and the loss of my dreams had been so gradual that confronted by Ferrante's indifference in this episode, I was no longer surprised. In pain, certainly. But I recognized, with a searing honesty, that I would never be the love of his life, as he was mine.

I had a role in his life, though; I had no doubt of that. And with resignation, I accepted it. I put away any hope that it might be otherwise, as I put away the ostentatious jewelry with which he'd expected to assuage my anger and purchase my absolution of his never-admitted betrayal.

At that moment I resolved to leave Ischia. I craved a change of scenery from the all-too-present memories of my marriage. Friends and family waited on the other side of the Tyrrhenian Sea. The emptiness left by this ordeal cried out to be filled. Costanza, although I hadn't taken her into my confidence, saw the change in me and endorsed my plan to travel.

"This winter has drained you, child, beyond any I can remember. You need some distraction. Fly away on the wind and send me a detailed account of your discoveries and adventures."

A door to my innocence was locked irrevocably that early spring. It was a dwelling to which I would never return.

1536

CHAPTER TWENTY-EIGHT

Let Your Suffering Pass to Me

Vittoria
1536
Rome

I am composing my thoughts on the drawings for the *Last Judgment* when I'm summoned by the convent's porter.

"A young man named Urbino is at the gate, my lady. He is quite distraught."

It is Michelangelo's Urbino, his trusted servant. He is breathing heavily as if he's run all the way from Michelangelo's house.

"My lady, forgive me for disturbing you at this hour. I bring a message from Michelangelo. He asks you to forgive him, but he cannot visit you this evening."

My disappointment is entwined with concern. Urbino's demeanor hints that he hasn't told me everything. The suora is right; he is distraught, which is quite an excessive state to be in for the simple cancellation of a visit. Michelangelo and I have been meeting and engaging in intense discussions with increasing frequency as his work on the wall proceeds. I would accept without question if he's unable to come. I brush aside the thought that Michelangelo is retreating from the intimate direction our conversations have taken. Nothing in our last exchange suggested anything other than joy in my presence. Something is amiss.

"Urbino, of course I forgive him. But has anything happened? Please tell me, or I'll worry all night."

"I cannot say, my lady. He ordered me to be silent if you asked."

"You're worried about him? At least you can tell me that."

He nods, twisting his hat in his hand.

I realize that out of loyalty to Michelangelo, Urbino won't reveal to me what has caused Michelangelo's change of plans. But Michelangelo has not asked him to keep me away. I make a decision.

"Urbino, please wait for a moment. I shall return immediately with an item for you to take to Michelangelo."

I run quickly back to my room, leave a note for my cousin Giulia and gather my cloak. To my great relief, Urbino is still pacing at the gate when I return. He looks up expectantly.

"What is it that I should bring home to Michelangelo?"

I look him firmly in the eye and say, "Me."

I expect him to protest, but his agitation leaves him and he utters a grateful "Thank you, my lady!" and takes my arm.

"We must hurry." He holds to his word and does not tell me what has befallen his master. When we arrive at the house, all is dark and still.

Urbino lights a lamp and calls out. "Maestro! Maestro! I have returned."

No response answers Urbino's call. In the lamplight I recognize the concern and fear on his face.

"Urbino, I must ask you, now that we're here, what happened that must be kept so secret?"

"I begged him to let me tell someone, anyone. But he was so angry."

"With you?" I am incredulous. I know Michelangelo loves Urbino.

"No! No! With himself."

"For the love of God, Urbino. Tell me!"

"He fell from the scaffolding this afternoon. The apprentices brought him back here on a board and he ordered them away. He extracted the same promise from them to tell no one." The young man is trembling.

I place my hand on his arm.

"You did the right thing in coming to me yourself. Now, tell me, does he have a doctor here in Rome?"

"He shouted at me that he wants no one. Someone came from the Vatican, sent by the pope, who somehow heard what had happened. But the Maestro locked his bedroom door and refused to see him. My lady, I saw his leg. The bone is sticking out."

"There must be someone he trusts, Urbino. Think!"

I doubt Michelangelo will let me near him. I assume it's unwise even to let him know I'm in the house. But I am determined to get him the medical care he clearly needs.

"There is a Florentine physician who comes for dinner sometimes. They seem to be old friends. They argue a lot, but in a good-natured way. The friend is as stubborn and strong-willed as the Maestro."

"What is his name?" I ask.

"Baccio Rontini."

"Do you know where he lives?"

Urbino nods.

"Then go immediately and fetch him. Do not come back without him."

The house remains uncomfortably quiet. Wherever Michelangelo has hidden himself is far enough away to muffle any groans. I am too impatient to sit and wait for Urbino and the physician to return. I need to feel useful, so I seize upon the task of building the fire and boiling water. More than likely, if Michelangelo's injury is as severe as Urbino described, both will be needed. I am grateful that I've adopted simpler dress in the last few years. It would be quite cumbersome to be on my knees in brocade stirring embers and adding kindling to the hearth. Once I get the fire caught, I hunt around in the kitchen for a large pot and the water jar. I am relieved to see it is full. I tie an apron around my waist, haul the heavy iron pot to the hearth and manage to hang it above the fire.

The water is coming to a boil when I hear voices in the garden and the key in the door. As I hoped, Urbino is not alone but was successful in locating Baccio Rontini and convincing him to come.

"Where is your master?" the doctor asks me.

Urbino grows red in the face and is about to correct him, but I silence him with a gesture.

"He has made no sound at all in the last hour. I assume he's hidden himself away. Urbino, can you lead Dottore Rontini through the house? When you find him, I have hot water and clean cloths ready if you need them."

Urbino looks at me in astonishment, but I wink at him and send them to their task up the stairs.

The physician turns back. "We'll need strong spirits as well if he is in the condition Urbino described. Also, wood for a splint and a stick wrapped on a rag for him to bite on."

As I rummage for wine and wood I can hear the repeated calls for Michelangelo as doors are opened and footsteps retreat further and further into the house. I am perversely impressed at the strength and will that have driven him to hide himself so thoroughly.

Nearly an hour passes before Urbino comes rushing into the kitchen.

"We have found him! The dottore is with him now, arguing with him, but Michelangelo cannot be moved. We are to bring everything above—the wine, the water, the cloths. I tried to tell Dottore Rontini that you are a marchesa, not a housekeeper, but he was too intent on finding the Maestro and he didn't seem to hear me."

"It's not important, Urbino. I'd rather he not know I'm a marchesa, and thus consider me too refined and delicate to do more than say the rosary. Come, there is work to be done."

We gather all the supplies I have prepared. Urbino hauls the cauldron of hot water and leads me through a series of hidden passageways deep into the house.

I do not want to upset Michelangelo with my presence and stay in the shadows behind Urbino. But when we reach him, I can see and hear that he's delirious with pain. He has no idea who is in the room.

Dottore Rontini works confidently and quickly, cleaning the wound and setting the bone. Urbino holds the thrashing Michelangelo firmly down and I stand at his side, swabbing Michelangelo's brow, still smeared with pigment.

By the time the leg is bound and splinted, Michelangelo has fainted.

"It's just as well. He needs to lie quietly if the leg is to heal." The dottore is wiping his hands and his instruments. He turns to Urbino and me. "Someone will need to sit with him through the night and watch for fever. It's probably best if we take shifts."

"You'll stay?" Urbino asks him, relief in his voice.

"Of course. As long as he needs me. I am his friend. I doubt he'll allow anyone else to touch him once he is conscious."

"I'll sit with him now. You two get some rest. You both did far more strenuous work than I did," I offer.

Rontini looks at me closely. "You are new to the household. I've never seen you before, or known Michelangelo to have a woman servant." He does not sound distrustful, but he clearly knows Michelangelo well.

It's time to clarify my identity now that the emergency is past. I do not want the doctor to feel like a fool.

"I am not a servant but a friend, who came as you did when I learned of the accident."

"Forgive me!"

"There is no need for apology. You were intent on saving your friend, and I could easily be mistaken for a housekeeper." I gesture toward my dress and smile.

"You are certainly as competent as a housekeeper. Your foresight in preparing everything saved us valuable time. Allow me to introduce myself. Baccio Rontini, physician of Florence."

"And I am Vittoria Colonna, of Ischia."

"The poet!" Rontini whispers.

At that moment Michelangelo groans. I turn toward him.

"Yes. And right now, also a nurse. Please, go rest. I am sure you will need your strength later in the night when he wakes enraged that you've saved him from himself."

I take my seat at Michelangelo's bedside and continue to sponge his paint-spattered face.

His stillness does not last long, as the wine that dulled the pain wears off. He moans and grabs for the bandaged leg. I am not strong enough to restrain him, but I clasp his hands in mine and bend to whisper in his ear. "Hold my hands and let your suffering pass from you to me."

He must hear me, for he clutches my fingers with such force that I cry out. *Good,* I reassure myself. Let me absorb as much as he can give me.

I sing to him, the lullabies with which I soothed Alfonso's bad dreams. I pray with him, the lyrical psalms that calm me in the chapel at San Silvestro. When he loosens his grip, I free one of my hands to squeeze out a cloth soaked in vinegar and cool his flesh.

I do not know how long into the night I sit with him. I offer him a few sips of wine when he is alert enough to drink and he drifts off again into a fitful sleep.

When Urbino comes to relieve me, I am asleep myself, my head resting on Michelangelo's chest, his heartbeat my own lullaby.

"My lady, I am ready to take your place," he whispers, gently nudging my shoulder. I sit up, slightly dazed, and then remember where I am. I touch Michelangelo's forehead to check for fever, but his skin is cool. I ease my hand from his and slowly stand.

Urbino passes me a candle. "I have prepared a bed for you close by," he says. "The second room on the right."

I nod in thanks and feel my way in the dim candlelight. When I reach my destination, I undo my shoes, remove my stockings and the borrowed apron, now bearing splotches of blood and aquamarine, and collapse onto the bed fully clothed.

Michelangelo's shouts awaken me in the morning. I should be surprised that he has the energy to make so much noise, but nothing shocks me about him anymore. His loud complaints are answered by the equally vociferous words of Baccio Rontini, who must have taken the early-morning watch from Urbino.

A finger of light is visible under the shutter in the window opposite the bed. I stretch and walk barefoot across the room to open the shutter. The window looks out over rooftops and chimneys toward the Vatican. We are quite high up in the house. How Michelangelo got here yesterday is beyond my imagination. Even more unknowable is why. From the position of the sun and the lack of activity in the street below, I surmise that it's still early. I survey the room. Beside the bed a small table holds the candle where I placed it during the night. Below a simple mirror is another small table with a wash bowl and ewer and a clean towel. To my relief, a chamber pot sits on the floor beneath the table. Urbino, bless him, has thought of everything.

I wash up, repin my hair and veil, and smooth my gown as best I can. Then I tiptoe out the door and turn in the opposite direction from Michelangelo's room. I have no intention of interrupting the shouting match. Descending through a complicated warren of rooms and passages, I reach the kitchen. There is no sign of Urbino, who must have collapsed as wearily as I had when his watch ended. The only living creature I encounter is a cat licking her paws by the barely glowing hearth.

I am used to the bustle of the Castello in early morning, when activity is always at its most frenetic, especially in the kitchen—fires to be stoked, bread to be baked, porridge to be stirred. If I expect to break my fast in this house, it is clear I will have to prepare my own meal.

Once again I am on my knees at the hearth. The cat rubs against my thigh and I stroke her. "Good morning, dear companion."

She purrs and then wanders off while I pile new kindling on top of the few remaining embers. It is good dry wood and the fire catches easily. I warm myself for a few minutes, spreading my hands in front of me. Although they bear no physical imprint of Michelangelo's desperate grip, they still retain the memory of his agony and calloused flesh. The last time I held a man's hand with such intimacy was Ferrante's a full three years before his death. I didn't expect I would ever touch or be touched again after he left me that final time.

I shake my head to dispel these memories. Last night, I held the hands of a suffering man, as a nurse would. Nothing more. He was not even aware I was there. For all he knew, in his pain and wine-fogged brain, I was an apparition. Not real. Not flesh and blood.

Footsteps on the staircase dispel my foolish wandering. The doctor appears at the bottom.

"How is our patient this morning?" I ask. "The strength of his voice leads me to believe that he withstood the night well."

"He has. As anticipated, he is angry that we didn't abandon him, but it's his pride that suffered the most damage. Like all of us, he rages against the infirmities of age. He cannot bear the thought that his body is impeding his ever-vital mind. He is sleeping again. Nevertheless, he is not out of danger yet. Fevers have a tendency to emerge on the second day. We still need to be watchful."

"I must admit I don't understand his unwillingness to seek help. I am grateful that you were able to come, and more than grateful that you were willing to endure his wrath."

"He is my friend," the doctor said simply. "As difficult as he may be at times, I love him and would do anything for him."

"I believe there's no middle ground for those of us who know him. One cannot hold back or hide behind the artificial courtesies of society with him. He demands all, if one is truly to be his friend."

"Then you know him well and must be a devoted friend, to have defied society's expectations and come to him as you did."

"I came without considering how it might appear to the rest of the world. Does that shock you?"

"On the contrary, my lady. I admire you. He is a most fortunate man to count you among his friends."

"Likewise, Dottore. He is equally fortunate in you."

"Now that we have settled how blessed Michelangelo is by our friendship, I propose we join forces to find something to eat. We will both need to be fortified if we are to cope with him today."

Together we hunt through the kitchen and uncover a half loaf of bread, some cheese and some pickled fish. I am ravenous, and realize that I have not eaten anything since the midday meal the day before—a simple lentil soup at the convent. But my appetite surprises me.

"Forgive me if I appear unladylike, Dottore," I say as I tear off a second chunk of bread and slice more cheese. "In the turmoil of last night, I seem to have forgotten to eat."

He laughs. "It is actually a delight to see you enjoying the food. Some women deny themselves out of vanity or a false sense of piety. I have never believed that God intended us to starve ourselves into heaven."

I thought back to how I had indeed starved myself after Ferrante's death. What has changed me?

"Perhaps it is the influence of Michelangelo himself that awakens me to the pleasure of a simple meal, the beauty of the human body, the gift of a loyal friend."

"I could not have said it better, my lady." And he lifts a cup of fermented cider we discovered in a barrel.

We continue to enjoy our breakfast, a respite from the night's labors and a preparation for the challenges that might lie ahead. As I clear away the crumbs and add wood to the fire, Dottore Rontini prepares to leave for the apothecary. He brought only a small amount of medication and wants to have more on hand.

"It would be best if you could go and sit with him again. When Urbino rises, tell him we'll need the ingredients for a hearty broth—a chicken or some marrow bones, onions, carrots, garlic and green herbs. Will you be all right alone with Michelangelo if he awakens restless and belligerent? Shout for Urbino if things get out of hand. I won't be gone long."

"I'll be fine," I assure him, although I have no idea how Michelangelo will react when he sees me or how I'll respond. Daylight forces hidden things out of the shadows. I will no longer be able to conceal myself in the darkness holding his hand.

I retrace my steps to the top of the house with a fresh ewer of water. About halfway up, I hear Urbino's snores behind a closed door. I enter Michelangelo's room cautiously, hoping not to wake him. His eyelids flutter in deep sleep and his breathing is regular. I carefully place the ewer on the bedside table and am tiptoeing out to empty the basin when a groan escapes his mouth.

I stop, my back to him, and hope that it's the voice of a dream. But no, he is awake.

"Urbino! Urbino! Where are you? Have I been dreaming or was that worthless son of Florence Rontini here in my house and ignoring my wishes?"

I freeze. He didn't see me, only sensed my movement, assuming I was Urbino.

"Urbino, why do you not answer me?"

I put the basin on the floor and face him.

"Because I am not Urbino."

"Vittoria!" He is silent for a moment, and then speaks softly. "Then it was not a dream. You were here during the night."

"Yes."

He turns his head away from me. I cannot tell if he is angry or ashamed.

"You should not see me like this. A broken man."

So it is shame. Anger I could have answered, shout for shout. But not this. I grope for words. I, the poet, whose words pour out of me like blood from a severed vein, cannot find anything to say.

But he does.

"Go away."

"No."

"Go away."

I take three swift, determined steps to his bed and clasp his head in my hands. His skin is so hot I almost pull my palms away.

"You're on fire with fever!"

"Let it rage. A fitting end for a clumsy old man."

"It's not time for you to die."

"How do you know?"

"God still has more work for you to do. You have to finish the wall."

"I hate the wall. I wish Giulio had never asked me to do it."

"You sound like a petulant schoolboy. Enough."

I reach for a clean towel and pour fresh water over it.

"What are you doing?"

I show him, as I reach across the bed to wipe his brow.

He grabs my wrist. "Don't. I don't deserve you, here, caring for me as if you were an Oblate of St. Frances ministering to a beggar."

"You let me care for you during the night."

"I thought you were a dream."

"So, you will permit me to touch you if I am a specter, a being of your mind's creation, but not if I'm flesh and blood, my own creature."

"Not if you are a marchesa."

"I am a woman before I am a marchesa. Look at me, Michelangelo. There are three people in this house who love you, who came, despite your fury, to care for you and keep you whole and safe. Allow us to love you. Allow me to love you."

He lets go of my wrist.

As I wipe the feverish sweat from his brow, he closes his eyes and turns away.

CHAPTER TWENTY-NINE

Vigil

Vittoria
1536
Rome

I stay with Michelangelo until his fever breaks in the late afternoon, spooning him Urbino's broth and Baccio Rontini's herbs infused in wine. He is resigned to my presence when he realizes he cannot order me away. But he does not speak to me or even look at me as I nurse him.

Despite his silence, I keep up a conversation with him, filling the void between us with my thoughts on the *Last Judgment*. It is the natural choice of topic and helps me avoid any mention of his condition or the odd circumstances that place me at his bedside. I reassure myself that our friendship is an intimacy of the mind, a sharing of lofty ideas. We both choose to ignore the fact that I flew to his side and spent the night in his home, sleeping only a few feet from his bed.

By the time his body is no longer aflame, I have exhausted my repertoire of critical ideas related to Matthew's Gospel and am relieved that I no longer have to grapple for some other intellectual topic. He drifts to sleep listening to my monologue, and his breathing is rhythmic and without struggle.

I stand, stretching the muscles of my back that are so tense, not just from bending over his body with wet cloths to soothe his discomfort, but also from the worry that he might not survive the trauma of his disastrous fall.

Baccio Rontini is on the main level of the house busy making notes in a journal.

"He is sleeping peacefully and I believe the fever has broken. I will rest more securely if you'll go and see for yourself."

Signaling his agreement, he closes his book and gets up. Before he leaves me to go to Michelangelo, he speaks.

"You have earned more than rest, my lady. Michelangelo may never express his gratitude to you, but I thank you from the bottom of my heart."

"And I also." Urbino stands in the doorway to the kitchen. "I have prepared something for you to eat after your long hours above. Wait just a moment."

He ducks into the kitchen and I take a seat at the worn table that is nevertheless scrubbed and oiled to a sheen.

Urbino brings out a trencher filled with an aromatic stew, chunks of meat and onions and greens bubbling in a thick sauce. As I was earlier in the day, I am ravenous. I feel a twinge of guilt at eating such a rich meal in comparison to the fare that sustains me at San Silvestro. But I realize this is a household of men, used to hearty food to nourish the strenuous work of painting monumental images. Urbino watches me eat with a smile of pride.

"This is delicious, Urbino. Thank you!" I utter my gratitude between bites.

Shortly after I finish, Baccio Rontini descends from Michelangelo's room.

"The fever has indeed broken. The worst is past."

"I fear the worst may still be ahead of us, Dottore," Urbino suggests. "The better he feels, the harder it will be to keep him still and rested enough for his leg to heal."

"Then you and I have our work cut out for us, Urbino," the doctor says.

"You? You will help me?"

"I am not leaving until Michelangelo is on his feet again. You can rely on me, if you can put up with me."

"Gladly, Dottore!"

I know that my own role in this catastrophe has come to an end. I will be useless in holding Michelangelo back from charging ahead. He more than likely no longer needs a nurse. He needs prison guards, for that is how he'll perceive them.

But the true reason I'm leaving is that Michelangelo cannot bear to have me caring for him.

I rise. "Gentleman, I believe I have done all I can. I should return to San Silvestro. Urbino, may I impose on you to accompany me back? Dottore, please call upon me at any time if I can be of service to our friend."

"We shall miss you, my lady. Your presence has given us more than an extra pair of hands to care for Michelangelo. You imparted both serenity and hope to our worried and weary spirits. Once again, I thank you."

Bundled tightly in my cloak against the bitter cold, I take my leave. Urbino and I don't speak on the journey back. We are both exhausted. I do not envy him the challenging days ahead, coping with a healing but still furiously angry Michelangelo.

I bid him farewell at the convent gate and draw myself up to face the questions that surely await me within the convent walls. Suora Angelica swings open the door when I announce myself at the grating that obscures the world from the convent, the convent from the world.

"My lady! Welcome back. Your cousin Giulia told us you had gone to care for a sick friend and we added her to our prayers. I hope she has recovered?"

"Thank you for your prayers, Suora. My friend has passed the crisis and it appears that all is well. Do you know where I can find my cousin? She'll be eager to hear my news."

"The Lady Giulia is in the garden."

I go immediately to Giulia, grateful that she has kept my whereabouts to herself but sure that she will want—and deserves—an explanation.

She sees me from where she sits in a small grove, wrapped in heavy wool, and comes to meet me as I cross the garden toward her.

"You're back! Tell me all." She kisses me and draws me back into the seclusion of the trees.

"First, thank you for being discreet about my sudden disappearance. I had no idea when I left with Michelangelo's servant how grave his condition was. I truly did not expect to be gone for more than an hour or two."

"I understand you well enough to recognize that it could only have been something compelling to keep you away. What happened?"

I recount the story of our arrival at the silent house, my charge to Urbino to bring the doctor, the gruesome injury and the onset of the fever. Although I am precise and thorough in my description of the actions we undertook to save Michelangelo, I hold back from Giulia the emotional upheaval I experienced. It is hard to fathom that it's merely twenty-four hours since Urbino came to announce the cancellation of our meeting. So much has changed between Michelangelo and me.

"You would have been either proud of me or amused, Giulia, if you'd seen me on my knees building a fire." I focus on my unexpected role as a competent keeper of the household, especially since I'm pleased with myself for being useful and resourceful. I avoid any mention of my place at Michelangelo's bedside. I am not ashamed of what I did, but it could so easily be misunderstood. I do not expect Giulia to disapprove, for she already accepts my absence without judgment. But if she knew how closely I cared for Michelangelo last night she might inadvertently reveal it in conversation with someone who would see nothing but scandal in my actions. So I keep silent.

"It must have been so draining! I remember my mother's experience with my brother when he injured himself as a child—the long vigil as the fever attacked, the helplessness and the lack of recognition when he was delirious and didn't even know that she was there. You must be exhausted!"

"I am indeed. We had very little sleep."

"And how did you leave him? Is he well? Or does he still suffer?"

"He will survive. But I left his physician and his servant with the unenviable task of managing his recuperation. Michelangelo is not a charming man under the best of circumstances. I can only imagine what the next few weeks will be like in that household."

I try to make light of Michelangelo's obstinate personality. And I don't reveal that I ache to be back there, to smooth the rough edges of his recovery. But he will not have me. That much is clear. It is not my sense of propriety that led to my departure once the crisis was past.

"Will you go back?"

I look up sharply. Giulia appears to be reading my mind. I suspect that she apprehends how the experience has affected me.

"Certainly, if they ask for me. But they have everything under control now. The doctor, who is a good friend of Michelangelo's, has agreed to stay until he's healed. The two are well-matched—both strong-willed and in possession of very loud voices."

Giulia smiles. She seems satisfied with my report and does not press me for more details.

"Thank you again for explaining my absence to the nuns. I never want to cause them worry or alarm. I am going to the chapel to pray. I've had scant time to talk to God in the last twenty-four hours."

She waves me off and returns to her book.

No word comes to me from either Michelangelo or Baccio Rontini over the following days. They no longer appear to need me. I am both grateful and regretful. Grateful because the emotional cost of the time I spend with Michelangelo is so high. I need a respite from the tumultuous feelings he engenders. He opens wounds in my soul, slashes the veil I place between myself and the world and elicits from me revelations that should remain hidden, especially from him. I tell him that I love him and he turns away from me. But I am also regretful. Despite the agitation into which my spirit is thrown, I find myself welcoming the sense of being fiercely alive—to beauty, to emotion, to yearning—that was missing in my solitude. I feel as if he rips away my widow's weeds and all they represent.

Once before, I experienced such turmoil—joy mingled with grief. In my loneliness as Ferrante's wife, I was cut off from him, not only by the battlefield but also by his withdrawal into silence whenever he returned to me in body but not in spirit. I'd known, deep in some hidden place, that he no longer loved me—perhaps wasn't even capable of love.

1522 – 1525

CHAPTER THIRTY

Solace and Apprehension

Vittoria
1522 – 1525
Arpino and Rocca

I found a welcome in Arpino among friends as spring emerged. Not far from my birthplace, the ancient town high in the mountains had a stark beauty that brought a familiar comfort to me. My friends didn't know Isabella de Cardona, and that was a comfort to me, as well. No one offered me soulful looks of concern or sought to ascertain how I was coping with Ferrante's infidelity. Far from the court of Napoli, tucked away in the mountains of central Italy, they enjoyed a blissful ignorance of political intrigue and illicit liaisons, which offered me a respite from the role I knew I'd have to play once I was among Ferrante's colleagues again.

More than the bracing mountain air and the clarity of light, it was freedom from oppressive memories that revived my spirit. But a letter from my brother broke the spell of my reveries. It arrived in early April, just as the carpet of mountain flowers was beginning to spread across the sward below the castle. The missive carried the crushing news of my mother's death. She had made a pilgrimage to the shrine of the Virgin Mary in Loreto—against Ascanio's wishes, he was clear in pointing out. He had assumed the role of our mother's guardian and protector upon the death of our father, but my mother had never been one to bend easily to her husband's will. It was no surprise that she'd set out on the journey in spite of her son's pronouncements. But when she returned to the castle at Rocca she was not well and succumbed to her illness. I suspect that my mother knew she was ill before she'd departed for Loreto, and sought to spend her final days on earth in communion with Our Lady, for whom she had a fervent devotion. I know that after my father died two years before, his loss was nearly unbearable to my mother. She longed to join him, and now she had.

My grief was without solace. Although I was a woman in my thirty-third year, I felt keenly that I was now an orphan. Ferrante was in Spain again. Even if he had been close by, I still would have had no hope of finding comfort in his arms. And I had no desire to darken the warmth of my welcome in Arpino with my sadness.

I bade farewell with a promise to return, and traveled north to my brother at Rocca.

I could see the black draping hung on the castle gate from the road below, and along the way as I approached the summit, peasants in the fields tipped their hats. My mother was well-loved by more than her family. I maintained my composure as I rode, focusing on the stone walls of the stronghold and the cadence of my escort's horses.

The gates swung open as we reached the summit, and Ascanio and Giovanna were waiting for me in the courtyard. I descended from my mount and fell wearily into my brother's arms. We were the elders now, and I could see not only grief but the burdens of responsibility and leadership in his eyes.

"Welcome, sister, despite the sad reason for your visit. Your presence is a great comfort to me."

"And yours to me, Ascanio. Come, tell me the whole story."

We withdrew to the family's quarters. We had not lived at Rocca as children, but our mother had chosen to retreat there after Papa's death. It was safer than Marino, and although she was a devout woman, the widow's refuge of the convent held no appeal for her.

But Rocca was more a garrison than a noble residence, and apart from her books and a few favorite works of art, my mother's quarters were simple and austere. These last years of her life had been spent in a kind of contemplative simplicity. It was a striking juxtaposition for me, who had lived so many years surrounded by the opulent vitality of Costanza's court.

I refreshed myself briefly from the dust of the journey and joined Ascanio and Giovanna at a table set before the fire.

"To our mother." Ascanio lifted his glass of wine from the Colonna vineyards terraced below the walls.

We spent the next few hours in conversation, starting with the immediate story of her death, but drifting further and further back to memories that brought her presence into the room with us.

"She was determined to make the trip to Loreto. I tried vainly to dissuade her, knowing how weak she was and how blind she was to her own frailty."

Giovanna placed her hand on his arm.

"Don't blame yourself, Ascanio. She was not as blind as you imagine. She knew the risk she was taking and, in a way, welcomed it. She felt called to Loreto."

"I always thought of Mama as a woman of the world," he said, "more at home negotiating Papa's ransom or discoursing with philosophers. Her spiritual life was a foundation, but a less visible part of who she was. I never considered her to be overtly pious."

"It's mainly been since your father's death that her devotions took more prominence," offered Giovanna. "She seemed at a loss for how to occupy herself after he was gone."

"I can imagine that she turned to *studying* the life of the Virgin before she dedicated her own life to praying to her." If I knew anything about Agnese di Montefeltro, it was that whatever she did had its roots in learning.

We talked well into the night. The next morning we accompanied my mother's body to Rome and buried her in the Colonna crypt beside my father in the Church of Santi

Apostoli. Our cousin, Cardinal Pompeo Colonna, conducted the funeral mass.

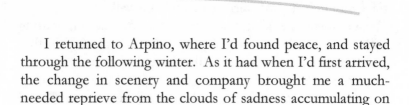

I returned to Arpino, where I'd found peace, and stayed through the following winter. As it had when I'd first arrived, the change in scenery and company brought me a much-needed reprieve from the clouds of sadness accumulating on my horizon.

By that time Ferrante had left Spain for Milan, under threat from the French. He did not attempt to visit me. I was no longer the patient wife, waiting dutifully at home for his return. Ferrante knew where to find me. My presence in Arpino wasn't hidden.

I was clear with my circle that I sought no secret liaisons to provide what my husband didn't. If truth be told, flattered as I was by the verses composed to honor my beauty or my wit, I found myself bereft of desire. I may have been inflaming the passions of the men surrounding me at Arpino—either figuratively in their poetry or actually in their heated imaginations—but I felt no flames myself.

It seemed that I'd erected walls around my emotions as stout as those surrounding Arpino, walls that had withstood millennia of attacks from both man and nature. Time was, I'd relished the untempered exuberance of physical love. But that kind of love without Ferrante held no appeal.

Instead of kisses I bestowed words—lilting, amusing, challenging—upon my would-be courtiers. That was how we passed our days, each bringing something of value to the others. The men, if they wanted more, refrained from pressing me, and poured their desire into Petrarchan sonnets.

At the start of Holy Week, I departed our congenial circle to join Ascanio and Giovanna at Marino. It had been two years since I'd seen Ferrante.

Following our mother's death, Ascanio and I had grown closer. Because our lives spent together as children had been curtailed by war and by my separation to Ischia, we had not shared the common experiences of childhood that bind sister and brother. But the loneliness precipitated by Ferrante's continued absence, coupled with my deep affection for my young sister-in-law, drew me to depend more on their counsel and company, and they seemed happy to reciprocate.

I was relieved that they'd chosen to spend Holy Week at Marino and not at the palazzo in Rome. After the headiness of the distractions at Arpino, I was content to immerse myself in Ascanio's family. His daughters surrounded us, and I was struck by their playfulness and exuberance. They reminded me of my own early childhood on the mountain, and I was happy to indulge them with visits to the nursery for stories at bedtime. I'd lost sight of how much joy children bring to one's life. My days in the nursery with Alfonso were long past, but they had bestowed upon me a great gift, despite the inherent challenges.

I cherished being called "Zia" by my nieces, grateful to have the title when I lacked the affection I still craved from my husband.

With Giovanna, I helped supervise the preparations for Easter in Marino's ancient kitchen, remembering my mother's lists and her organization of my wedding as if it were a military campaign. A lamb would be slaughtered at the end of the week, breads kneaded and baked, the last of the winter vegetables roasted and spring greens plucked for salad. The tempo of our industry was interrupted early in the week by a messenger from Rome. He delivered a gift from my dear friend Giovan Matteo Giberti—a palm blessed by His Holiness Pope Clement VII and a letter that was even more precious to me. Giovan, as head of the papal secretaries, had access to news of the warfront. I'd learned weeks before that Ferrante was seriously ill, but since then had received no word either from him or about his condition. Giovan, realizing what it would mean to me, had secured the news that Ferrante had recovered. For reasons of security, he couldn't tell me where he was, only that he was once again on the move with his troops.

I was overcome with gratitude, and touched by Giovan's thoughtfulness. I slid the palm behind the crucifix that hung in my chamber and placed the letter in the carved wooden box that held my most important papers. It was enough to know that Ferrante still strode across his battlefield, however distant it might be from Marino.

The following months brought more of the same pattern that had marked my life since the war had intensified. Reports from Giovan or other knowledgeable friends about skirmishes or full-blown battles. Requests from Ferrante that I use my influence to exhort those who still owed him ransom money to pay their debts. Word from those close to the emperor or the pope regarding expectations or manipulations. It was a dark time, made more troubling by Ferrante's first retreat. His attempt to invade France and lay siege to Marseilles with the imperial army failed against an embittered and powerful city. He returned to Italy, pursued by the young French king, François.

It was winter once again, and François set out to besiege the city of Pavia, a rash decision that had dire consequences for both him and Ferrante. The news that reached me of the ferocious battle there in late February was both exhilarating and deeply disturbing. Ferrante had led the imperial forces to a decisive victory. François, the inexperienced and eager warrior king, had been taken prisoner. There was no question that Pavia was Ferrante's victory. My heart swelled when I learned the news. This was what he lived for, and the reward for which I'd paid with my marriage. I felt an equal in his victory, as if I'd donned armor and wielded a sword. My weapon had been my pen, my powerful friendships, my steadfastness in supporting his long and arduous journey to leadership. Isabella might have given him a few hours of pleasure, but she had not fostered the honor and honed the skill of the warrior he became as my husband. Pavia was my vindication.

But it was also my terror. Ferrante had been wounded. "Covered in wounds," the message said, after extolling his victory. He had been carried to Milan to recover. I wrote immediately. "Shall I come to nurse you?"

Ever the soldier, his reply was that the wounds, although many, were superficial. "Wait," he wrote. "If I need you, I will send word at once, but I am already regaining my strength."

CHAPTER THIRTY-ONE

Betrayal

Ferrante
1525
Milan

The wounds were not severe. He'd managed to stanch the blood even before he left the battlefield, and the pain merely hovered at the edge of his consciousness, overshadowed by the elation of his victory. It was *his* strategy, forged in the bitter lessons learned at Ravenna and refined in the combative years following it, that had finally defeated the French at Pavia. Word had come to him on the field that King François had relinquished his sword, a prisoner now and not the impetuous, headstrong warrior who had led the charge only a few hours before. Ferrante's satisfaction flooded and uplifted him, comforting his battered body.

He limped to his tent, the exhaustion beginning to sap him as he entered its sheltering walls. The weight of his armor pressed against the jagged flesh of his shoulder where a French bullet had lodged itself. He winced and felt a wave of nausea sweep through him.

His squire, Marco, moved swiftly to his side and eased him onto a stool. "Shall I call for the surgeon, sir?" He was gently stripping the steel from Ferrante's rapidly stiffening limbs. Fresh blood oozed from the torn flesh.

"Later. Get me some wine and pen and paper. Have Commander Lannoy and the Duke of Bourbon returned to their tents? Who is holding the king?" During the intensity of the battle he'd lost contact with his fellow commanders. But now, they must regroup.

Ever the strategist, he'd already shifted from the battlefield to the bargaining table. Word needed to be sent to the emperor. Even in his exhausted and dazed state, he savored the honor and the rewards this victory would mean for him personally, as well as the decisive power it placed in the hands of Charles V.

The emperor would be grateful. The condemnations of brutality that had clung to Ferrante after his troops had rampaged in Bicocca would be forgotten in this triumph. He was vindicated, he told himself, as the pen fell from his hand, and his body, asserting its dominance, slipped into unconsciousness.

He spent the next several weeks recovering in the castello of Francesco II Sforza in Milan, drifting in and out of a feverish delirium, unable to wield any control over the critical political aftermath of his military victory. At the moment of his greatest triumph as a general, when the world—or at least those territories he had wrested from the French—should have been his, he was incomprehensively sickly and isolated.

His only solace was the presence of his mistress Delia, who had learned of his wounds as well as his victory.

When she arrived, he had the strength to sit up, the awareness to sense her cool, smooth hand against his battered cheek, the words to share with her the longing that had consumed him all the months of the campaign. It had been a year since he'd seen her. And although there'd been others— the spiteful Isabella, for example, who had maliciously sent Vittoria her necklace back—none had ever surpassed Delia in his need for her.

"Hush. Don't waste energy speaking. You need your strength to recover. Just let me sit with you in silence and gaze on your countenance. Even rough and scarred, it is still beautiful to me."

She was his medicine, far better than any draughts Sforza's physicians could have prepared. Far better, he acknowledged with neither guilt nor regret, than what Vittoria could have provided. His wife was a stranger to him, untouched by the horrors he had witnessed, immersed in her

392 ~ Linda Cardillo

books and her conversations with poets and philosophers and ignorant of the world of flesh and clamor and deceit and power that had defined him for so long. Vittoria didn't understand his needs. And she didn't need *him*, the way Delia did.

But even Delia's attendance at his bedside could not protect him from his realization that, for the first time in his career, he was at the periphery—of power, of recognition and control. He had heard nothing from Emperor Charles V acknowledging his victory, a silence that ate away at his pride like acid. When a messenger arrived from Spain reporting that Charles de Lannoy, his fellow commander at Pavia, had claimed sole responsibility for the capture of Francois, Ferrante exploded in rage. The rewards he had anticipated from the emperor—lands, honor, gratitude—had been wrenched from his grasp while he lay impotent, a prisoner not of a military enemy but of his own weak flesh.

His disaffection and vulnerability were no secret in Milan; before long, word reached the Vatican. One of Pope Clement's cardinals made a secret journey north to probe the depths of his estrangement from the emperor. Would he be willing to join a union of Italian cities ready to throw off the yoke of foreign occupation?

Ferrante concealed his reaction as the terms of his potential betrayal were presented to him. The enormity of what he was being asked to do—violate his oath of loyalty to Charles—was offset by the magnitude of what he was being offered in return. The crown of the Kingdom of Napoli. Not just a few scattered territories from the land taken back from the French, but a kingdom.

"You realize the risk to my honor that my participation would cause?"

"Of course. But His Holiness is prepared to absolve you of your oath to Charles by invoking his own authority over you. Your allegiance to Pope Clement takes priority over your loyalty to the emperor."

They had thought of the major obstacle standing in his way and had extended a proposal to overcome it.

He despised the situation in which he found himself—prey for the ambitions of others who wished to use him for their own ends and torn by a sense of duty and loyalty to an emperor who had abandoned him. After a restless night, fueled by both wine and bitterness, betrayed by Lannoy and ignored by Charles V, he decided there was one person in whom he could confide, and wrote to his wife.

CHAPTER THIRTY-TWO

A Broken Man

Vittoria
1525
Ischia and on the road to Milan

When my offer to nurse Ferrante back to health after the wounds he'd suffered at Pavia was refused, I remained on Ischia, where I'd once again returned to Costanza's court. She shared my worries, but also reassured me. "If he is confident of his recovery, I see no reason to doubt him. He's been doing this long enough to know the severity of his condition."

I sensed her attempt to assuage not only my concerns for Ferrante's health, but also my disappointment that he was yet again pushing me away.

Had I realized it was his spiritual health that was more at risk than his flesh wounds, I would have ignored his bravado and traveled immediately to Milan. But it took several months before the real damage to Ferrante was apparent to me, and by then, it was too late.

I fault myself for not recognizing the depth of his despair when the emperor failed to honor him for his role in winning Pavia. Charles had remained silent when he could have rewarded Ferrante with a title or a portion of the lands he'd fought so bravely to defend. And he'd denied Ferrante even the token recognition one would expect for lesser conquests. The significance of the emperor's inaction was not lost on me, and when Ferrante sent me a message suggesting I could help him more with my pen than my nursing skills, I gladly wrote to Charles on his behalf. It was a task I'd often performed for Ferrante, shaping his intentions into words that smoothed the sharp edges of alliances that had veered off course or sought to allay unwarranted suspicions. My husband, though unsurpassed with a sword in his hand, was much less adept with a pen and had gratefully acceded that role to me.

Attempting to express my expectations and hopes for Ferrante without appearing to beg was a precarious, delicate task that demanded all my skills of persuasion. My hand clenched the pen as tightly as I might have clenched my teeth if I had the opportunity to speak to the emperor directly. I believed fervently that Ferrante was worthy of acknowledgment. He had earned the emperor's gratitude. Why was it not forthcoming? I couldn't declare outright our profound disappointment or appear to be greedy for the spoils of war. But I defended Ferrante's service, faithfulness and sincerity as the true basis for any reward from Charles. There was no doubt in my mind that he'd fought only to advance the emperor's objectives—and my belief was confirmed in all the accounts of Ferrante's accomplishments throughout this ambitious imperial campaign.

These were complicated times. I was weary—of my husband's absence, of unmet expectations, of constantly shifting alliances. I would've been content to withdraw from the maelstrom of uncertainty that had convulsed the seas of power in which we navigated. But my husband's discontent didn't allow me that reprieve.

Costanza summoned me one afternoon in a state of agitation. She had received a letter from one of her many confidants.

"Words are being whispered about Ferrante. You need to be aware." Her face revealed anguish, but also the ferocity of a mother ready to defend her child.

"What sort of words?" I couldn't take much more of the dismantling of my husband's honor.

"A man of uncertain loyalty. Weak in spirit. Easily tempted." She threw the letter down on the marble table between us, but I didn't move to pick it up. I looked across at Costanza and saw my own weariness mirrored.

"What does that mean, 'easily tempted'?" I asked warily. Was she about to tell me what I already knew, that the epithet referred to his weakness for other men's wives?

"It means he's vulnerable to dangerous plots devised by men who want to betray the emperor. They believe they can dangle a prize in front of him and he'll grab it like a child at Carneval chasing after a float in hopes of capturing a sweet."

"I don't believe it!" I was vehement. A betrayal of this magnitude overshadowed his infidelity to me. I *could* not believe it.

But within days, I was forced to accept it when a letter arrived from my husband that threatened to undermine all the validation of his honor that the victory at Pavia had brought me. He *had* been offered a prize, as Costanza had predicted. The kingdom of Napoli in return for participating in a plot driven by Milan—for Venice, Florence and Napoli to join Milan in an alliance with the Pope to betray the emperor. But the fact that Ferrante had turned to me and sought my counsel was enough for me to know that he had not yet succumbed to the conspiracy. With profound despair, I grasped the state of mind that had left him so vulnerable.

My writing hand, recently employed in supplication to the emperor, now scratched out a hurried missive to forestall and, with God's grace, undo any rash decision Ferrante might make. I implored him to refuse the crown that was being offered to him by the hands of traitors. I had no wish to be the wife of a king; I wanted simply to be the wife of a noble warrior.

He did, in the end, listen to my appeal, and remained steadfastly loyal to Charles. He convinced the chancellor of Milan that he was still interested in the plot, and persuaded him to come to discuss the final details. But he arranged for another of the emperor's generals to overhear the conversation describing the specifics. Ferrante arrested the chancellor on the spot and delivered him to the emperor. His actions should have quieted the whispers. They should have restored his reputation as a man of honor, loyal to the empire for which he fought.

He had heeded my entreaty, but not in time to save his good name.

The damage had been done, by Ferrante's own weakness and willingness even to consider joining the plot. Too many knew of his involvement; too few believed that he was merely gathering information as the emperor's man.

My husband was an isolated, shunned man after that disastrous episode, trusted by no one. Alone and disgraced, despairing of his health, he finally sent for me.

And I went to him.

Costanza accompanied me to the ship and embraced me, her face and her entire being once again reflecting my own emotions about the man who'd been so difficult to love and yet to whom I'd given my life and my soul.

"Godspeed. Bring him home." She kissed me and released me to my journey, burdened by so many ghosts, so many moments of loss and disappointment.

Once the ship made anchor at Napoli, we rode hard northward. I eschewed the need for rest, so urgent was my desire to reach Ferrante. I'd waited almost three years for him to call for me. I couldn't wait a day longer.

We were on the road near Viterbo, moving swiftly, when a soldier bearing my husband's colors approached from the north, his horse frothing with the exertion of a demanding pace.

He pulled up abruptly when he recognized who we were and spoke quietly to Costanza's guard leading my party. The captain looked back at me and then nodded to the soldier, who turned his horse and approached me.

He doffed his plumed hat and held it, trembling, in his hand. He bore the strain of his journey, sweat pouring down his brow despite the November temperature.

"My lady, if you will, I bring word from Milan."

My heart leaped that Ferrante had sent someone out to meet me, a reassurance to quell my anxiety.

"Word from the marchese?" I asked expectantly.

"No, my lady."

He handed me a letter sealed with an unknown signet. I slit it open and read the brief message.

"With deep regret, I inform you that His Excellency, Ferrante d'Avalos, Marchese de Pescara, passed from this world on 25 November 1525. May God have mercy on his soul."

The note slipped from my hand as my body slipped from my horse. I tasted the dust of the road, the dust to which his once-vibrant body would now return, and wished only to be swallowed up by the earth along with him.

My life was over.

1526 – 1529

CHAPTER THIRTY-THREE

Refuge

Vittoria
1526 – 1527
Rome

The knock on the door came as I sat at my writing table in the late afternoon.

"My lady, you have a visitor." It was the raspy voice of Suora Carita, the nun who served as the gatekeeper of the Convent of San Silvestro.

"Suora, please inform whoever it is that I remain in mourning. I will not receive visitors."

"I did so, my lady. But he insisted and would not leave until I fetched you."

It was unlike Suora Carita to falter in her vigilance as protector of the convent's peace and security.

"Who makes such a demand?"

"Your brother, my lady. He claims to bear a message from his Holiness."

I tensed. With Ferrante's death, Ascanio had taken on the mantle of my guardian with far more zeal than he had ever shown before. I could not burden the suora with the task of sending him away.

"I apologize for this disruption, Suora. I will see him and tell him myself to leave."

I followed the nun through the labyrinth of dim corridors in the convent's guest quarters. These halls had been my refuge since Ferrante's death. I'd fled here only days after I'd seen my husband entombed in the crypt of San Domenico in Napoli. I could not return to Ischia, where every stone, every glimpse of the sea, every breath of the wind seared my spirit with memories of my life with Ferrante—first as children and then as husband and wife.

Before we entered the visitors' salon, Suora Carita turned to me. "Would you like me to stay, my lady?"

I knew Suora Carita could be a formidable barrier to those who would disturb or breach the solitude within these walls. More than one young man had hoped to "rescue" daughters destined for convent life by their parents. None had ever succeeded.

I smiled. "Thank you, Suora. But I used to wipe Ascanio's behind when he was a boy. I can handle my brother."

"If you need me, I'll be in the outer foyer." She opened the salon door, nodded to Ascanio and disappeared to her post. I went to my brother and kissed his cheek.

"Ascanio. What brings you here with such urgency that you disrupt both my mourning and the convent's peace?"

"Good God, Vittoria! You're even dressing like a nun. Where is my beautiful golden-haired sister beneath these coarse rags?"

"It is you who are being coarse right now. I won't honor your disrespect with an answer. But I do demand an answer to my own question. Why are you here?"

"Word has come to me that you are considering taking the veil and joining this community as a sister, not just a guest. I don't dispute your need to withdraw and mourn, but I will not allow you to throw away your life by hiding behind these walls."

"You will not *allow*? Neither our father nor my husband ever spoke to me in this manner! Who are you to interject yourself between me and my God?"

"It is not I, but the Holy Father." He showed me a letter with the pope's seal. I stretched out my hand for it, not believing it contained the pope's prohibition. But Ascanio held it back.

"The letter is addressed to the Reverend Mother, and I've been charged with delivering it. But I felt I should tell you personally first, to prepare you."

"Why should his Holiness want to keep me from professing vows?" I was truly puzzled until I saw the look of complicity on Ascanio's face. I'd been schooled by Costanza and Mama to present a dispassionate façade in the service of negotiating the constraints of our women's lives; Ascanio had no need to keep his motives or true desires hidden. He could command and it was done.

"Or should I ask why did *you* request this dictate of the pope?"

"I did it for you and for our family. But the pope would not have agreed if he didn't also believe that the Church and Italy need you *in* the world, not hidden from it."

"First of all, I haven't voiced any intention to take vows. I don't know who told you such a thing, but whoever it is does not know my heart. I am still suffering the loss of my husband and have no room to consider taking another, not even Christ."

"That is precisely why I went to the pope—to ensure that in your profound grief you should be protected from making any rash decisions. I am relieved that you recognize as well that you are in a fragile state."

"Not so fragile that I don't see your intention here, Ascanio. You don't want me to become a nun because you want me free to become a wife again."

His face reddened. "Not now, not in your grief. But the day may come. . . . You are still young, still beautiful, Vittoria, despite how you have disguised yourself. Think of the family, and what a strategic second marriage can do for us."

"I wish to contemplate nothing right now except my dead husband. Now please leave. I've granted you far more of my time and energy than I can afford. You have exhausted me and depleted me in ways you cannot possibly comprehend. You can give the pope's letter to Suora Carita and she will see that it reaches the Reverend Mother's hand."

"I shall take my leave as you ask. When you are ready, know that Giovanna and I welcome you, at the palazzo here in Rome or at Marino. Wherever you wish to abide."

"It is here that I wish to abide. But I thank you and, especially, Giovanna, whom I miss. My love to her and the children."

"They long to see you."

"In time, Ascanio. In time."

When he left, I remained in the salon, unable to lift my body from the chair. Its rigid back and carved arms were all that held me together. As if the acute pain of my grief wasn't enough, this visit from Ascanio had felt like an assault, ripping through what little peace I'd found in the convent.

Suora Carita poked her head through the doorway. "My lady, are you distressed? Has your brother brought you disturbing family news? I can call for one of the sisters if you need someone."

"Thank you, Suora. The family is well. My solitude has made me unused to prolonged conversation." I didn't add that I was also unused to being told what to do by a man. I'd learned this afternoon that Ferrante's death had exposed me to an unexpected risk. My years as his wife had offered me a great deal of autonomy because he'd spent so much of our marriage on the battlefield. This brief encounter with Ascanio was an object lesson on my future as a widow. His words, his arrogance had served as a warning to be on the alert, suffusing my entire spirit with vigilance. If Ascanio, whom I knew and loved, could step into my life as he had that day, to try to force me to take an unwanted direction, how much more uncertain would another marriage be?

I rose and returned to my rooms, lit the lamp and resumed the poem that had been interrupted by Ascanio's violation of my privacy and seclusion.

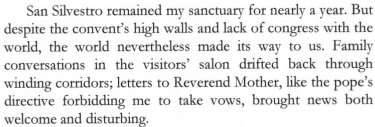

San Silvestro remained my sanctuary for nearly a year. But despite the convent's high walls and lack of congress with the world, the world nevertheless made its way to us. Family conversations in the visitors' salon drifted back through winding corridors; letters to Reverend Mother, like the pope's directive forbidding me to take vows, brought news both welcome and disturbing.

Ultimately it was the world that ended my sojourn at San Silvestro. We didn't hear the cannons, but they might as well have been in the courtyard for the damage they did to my refuge. The Colonna were at war with the pope. Again. Not only in my lifetime but for generations before, the Colonna had often been at war with whoever wore the ring of St. Peter. This time the conflict had its origins in the rivalry that had existed between our cousin Cardinal Pompeo Colonna and Giulio de' Medici long before he became Pope Clement VII.

It was Giovanna, Ascanio's wife, who brought the news. She was no stranger to the visitors' salon. Following Ascanio's disruptive visit to me, Giovanna was the one who came regularly. After five years of marriage to my brother and the birth of three children, she was far from the young girl who had shared the classroom with Alfonso and her irrepressible younger sister, Maria. Giovanna had been the serious, studious one of the trio of scholars. She had retained her calm demeanor and inquisitive spirit despite the demands of motherhood and, I imagined, Ascanio. We had formed a close bond since Ferrante's death, so I immediately detected her distress when I arrived in the salon to greet her.

"Vittoria! I bring troubling news. Rome is no longer a safe haven for the Colonna. War has broken out with Pope

Clement. The pope knows you're here and Ascanio fears that you may become a hostage. We are leaving for Marino imminently and I have come to beg you to go with us."

The anguish in her voice was more convincing to me than if Ascanio had come himself and ordered me to leave with him. For all the years of my marriage, I'd been able to keep myself buffered from the clan warfare that had defined the relationship between the Colonna and the Vatican. But I was no longer on Ischia, a world and a lifetime away from Rome and its feuds. I acquiesced to Giovanna's request, aware that without a doubt it had come from Ascanio. I didn't want to know what exaggerated slight or misspoken words had triggered this latest fanning of the flames of hatred. I knew it would only anger and frustrate me.

"How soon must I be ready to leave?" I could see the relief in Giovanna's face that I was not going to resist.

"Tonight. We will travel under the cover of dark."

I kissed my sister-in-law. "Till this evening. I must go and pack."

"It would be best not to say anything to the sisters until just before your departure."

"Of course." We both understood that somewhere underneath the wimples and habits could be a cousin or aunt of Colonna enemies.

When my trunks were packed and waiting in the foyer, I spoke to Reverend Mother.

"I regret that I must leave so unexpectedly, Reverend Mother. But a family emergency calls me. I am truly grateful for the refuge you have given me."

"You will always be welcome here, my dear. You have enriched us with your presence and have become part of this house. Godspeed."

She pressed a small prayer book into my hands. "Let God speak to you through this when you are absent from us and our prayers."

"Thank you, Reverend Mother."

Ascanio was waiting at the gate. Giovanna and the children were in a curtained carriage surrounded by his soldiers.

"Do you have an extra horse for me?"

He smiled and handed me the reins of a palfrey. "She's small, but she knows the way to Marino in the dark."

With that, our party proceeded with stealth through the streets of Rome and out into the Alban Hills. It was nearly dawn when we reached the fortress that had been our childhood home.

All along the ramparts, I saw Ascanio's men, watchful with arms ready. My heart sank. My months at San Silvestro had helped me forget the ravages of war even as I grieved for a husband taken from me by war. But here it was again, confronting me. I spurred the horse through the gate, dismounted and strode into the keep, unable to speak a civil word to my brother.

Because we had left Rome so precipitously the household was unprepared for our arrival. Although I was exhausted from the long night of travel, no bed awaited me. Ignoring my fatigue, I offered my help to Giovanna, even wearier than I was, and gathered the children by the fire in the kitchen. I tried to amuse them with stories while the servants scrambled to prepare a hot meal and make up beds.

"It's at times like this that I desperately miss Ischia," Giovanna confided as she rocked her youngest, a baby of less than a year who fussed and fretted, finding no comfort in his mother's arms. Giovanna herself looked incapable of being comforted, her body tensing with every scream from the baby, her pale eyes smudged with dark circles.

"Let me have Fabrizio. I'll walk with him. Where is the nurse?"

"She's gone with the others to set up the children's room. She had Fabrizio in the carriage throughout the night while I tried to soothe the girls. They were frightened, of course. Even when they don't understand what's happening, children sense that something is terribly wrong. They could hear Ascanio shouting orders in the courtyard before we left, saw the tumult in the palazzo as we lifted them from their beds in the middle of the night." She looked around her at the smoky kitchen. "I don't believe they have any memories of ever having been here."

"Children are resilient, even if we aren't. I wasn't spirited away in the middle of the night when war came to Marino in my childhood, but I felt as if I'd been ripped from my family...and I recovered. At least your children have you with them. You are more important to them than whether the walls encompassing them are familiar. *You* are their walls."

She smiled weakly. "Thank you, Vittoria. I'd forgotten that you were only a child when you were sent to Ischia. We led such a charmed life there, didn't we? Untouched by the never-healed wounds of these clan wars. How many centuries have these families been at each other's throats? I will never comprehend it."

No, I didn't think she would. Not in the way I had, fiercely loyal to my father, hating his enemies and what they had done to my childhood. But I was no longer a child, and now I saw only futility and emptiness in the fighting between these bitter rivals. I saw nothing noble, as I believed Ferrante's war against the French had been.

Fabrizio, my father's namesake, finally quieted as I paced the floor with him, and Giovanna cast me a grateful glance.

By midmorning the beds were made, the children were fed and fires were dispelling the late-September chill from the stone walls of Marino. The nurse took the children, and both Giovanna and I retreated to our rooms and slept.

It was two days before I saw my brother again. I woke in the middle of the night to a commotion in the great hall. Fearing the worst, I threw on a cloak to investigate. I listened from the landing and realized that the voices I heard were those of Ascanio and his men calling for food and wine. I had no desire to descend into their raucous company and retreated to my room. Like Giovanna and her children, my life had been disrupted, too. Marino, despite its familiarity as my childhood home, was a far cry from the convent of San Silvestro.

When I rose the next morning, Ascanio was at the table, his wrist bandaged and a bruise spreading purple and blue across his forehead.

"Have you and Pompeo already engaged the pope's men?" I asked.

"Engaged and prevailed. In just two days, we sacked the Vatican and burned everything within the Burgo. The pope is in hiding, furiously issuing decrees against us, but those are only words."

"Do you not expect retaliation?"

"Of course, but we are ready. Don't worry, you're safe here. I wouldn't have brought you, Giovanna and the children if I thought otherwise."

"When and how does it end, Ascanio?"

"When they admit defeat."

"When have they *ever* admitted defeat? Your infant son and his sons and grandsons will still be fighting, just as our father and grandfather before you."

Whoever was pope would be as fierce and proud as the Colonna, with no intention of surrendering.

I endured the chaos and uncertainty for a few months, but only to comfort Giovanna. By January, I had to admit to myself that my concern for my sister-in-law was not enough to keep me at Marino. I longed for the peace I'd found in San Silvestro, but that retreat was no longer open to me. I would have put the convent at risk if I'd returned, to say nothing of my own safety.

It was a dark time—for Italy and for my soul.

I traveled south with only a servant and a handful of Ascanio's men. We pressed on to the coast and sailed for Ischia as soon as we had a day of calm seas.

"Welcome home, my dearest!" Costanza greeted me when we landed. "You do know that this will always be your home, don't you? I worried that your retreat to the convent and then to your brother's fortress signaled that you no longer felt welcome here."

Costanza had aged in the year and a half since I'd last seen her at Ferrante's funeral. But it was more than her 65 years that had caused the deep lines and dark shadows that encircled her eyes—eyes that had seen and assessed the world with such piercing clarity in all the time I'd known her. Ferrante's death had taken its toll on her as well as me. I embraced her.

"Of course I know I'm welcome here! I will never abandon you, Tia. It was only the agony of memory that kept me away."

"I suspected as much. Come, we have a great deal to tell each other, as well as comfort to offer. I have missed you so!" She squeezed my hand as we climbed to her studiolo.

As it always had, the room reflected her engagement with the worlds of both the court and the arts. A painting by Titian, so recent it hadn't yet been hung, stood propped against the wall above a chest. Letters—from Pope Clement, from the Neapolitan viceroy—lay open on her desk, joined by unfinished replies in her own hand. She had a secretary, but I knew that some missives she considered too sensitive even for that trusted scribe. "I find I think better when I write," she'd told me once, and I'd followed her practice.

A book, closed but marked with a thin strip of embossed leather, lay on a table near the fire, which was where she drew me. The winter chill had permeated my weary bones on the crossing from Napoli, and I was grateful for the warmth.

"Alfonso is here. He arrived a few days ago," she said, handing me a cup of wine. "I thought that would cheer you."

I smiled and nodded. "He wrote me about his plan, but didn't know when he'd be able to leave the field. I have missed him more than I could have fathomed."

"He has news. He wouldn't reveal it, said he was waiting for you. I suspect it has something to do with Maria. They assume they're unobserved, but only a blind man could miss what passes between them. They remind me of you and Ferrante."

Flinching at the memory, I forced myself to push away the heartache. If I was to have any peace at all on Ischia, I could not react to every mention of my marriage.

"It's not surprising, given how they were raised and educated together," I managed to respond. Silently, I hoped their union would be happier than ours.

"Try not to look so stricken when he tells you, Vittoria. I know it can be a challenge when you're still in mourning, but he is your son. Don't deny him his joy because of your sorrow."

"I *am* happy for him, Tia. I cannot imagine a better match for either of them, and will bestow my blessing without hesitation. I am still learning this widowhood role. Forgive me if I burden you. The complications of the last several months, with the Colonna at war with Clement, have robbed me of the emotional strength I was able to muster in the peace of San Silvestro. I feel depleted and angry."

"Oh, my dear, I didn't mean my words as a rebuke, only as advice. I do not want you to lose Alfonso, that's all."

Later that evening I followed Costanza's counsel and expressed both my approval and my happiness when Alfonso revealed his intention of requesting the hand of Maria d'Aragona from her father.

We laughed in reminiscence of their childhood squabbles, of Maria's vibrant imagination and spirit, and Alfonso's logical defenses.

"Do you anticipate any objections, any obstacles in our way? Her parents haven't betrothed her to someone else while I've been at war, have they?"

My earnest boy, halfway to his heart's desire with my blessing, was suddenly stricken with doubt that it might elude him.

"Not that I am aware," Costanza assured him. "And surely the duke and Castellana would have discussed it with Maria if they were considering another offer. As members of my court all these years, they're certainly aware that they need to include her."

Indeed, Maria's parents were as pleased as Costanza and I, and plans for their marriage moved quickly, given the state of unrest and Alfonso's obligations as a commander in the imperial forces. They married in March, as soon as the banns had been announced on three consecutive Sundays in the cathedral, and enjoyed two brief months as husband and wife before the darkness descended upon us at the beginning of May.

Our peaceful isle was shattered with the influx of the survivors from the ravaged city of Rome, sacked by imperial troops under the leadership of the Duke of Bourbon. Unpaid for months, starving and driven by the frenzy of the mob, the soldiers rampaged through the city unchecked by lesser officers who were unable to take command when Bourbon was killed.

Giovanna was among the first to reach us. Clutching her children, she collapsed in our arms in defeat.

"Once again, we were driven from our home in the middle of the night, racing ahead of our own allies. News followed us on the road south. Thousands are dead. The Tiber is choked with bodies. Ascanio and your cousin

Cardinal Pompeo have ridden into the city to take advantage of the chaos for their own ends."

She spat out the words, her horror and anger unconcealed.

"I cannot do this anymore, Vittoria. I am pregnant again. How many times can I gather my children from their beds and carry them to safety? Ascanio said Marino was safe, but I don't expect it will be spared. How can we even be sure we'll be protected here on Ischia? Word on the ship was that the French fleet was heading south."

We gave her wine, tried to calm her agitation. She could not stop talking, describing a catastrophe so unimaginable that I feared for her sanity. When she'd drained herself of her rage, Castellana and I put her to bed like a child.

"Even escaping Napoli a quarter-century ago, when we left with only the clothes on our backs, does not compare to what my daughter has endured. I have never been so afraid, not just for the lives of my children and grandchildren, but for the world itself." Castellana paced the floor. What we had heard from Giovanna's lips was incomprehensible.

As the days brought more refugees, their stories confirmed and expanded the horror of the sack of Rome. Costanza and I spent our waking hours opening long-empty rooms in the citadel to accommodate them, organizing the kitchen to feed them, sending to Napoli for physicians to treat them, finding the funds to restore some dignity to their destroyed lives.

At night, I retreated, exhausted, to my own quarters and knelt on the stone floor for hours, imploring God, questioning God.

"What do you want from me, that you might heal the horrific wound that has been inflicted on my city, my people?"

I didn't hear an answer.

CHAPTER THIRTY-FOUR

Visit from a Friend

Paolo Giovio
1527
Rome

Paolo Giovio—physician, historian and companion to Pope Clement—had been at the pope's side the morning of the catastrophe that descended upon Rome. The imperial troops, unpaid for months, starving and misled by unfulfilled promises, defied the truce the misguided pope thought he had secured. Paolo had dragged the pope to safety through the Passetto, the raised passageway that connected the Vatican to the fortress of the Castel Sant'Angelo, only minutes before the raging soldiers stormed the pope's residence. Nearly a thousand refugees from the Vatican had sought protection in the Castel, expecting to be saved by their allies within a few days. But the rescue never came. Without deliverance, the pope remained under siege for months, a prisoner of his rivals, Pompeo and Ascanio Colonna, who had taken advantage of the chaos. Paolo remained at the Castel until the Spanish troops guarding the pope ordered Paolo to leave, denying Pope Clement the solace, intelligence and judgment Paolo had sought to provide to the despairing pontiff.

He was preparing to return to his brother's home in Como when a letter arrived from the Marchesa di Pescara.

"I am reminded of how kind you were to me, a young wife desperate for news of her husband on the battlefield. Your loyalty to the marchese and your stories recounting his bravery meant a great deal to me. When I learned of your ordeal at Castel Sant'Angelo, my heart broke. I entreat you to take refuge with us in the safety of Ischia."

He put the letter away, took up his pen and replied to the marchesa that he was on his way, for in his mind, he already was.

When he arrived at Ischia a few weeks later, two of the marchesa's men met him at the wharf with a horse, and he followed them through the mountain and the crowded borgos, past the cathedral and the lesser churches, up beyond the vineyards and the orchards to the gates of the citadel.

No one was waiting to greet him in the deserted courtyard. A groomsman took his horse and the guards escorted him inside, where only the chamberlain waited.

"Signor Giovio, my lady offers you her warmest welcome, but begs your forbearance because she is not here to greet you. She has set aside quarters for you and asks that you consider them your home for as long as you wish to abide on Ischia. You are most welcome to explore the citadel and gardens until dinner this evening. Lady Pescara has been in seclusion since the death of her husband, but she will join you, the other guests and members of the court for dinner. If there is anything you require, I am at your disposal."

Paolo followed him through the citadel to his rooms. As the chamberlain opened the door a swath of brilliant sunlight spilled into the dim corridor. He blinked, his vision momentarily stunned by the brightness of the light. As his eyes adjusted, they took in his surroundings. Across from the door was the source of the light, an immense arched window overlooking the sea. Paolo moved toward it as if pulled by a siren call. The window was open and he gulped in the sea air, the sapphire blue of the Tyrrhenian Sea, the shriek of a bird of prey diving from above the parapets.

He turned to the room itself. A large writing table stood perpendicular to the window, positioned to make use of the abundant light, although a sturdy lantern had been placed at the ready.

"Lady Pescara didn't know your preference for the hours when you write and thought it best to be prepared for both an early riser and a night owl."

The furnishings in the rest of the room—carpet, tapestries, chests, a finely carved bed hung with damask—bespoke an attention to his every comfort. As if the marchesa was whispering to him, *I am here in the choices I have made for you. I hope you are happy with them.*

"Please tell Lady Pescara that I am most grateful for the comfort she has provided for me. No, I am more than grateful. I am humbled."

The chamberlain nodded and withdrew.

Paolo removed his outer clothing, stripped off his boots and threw himself onto the bed, his head sinking into a pillow that sighed and released the fragrance of lavender. He reveled in the comfort, but was sharply reminded of the contrast to his surroundings only a few weeks before at the Castel Sant'Angelo. Weary not just from his journey but from his months of captivity, he drifted off to sleep.

Several hours later, he was following a servant who had come to announce dinner, although he scarcely needed a guide. He had only to use his ears, like a stag in the forest, to locate the source of a din rising and falling in a rhythm of greeting.

"Are there many guests in the citadel?" he inquired.

The servant answered, "Since the terrible events in Rome, Principessa Costanza and Lady Pescara have opened their home to many lost souls like you, Dottore. If you know them, you surely recognize that there is no limit to their hospitality." With a flourish of his hand and a slight bow, he directed Paolo to a salon bathed in the amber light of the setting sun pouring through tall windows that were open to the sea.

A few eyes directed their gaze to him as he entered the room, but most people were deeply engrossed in conversation. Many, like him, bore the ravaged signs of the past three months: bodies gaunt from near-starvation, eyes darkened from the sleeplessness brought on by nightmares, skin sallow from the lack of sunlight in whatever cellar they had hidden or been held prisoner. He recognized no one, until a young man with military bearing crossed the room, hand extended.

"Paolo, my friend, welcome! My mother told me you were expected."

"Alfonso! I didn't expect to see you. I thought you were in the field."

Alfonso del Vasto shrugged but, like the soldier he was, made no answer to explain his presence on the island. Paolo stored away the knowledge. It meant that the troops del Vasto commanded could not be far.

"Come, let us find my mother. I know she has eagerly awaited your arrival." Alfonso handed him a goblet of wine and led him across the crowded room.

Vittoria Colonna stood surrounded by a small group of men. Her attention was focused on the oldest, who was speaking fervently. Paolo hardly recognized her. It had been several years since he'd seen her, true, but the transformation in her appearance shocked him. She might have been one of the refugees from Rome, she was so emaciated. And although she gave the elderly speaker her undivided gaze, her eyes no longer flashed with the curiosity and vibrancy that had so captivated him and others many years ago in Rome. How long had it been since the death of her husband? Almost two years. Most women widowed at Vittoria's age would already have another husband warming their beds.

"Vittoria, look who I found on the other side of the room." Alfonso's enthusiasm caused everyone in Vittoria's circle to turn their heads.

"Oh, Dottore Giovio! Welcome, welcome. It gives me great comfort to know you are safe at last on our shore."

He bent over her extended hand and took it in his own long enough to detect how cold it was, how rough and dry the skin. He released it and rose to face her. Now was not the time to question her about her health, in front of guests. But he resolved to speak with her privately. She had invited him to take refuge with her as a historian, not as a physician, but he could put aside neither his concern for her nor his ability to help her if he could.

The opportunity arrived more quickly than he had hoped. She came to his quarters the next day.

He jumped to his feet when she glided into the room.

"My lady, you honor me with your visit!"

"Nonsense, Dottore Giovio. It is you who honor me by accepting my invitation. I learned of your plight through my brother, who accompanied our cousin Cardinal Colonna in his negotiations with the Holy Father. You continue to be a witness to Italy's history, Dottore, although I fear that the price you pay for your proximity to momentous events may often be excessive."

"I didn't suffer as so many did. While conditions in the Castel Sant'Angelo were deplorable, they were not unbearable, except perhaps the constant squabbling of the bishops."

"Nevertheless, I'm glad you are here and not there."

"As am I, my lady. I would not have left the Holy Father if I hadn't been ordered to by our captors. But I'm grateful that I was finally free and able to accept your most gracious invitation."

"I trust that you are comfortable and have everything you need?"

"Of course! More than enough."

"I wonder if I might impose upon you so soon in your stay, but I find I have lost my ability to be patient and circumspect since the advent of so many catastrophes—not only in Italy's life but in my own."

"Please, my lady. I am eager to learn of your need for me—whatever it is!" He hoped she might take this opportunity to speak not of some history she wished to commission but of her troubling physical condition. But that was not to be.

"My husband's life, Dottore Giovio. He must not be forgotten, must not be lost to obscurity. After only two years, I fear that he has already disappeared, his bravery overshadowed by the latest crisis. I cannot allow his accomplishments, all that he sacrificed for Italy, to recede from memory. I *will* not allow it."

Her emotional distress was palpable, magnified by the extremity of her physical state. But she recovered her composure and her tone shifted.

"I have spent many hours in contemplation, searching for a solution to my dilemma, Dottore, and have devised a plan—a partnership. I extend an invitation to you. I am a poet. You are a historian. Each of us brings a specific talent and unique knowledge of my husband to the telling of his story. Alone, my poems might be dismissed as the sweet illusions of a lonely widow. Coupled with the authority of your historical account of his life, I believe that together we can resurrect his memory."

"Your love for your husband is obvious, my lady. With your intimate knowledge of his life and my own experience of his actions on the battlefield, I am confident we can create a noble record of his life."

"I share your confidence, Dottore Giovio. It's why I knew you would be the only one to whom I could entrust this endeavor. I will be frank with you. My husband was an imperfect man. In his final days, especially, he gave others the opportunity to malign his reputation and to cloud, if not obliterate, his earlier glory. I do not want the shadow that hovered over him after his victory at Pavia to define him."

"I have learned in my observation of the human condition, both as a historian and a physician, that we are complex creatures who cannot be painted in one stroke of the brush or described by a single act."

His words appeared to calm the marchesa or at least bring a moment of respite to her agitation. Her face softened into a smile and he saw a glimmer of her former beauty and vivaciousness.

"The more you speak, Dottore Giovio, the more you confirm that I made the right choice in asking you to take on this task. I am not looking for a sycophant to write the myth of a man who didn't exist. To approach his life without acknowledging his weaknesses would only give the world a reason to dismiss your words as false, written to please your wealthy patron. I simply ask you to take care in how you depict him. I know he had reasons for whatever decisions he made. If you can, find out what they were. Present him in all his complexity."

"That I will do, my lady, as it corresponds to my own belief in the power of history. We cannot draw a veil across our errors if generations after us are to learn from them."

"Then we understand each other. I shall make myself available to you two afternoons a week for interviews and discussion. Beyond that, I shall not be hosting salons and only rarely will I join guests for dinner. If I had my preference, I would still be at the convent of San Silvestro. But since that's not possible, I am attempting to recreate my solitude here. Please do not take my withdrawal personally in any way. You are welcome to all that Ischia offers. Enjoy the company of your fellow guests, wander the gardens, hunt, fish, partake of the evening entertainments for which our court here is well-known. And write!" She said those last words with a smile that reminded Paolo of the young marchesa.

He bowed. "With pleasure, my lady. I am eager to begin this adventure."

She turned to leave him and he watched her stately progress as she retreated. She seemed to him a woman on a mission, like a soldier girded for battle.

He knew enough of Ferrante d'Avalos to question her fierce loyalty to him. Vittoria Colonna was not a naïf, sheltered from the world of men. She was an astute observer, curious, brilliant. In Paolo's estimation, her intention to restore her husband's damaged reputation bordered on obsession. It was not unusual, of course, for the widow of a famous—or infamous—man to secure a paean to honor him as a hero. But it troubled Paolo that Vittoria was going to such calculated efforts to protect the honor of a man who had more than likely betrayed both her and the empire.

Perhaps it was to protect her own honor. And he admitted to himself that he was quite willing to help her do that.

His sojourn on Ischia lasted longer than he'd expected. Rome was both uninhabitable and without work for him, and nothing else beckoned with such compelling force as his relationship with the marchesa.

Despite the limits she'd set on their interactions, the time she *did* spend with him was deeply satisfying. She was his equal in both intellect and learning, offering examples from ancient Rome to which her husband might be compared and grasping the realities of Italy's precarious position between France and Spain. Their intellectual equality led to a friendship that allowed them to loosen the formalities that had governed their earlier relationship.

"You are remarkably knowledgeable, Vittoria."

"You mean, for a woman," she teased him.

He blushed and stammered. "On the contrary. I know many men who either do not grasp the complexity of our time or choose to ignore it, charging ahead into action without a thought as to how what's gone before might guide them."

"You are ever the historian, Paolo, justifying the importance of your profession! No, no, don't be embarrassed. I agree with you! And I owe much of my understanding to a young physician who came to Rome many years ago and agreed to be my eyes and ears at those times and in those places I couldn't go. I am indebted to you, Paolo. How can I repay you for this education?"

She had stopped her teasing and regarded him with seriousness.

He was about to tell her that she'd already repaid him, not only with this commission for her husband's biography but also with her friendship. Then he stopped and, emboldened by her question, plunged ahead with the concern that had gnawed at him since his arrival at the Castello.

"You can allow me to be not just your historian, but your physician."

Her head jerked up and he saw that her expression had become impenetrable. Guarded.

"I have no need of a physician."

"Then let me speak as a friend. You are not the same woman I last saw in Rome…"

"Indeed I am not. I'm a widow now, not a young bride on the cusp of life. My life is over."

"I do not believe that! Yes, a husband's death exacts its toll on the wife left behind, especially when the bond between them was intense."

"As mine was," she interrupted. She didn't say, "As *ours* was."

"But in my practice of medicine, I have not seen a case as extreme as yours."

"There is always a first time. Consider me a precedent, an example of the ravages of mourning."

"Let me help you. Let me prescribe a medication to ease your suffering."

"I do not wish to be relieved of my suffering. It fuels my poetry, and my poems are my medication."

Rebuffed by her adamant refusal, he acquiesced. He could not force her to accept his assistance.

"You assuage my pain more with Ferrante's biography than with tonics and potions." She stretched out her hand

and squeezed his. "You cannot cure my despair, but you can heal the wound of my husband's lost honor. And that is worth more to me than any relief you might provide to my body. It is only a body. Like Ferrante's, it will one day be no more than a handful of dust."

He sought another pathway to reach the woman behind the mask that had closed her off during this conversation.

"Will you share your poems with me? They will certainly enlighten me about aspects of your husband's life as I seek to portray him."

He didn't add that they would reveal more of her than her husband. She agreed, and the next day brought several sheets, some still in draft form but others completed in her elegant hand.

What he read astonished him on many levels. The depth of her love for her husband was no surprise, given the suffering his death had caused her. But the form of her poetry and the language she had chosen were unknown to him in the poetry of women. The day before she had described her physical state as unprecedented. But it was her poetry that he found unparalleled. No woman had seized Petrarch's mode as she had; no woman had described her lover and his effect on her as Vittoria Colonna had created Ferrante d'Avalos on the page.

He was in awe of the power she wielded with language, fascinated by her ability to transform a man Paolo knew and didn't love into a hero to be celebrated. She had earlier spoken to him about resurrecting her husband's reputation. But she'd done more than resurrect him with her words. She had breathed life into a decaying corpse and presented to the world not only a man restored to life but a god. And Paolo believed her.

In reading the poems, he began to sense what had depleted her physically. All her energy and all her strength were being poured into shaping this idealized image of her husband, as if she were wresting control of Ferrante's story from some demon. It occurred to Paolo that the demon was Ferrante himself—or rather, Vittoria's experience of Ferrante in life.

Paolo didn't know if he would ever be willing to pay the price Vittoria was demanding of herself. She had worried over him when he'd first arrived, troubled that he placed himself too often in harm's way in order to be the witness to history. But no battle he had ever experienced, not even the Sack, had demanded of him what Vittoria's poetry exacted from her.

He acknowledged that there was nothing he could offer her to quell the grief, since it was the grief that fed the brilliance he held in his hands. He could only hope that she would complete this masterpiece before it drove her mad. But he could ensure that the world would know of it. That was something she couldn't do for herself. She had shown him that she could overcome creative barriers no one had expected a woman to topple. But for her to take any steps to distribute her words publicly would dishonor her in the world in which they moved. And Paolo knew that honor to Vittoria was second only to her love for her husband. He also knew that Vittoria had not written her poems for herself alone, as a personal meditation. She had written them for the world to read.

CHAPTER THIRTY-FIVE

A Promise Fulfilled

Paolo Giovio
1529
Bologna

It was two years before Paolo could fulfill the promise he'd made to himself to bring Vittoria's poetry to the world.

He was summoned to the pope's bedside when Pope Clement fell critically ill. Paolo moved through the chamber crowded with physicians, courtiers and cardinals expecting to be called to a conclave within days. The air was thick with incense, unguents and the oil for the anointing of Last Rites. The low murmur of prayers and gossip was occasionally punctuated by the Holy Father's rasping cough.

Clement beckoned for Paolo with a bony finger. "I have need of you, Paolo. Because I am dying, the Sacred College has agreed to my wish to make Ippolito a cardinal."

Ippolito de' Medici was Clement's young cousin, an illegitimate nephew Pope Leo had brought to the Vatican when he was three years old to educate him and prepare him for a life in the church.

"He is young, only eighteen. Despite being raised here, he'll either be eaten alive by the vipers after my death or follow Leo's footsteps into a life of profligacy and excess. I need to protect him and the Medici family's name, as well. I want you at his side. He needs an adviser I can trust."

"Of course, Your Holiness. It will be my honor to serve you in this role."

"It is Ippolito and the Medicis you will serve."

Paolo withdrew quietly, found Ippolito and presented himself.

"The Holy Father told me to expect you. I didn't want to be a cardinal, you know. He tapped my cousin Alessandro, as illegitimate as I am, to lead Florence when the Medicis regain control from the Republic. Why not me? I'll tell you why. Because Alessandro is his own son, his favorite. The family, and especially the Holy Father, have kept that hidden."

"You should, too, Eminence." And thus began Paolo's role as adviser to the headstrong, frustrated and entirely imprudent young cardinal.

A few days later, word began to spread through the corridors and chapels of the Vatican. "The Holy Father is up, asking for wine and beef, and wants to see his secretary of state. He announced that he is not ready to die, after all."

His recovery precipitated his willingness to make peace with Charles V—not so much for the benefit of the Church as for the Medici. The citizens of his native city of Florence had taken advantage of the pope's powerlessness and imprisonment after the Sack of Rome two years earlier to expel the Medici and reestablish the Republic. It had driven Clement to despair and made him willing to negotiate and reconcile with the emperor in order to regain control of Florence. He wanted Florence back for his family, and Charles V was the only one who could give it to him.

A treaty was signed at Barcelona in June, and Clement announced a congress to be held in Bologna, during which he agreed finally to crown Charles as Holy Roman Emperor., ten years after his election to the post.

Ippolito called for Paolo immediately. "Paolo, we are to travel to Genoa to welcome the emperor to Italy. My illustrious cousin has named me a legate. As I'm sure you realize, he doesn't want me to undo whatever deal he's made for Florence, so you are to be my right hand."

Managing Ippolito was no small task during the months between Charles's arrival on Italian soil in August and his coronation at the end of February. The emperor and the pope took up residence in adjoining apartments in the Palazzo Pubblico and continued to work out the details of their agreement. Half of Europe's clerics and nobility descended on the city to witness the historic reconciliation between the papal throne and the empire. While they waited, they amused themselves with a constant stream of entertainments. Ippolito embraced every opportunity. Each fête was more extravagant than the one preceding it, and Ippolito attended them all.

"We have been invited by Isabella d'Este at the Palazzo Manzoli on Tuesday, and the following day there is a poetry recitation at the Academia. Pietro Bembo has arrived in town, have you heard? The clarion call seems to have gone out to every poet, artist and philosopher in all of Europe. It's like being back in Rome when my Uncle Giovanni was pope— the music, the plays, the parties!" Ippolito practically danced with glee.

Paolo couldn't fault him for his excitement. He, too, felt the energy with which the city was vibrating, and to find himself in the midst of it was an extraordinary gift for a historian. It was more than a civic moment he was witnessing, although this meeting of pope and emperor was unprecedented in its importance not only to Italy but all of Christendom. It was also a cultural moment, exploding like fireworks over every palazzo in the city.

Something was *happening*, and he, Paolo Giovio, was in Bologna to sear it into his brain and recreate it on the page. The words of his history were forming almost as he heard them proclaimed or whispered; the descriptions were taking shape in his memory as the plays unfolded before rapt audiences and the triumphal arches were constructed for the coronation procession.

After the deprivations at the Castel Sant'Angelo only two years before, he smiled to himself at his own good fortune. Ippolito was carousing in the wine and song and elegant women filling his evenings; Paolo was reveling in the anticipation of renown and prosperity with which he would be rewarded after weaving his experience of Bologna into a historical account for the ages. He almost wanted to dance himself.

But one afternoon as he was searching for a misplaced document, he came across a sheaf of papers carefully stored in a leather portfolio at the bottom of his writing chest. A brief shiver of guilt passed through him. The papers contained the poems Vittoria had given him during his sojourn on Ischia.

He realized that Bologna would be a perfect opportunity for Vittoria, with every poet of any importance gathering here. Pietro Bembo had even suggested the other night that the literary world ought to hold its own congress while the politicians worked out their treaties, since so many writers were in the city. Paolo decided to write her at once to urge her to come.

"As the widow of the hero of Pavia, the fifth anniversary of which has been set as the date of the coronation, you are the symbol of the new order about to be inaugurated. A Roman united by your marriage to the house of d'Avalos, you represent the unity we have all longed for. Please come and be welcomed by a city who will revere you!"

The very night he sent the letter, he found himself seated at dinner next to Alfonso del Vasto.

"Alfonso! I had no idea you were here! Had I been aware, I would already have invited you to one of Cardinal Ippolito's evenings."

"Thank you, my friend. But I've only just arrived and I won't be staying more than a few days. The pope and the emperor have work for me to do." The last sentence was uttered *sota voce*.

Paolo had been with Pope Clement long enough to know the "work" involved the retaking of Florence. He nodded to acknowledge that he understood.

"I am so glad to see you and perhaps take this opportunity to enlist your help," he said.

"For you, Paolo, anything. Or *almost* anything."

"It involves your mother. I have written to Vittoria today, entreating her to come to Bologna. As a poet as well as a military man, surely you've sensed that the coronation is more than a civic celebration."

Alfonso laughed. "I can't walk into any palazzo or across the Piazza Maggiore without tripping over at least three poets." His tone shifted. "Paolo, to be serious, even our combined voices could not persuade Vittoria to rise from her knees and journey here. She insists that she's still in mourning, despite every argument, every enticement my aunt, my wife and I have laid in front of her. To my profound dismay, our attempts have all been futile."

"I feared as much. When I left Ischia I'd hoped that time would ease her sorrow, or in some way smooth its edges. I share your dismay."

Vittoria confirmed Alfonso's prediction with a letter to Paolo thanking him for his invitation and asking him to convey her greetings to His Holiness, His Imperial Majesty and all her friends gathering in the city.

Vittoria's refusal to come to Bologna intensified Paolo's guilt that he'd been unable to rescue her from despair. That was what had caused him such discomfort the day he'd discovered her poems, packed away and abandoned as he pursued his own ends in the heady, intoxicating air of a celebrating Bologna. He was determined not to abandon them again.

His opportunity to redeem himself and fulfill the vow he'd made on Ischia came quickly and almost effortlessly. The pace of entertaining was reaching a frenetic tempo as the date of the coronation approached. The teeming streets of the city reflected the exuberant mood that reverberated within the walls of every palazzo and villa. Alfonso del Vasto was hosting one final extravagant party before he left on his military mission. When Paolo and Cardinal Ippolito arrived, they were struck by the profuse bounty that greeted them—copious amounts of wine, platters piled with roasted meats, confections of spun sugar constructed in the form of the emperor's coat of arms—the double-headed eagle between the Pillars of Hercules, around which the words of his motto, "Plus Ultra," had been inscribed in almond paste.

"There's no one more entitled than del Vasto to celebrate Charles's ascendancy and triumph," murmured Ippolito as they surveyed the excess arrayed in front of them.

Paolo took it all in, swallowing with his eyes what he would later enjoy as a repast, and then moved on, a goblet of Venetian glass filled with Castilian wine in his hand.

Pietro Bembo saw him first and moved toward him.

"Paolo Giovio, one of the most essential men in Bologna! Without your eyes as witness and your hand as scribe, the events that are upon us would be lost to faulty memory. I don't know of anyone else who could capture these momentous days better than you."

Paolo bowed, his pleasure in Bembo's greeting spreading across his face. "You honor me, Signor Bembo, but my humble prose cannot compare to the images you paint with your poems."

"We are the servants of our muses, my friend. Come, tell me what you've seen and learned in the company of the young cardinal."

The two retreated to a quiet alcove to escape the tumult of the circulating guests. They shared tidbits from their separate experiences in the city, and then Bembo brought up his idea of a literary congress again.

"With so many of us in the city, it seems the time is ripe for a long-overdue discussion about adopting rules for our native tongue. You know how critical I believe it is for us to elevate Italian as the language of our literature."

Bembo's passion for Italian was well known. It had become his life's work, the cause with which he was most identified—and, at times, he was vilified because of it. Paolo saw an opening and leapt through it, not knowing what he might find on the other side.

"Signor Bembo, I am in possession of something that may help further your cause—a collection of poems written in an Italian so lyrical and powerful that I believe it will silence any critics who hold tenaciously to the supremacy of Latin. Do you know of Vittoria Colonna, the Marchesa di Pescara and widow of Ferrante d'Avalos, the hero of Pavia?" He omitted no part of Vittoria's identity and titles, hoping to find some recognition by Bembo of who she was.

"Of course I know of her. We met in Rome when she was a young woman and had an audience with Pope Leo. She was a budding poet then, with a nascent talent I found intriguing. But I've heard nothing of her for many years. Is it her poems of which you speak?"

"It is. May I recommend them to you and ask for your learned opinion? I'm no poet myself, and my reading of her work may be limited. I would be honored if you'd consider reading them."

"I'd be most interested in seeing the poems, signor. Do you have them here in Bologna?"

"I do. If you will give me a few days to have them copied, I'll send them to you."

The two men bowed to each other in agreement as Alfonso del Vasto approached them in hearty welcome and pulled them back into his festivities.

Once Pietro Bembo had received the poems, Paolo didn't have long to wait before the reaction he hoped for began to surface. At first, it was a note of thanks from Bembo—complimentary of Vittoria's style, although without effusive praise. As Paolo anticipated, however, Bembo didn't keep the poems to himself but introduced them at various salons and even had more copies transcribed as curiosity was piqued among the throngs of literati. Paolo didn't care that Bembo seemed to be taking credit for "discovering" Vittoria as word began to spread. He realized in retrospect that it was better that Vittoria was far from Bologna as her poems circulated. Her absence protected her from any embarrassment the attention might have caused her and also allowed the poems to be discussed freely throughout the city, passing from hand to hand, lips to ears. Her seclusion and virtual disappearance from the social interaction that was the lifeblood of the court only seemed to enhance everyone's desire to possess the poetry of the elusive marchesa.

On the day of the coronation, Paolo woke free of the burden of his promise regarding Vittoria's poems. He had kept his vow, the vow he'd made to himself two years earlier. The visitors who'd converged on Bologna to witness the crowning of an emperor would bring back to their homes not just the resplendent images of Pope Clement and Charles V in procession through the city, or the glint of gold in the sunlight as Clement placed the crown on Charles's head. They would also bring Vittoria's poetry.

1537 – 1547

CHAPTER THIRTY-SIX

Pilgrim

Vittoria
1537 – 1538
Ferrara

If I didn't recognize the character of my life before, by 1537 I cannot deny that I am a wanderer, a pilgrim. I am welcomed wherever I go, sought after, even. But I am always a guest, never home.

When Michelangelo refuses to see me during his long and painful recuperation, my reason for remaining in Rome disperses like the dust carried down from the Alps by the tramontana wind in early morning. My cousin Giulia has returned to Napoli, and I consider following her south when I receive an invitation from Renata di Francia, the Duchessa of Ferrara and wife of Duke Ercole d'Este. Nearly ten years before, I attended her wedding and was among the women who led her to the marriage bed. We have remained close through the years via our correspondence. I am especially fond of her and consider her almost as a daughter—a bright, inquisitive woman who, despite her youth, has established a vibrant court at Ferrara. The artists, poets and philosophers who find a home there reflect the ideals that flourish under Costanza on Ischia. Through our correspondence, Renata and I have discovered a common bond in our hunger to explore the meaning of Scripture.

I welcome her invitation and the opportunity to experience for myself the vitality and intellectual feast that Renata's court has become.

As I have in Rome, however, I choose to reside at a convent in Ferrara rather than at court. I have grown so accustomed to the simplicity and peace of convent life that I am reluctant to become caught up in the display and intrigue of court, even one as refined as Ferrara.

My entourage has grown from my two steadfast servants, Salviata and Nicolo, to include six women—not to hover in service to me personally but to carry on the work I have begun in ministering to the poor and infirm in Rome.

It was Michelangelo's comment to me as I nursed him, comparing me to an Oblate of St. Frances, that inspired me. His words bored into my soul, as powerful as the words of Matthew's Gospel: "I was hungry and you gave me food; I was thirsty and you gave me drink; I was a stranger and you welcome me; naked and you clothed me, sick and you visited me, in prison and you came to see me."

My women and I found ample opportunities to carry out Christ's message in Rome, and I do not doubt that as time unfolds, Ferrara will reveal to us its own needs.

We arrive at the Dominican Convent of Santa Caterina at the beginning of April after a wet, cold journey over muddy roads. Our little party is bedraggled and tired as we enter the massive walls of the convent. Despite our efforts to be humble and undemanding, we are human, after all, strangers here, and uncertain of the form of hospitality or even the spiritual climate at the convent.

As we wait for the convent's gatekeeper to announce us to the Mother Superior, the exhaustion and tension of the journey surface. The convent is much larger than our familiar San Silvestro, and its vastness is overwhelming to our close-knit group.

I try to reassure them, weary as I am and as uncertain as they are as to how well our little band will fit in. We are an unusual group, women who seek refuge from the world as widows unwilling to enter into another marriage or second daughters destined for the convent but not yet ready to take vows. They entrusted themselves to me, or were entrusted by their fathers. Our common bonds are our belief in the message of Bernardino Ochino and our dedication to the poor, the hungry, the sick. Unlike the sisters in the convents that house us, we go out into the world.

Fra Bernardino spoke to me of his desire to establish a Capuchin convent in Ferrara, and part of the reason for my visit is to request permission for him from the duke. But for now, we are the guests of Santa Caterina.

We wait for quite some time before the gatekeeper returns, not with the Mother Superior but with the suora who oversees the guest quarters.

"In the name of Santa Caterina, I welcome you. Come follow me, but without your chattering. The convent is observing silence in preparation for Holy Week."

She leads us from the visitors' reception room through a locked set of doors and into a dim corridor, the keys at her waist jangling in the hushed surroundings.

Our group exchanges uneasy glances. A simple explanation may be that this suora has a personality not given to effusive warmth and that she's not reflective of the convent's character. But it seems odd to me that someone like her has been assigned responsibility for the convent's guests.

She stops to unlock each door in the corridor we have been assigned and flings them open without ceremony.

"There are so many of you. I leave it to Lady Pescara to decide who shall sleep where. Vespers begins in the chapel within the hour. You'll find it to the left at the end of the cloister. If you have any needs, you may place a note for me in the basket at the door of the chapel."

She departs without introducing herself. Everyone clusters around me, exhaustion now exacerbated by the lack of sympathy.

"Come, let us not stand here in the damp and dark. We can unpack, change into warm clothes and be ready to offer our prayers of thanksgiving for a safe journey and a roof over our heads."

I move from room to room, directing each woman to a space, taking the last for myself. The quarters are spare and austere. A bed, a small table and chair, high windows that offer only a glimpse of sky and treetops. The linens are rough; the candles of tallow, not beeswax. But the straw in the mattresses is fresh and the rooms have been well-scrubbed.

"We have seen worse hovels where we've ministered," I say softly. After each of my charges has retreated to her room, I close my door and lean my forehead against the wood. The simplicity of our surroundings, while lacking the comfort of San Silvestro, nevertheless meets our basic physical needs. It is our spiritual comfort that concerns me. If Santa Caterina is so unwelcoming to its guests, I wonder how open it is to the new ideas rippling through the Church. I thought that under Renata's influence, the Ferrara convent would be vibrant with discussion. But if the nuns are forbidden to speak....

I shake away my concern. I resolve to give the convent time to reveal itself. But I caution my women to refrain from taking their Bibles with them when we go to pray. My limited impressions warn me that this is a convent where the nuns are not free to read and interpret Scripture on their own.

Our sense of unease is heightened when we are called to chapel. Although the space has a lavish beauty, with a fresco of the life of Santa Caterina of Sienna decorating the altar wall, the art fails to elicit a call to the spirit. I recall my discussion with Michelangelo on the purpose of religious art and wish I could continue the conversation with him, telling him of my experience in this cold and uninviting space. As the sisters begin their recitation of the Divine Office, I am struck by the lack of any emotion in their voices. In my own practice of seeking God's presence, prayer is many things—questioning, entreaty, unburdening of sorrow, gratitude, release. I hear none of those as I listen. The sisters even have difficulty reciting in unison. Where the litanies of the Office at San Silvestro often transport me with their cadences and lyricism, the prayers at Santa Caterina are disruptive, interfering with my own conversation with God.

I glance around at my companions and read on their faces the same sense of dissonance. I close my eyes to block out my visual surroundings, hoping to spare myself the soulless images towering over us on the wall. I cannot find the rhythm to join in the recitation with the sisters, and withdraw into silent contemplation.

By the time the Divine Office is finished I am exhausted. In other circumstances I might attribute my fatigue to the journey, but I know that it's the effort required to erect a barrier between myself and the discontent and dissension smothering the community in the chapel.

As we file out, the suora who greeted us gestures to me with an age-spotted finger, a rim of dirt lining her fingernail. I approach her.

"Supper is in the refectory. Now. Follow me."

I motion silently to the others, and we trail the suora. Weariness and wariness flicker across all their faces, and I cannot summon within myself answers for their questions or comfort for their disquiet.

The meal is plain, which is no surprise. A bean soup and coarse dark bread, a supper we often eat at San Silvestro. But this is tasteless, almost careless in its preparation. Sustenance but not nourishment. I am not one to pay great attention to food, but since Urbino presented me with his hearty stew after my vigil with Michelangelo, I have gained an appreciation for simple meals that are lovingly prepared. Love is decidedly missing from this soup. It seems to me that so far, the convent has presented me with two examples of people whose talents have been mismatched with their roles—the inhospitable suora responsible for guests and the indifferent cook charged with feeding the community.

We all nibble at our food as we listen to the monotonous reading by a suora at the lectern under a grotesque crucifix.

Like Vespers, the words do not inspire. I shut them out as I push my spoon around in the bowl.

After the meal we retreat to the guest quarters. I know I can't let our unease fester, so I invite everyone into my room. They arrange themselves as best they can in the cramped space—some on the bed, the eldest in the chair, the younger ones on the floor.

"We need our own prayer to start," I say. Nods of agreement and relief greet me. I bow my head and offer a simple petition for a fruitful mission for us and a healing for this troubled convent. Acknowledging what we all sensed in these disturbing first hours helps to dispel the isolation that the silence and disunity cast over us. It is Clara, a widow and quickest among us to form an opinion, who speaks first.

"I knew, before we even entered the house, that something was wrong here. Something evil." She holds herself, arms wrapped tightly against whatever she believes lurks in the dark corners of this vast place.

"Evil is a powerful word." Innocenza, the youngest and closest to my heart, speaks up from the floor, her knees drawn to her chin. She is the daughter of my secretary and agent, Carlo Gualteruzzi, who has entrusted me with her education since her mother died.

"I agree, Innocenza," I assure her. "I do not believe evil is at work here, but silence, in the broadest sense of the word. Something within this house is unspoken, and it has divided the sisters." I look around at them. "That's why I believe it's so important that we find the words—with one another, with God—to express our fears, our hopes, our dissatisfactions and, especially, our joy."

I clasp Clara's hand. "You have a gift, Clara, a perceptive and receptive spirit. But— whatever you discern—let it sit within you a while before you judge it."

I turn to the others. "My expectation is that we cannot repair what has damaged this place, or even discover what secret they're protecting. If they don't speak to one another, they surely won't speak to us. But we can pray for them. And we can band together to create our own place of peace in which we can pray and work. Let us vow that we will not allow the silence of Santa Caterina to infect us with dissension. Are we agreed?"

I wait until each one voices her assent. Then I send them off with a blessing and fall into my narrow bed.

When I am awakened in the middle of the night by muffled weeping, I assume that one of our little group is suffering from a nightmare. I sit up, my sleep-fogged brain suddenly sharp and on alert. I fumble for my shawl in the dark and draw it around my shoulders as I unlatch the heavy wooden door and move into the corridor. The moon is full and suffuses the gallery, which is open to the courtyard, with enough light for me to move from door to door, listening for the sounds of distress that summoned me from my sleep. But all is quiet, except for the snoring of Barbara, the oldest of our group, a steady grandmother who mothers us all. I smile at the familiar, reassuring sound. I'm ready to return to bed, assuming I imagined the weeping in a dream, when I hear it again. It is coming from a distant corner of the convent, well beyond the guest quarters. I hear footsteps and see the bobbing glimmer of a candle passing through the colonnade of an upper gallery. The light is moving in the direction of the mournful sound. Reassured that someone is going to help and recognizing, reluctantly, that it's not my place to rescue the troubled soul, I retreat to my room. But I cannot shake the feeling that the cries I heard are connected to the secret plaguing the sisters of Santa Caterina.

In the morning I detect no sign that anyone else in our group heard the weeping. We pray together in the garden before joining the sisters in the silent refectory for breakfast and then we meet in the visitors' parlor to plan the day.

"I will send word to the duchessa this morning that we have arrived and await her invitation to visit at court. I suggest we occupy ourselves with study and writing today. I will offer our help to the convent in areas where we have skills. We can at least serve their temporal needs in the garden or in the sewing room, if we cannot heal their spiritual wounds."

"Perhaps we can assist in the kitchen?" It is Barbara who speaks, and the others break into grins. We have all eaten Barbara's food, and the memory of its soul-satisfying flavor brightens the mood in the room.

I laugh. "I will certainly propose it!" I wish I can be confident that the Mother Superior will accept, but I doubt she will. It's still Lent, and the pall of a deep and unrelenting penance is layered on top of the secrets hidden within these walls.

I leave my friends to their quiet pursuits and find the gatekeeper at her post.

"Suora, my manservant Nicolo will be stopping by this morning for my instructions. Please ask him to take this letter to the duchessa." Nicolo is staying at a nearby inn. He will come to the convent every day to accompany us when we venture out into the city or to secure what we might need outside the walls.

The suora smiles as she accepts the letter. She reminds me of Suora Carita, the old nun charged with guarding the gate at San Silvestro long ago. Her smile is unexpected, the first sign of warmth since our arrival. She looks around, as if to reassure herself that I am alone, and then she speaks.

"Good morning, my lady. I hope you've found your quarters comfortable. Sometimes we forget Christ's words when we open the gates to travelers." She seems to be referring to her fellow sister, the sour-faced keeper of the guest quarters.

"Thank you for asking, Suora. We do not require much and are quite comfortable." I consider drawing her out with more conversation, but her eyes continue to dart behind me. She is clearly nervous about being discovered breaking the convent's rule of silence. I thank her and leave to seek out the Mother Superior.

Her office is not far from the visitors' parlor, and she bids me enter in a strong voice when I knock. She bows to me in stiff formality.

"My lady, allow me to welcome you and also to apologize for not greeting you when you arrived yesterday. My duties prevented me from receiving you, but I trust that Suora Annunziata provided for your needs."

"Thank you, Madre. We are comfortable. I have come to offer our assistance during our stay. We are gardeners, seamstresses, cooks—whatever you might need to ease the extra work caused by our presence. We will occasionally be spending time away from the convent—in our visits to the court but also in our charitable works."

"Ah, yes, your reputation has preceded you. We at Santa Caterina, of course, serve God within the walls with our prayers."

"There are many ways to serve Our Lord," I acknowledge, although her tone implies that the prayers of the sisters of Santa Caterina far outweigh the value of our ministering to the poor and the sick.

"I shall consider your proposal, my lady. But our sisters consider their work sacred and would not wish to lighten their burdens."

She picks up a document from her desk and nods at me. "If you will excuse me, my lady, I have important work that needs my attention."

I bow in acquiescence and depart, relieved to be out of the oppressive atmosphere that surrounds her like the miasma rising from a putrid swamp. I step from the cloister into the sunlight of the garden. Under straw hats, their sleeves rolled up to their elbows, I see a group of sisters preparing a bed for planting in a far corner of the garden near the outer wall. They hoe vigorously, breaking up clods of dirt that have been hardened by winter frosts. Despite the rigor of the work, they seem far more attuned to one another than they had been at prayer the previous evening. The rain that followed us all the way from Rome has cleared and a warm breeze hints at the spring to come. At my feet, tiny shoots of green are spiking along the path. Flowers, I hope, to brighten the shadowed life that pervades the convent. I do not wish to disturb the sisters during their precious few moments of respite and freedom in the open air.

I return to the cloister, passing the Mother Superior's closed door, and rejoin my group in the parlor.

They all look up expectantly as I enter. I wish I had work to offer them, tasks with meaning and usefulness that can do good for them and for the sisters whose "burdens" the Mother Superior does not wish to relieve. I shake my head and acknowledge their disappointment.

However, we don't have long to wonder about the ever-widening dysfunction of the convent. Suora Ursula, the gatekeeper, sticks her sun-wizened face in the door.

"My lady, your servant has returned with a message from the palazzo." She holds out a cream-colored folded sheet sealed with the d'Este crest.

I thank her and take the letter. She seems reluctant to go, and I gather that the convent does not often receive messages from the palazzo. For the benefit of the entire group, including Suora Ursula, I read the contents of the Duchessa Renata's letter aloud.

"A most gracious welcome to you and your ladies, my dear Vittoria. We are eager to see your face and hear your words and beg you all to join us today for dinner, conversation and a small gathering in your honor. We are graced with the presence of many of the region's most brilliant minds, and they are all eager to make the acquaintance of the illustrious and equally brilliant Marchesa di Pescara." I skip over that effusive description when I read the letter aloud. I am not comfortable with praise and am troubled by the expectations Renata's guests are bringing to their encounter with me. But I can't retreat from the invitation, especially when I see the excitement bubbling over among the women. Even Barbara, solid and without artifice, is beaming. I cannot deny them the pleasure promised by Renata after the cold and ungracious lack of welcome at Santa Caterina.

"Is Nicolo still at the gate, Suora?"

"He is, my lady, awaiting your reply to the duchessa. He has found a bit of shade under the tree across the road and I gave him a cup of wine."

The more I learn of Suora Ursula, the more I like her, and see her as an ally in this inhospitable environment.

"Please tell him to bring our delighted acceptance to Duchessa Renata and then return to the convent to escort us."

"With pleasure, my lady!"

We then disperse to our rooms to dress for our visit and are ready when Nicolo returns. As we depart, Suora Ursula squeezes my hand.

"Have a wonderful visit, my lady. Bring back lots of stories!"

I assure her that I will. Perhaps in exchange for my story, she might be willing to tell me a story of her own about why the convent is so divided. I do not expect to be told the secret, but even an acknowledgment that a secret exists might help ease the sickness with which Santa Caterina is afflicted.

We set out with lightened hearts. The palazzo is not far from the convent, and the walk seems to release the pent-up anxiety of the last twenty-four hours. My companions drink in the sunlit sights that were obscured by the rain when we arrived. Ferrara is a well-planned and elegant city, reflecting the erudite passion of the d'Este family. The current duke's grandfather was a great lover of the arts, and that is evident in the broad avenues and well-designed buildings.

Renata is waiting for us eagerly on the steps of the palace, her lovely face lit with an inner grace. She rushes down to meet as soon as we enter the grounds of the palazzo.

"Oh, my dear friend! How wonderful it is to see you at last!" She grabs my hands and kisses me on both cheeks. Although married nearly ten years and the mother of two daughters, she has not lost her childlike exuberance. It's an attitude she brings to all her endeavors—her friendships, her scholarship, her spirituality. It infuses me with an energy the convent has drained from me.

I introduce Renata to my wonderful women, all of them radiating smiles in the glow of her fervent welcome. We follow her into the palazzo and up to her chamber. Each of Renata's ladies-in-waiting pairs off with one of mine, leaving Renata and me the luxury of a private dialogue. At first, the topics are domestic—the health and progress of her daughters, Anna and Lucrezia, and her growing closeness to her cousin, Marguerite de Navarre, the sister of King François.

"I long for the two of you to meet. You would be kindred spirits, I just know it."

But then our conversation shifts.

"Vittoria, have you ever heard Bernardino Ochino preach?" she asks. When my face lights up as I answer her, she laughs in response.

"I knew it! I knew you would've discovered him. He is in Ferrara now! We must go together to hear him preach at the cathedral, and I want you to join my circle when we discuss his sermon. I must warn you, we're a noisy and argumentative bunch. Ercole fears we're treading on dangerous ground with the books we read and the ideas we entertain. I try to reassure him that God encourages us to question and debate and rely upon our own insights to interpret his Word. If you've been moved by Fra Bernardino, then you understand. Ercole has not opened his heart to the monk. If he did, he would realize the sheer joy it brings to know God unfiltered by some dissolute priest whose only aim is to enrich the coffers of the church."

Renata's enthusiasm for her spiritual circle is infectious and reflects the passion that makes her court so sought after by the intellectuals and artists of the region.

Dinner is an ebullient event, with topics leaping from philosophy to poetry to painting to the education of women. As Renata warned me, many of her guests are present specifically to meet me. I flush with the effort of responding to myriad calls for my attention and opinions on everything from Pietro Bembo's promotion of Italian as the language of literature to Pope Paul's revival of the carnival in Rome and his restoration of extravagant ceremonies like the one receiving the emperor. But when the conversation shifts to a discussion of Michelangelo, I find myself growing silent. I cannot bear to participate in the conjecture and curiosity surrounding the *Last Judgment*. I don't trust myself, afraid that I might reveal my intimate connection to both the theology behind the painting and the artist himself. I make an excuse to withdraw from the heated discussion and take a moment to sip my wine and survey the room.

The duke catches my eye, smiles and approaches me from across the salon.

"Although I have offered you my formal greeting already, I am delighted to discover you momentarily unaccompanied. I shall selfishly claim you as my own until one of your many admirers spirits you away."

"I am equally delighted, Ercole. Help me escape for a few minutes on the terrace. I'm not used to such a clamor for my attention."

"You will have to learn to accept it as the price of fame, I'm afraid." He takes my arm and we retreat to the terrace.

"Vittoria, I need to discuss something with you away from Renata."

He has my attention. I tense, wary of what he might say. Renata is my friend, my surrogate daughter. I do not want to be placed between her and her husband, whom I also count among my friends.

"What is it, Ercole?" I am genuinely worried.

"I assume she has spoken to you about her immersion in this reformist thinking?"

"Yes, of course."

"Are you aware that she harbored John Calvin here last summer?"

My widened eyes answer his question.

"He traveled under an assumed name, and only a handful of our confidants knew it was him. But it was an extraordinarily risky thing for her to do. She put herself in jeopardy simply by entertaining him, and then spent hours every day soaking up his heresy and working with him on his treatise. She had it printed and circulated here at court. I don't know whether to be enraged or protective."

"What would you like me to do?" It's just as I feared. He's putting me in an untenable position between my two friends.

"Speak to her. Try to impart some reason. She trusts and respects you."

"Ercole, while I'm as shocked as you are that she offered asylum to Calvin, I must tell you that I'm in sympathy with the reformers. Surely you agree that the Church must recognize its sins and change."

"But she's in danger of losing her very soul if she continues along this path!"

I hear his anguish.

"One can believe in reform and remain a Catholic," I reassure him. "From what she told me today, she's an avid follower of Bernardino Ochino, who has the pope's blessing. I know Pope Paul. He recognizes the need for change and is moving in that direction to save the Church from the corruption that has undermined it. He's a good man, Ercole."

"I wish I could believe you that her soul is safe from damnation. I beg you, be a guide to Renata while you're here."

"I promise you, I will."

"Thank you, Vittoria. I blame her cousin most of all for these perilous notions. It was Marguerite who saw to Renata's religious education and who planted outrageous ideas in her head about thinking independently."

I listen, but do not sympathize with his criticism of Marguerite de Navarre. Everything Renata has told me about her leads me to believe that she's been a blessing in Renata's life.

I decide it's wise to divert him from his tirade.

"Ercole, may I ask you an unrelated question? You know that my women and I are staying at the Convent of Santa Caterina?"

He nods, but his expression becomes guarded.

"Your grandfather built the convent, did he not? What prompted him?"

"He built it for the mystic, Lucia of Narni. Did you never hear of her?"

I have a vague recollection of stories about a young woman with stigmata. But from the distance of Ischia they were the stuff of legend, often embellished.

"Is she still alive? She must be in her sixties if she is."

"I don't know. She was my grandfather's. . ." He starts to say "obsession," but apparently reconsiders. "My grandfather was her champion and her patron, but after he died she withdrew from public view. For all I know, she went back to Viterbo, where he discovered her. I don't pay much attention to the convent. We support it, of course, and the girls will have their bridal linens embroidered there, but neither Renata nor I have taken much interest in it."

He seems dismissive and genuinely unaware of the climate there. I doubt I'll learn more from him, either because he doesn't know or doesn't want me to know. But I am now convinced that the secret being kept at Santa Caterina has something to do with Lucia.

We reenter the salon in time for the entertainment Renata has planned. I am relieved not to be asked to recite and only expected to enjoy the poetry and music prepared by others. As I listen, I mull over how to balance Ercole's frantic fears with my support of Renata's reformist ideas. And simmering underneath that immediate concern is my memory of the weeping that disturbed my sleep.

Because of the lateness of the evening, Renata and Ercole insist we spend the night in the palazzo and send word to the convent that we will not return until the next day. It is a blessing for all of us to be surrounded by genuine affection and warmth as we begin our sojourn in Ferrara. In the morning, Renata and I meet to identify where my women and I can offer succor. It is just as well that the convent has no need of our talents, as we discover more than enough to occupy us behind the façades of the Este's elegant city.

When we return to the convent, I keep my promise to Suora Ursula and regale her with a description of the beauty of the palazzo, lit with hundreds of candles and humming with the conversation of poets and philosophers. I describe the women's dresses, the feast, the haunting music. She relishes it all with gleaming eyes.

"I was a young woman when the old duke was ruling," she reminisces. "I remember the parties from before I was sent here. It was an innocent and magical time. Before this." She waves her hand at the walls of the convent.

I squeeze that hand, glad I'm able to recreate for her a fragment of her past, however bittersweet. Her comment suggests that the choice to enter Santa Caterina wasn't hers. Her willingness to overcome the stricture of silence imposed by Mother Superior is further evidence that perhaps she is a key to dispelling the shadow of hostility and dissension that darkens this house full of holy women.

But I bide my time. The next few nights are quiet, interrupted only by the murmur of night creatures in the gardens. We spend our days in the city doing the work we've been called to do in the orphanage and the hospital, at the palazzo engaged in serious discussion of scripture, or at the cathedral listening intently to Fra Bernardino. I continue to bring our lives outside the walls back to Suora Ursula.

But on Good Friday, the peace into which we've been lulled breaks apart just as the temple curtain was rent on the afternoon Christ was crucified. The clamor explodes well past midnight, jolting me from my sleep. There is no full moon to guide me this time and I grope for the door to the corridor. Outside I find several of my women shivering with fear. The cries come from a different location than the first night. They are closer, out in the garden.

I move toward them, but feel the grip of a firm hand restraining me.

"Go back to bed, my lady, and send your women to their rooms. It's nothing. An old owl in the trees disturbed by young men in the street who ignore the curfew on this holiest of nights."

I hear the rustle of movement and whispers in the garden, but say nothing. Someone is searching for the source of the disturbance and that person is not looking for an owl.

The hand still grips my forearm.

"There is no need to hurt me, Suora. We shall leave you to catch your owl. I will say goodnight to everyone," I tell her. She releases my arm but bars the way to the garden. I expect she'll remain there for the rest of the night. "They are frightened and need reassurance."

I shepherd my women back to their rooms.

I enter each room, speak calming words and embrace those in need of human contact. When I return to my own bed I'm unable to sleep, and in the remaining hours of darkness I pray for the woman whose anguished cry for help has so pierced my soul.

Shortly before sunrise I leave my bed. The commotion in the garden has finally subsided and the nun guarding the passageway that leads to the garden has apparently given up her post. As I did on Ischia when troubled in spirit, I need to walk in the open air. Santa Caterina offers no expansive vistas of the sea, but its grounds are immense, lush with early spring greenery and tall trees, despite being bound by high walls. I gather my cloak around me and set foot on the garden path that I was forbidden to tread the night before.

The earth is still damp with dew and my nightgown wicks up moisture from the wet stones of the path. I draw my cloak tighter around me, more for comfort from the uneasy silence than for warmth. No birds have begun their morning song and the "owl" the nun spoke of during the night has ceased its calls of distress.

I venture further into the garden, my footsteps taking me in the direction from which I heard the night voices. I do not know what I'm seeking or even if, after so many hours, there'll be any sign of what occurred during the night. Although I started my walk to clear my head and release the oppression of the mounting secrecy within the convent, I feel myself pulled deeper into its mystery. If I were thinking rationally, I would pursue an entirely different course and go directly to Suora Ursula at the gate to try to unravel what took place. Instead, what I admit to myself is that against all reason, I'm searching blindly for something that has most likely disappeared or at least been hidden away.

As I expect, I see nothing that so much as hints at the source of the distress I heard during the night. I am about to turn back, planning to retrace my steps with far more vigor. If I walk with a fierce energy, I might be able to dispel the fog that hovers over my spirit. In my haste, I trip and reach out to catch myself. My hand grasps what I mistakenly assume is a sturdy branch. But it's the post of a rusted gate that swings with a melancholy whine. Beyond the gate is an overgrown path that leads to another wing of the cloister. I know the convent was built with the anticipation of housing a large number of nuns—at least 140. The size of the community we saw at chapel is far smaller, perhaps half that number. And the part of the cloister we guests are permitted to see can easily house them. What stands beyond the gate must be an unused portion of the house.

I rub the rust from my hands and brush my skirt, stroking away the flecks of dead leaves and burrs that attached themselves when I fell. As I do so, I notice a cluster of footprints on the muddy path just past the gate. Some are of bare feet; others bear the imprint of the simple sandals the sisters wear. Close to the iron barrier the prints are distinct, but as they approach the cloister, the bare prints are smeared, as if the feet have been dragged.

I push open the gate carefully, trying not to cause the moaning sound that accompanied my fall. I move down the path toward the cloister, following the footprints until they end at an opening in the outer gallery. I listen for signs of life, but hear nothing.

The sun is about to rim the top of the convent wall to the east. Within a few minutes the convent will be awake, the bells for Matins will ring and the garden will be populated with sisters on their way to chapel.

I reluctantly end my search, turning to walk briskly back to my room. As I approach the gate, my eye catches a fragment of light-colored cloth hanging from a bush on the side of the path. It is a scapular of San Domenico, torn on one edge and flecked with tiny drops of dried blood.

I take it, closing my fingers around it as I hurry back to the guest quarters.

We spend Holy Saturday in silent prayer in preparation for the Easter celebration. My women and I will not be attending services in the convent on Sunday morning. We are invited to attend Mass in the cathedral with Renata and the duke. We keep the Easter Vigil together with the sisters in the chapel overnight. It is both to honor the solemnity of Christ's crucifixion and burial, and to stay together in a holy place as protection from the anger that seems to lurk in the garden. During the night I stroke the tattered and worn scapular in my pocket as if I could identify its owner through my touch. No sounds disturb our vigil.

At dawn, our faces washed of the long night's watch, our hair re-pinned and our gowns changed, we wait at the convent gate for Nicolo to escort us.

Ahead in the piazza, we can see the flames of the bonfire from which the Paschal candle will be lit.

As the sun rises, trumpets announce the Resurrection, and Renata and Ercole lead the procession of people into the cathedral, following the cardinal, his acolytes and the lit candle.

The celebration at the palazzo after Mass lasts for two days. Renata sent baskets of food and a whole roasted lamb to the convent for their feast, but I wonder how much celebration the nuns are able to enjoy even though Lent is over.

In a lull during the festivities, I seek out one of the older members of the court, a woman who was a lady-in-waiting to Lucrezia Borgia, Ercole's mother, when she arrived in Ferrara to become the bride of Alfonso d'Este—the man who defeated my father and Ferrante at Ravenna.

"Lady Alessandra, I've learned that you're something of a historian of the court," I tell her. "I'm fascinated by the place women have had in Ferrara's history and would be grateful to hear your account of life when the Duchessa Lucrezia ruled."

"There aren't many willing to listen to an old woman's stories, my dear. The young girls believe in making their own history these days and don't think they can learn anything from the past. But come, sit with me a while and I'll entertain you, if that's what you want."

She pats the cushion next to her on a window seat and beckons a passing servant to bring us wine.

Lady Alessandra meanders through her memories, starting with her arrival in Ferrara with Lucrezia Borgia. Among the details of Lucrezia's dowry was a gift of eleven women for the Convent of Santa Caterina.

"Old Duke Ercole, Alfonso d'Este's father, wasn't happy when Pope Alexander, Lucrezia's father, proposed that Alfonso marry her. She'd already had two husbands. Duke Ercole refused to consider the offer for nearly a year. Lucrezia's gift of the nuns was really to appease her future father-in-law."

"Why was that?"

"Because of Lucia of Narni, of course! Duke Ercole had spent years winning her away from Viterbo and had finally succeeded in bringing her to Ferrara as his spiritual guide and personal adviser. He had the convent built for her and even got the pope to name her as prioress. Why, Duke Ercole laid the first stone! It was vitally important to him that the convent flourish. That's why he insisted it be so big. Lucrezia realized that by helping fill it, she would gain favor with the duke. Even after the wedding, she continued to recruit women to take their vows there."

"Did you ever meet Lucia?"

"Oh, yes. She had unusual freedom when the old duke was alive. She came to the palazzo often."

"What was she like?"

"She was quite the celebrity in those days. In Viterbo hundreds of people had flocked to the convent where she lived when it was discovered that she had the stigmata and was seeing visions. That's why they didn't want her to leave. When she spoke here at the palazzo, everyone listened to her. She was beautiful, she was wise and she was also tragic."

"In what way?"

"She was so isolated by her gifts. She elicited either profound awe or vicious jealousy—especially because she was so honored by the duke. If you ask me, although no one does anymore, she had bewitched him. From the time he met her, he was obsessed with possessing her as his own saint." She takes a sip of wine.

"Fame is not a blessing, my dear." She looks at me knowingly and I shiver. Lady Alessandra was at the salon when Renata welcomed me to Ferrara. She is well aware of the attention I've received since coming to court. I tuck her warning away in my heart and shift the conversation back to Lucia and the convent.

"What happened to Lucia after the duke died?"

"She was silenced. I myself witnessed the signing of the document that stripped her of her authority and privileges. The Vicar General of the Dominicans himself came to Ferrara and made a great public showing in front of Lucrezia and Alfonso and their entire court less than a month after the old duke's death. Lucia returned to the convent, where she was forbidden to speak to anyone, and no one ever saw her again."

"She fell very far, to have disappeared so completely."

"It's not difficult to disappear in that place."

She shudders with a distant look in her eyes. "I was meant to take the veil," she says quietly. "It was in the early years of Lucrezia's marriage, when she was still trying to please the old duke by building the population of Santa Caterina. She wanted me and two of her other ladies-in-waiting to profess vows. I was young and desperately unhappy about it. I'd heard stories from women whose sisters were there. It was not a holy place. I wrote my father and begged him to find me a husband. He went to the pope and somehow persuaded him to spare me. I was betrothed to a distant cousin of the duke's and, to compensate for my withdrawal, six young women were sent from Rome to enter the convent."

"Was it a good outcome for you?"

"Alfredo was an undemanding husband. He gave me seven children, spent most of his time away at war and left me alone to manage his household as I saw fit. Now that he's gone, I enjoy my grandchildren and get to reminisce with the curious and inquisitive, like you."

I feel myself redden with embarrassment. "Have I been too inquisitive?"

She takes my hand between her bony fingers. "I'm an old woman, my dear, who has seen many things. You do not fool me with your broad question about the role women have played in Ferrara's history. You've only lived at the convent a week and already I can see the effect it's had on you and your women. You're not sleeping, are you? And prayer is difficult in the cacophony of that chapel."

She knows.

"I think Lucia is still alive. Hidden away in the depths of the cloister." I speak my suspicion aloud.

She makes the sign of the cross. "I have often suspected that. As long as she lives she is a source of divisiveness."

"I feel the need to do something, if only to give my women a safe haven."

"There I cannot advise you, my dear. I chose to run away from Santa Caterina into marriage. I knew I lacked the strength to live amid such dissension."

"Thank you for your honesty, Lady Alessandra."

"Now, enough of this dark story. It is Easter, and we should be rejoicing. Let go of your worries for a few hours. You strike me as a woman who will find a solution. Be patient with yourself." She rises and leads me away in the direction of music and laughter.

Later that night, in the peace of Renata's guest room, I sleep soundly. As Alessandra generously advised, I trust that the answer lies within me.

On the evening of Easter Monday, we return to the convent well-rested and filled with the bounty of stimulating conversation, lyrical entertainment and an abiding spirituality that reflects Renata's charismatic presence. We are restored, renewed. The Easter message of redemption has invigorated us.

In my own prayers I seek God's help for my role in alleviating the misery that pervades Santa Caterina. I contemplate the punishment meted out to Lucia, denying her any contact. No wonder the nights are shattered by that keening. She is in mourning for herself, sentenced to a kind of living death.

As an outsider, I do not believe I can change the character of the convent. It seems too entrenched in its history, tied to Lucia's rise and fall. But something gnaws at me to ease Lucia's suffering, as if God has brought me to Santa Caterina not only to do His work in the streets, but also to minister within these walls. I have the sense that her moans in the night are a call directed at me, and I know I must find a way to answer them.

I continue to be drawn to the sympathetic warmth of Suora Ursula, who is once again eager to hear about our outing to court. Over several days I share small vignettes of the Easter celebration as I wait with her for Nicolo to return with a message or an errand from the market. When I've exhausted such safe topics as the bonfire or the poetry recitation, I shift to my conversation with Alessandra.

At the mention of her name I detect a shift in Suora Ursula's attention, a wariness that hints to me she knows her.

"Do you know Lady Alessandra?" I ask her outright.

"Yes." I cannot read the expression on her face. It is guarded, clouded, as if she were struggling to hold back anger. I cannot imagine why Suora Ursula has such intense feelings about her, or how they might have known each other. Lady Alessandra was quite clear that she stays away from Santa Caterina.

Then I realize they must have known each other before Suora Ursula entered the convent. "You knew her when you were at court?"

She speaks, tears filling her eyes. "I was one of the Duchessa Lucrezia's ladies-in-waiting, along with Alessandra. One of the ones Lucrezia offered to the convent."

Unlike Alessandra, she must have had no father powerful enough to prevent her from being swallowed up behind the walls.

"You've accepted with grace what must have been a bitter and hurtful charge, Suora. Please know that you are a ray of light in this very dark place."

"Your words are like a tonic, my lady. It is a blessing you are here."

"Thank you, Suora. But I feel I've done nothing to ease the sorrow I sense in this house. If anything, I believe our presence—and mine especially—has been disruptive."

She looks at me sharply, as if to assess the wisdom of what she might say next. Then she takes a deep breath. "You mean the night disturbances."

"Yes. Are they common?"

"No. Not for a long time. But since you arrived...."

This confirms for me that I *am* the cause—or at least the recipient for whom the cries are meant. I decide to be as forthright as Suora Ursula.

"It is Lucia of Narni, the mystic, is it not?"

She nods. "We do not speak her name. The younger nuns don't even know of her existence. She is forgotten, by order of the Vicar General."

"But not forgotten by you."

She shakes her head. "Please, my lady. I can speak of this no longer." She dismisses me. I do not wish to trouble her further or bring the wrath of the Mother Superior down upon her. I especially don't want to lose her companionship and I'm afraid she might be reassigned away from contact with us. For several days I refrain from engaging her in any conversation at all, not just the topic of Lucia.

After Easter, the convent settles into a less restrictive atmosphere. The coming of spring means more work outdoors for most of the sisters, and the fresh air, sunshine and rigorous labor in the vegetable gardens eases some of the tension. The nights remain quiet, and I am lulled into thinking that God has freed me of any responsibility.

It's June when I learn God has no such plan. On the eve of the feast of St. John, the excitement in the streets spills over into the convent. The walls can't hold back the insistent rhythm of the drums, the acrid smell of gunpowder from the fireworks exploding in the cathedral piazza or the orange glow in the sky from the bonfires encircling the city. There is an agitation within the convent, but instead of allowing it to dissipate with some form of communal celebration, the Mother Superior only exacerbates it by clamping down on the excitement.

"This is a pagan celebration, nothing more. No one is to be out in the garden," she decrees. Cooped up in the heat and airlessness of the refectory, tempers simmer and resentments become heightened, stoked by the arbitrary rule.

When everyone grudgingly retires, sleep is fitful. The heat, the noise from the streets, the longing for even the simplest pleasures, creates a storm of discontent like a squall rising out of a tempestuous sea.

It is no surprise to me that a night like this will engender a reawakening of Lucia's sorrow. The moans are barely discernible in the tumult from the streets and the restless stirring in the beds within the cloister. But I hear them. I listen intently, waiting for the sound of footsteps and murmuring voices heading off to silence her. But all is quiet. It occurs to me that everyone is exhausted, drained of energy, and tonight Lucia will be ignored.

I creep from my bed, wrap a light shawl over my nightgown and inch my way quietly into the corridor. No one is about and I tiptoe in the dark toward the hidden wing of the cloister. As I get closer, the keening is stronger and has an almost song-like quality to it. When I reach the gallery, I move from door to door, pressing my ear against the wood in search of the source of the sound. At the last door, farthest from the main house, I stop, frozen. In addition to the keening, I now hear a faint tattoo, as if she were tapping her hands on a table in imitation of the drumming going on in the streets. Even as hidden away as she is, deep in the far recesses of the convent grounds, Lucia is aware that it's St. John's Eve.

I do not want to frighten her with my voice. But I carry in my hand the tattered scapular I found on the bushes. I kneel and push it partway through the crack at the bottom of the door. For a moment it lies there, the strings still on my side of the door and the badge inside. The keening and thrumming stop. And then the strings slide away from me, pulled into the lonely prison on the other side.

There is no further sound. I stay for a few more minutes and utter a prayer out loud for her ears as well as God's. And then I go back to bed.

CHAPTER THIRTY-SEVEN

Caritas

Vittoria
1538
Ferrara

From the moment I make contact with Lucia, I know I've done the right thing. A peace settles over me in the same way my gesture of returning the scapular quieted her mournful keening. I resolve to find ways to return to her with other gifts that will soothe her lonely soul.

I pray for her—both in the chapel during the Divine Office and at her door deep in the night when the convent has retired after Compline. I learn quickly to find my way in the dark, silent as a hunter in the forest taking care not to alert her prey. I move as if invisible, covering myself even in the heat of summer with a dark cloak. I don't go every night, especially not when the moon illuminates every leaf and casts sharp shadows on the path. I am unafraid, but I do not wish to damage Lucia further if it were to be discovered that I visit her. I cannot imagine how much more they can punish her, but I don't want to find out.

I write poems for her. I plan at first to slide them under the door as I did with the scapular. But I worry that she has no place for safekeeping even a small sheet of paper. As an alternative, I recite the poems to her.

I send a letter of entreaty to the pope to release her or at least ease the isolation in which she's been confined. I do so cautiously. I suspect he might be aware of her history, although I doubt he played a role in her banishment. Before he rose as a cardinal, Alessandro Farnese was closely connected to the Borgia pope. His sister Giulia had been the pope's mistress, and it was likely Alessandro knew of Lucrezia Borgia's gift of women for Duke Ercole's convent. I appeal to his sense of justice, but I also assure him that I am acting on my own—no one else knows of my request nor is anyone aware that I even know of Lucia's existence. I understand papal power. No pope wants to be forced into a decision that will make him appear weak. He can only be magnanimous and compassionate if the idea to release Lucia appears to be his alone.

I wait for an answer, adding a nightly prayer that Pope Paul will consider my request with an open heart. When his reply comes, it causes a stir in the convent. A message from the pope is no small matter, and I expect the Mother Superior to question me, no matter what the pope has decided.

I retreat with the letter to my room and open it, smoothing the thick sheet on my writing table. I scan the document quickly, impatient for his final word. I will go over it slowly to read the reasoning behind his decision, but first I want his answer. Which is "No." Disappointed but not surprised, I go back to the beginning. Although couched in spiritual terms, it is clear to me that Paul has considered the ramifications of freeing Lucia. The Church is already in turmoil. The sudden reappearance of a celebrated mystic could precipitate the kind of frenzy and religious excess that easily rages out of control. Paul's foremost priority is maintaining his authority over a splintering Church. I appreciate his position. I have placed great hope for the Church in Paul's papacy. The Church needs someone both formidable enough to demand respect, yet open enough to reform to save it from itself. I know that Lucia is a distraction. It fills me with sorrow that the state of the world can have such an impact on a single life.

I burn the letter. When the Mother Superior asks me about it, I tell her it's a personal spiritual matter. She is not happy. But I'm her guest, not one of her sisters.

"If you need a confessor, our own padre is here every morning to say Mass," she offers, as though I've been blind to the ancient, mumbling priest all these months. Suora

Ursula has whispered to me that the priest is Lucia's confessor, the only one allowed to speak with her.

"Thank you, Madre. But I am well counseled by both the Holy Father and the duchessa's chaplain. My spiritual needs are being met."

Because I spoke to no one about my petition to the pope, I seek consolation within myself. I did not hint to Lucia what I did, for fear of raising false hopes. I continue with my nightly visits, hearing only her soft breath on the other side of the door. She never responds, not even with an "Amen." I wonder if she might have forgotten how to speak after so many years of silence—until one night not long after I received the pope's letter.

I try to keep my melancholy separate from what I consider my mission to Lucia. But perhaps she detects a change in my voice, a raggedness that I do not recognize. For whatever reason, she breaks her silence not with prayer but with song. I struggle to decipher the words until I realize there are no words, only a melody that mimics the songbirds that live in the trees surrounding her cell. It is beautiful and comforting and transformative.

I shake my head in bewilderment and also shame. I wrongly presumed that I was the one bringing solace to Lucia, that I am the one who is whole, offering a refuge in the night to one who is broken. But she sings to reassure and lift me.

I weep when I leave her that night.

As winter approaches, our work in the city becomes all-consuming. The problems of the poor are compounded as the air turns frigid and the earth shrivels and dies, no longer providing bounty for foraging. I am spending more in the market than I expected—for food, for blankets and warm clothing. The long hours of caring for the needy, combined with concern over my diminishing funds and the very short amount of time I sleep every night— all lead to my collapse one day. A spasm of uncontrollable coughing overwhelms me as we return to the convent.

Barbara takes me back to my room and settles me in bed propped up against a pillow. She rubs my hands between hers.

"You're freezing, Vittoria! Here, wrap yourself in this extra shawl and I will build up the fire. I've sent Clara to the kitchen for something warm to drink."

The illness confines me to bed for several days. My difficulty breathing and its accompanying sleeplessness are compounded by my dismay that I cannot visit Lucia. Someone sits with me every night, so I can't leave my bed unnoticed, even if I were physically able.

As I lie there struggling to clear my lungs, I face a difficult truth. This illness is a warning, and not merely of my own mortality. The humid air of Ferrara is destroying my health and I know I cannot remain at Santa Caterina much longer. I do not want to abandon Lucia, but because I am the sole source of prayer and companionship to her, that is exactly what I'll be doing when I leave. During the many hours of my recuperation, I resolve to find someone willing to carry on in my place.

The choice is not difficult. I know only one sister with the courage and compassion to form a connection with Lucia as I have. Suora Ursula.

When I'm well enough to be on my feet, I visit her at her gatekeeper's post. My women, assured that I have recovered, are out in the city again.

"My lady! Are you sure you should be up? I have been so worried for you."

"Thank you, Suora. I'm taking a few steps today to remind myself how it feels to be upright. I missed you and thought it would cheer me to spend a few moments in your company."

The old nun smiles. "I have missed you, too, my lady. Look, I have some warm chestnuts. May I offer you one?" She opens a cloth bundle tucked into a corner.

"Are these from the convent garden?" I ask as I peel away the charred skin.

"No. Alberto, the street vendor who sometimes stops at the gate to sell things or bring me news, gave them to me. He needed a salve for his wife and I was able to persuade Suora Immaculata to make some up for him. He paid, of course. The chestnuts were a gesture of thanks to me for arranging it." She seems anxious to reassure me.

"You are a kind woman, Suora. I'm not surprised he wished to thank you."

We eat the chestnuts in companionable silence.

"Suora, may I ask you something?"

"Of course, my lady. Anything."

"Have you noticed that Lucia has not disturbed the peace of the convent for several months?"

She nods but says nothing.

"I have been praying for her."

"Thank you, my lady. Then God has heard your prayers."

"I have also been praying *with* her." I wait. I take the risk of telling her, trusting that she will not report my breach to the Mother Superior.

"But how, my lady?"

"I go to her at night after the convent is asleep. It seems that neither she nor I sleep well."

"And no one has seen or heard you?"

"Apparently not."

"Then God must be watching out for both of you." She makes the sign of the cross.

"I feel that He meant for me to be a comfort to her. But to my astonishment, *she* has become a comfort to me."

"I am not surprised. She had that effect on the people who believed she was blessed."

"Suora, my illness has made me realize that I cannot remain at Santa Caterina much longer. The Ferrara air is not healthy for me."

"Oh, my lady! I knew you couldn't stay forever, but the thought of losing you troubles me. Especially after what you've just told me. You have brought us a measure of goodness that we have not known for many years."

"The goodness need not depart with me, Suora."

"I don't see how." Her doubt is pervasive, defeating.

"Suora, when I first came here I sensed something was very wrong. I thought at first it was the silence. The sisters do not communicate with one another on any level. But I have since come to realize that the silence is a symptom, not a cause of the unrest."

"What do you believe has damaged us so?" She waits expectantly, eager for my answer.

"The lack of love, of *caritas*."

She gasps. Caritas is the foundation of Christian life, spoken of by Christ and echoed by Saint Paul in his epistle to the Corinthians: "In short, there are three things that last: faith, hope and love; and the greatest of these is love."

I know I'm using strong words. But I trust she will hear me in her heart.

"You can bring the love back, Suora. You already do in so many ways." I hold up my chestnut as an example. "Your kindness to Alberto; your warmth to me and my women. I ask you, after I'm gone, to carry on my night-time visits to Lucia. Not only for her, but for you and ultimately the whole convent."

Suora Ursula looks away from me, her brow knit in distress and her mouth moving as if in silent conversation with herself or God.

"You are asking me to go against the order of the Vicar General."

"Is his order not to pray for Lucia?"

"No. It is that she is to see no one, speak to no one except her confessor."

"I do not see Lucia and I do not speak to her. I only speak *with* her to God."

Suora Ursula considers my distinction. We both know that Mother Superior will not see a difference. My hope is that Suora Ursula will perceive that God sees the difference.

She turns back to me.

"You have shown Lucia love. I see that. And I agree with you, that love has been missing within these walls. I will try to bring it back."

I want to embrace her for her courage. I hesitate, not wanting to overstep any further the rules that bind her.

Respecting her constraints, I bow my head in gratitude. "Thank you, Suora."

In January, still beset with ill health, I leave Ferrara for a respite in the mountains to the north, to clear my lungs and my head. My sojourn here will be brief, as I received a letter from Pope Paul before I left Santa Caterina, requesting my presence in Rome.

Alfonso comes to me from Milan, where Emperor Charles V had just named him governor. I am sitting on the terrace in the sun, well-wrapped in heavy furs to keep me warm in the biting cold but pure mountain air.

"Vittoria! They told me the crazy marchesa could not be convinced to stay indoors. I assured them you were not crazy at all, but had lived almost your entire life on a mountaintop and had become enamored of wind and sun and distant vistas."

He envelopes me in his warrior's arms, a wide grin on his face and a surfeit of love in his eyes.

"I cannot express how wonderful it is to see you, my dearest boy! Tell me everything. I long to hear about you, Maria and the children. I have missed you all."

"You must come and visit us in Milan. It may not be as elegant or as daring as Ferrara, although we're trying to measure up." He speaks lightly but I know from my correspondence with friends that he has developed into a remarkable military leader, distinguishing himself not only at Pavia in 1525, but also in Tunis only three years ago. A captain of the imperial troops, he had led his forces to victory over eighty thousand Turks. But perhaps of most joy to me, he has become recognized as an accomplished poet. Smiling to myself in recollection of the literary seeds planted so long ago by Giancarlo Brittonio, I prod him gently.

"You continue to compose your sonnets, despite your responsibilities on the battlefield?"

"I shall write poetry until I die. At times, I find it a solace and a balm; but I have also discovered that committing my words to the page can be as thrilling as the execution of a sharply honed military strategy."

We sit deep in conversation amidst the snow-clad mountains until the winter sun retreats beyond the western ridge. He takes my arm as we step inside to a room glowing with fire and candlelight and aromatic with a wine-simmered stew.

Alfonso sniffs the air. "I'm ravenous after my climb to reach you here in the heights."

We sit down to eat, continuing our far-ranging discussion of family, the emperor and the pope.

"I hear the Holy Father has recalled you to Rome," he says when dinner is finished and we are sated by both the meal and the intimate talk. "I've come not just for this visit but to escort you south."

"As much as I would relish your companionship, Alfonso, there is no need. I have Nicolo and my women. I am far from a lonely wanderer."

"But *I* have a need to be with you, Vi." He uses a childhood nickname. It touches me deeply.

"Then I will not refuse you. You're not worried about me, are you?"

"Your illness in Ferrara provoked distress in us all. You have a reputation for driving yourself beyond your own limits."

He holds my glance. We both acknowledge he is referring to my long and devastating period of mourning, when I wrongly believed that an austere life of self-discipline and self-denial was what God had asked of me.

I long to tell him of the changes my friendship with Michelangelo has wrought in me, but I hold back. Even thinking of Michelangelo causes me anguish, especially since returning to Rome means I will constantly be reminded of his presence.

"I am no longer that woman, Alfonso. Rest assured, I am changed, whole, in ways that I could not have imagined. Ferrara was bad air, not misguided action on my part. I am here, in the mountains, taking responsibility for my health. Look at my rosy cheeks!"

He smiles and leans across the table to kiss the cheeks with which I am so pleased.

A few days later we begin our trek south, stopping wherever Bernardino Ochino is preaching—a sustenance as vital as the food and water we carry. It does not surprise me that Alfonso is as drawn to Ochino as I am—the simplicity of his life in contrast to the excesses of the Church; the challenge in his passionate message of faith. Alfonso, even as a child, was quick to question assumptions and plunge deeply into issues that intrigued him. And from our conversations, I am aware how much Maria has played a role in introducing him to the ideas of Ochino and Juan de Valdés. Their marriage, from my perspective, is a fruitful one—not only in their five exuberant and flourishing children but in their ability to nourish one another's ideas. How fortunate for both of them!

When we arrive in Rome, I settle at San Silvestro again, where I find letters waiting for me from Paolo Giovio, Pietro Bembo and, at the bottom of the pile, Michelangelo.

My hands clutch the letter as if it might fly away. It's more than a year since I have seen or heard from him. Tracing my name on the outside of the letter, seeing his distinctive handwriting, reminds me that he has never been far from my thoughts, despite everything I lived through in the intervening months. I miss him desperately.

I open the letter.

Wrapped within it is a drawing, an evocative image of Christ and a woman at a well—the Samaritan woman who gave Christ a drink of water. The drawing conveys both tenderness and defiance.

The letter itself is brief, without embellishment. It reads, "Forgive me."

I write to him immediately, the words I held so tightly within me all those months in Ferrara now flying from my pen. I end with a suggestion. "If you are not too occupied with your work today, you might visit at your leisure and talk with me."

He comes to see me that afternoon. He must have been at work on the Sistine wall when my letter was delivered to him, but he's taken the time to change his clothes before coming here. Gone are the usual vestiges of paint on his face and hands. He is dressed in clean linen and a well-fitting jacket of black damask. Like his letter, his appearance is without ornament but conveys an aura of dignity. I am touched by the care and attention he has paid to preparing himself.

I greet him in the convent's visitors' parlor. "My dearest friend, how I have longed to see you!"

"And I you, Vittoria. Welcome back to Rome." He encloses both my hands within his and brings them to his lips.

"The day is too beautiful to remain inside. Come with me for a walk." When I retrieve my cloak, we depart. Although still early March, the sun is dazzling and the day is without wind.

At first we walk without speaking. The simple pleasure of sharing each other's presence, my arm in his, is enough. Although we do not discuss where we are headed, our footsteps take us in the direction of some of Rome's ancient ruins. Amidst the shattered columns and fragments of once-glorious buildings, we stop to confront our own past.

"You saved my life." He speaks without preface.

"Baccio Rontini saved your life. All I did was wash your face."

"Without you, Baccio would not have known what had happened to me. Without you, I would not have had the will to survive."

"And without you, *I* would not have wanted to survive."

"When I realized you had left Rome without any word, I grasped how deeply I'd hurt you."

"Please understand. I wasn't angry with you. But I couldn't bear to be in Rome and not be with you. I hoped that in time, as your body healed, your heart would heal, as well."

"Forgive me for not accepting your love when it was offered. I felt desperately unworthy of you."

"Please don't return to that tired refrain of 'you are a marchesa and I am only an artist.'" I can feel my ire rising as it had that night when I'd bullied him into recovering.

He smiles and teases me. "You are still a marchesa, unless you married a duke or a prince since you've been away. And I am still an artist. Although I will accede to your request and eliminate the 'only.'"

He starts counting off on his fingers. "I am also a poet, a Florentine, a pilgrim and a man."

He has disarmed me. But he hasn't convinced me that he no longer believes himself unworthy.

"Do you recognize how unimportant our status in society is to me? If you wish to play this game of words, I can counter with your position in the constellation of great artists. You are the zenith, Michelangelo. No one surpasses you, not in our own age and not among the ancients. It is I who should feel unworthy of you. But," I add, "I don't."

He laughs out loud. "You have always insisted on our equality. We are not teacher and pupil, not leader and follower. However, we *are* man and woman, are we not?"

His words stop me. Throughout my life I have remained vigilant to present myself as virtuous and modest, conforming to society's expectations for a woman of my class. But I have also taken my place among philosophers and writers and poets as their intellectual equal. My pious demeanor is the cloak that allows me to move undisturbed and protected through the world, but underneath the cloak is fervor and passion and curiosity—the same fires that drive men.

"How am I to answer that?" I ask him.

"You are a contradiction to me, you know. In your intellect and eloquence you are a man within a woman—the equal of any. But in your vulnerability and tenderness and beauty, you are a woman. Not just *a* woman, but *the* woman in my life. I love you, Vittoria. I could not tell you that last year because I could not admit it to myself."

Had we not already been sitting side by side on an overturned block of marble I would have run into his arms. I take his hand and bring it to my lips.

"What are we to do now?"

"I believe neither of us wishes to marry?"

I shake my head. "We are too independent, you and I. Our joint household would not be a peaceful one."

"I have observed that it is easier to sustain love when one is not married."

A brief memory of the love lost in my marriage to Ferrante wells up within me and I cannot hide the pain it causes me.

"I have said something to hurt you. Forgive me."

"You've done nothing. It's only a memory that disturbs me."

"Do you trust me enough to tell me?"

I take a deep breath. "My marriage to Ferrante…" I hesitate.

"Was an unhappy one." He finishes my sentence.

"How did you know? *When* did you know?"

"A moment ago, as I saw your face when I said it was easier to hold onto love if one doesn't marry."

"I held onto love. It was he who stopped loving."

"You know that I will never stop loving you. You can ask my family, my friends. Once a powerful emotion seizes me, I can't relinquish it. Some of them will tell you it's my willful, stubborn character."

He smiles, and I smile in return.

"I will warn you, as well, that I can be just as willful," I tell him.

"I know. I would not be alive, I would not be walking if you hadn't been so immovable last year."

"That reminds me—we have a whole year of life lived apart to recount to each other. So many times I found myself longing to tell you what I was experiencing or learning or feeling."

"Then tell me now."

And so I do. I describe the loneliness and darkness of Santa Caterina; Lucia di Narni; Renata's spiritual circle; the music and poetry and plays of the Ferrara court; the poverty and despair in the streets; the inspiration of Fra Bernardino's sermons.

He absorbs it all, never taking his eyes from my face. Michelangelo the observer, listening to my stories in the same way he studies the muscles and sinews of the human body. I feel that I am laying myself bare before him—my fears, my joys, my hunger. Will he take these secrets of mine and transform them? Will I become one of the writhing souls on his wall, or one of the hopeful ones lifted to heaven on Christ's gesture?

The sun is low in the sky by the time I exhaust my account of my year away from him.

"I have left no time for your tales," I apologize as we make ready to return to the convent.

"I shall save them for another day," he promises.

"It gives me such joy to know there will be another day with you."

"There will be many days, God willing. I need to go back to the wall tomorrow. If I disappear for more than a day, the pope and twenty cardinals will descend upon my house like they did last summer."

"Did he really? And I thought no one could be more demanding of you than Pope Clement."

"Each pope has found his own means to be a gnat buzzing around my head, from Julius on."

We reach the gate of San Silvestro.

"Send me word whenever you're free, and I will make the time to be with you," I pledge.

"I do not want to be parted from you again, Vittoria."

"Nor I from you."

I watch him walk briskly down the hill. Baccio Rontini did a fine job in healing his broken body. He does not have a limp; his back is straight and strong. Michelangelo moves like a much younger man, a man alive in spirit. A man in love.

I turn back to the convent, my own spirit restored.

Finding time for Michelangelo is the starting point for each day after that, but I didn't realize how many demands would clamor for my attention once I returned to Rome.

Pietro Bembo is the first of many to call upon me.

"I come first in gratitude, my lady."

"For what?" I ask, bewildered.

"My elevation to cardinal. I know Pope Paul asked for your opinion, and I believe I would not be wearing the crimson without your mediation. Some men are called kingmakers because of their influence over who sits on the throne, but I believe you wield as much power in the rise of princes of the Church."

"You place far too much importance on one of many voices to whom the pope listens. You achieved your rank as a result of your own accomplishments, Cardinal Bembo, not through any words I might have whispered in the pope's ear." It is only recently that Pietro has embraced the life of a man of the church. His love of language had at times been overshadowed by his love of women, and one woman in particular, the courtesan Morosina. Although I'd never met her, I knew he loved her and it was not until after her death that he was willing to be ordained.

"The honor of cardinal was not bestowed exclusively on me, my lady. Reginald Pole, Federico Fregoso and Jacopo Sadoleto have also risen thanks to their association with you."

I wave away his pronouncements. "Cardinal Bembo, you are being excessive. I am thrilled for all of you and know of no better choices, but as for my role in the pope's decisions, I advise you to look to yourselves, not me. Now, enough of this. What is far more important to me, other than my congratulations, is your poetry."

He lets go of this obsession with my power. I learned over the years that influence is more effective when it is subtle, not flaunted. I am listened to because I do not shout or demand. And I choose wisely the causes and individuals I champion. The men Pietro Bembo named were friends, well-known to me in their thinking and their character. And none of them had asked me to place his name in front of the pope.

I am happy for all of them and for the Church. I impressed upon the Holy Father the need for men like this to lead us out of the morass into which we are sinking. It is now up to them. Among those Pietro Bembo named is one particularly close to my heart—Reginald Pole, an Englishman whom Pietro brought into my circle of friends. They met as young men studying at Padua. Reginald Pole has his demons, especially his king, Henry VIII. He suffers immeasurably trying to serve both Henry and his conscience with regard to Henry's desire to put aside his wife to marry Anne Boleyn. His very life has been in danger after he severed his ties with the king and denounced Henry's policies in a published treatise. He has escaped spies and an attempted assassination in Venice. But the danger to him pales in comparison to the revenge Henry has taken on Reginald's family. I do not learn of his immense burden until he comes to visit me, like Pietro, to acknowledge my involvement in his being named a cardinal. His political role has obscured what I recognized early on to be an ardent spiritual life. It is that openness to a direct relationship with Christ that so impressed me when we first met. I am therefore unprepared for the ragged, tortured man who waits for me in the visitors' parlor.

"My lady! When Pietro told me you had returned to Rome, I had to see you."

"Your Eminence." I bow to him. "I'm honored by your visit."

"Please, don't use titles with me. I am still Reginald. I didn't ask for this cardinal's hat, you know. I begged the pope not to name me."

"But why? There are few more qualified than you."

I am dismayed by his reluctance to be elevated, but more worried about his agitated state of mind.

"You are troubled, Reginald. And not just by the pope's decision to honor you. What has happened to distress you?"

I recognize the signs because I have experienced the ravages of unfathomable grief in my own life.

His face contorts into profound sorrow and he sobs an almost undecipherable answer that I strain to hear.

"My brothers, my mother. King Henry has arrested them for treason. Because of me!"

He flings himself into my arms and I hold him while he cries. He is only ten years younger than I am, but I feel incredibly old. The brilliant mind, the spiritual depth and the political astuteness that have protected him for years as he navigated the dangerous waters of Henry's obsession have not protected him where he is most vulnerable—with his family.

"I'm the one Henry wants to punish! Let him take me, not my mother, not my brothers! I wish I hadn't escaped the assassin. If he'd killed me, Henry would never have gone after my family. When the pope made me a cardinal, it was the final sign to Henry that I was Paul's man, not his."

His grief and his guilt fill the room, joining all the other sorrowful family news that has been told here for generations.

When his tears are spent, he recovers his composure.

"Forgive me, my lady. I should not have placed my burden in your lap."

"There is nothing to forgive, Reginald. I prompted you to reveal what was troubling you."

He does not stay longer than a few minutes after that. I understand he has much to do if he has any hope of saving his family. I wish him Godspeed and promise to pray for them.

"If there's *anything* I can do for you, please call upon me."

He leaves me. I hope that my comfort has eased his suffering, but everything I've heard about King Henry warns me that Reginald's agony has only just begun.

CHAPTER THIRTY-EIGHT

Flight

Vittoria
1539 – 1541
Rome and Orvieto

Michelangelo continues his work on the monumental wall, and I savor the hours we spend together envisioning the exultant message of the *Last Judgment*. My faith, honed in meditation on the teachings of Juan de Valdés and Bernardino Ochino, finds expression in both my poetry and my conversations with Michelangelo on the meaning of Christ's second coming.

"The second time," I tell him, "Christ will come armed and show his justice, his majesty, his grandeur and his almighty power, and there will no longer be any time for pity or room for pardon."

"My desire is to catch the fire of your words and make it mine in images."

But it is not only Michelangelo's art that occupies us. Whether our time together is spent poring over his red-chalk studies in his workroom or sitting in the garden of San Silvestro reciting sonnets or reading aloud from *The Divine Comedy*, we are shedding layers of emotional armor. In the journey we are on to find God—in my writing and his art—we are also discovering each other.

The joy I feel in his presence expands me, opening my constrained heart to receive the grace I have long sought. I believed I'd known love with Ferrante. But I've come to see those feelings as stunted, like a limb not fully formed; unnourished by my husband, my love withered.

With Michelangelo I *grow*, like a budding peony bursting into bloom when nurtured by an attentive gardener. Instead of the muted colors of my mourning and my descent into self-punishment, I experience myself in vivid pigments, another wall on which he paints.

Soon this luminous intensity of ours begins to be noticed.

"They are talking about us," he tells me one afternoon in the garden. "I have lived many years with the knowledge that my life is not my own. Whether it is Alessandro de' Medici's spies in Florence or gossiping clerics in the Vatican, everyone has an opinion about me—not just my art, but how I live, how I dress, whom I befriend. I do not wish to subject you to dishonor."

Fame is not a blessing, I remind myself of the Lady Alessandra's warning.

"We cannot hide our friendship any longer. But I wish to protect you from those who would harm your reputation. I would like to think that my rough and tarnished name might be smoothed and polished by my association with you, but I'm afraid that instead, you will be tainted."

"I don't want to hide my affection for you from the world."

"No, that's impossible now. Rome is feasting on the story of the friendship between the beautiful and brilliant poet and the inelegant, gruff artist who has never before loved a woman."

"Then we must hide in plain sight. We can give them a public banquet to satisfy their appetite. The more they believe we're hiding something, the more they will imagine it to be salacious and scandalous. I am not ashamed of our friendship, Michelangelo. And I will not let gossips deny us the profound connection we're forging. I will follow the path we're on, wherever it takes us."

He looks at me, and once again I feel the heat of his inner fire leaping across the stillness of the garden. The air shimmers, rippling with promise. His glance conveys more than any embrace from Ferrante.

"You're right. If we were to stop seeing each other in public, it would only fuel suspicions that we've taken our relationship behind closed doors. I just don't want any misconceptions to harm you."

"Michelangelo, I live in a convent. You and I visit in the Sistine Chapel and the garden of San Silvestro. We talk of God's goodness and grace. That's all people need to know."

I am touched by his concern for me and his desire to protect me. Neither one of us will abandon our friendship because the world has taken note of it and might judge us wrongly. But I recognize the danger he alludes to. So much depends on how the world perceives *me*, not him. I promise both of us that I will be a careful navigator as we explore this uncharted territory.

In fact, it is not my friendship with Michelangelo that threatens my public name, but my poetry. Or rather, a printed version of my poetry.

It is delivered to me at the convent with no accompanying letter. I open the plainly wrapped package and stare at a book cover with a simple woodcut of a pious woman in prayer before a crucifix. I don't know what it is at first. I assume someone has sent me the book to appraise. I often receive requests from both aspiring and established poets. I am honored to offer my analysis and am conscientious about being thorough, even when critical reading takes time and energy away from my own poems.

I open the book, curious to see whose poems these are, and immediately slam it shut in a rage. *My* name is on the frontispiece.

I am furious. Who has done this? Who has taken my manuscript and set it into type? I open the book again. If I read the poems that are included, I might be able to identify who has betrayed my trust.

As I turn the pages I become even more upset. Many of the poems are earlier drafts that I have since refined. I feel unmasked and violated. And I fear that my pious and modest persona is about to be obliterated. To publish one's poetry in print is an egregious breach of the rules society sets for a woman like me.

I have always chafed under that ridiculous constraint, but I've followed the rules in spirit, allowing my poems to be disseminated only in manuscript form through intermediaries like Pietro Bembo and Paolo Giovio. A delicate balance must be maintained—release a few poems to close friends but not so many that it appears I am promoting myself. And now this! I feel tears stinging my eyes in frustration and loss.

Once my eyes are dry, I go back to the book.

I want to rip it to shreds. But I remind myself that destroying one printed book is futile. How many more are out in the world, beyond my control?

I send a message to Pietro. I am sure he'll know who has done this.

When he arrives at the convent, I greet him with the book gripped tightly in my hand.

"I came quickly. Your note sounded so distressed. What happened?"

I thrust the book at him. "Do you know about this? Do you know who did it?"

He takes the book from my hand and begins to turn the pages. "These are your poems."

"Yes! Printed without my permission. But who will believe me?" I slump into a chair.

"I believe you. These are older versions. You would never have included them. And the woodcut is not a very good likeness. You are much more beautiful."

"You're making light of this, Your Eminence, because you are a man. You must know how damaging this is to me—how precarious my position as a woman who dares to write like a man."

"I'm sorry, my lady. I don't mean to tease you or imply that this isn't a problem. But it's a problem that can be fixed."

"How? Will you ride around the countryside gathering up every copy?"

"No. But I can spread the news around the countryside that the Marchesa di Pescara is dismayed that someone published her early work without her permission. You are revered. Your reputation as both a brilliant writer and a modest woman is secure. If anything, this collection will only enhance your fame."

"How can it?"

"You're seeing the book from the perspective of a privileged woman who has nevertheless had to shape herself to meet the constraints her position in society demands."

"Please, Cardinal Bembo. You have no idea what constraints are! You've never had to give up anything in order to pursue your art or your life." As soon as I say the words, I regret them. He had loved a woman who didn't have the advantages I had, but who was bound by another set of constraints. He could never marry Morosina, even though she was the mother of his children. I know he suffered greatly when she died.

"Forgive me," I say quietly.

He nods. "Perhaps I'm using the wrong argument. Let me start again. Your poetry has reached a wide audience in manuscript form and no one has questioned the propriety of its dissemination. You are celebrated. When this little book falls into the hands of those who have never read you before, your words will touch the hearts and minds of readers who cannot afford to pay for a hand-copied manuscript or who do not move in literary circles where those manuscripts are passed from hand to hand. Do you really believe your poems have meaning only for the elite?"

I think of the nuns of San Silvestro. I think of Lucia di Narni.

"You have convinced me."

"I understand your dismay, my lady. I do not mean to berate you for a social attitude you can't control. I recognize that you can't be associated with the publication of your poems, and I will make sure the world is aware of your distance from this book. But I still believe the book will benefit you, my lady. Not harm you."

"Thank you, Cardinal. I'm sorry for my outburst. The world is changing and I'm sometimes caught by surprise. Each time I believe I've mastered one more step on my path as a poet, another steeper climb presents itself."

"You will surpass us all, my lady. I'll take my leave now. I have a ride to make through the countryside," he says, with a broad smile. "Do you mind if I take the book? I'll return it."

"I'm not sure I want to see it again."

"This won't be the only edition that appears in your lifetime, my lady. Prepare yourself."

I resign myself to his prediction. He is right, of course, about the effect the publication of the poems has. I'm already known in the literary salons of Rome and Napoli and Ferrara. Soon I begin hearing from women in small fiefdoms and large towns, writing to me as a model for their own lives.

My words reach beyond Italy's borders, as well. I receive an unexpected letter from Marguerite d'Angouleme, the Queen of Navarre, sister of François I and Renata di Francia's cousin, about whom I heard so much when I was in Ferrara. Renata was perceptive in expecting that Marguerite and I would find a real affinity with each other. After she writes, we begin a correspondence that both nourishes and challenges me. At first, the disparity in our positions in society—she a queen and I a soldier's widow—cause me to address her with formality and distance, not with the personal thoughts I long to share with her. But she soon closes the distance between us and we use our letters as a wide-ranging conversation about our spiritual quests and our very public visibility as well-known women in a world ruled by men. She is a true friend, who shares my vision in so many ways.

Her friendship becomes a refuge for me as the world of men and the wars of men again cast their shadows over my life.

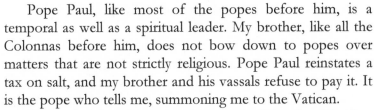

Pope Paul, like most of the popes before him, is a temporal as well as a spiritual leader. My brother, like all the Colonnas before him, does not bow down to popes over matters that are not strictly religious. Pope Paul reinstates a tax on salt, and my brother and his vassals refuse to pay it. It is the pope who tells me, summoning me to the Vatican.

"Your brother is an outlaw, Lady Vittoria. His first provocation was to order his vassals not to pay the salt tax, and now he's escalated his defiance by hindering the passage of travelers to Rome on roads that pass through his land. Last night was the final outrage. Hundreds of head of cattle disappeared from my land in Ostia, stolen by your brother. I have demanded that he appear before me to explain himself, make reparation and pay the tax."

"And you have called on me, Your Holiness, because you believe I have influence with my brother?"

I do not reveal to the pope my serious doubts that Ascanio will listen to me.

"I shall do my best," I say as I kneel to kiss his ring and then leave his chamber. As I move through the corridors of the Vatican, I feel eyes on me who see not Vittoria Colonna, the poet, or even Vittoria Colonna, the friend of Michelangelo, but Vittoria Colonna, the sister of the pope's enemy.

When I return to San Silvestro, I find a letter from Giovanna. Although she has never resumed living with Ascanio after leaving him eleven years ago, she is still his wife. Word has reached her of his belligerence.

"I can only thank God that I am safe here with the children on Ischia, or once again I would be fleeing in the middle of the night. I worry for you in Rome. I will do what I can to help deflect this pointless conflict."

I take up my pen and paper to send a message to my brother, urging him in the interest of our family's honor to meet with the pope. I send it with Nicolo, who knows hidden trails through the Alban Hills and can avoid a confrontation with the pope's army.

I wait nervously through the night, sleepless with worry and frustrated that I've been forced into this role of intermediary. I regret that I didn't speak to Michelangelo after my summons from the pope. But at the time, I thought better of dragging him into my family's conflict. Pope Paul knows of my friendship with Michelangelo, as nearly everyone in Rome does. But, despite my need for Michelangelo's solace, it is best for him if the pope does not see us together.

Nicolo returns to San Silvestro just after dawn. He carries no letter from Ascanio, only his message spat out to Nicolo in defiant words.

"During the night your brother moved with 2,000 men from Genezzano to the fortress at Paliano. He told me to tell you he refuses to obey the pope's order to appear."

"Thank you, Nicolo. Go rest and have something to eat. I'll have more messages for you to deliver later. I must think."

"My lady, if I may, I have never known your brother to be so obsessed. I am no soldier, but I've seen my share of sieges. He is acting without wisdom, without recognition of the consequences."

"I appreciate your frankness, Nicolo."

I have no one to turn to for advice. Our cousin, Cardinal Pompeo Colonna, who had been both warrior colleague and rival to Ascanio, is dead. He might have been able to talk reason to my brother or he might have joined him on the ramparts at Paliano. I should be grateful that I'm not faced with the dilemma of consulting him.

I have no army. I have no ambassadors. I have no weapons other than my pen and my brain. And, by some gift of God, I have time. For two weeks the situation remains unchanged—with Ascanio battle-ready in Paliano, Pope Paul fuming and plotting but not yet acting in the Vatican. I run Nicolo ragged delivering my letters. I summon every argument I can devise to convince my brother to avoid this senseless war. I invoke the memory of our parents and the legacy of our strongholds. I beg him to consider the lives as well as the castles that could be lost. I urge him to save his strength and his men for battle with our enemy in the Holy Land—not at the walls of Paliano.

While I wait for my brother to consider my entreaty, I send equally fierce words to the ambassadors of Charles V in Rome, beseeching them to intervene with the pope. The Colonna and the d'Avalos families have been warriors for Spanish interests since my father and Ferrante's father before him. I ask the emperor's men to honor that loyalty.

Will men never learn the stupidity of war? Neither the Spanish ambassadors nor Ascanio heeds my words.

In the middle of March, Nicolo returns once again from Paliano with Ascanio's refusal to put down his arms.

"My lady, as I passed over the crest of the mountain on my return, I saw the pope's army massing on the plain. They are making camp and will no doubt attack Paliano by sunrise tomorrow. War is inevitable."

Michelangelo comes to me early in the day shortly after I receive Nicolo's report.

"Vittoria, I know you have not confided in me about the conflict between the pope and your brother for a reason, but I am going to override your concerns and involve myself."

"Please, Michelangelo. Don't place yourself in danger."

"*You* are the one who's in danger. I overhear things in the Sistine Chapel. The whisperers forget that I am above them on the scaffold or presume I cannot hear so high up. The pope plans to take you hostage. Today. You must leave Rome."

I see the anguish in his face, the concern for my safety.

"I thought he would respect my role as Ascanio's diplomat. I must have angered him by appealing to the emperor."

"Do you have a safe haven? If not, I can arrange a hiding place for you."

"That's not necessary. As a precaution last week, I spoke to Suora Francesca when I sensed the situation deteriorating. She's arranged a refuge for me at a convent in Orvieto. I'd hoped I wouldn't need it."

"You must go there now. I will send Urbino with you."

"That isn't necessary. I have Nicolo."

"Two men will be better protection. Get ready to go. I'll take you and Nicolo to my house and we'll fetch Urbino. He is already arranging for horses."

I pack hurriedly, embrace Francesca and leave with Michelangelo and Nicolo by a little-used side gate. Avoiding the usual route to Michelangelo's house, which would take us in the direction of the Vatican, we skirt the main thoroughfares through alleys just coming to life with the morning's activity.

When we reach Michelangelo's gate, Urbino is waiting in the courtyard with three horses saddled.

As Nicolo and Urbino load saddlebags with provisions and my possessions, Michelangelo draws me aside. He pulls my hood up over my hair and arranges it to hide my face. He keeps his hands on either side of my head as he looks at me.

"Stay safe. I would come with you, but I fear that would bring even more of Paul's wrath down on your beautiful head. I will miss you. But I would miss you far more if you were imprisoned or killed."

He kisses me tenderly. I breathe in his scent to hold it in my memory—the cinnamon and nutmeg of the drink Urbino makes him every morning; the acrid metallic odor of the ground pigments that never seem to fade from his beard and his skin. I close my eyes to savor him. He kisses me again, this time on my eyelids, and then says, "You need to go. Now."

He lifts me into the saddle, his sinewy arms strong and enveloping.

We have not been apart since I returned from Ferrara three years ago. I do not believe I can bear the separation and choke back my anger at my brother for forcing me away.

Michelangelo holds my ankle until we depart, his long fingers circling it above my boot. Like his scent, I lock his touch into my memory to sustain me.

The sun is high on the third day of our journey as we make the final ascent to Orvieto, perched above cliff walls on a plateau that commands a view of the plains surrounding it. Orvieto is nearly ninety miles north of Rome; Paliano is forty miles to the south. With God's grace, we have fooled Paul's men at least for a few days.

The sisters of the Convent of San Paolo welcome me warmly. They feed Nicolo and Urbino before sending them to a nearby inn.

"The food is not so good there. Eat with us," they urge them.

I follow the nuns to my quarters after the meal. The windows overlook a courtyard with a fountain.

"In the spring the flowers will bloom and the fountain will flow like a stream in the mountains," Suora Angela assures me.

I wonder how long I'll need to seek refuge here. Will the war last days or seasons? I am exhausted by the ride, by the uncertainty.

"Suora, I need to rest. The journey and the upheaval in my peaceful life have overwhelmed me."

"Of course, my lady. Sleep as long as you wish. You are safe here."

She closes the door and leaves me to my solitude. I lean back against the pillow. I am once again a stranger, a guest. I ache with the loss of Michelangelo, who has become my home and my sanctuary. I do not know when I will see him again.

I sleep. The weeks of tension, the obstinacy of my brother and the pope, and the loss of Michelangelo have all taken their toll. I do not wake until the next morning.

My first full day at San Paolo passes without incident. Urbino returns to Rome. Nicolo takes it upon himself to keep watch on the convent from an unobtrusive distance.

At the end of the first week, a messenger arrives from my brother. He stays briefly to pass on news of the siege, but he brings no letters and will take nothing in writing back to Ascanio.

"The risk of my capture is too great, my lady. Your brother ordered me to carry back only what you say to me."

"Very well. Tell my brother to consider his people and his heritage and not to squander them with his misguided pride."

The young soldier looks at me and I see that he is about to question the wisdom of my words. He's evidently as familiar with Ascanio's volatile temper as I am. But he acquiesces, bows and leaves as soon as it's dark.

The next morning Nicolo comes to the convent gate. "My lady, there are spies in Orvieto watching the convent."

"The pope's spies or my brother's?"

"The pope's. They were careless at the inn last night. They don't know that I'm your man."

"Did they see or follow my brother's messenger?"

"No. They were already drinking."

The spies are not the only impediment placed in my path. It's clear that every letter addressed to me is being intercepted and read before reaching me. Broken seals, dirty fingerprints on the page, even a torn corner where a letter had been carelessly opened were all coarse signs to let me know that I'm under scrutiny. Is the pope trying to frighten me into urging my brother to surrender? How little he grasps of what motivates Ascanio Colonna.

To answer the pope's thinly disguised surveillance of my activities, I appeal to him directly, not with a letter but with two sonnets. Words have always been my weapons. They are not lethal, but they are as true as arrows meeting their target.

By May, no words will save my brother from his defiance. The pope's siege is successful. Ascanio's troops surrender. Ascanio himself flees to Napoli. And the pope razes every Colonna stronghold—my childhood home in Marino, my mother's final refuge at Rocca di Papa and Ascanio's last defense at Paliano. Our lands are confiscated; our castles are rubble.

I pack my meager belongings and bid farewell to the sisters of San Paolo who gave me shelter without question. I ride hard for Rome. I dismiss Nicolo when we reach the convent gates. But I refrain from making my presence known to the gatekeeper and ride on to Michelangelo's house.

Urbino lets me into the courtyard, takes the horse and brings me wine in the garden. When Michelangelo returns late in the day from the Vatican, he stops when he sees me.

I put down my goblet, rise from my seat and cross the distance between us into his waiting arms.

CHAPTER THIRTY-NINE

Spiritual Hunger

Vittoria
1541
Viterbo

Shortly after I return from Orvieto, word reaches me from Giovanna in Ischia that Costanza is ill and asking for me.

"She insists that she will not die until she sees you."

It has been five years since I breathed the mountain air of my Ischian home and walked its conch-shell covered paths, reciting a sonnet or delving into the meaning of a Gospel passage with Costanza and the circle of women she has nurtured, sheltered and challenged over the course of her nearly eighty-one years. As exhausted as I am from my exile and my failed attempt to negotiate a truce between the pope and my brother; as eager as I am to replenish my weary spirit in the encompassing presence of Michelangelo, I depart Rome within a day of receiving the message.

The seas do not recognize that it is June. The passage is rough, the weather wet and cold. I cannot bear to be below in the stale and dank quarters and take myself to the deck, enshrouded in heavy wool that too soon is drenched. I do not care. My outward discomfort is merely a shadow of the gnawing emptiness I feel within. The child I once was rails against the injustice of losing a mother for the second time. All my faith in the heaven that awaits Costanza fails me in my contemplation of my own despair that once again, someone I love is leaving me.

Arturo, Costanza's chamberlain and nearly as old as she is, greets me when I disembark in a state of agitation, far from the serenity I should be bringing Costanza in her final hours. Ashamed of my selfishness, I ask that we stop to pray at the cathedral on our way up the mountain. By the altar of Saint Rocco I light a candle, remembering that day forty years before when Costanza's kindness and discipline eased my fear and resentment. We continue the journey to the Castello, my own self-control reasserting itself, acknowledging the influence of the woman I am on my way to embrace.

When we arrive, I refuse the opportunity to rest or change my damp clothing and ask to be taken to Costanza immediately. No one attempts to dissuade me. They are too familiar with my stubbornness, my single-minded drive to act when perhaps I should take a step back.

It is late afternoon and the sun has finally emerged after the downpour I endured on the journey. The windows in Costanza's bedroom are open to the vista of the sea she has always cherished. She is in her bed, propped against several pillows, and turns from the windows as I enter.

"I've been watching the sea for your ship," she greets me, extending her hand. Her rings are loose; the wrists that emerge from the sleeves of her shift can be encircled with no more than my thumb and forefinger; her face, while still beautiful, is no longer brimming with the robust energy I remember. Her eyes, however, gleam with intelligence.

"Tia." I lean toward her and take her in my arms, even more aware of her fragility than I had perceived with my eyes.

We hold each other for a long moment and I swallow my tears. There will be time enough for those in the days ahead.

She releases me and pats the bed. "Sit here with me. Tell me everything. As eloquent as your words are on the page in your letters, hearing them from your mouth is far more satisfying."

She listens, questions and makes her penetrating observations as I recount my frustrations with Ascanio and my futile diplomacy. As I speak, the full impact of the destruction wrought by the pope's war with my family engulfs me. The awareness of loss that descended upon me on the ship now accelerates. The ruins of our castles and the shell of the woman beside me merge, and I experience a profound rage.

And then, I catch myself. I am pouring out my distress into the well of her understanding as if I am still a girl, uncertain and awkward. I take a breath.

"Enough of my sorrows. That is not why I am here, Tia. Forgive me."

"There is nothing to forgive, my dearest. Listening to you takes me away from my pain and loneliness. I have lived too long and lost too many—family, friends, lovers....Your presence restores me, reminds me that I still have something to give to the world."

"You've given me so much!"

"Thank you, Vittoria." She smiles as she touches my cheek.

"I've tired you. Rest. I'll sit with you while you sleep."

She acquiesces and closes her eyes. I settle in a chair by the window to wait and watch. My eyes roam around the familiar room and I notice that she has moved some of her favorite paintings here from the more public rooms of the Castello. I recognize and remember almost all of them—who painted them and when she acquired them, lavishing her patronage on both the aspiring and the accomplished artists who sought her attention. But one is new to me, a small, informal portrait that looks like a preliminary sketch. It is a striking likeness of Costanza as a young woman and it is propped on the table next to her bed, clearly a place of honor. Whoever has drawn the image has captured not only her beauty but her spirit. Her smile seems to convey an inner joy and a knowing acknowledgment of some secret, perhaps between her and the artist.

The painting is a reminder of how much Costanza has kept hidden in her life. She has been a widow for over forty years and never remarried—a lesson I took to heart in the power it gave her. But I've always been convinced that she has known love. She speaks of it too profoundly not to have experienced it.

I am holding the painting in my hand, studying it, when she wakes.

"Ah, you've discovered Leonardo's sketch."

"Da Vinci did this?"

"It was the preliminary drawing for a painting. He gave it to me when he left for France. A memento of a brief time when we... when I sat for him as a model." She gestures for the drawing and I hand it back to her. A smile lights up her face, the same enigmatic smile that graces the image.

"I've lived a wonderful life, Vittoria. May you as well."

I spend the next two weeks at Costanza's side, reading to her, feeding her sips of wine and broth, and finally, holding her hand and praying for her in her final, peaceful hours.

After her burial in the crypt in the cathedral, I return to Rome.

I become mother to another son when Margaret Pole is brutally executed after more than two years of imprisonment in the Tower of London. I hear the news not from Reginald but from the emperor's ambassador to England.

"The scene was horrific," he writes me. "Her sentencing was unjust and her executioner was either exceptionally incompetent or had been ordered to be viciously cruel." It took eleven blows of the sword to kill her.

I cannot imagine Reginald's despair and write to him immediately. Something precious was stolen from him by his mother's violent death, and I fear that his extraordinary brilliance and insightful embrace of God's love will be useless to him in his grief.

I find words to offer as a hand along the treacherous path I know lies ahead of him. I do not present myself as a replacement for his mother. No one can, especially a mother as close to Reginald and as influential as Margaret Pole had been.

But my words speak to Reginald and he calls on me, a humble supplicant and not the leader he has become to an intense and deeply spiritual group of seekers.

"My lady, I am so grateful for your message. It reached me at my darkest moment after I learned of my mother's death. She is a martyr, of that I am sure. She came to me in a dream, whole and unharmed, and her words reflected the same sentiments that I later read in your letter. You are her echo. Your words reverberate across the chasm that was carved between God and me by her murder."

I hold his hand, remembering his anguish two years before when Margaret was first imprisoned.

I foresee Reginald being torn apart by both his personal suffering and his country's disorder. As much as he feels compelled to intervene in the disastrous consequences of Henry's reign, his gifts are being squandered. The pope, fortunately, agrees with me. He considers it best to give Reginald a respite from the throes of his mission to bring England back into the fold of the Church, and assigns him to govern a portion of the Papal States in Viterbo. Wisely, he also assigns Reginald a bodyguard.

Reginald's appointment to Viterbo comes between Michelangelo and me, an unexpected rift as I struggle to find a balance among the many competing cries for my heart.

I speak to Michelangelo over dinner. The *Last Judgment* is in its final stages and he is working at an intense pace to finish it. Finding time for each other has become complicated, and both of us are suffering from the strain. I know I am about to add to it.

"I am going to Viterbo next week," I tell him.

"Why? For how long?" He stops eating to question me.

"I'm following Cardinal Pole. I'm uncertain how long I'll be away. He is in despair over the execution of his mother. I will try to be a lodestar for him and guide him out of his hopelessness with God's help."

"I know I should be sympathetic, Vittoria. You have been the same bright star for me in my own wretchedness. But I have watched you over the years empty yourself to refill the hollow soul of every man who turned to you as his goddess."

"That is a harsh assessment."

"I have long accepted a difficult truth. You are the only woman in my life. I am not the only man in yours."

"I can't be anyone other than who I am."

"And I love you for who you are. But there is a price we both pay. Mine is to bear your absence from me—whether it's caused by your following Reginald Pole to Viterbo or by loving those in need of your spirit and kindness. The price you have to pay is your awareness of how deep is the ache of my loneliness when you are gone from me."

"I do not love them as I love you, Michelangelo. Surely you know that."

"I thought I did. But the more I see the world bombarding you with demands, clamoring for your attention, the more I see you withdrawing from me."

I am at a loss about how to answer him or assuage the pain I hear expressed in every word. Michelangelo and I deal with our fame and our art very differently. He closes himself off from all but a few of his closest friends, because each person he loves takes a part of him that is then no longer his. He believes that to protect his talent and to create requires solitude and concentration to the exclusion of anything else. He has built high walls around himself to shut out the world.

Since I emerged from the devastation of my mourning, I have been nurtured by my friendships. Every conversation, every shared experience, every letter enriches me. I give, but I also receive. As much as Michelangelo sees me being drained by those whose lives intersect with mine, I feel that I am being filled up.

"You are right, my dearest," I tell him. "I am overwhelmed with sadness that this decision of mine is hurting you so. I am not abandoning you, and Cardinal Pole is not stealing me away from you. I shall write to you every day and think of you more often than that. Please know that something beyond my understanding is calling me to Viterbo."

"I thought I might lose you forever during your brother's war, and it drove me mad. To have you back for such a brief but profound time, only to have you leave me again, is more than I can bear. I must ask you, are you afraid of what has happened between us?"

It is now my turn in this conversation to be riven by agony.

"Are you running away from me, from us, Vittoria?"

The "No!" jumps from my lips too vehemently, too quickly, to be the truth. We both realize it. I bury my face in my hands, struggling with my thoughts. Am I truly using Reginald Pole's misery as an excuse to distance myself from the overwhelming power of my love for Michelangelo? Perhaps we are not so different, after all, and I, too, need barriers.

Michelangelo reaches across the table and gently pries my fingers away from my troubled brow. He holds my hands as he speaks. "Be honest with me and with yourself, Vittoria. If you're afraid, that's something I, of all people, comprehend. I don't condemn you."

I blink away tears as I nod. "If I'm honest, as I'm trying to be right now, I do not know the answer to that myself. What has happened between us since my return from Orvieto surpasses what I understood of love. I need to breathe other air, look out my window and see another landscape, while I sort this through. It could have been any place, but Viterbo presents itself. I am not going away to lose you. I am going to find myself."

"Then go in peace. I will pray that you come back to me, but I will not punish you or burden you with my sorrow. You are free."

Despite Michelangelo's releasing me, I ride away from Rome the next week in a state of confusion and uneasiness. It does not help that the road to Viterbo is the same one on which I learned of Ferrante's death so many years ago. But as we travel I realize I cannot identify the spot where the messenger met me and I fell in agonizing grief. We push on. I no longer need to erect a shrine to my dead husband, either on the side of the highway or in my memory.

Viterbo is closer to Rome than I remembered. In less than a day and a half, we make the climb to the mountaintop town and arrive at the Convent of Santa Caterina. Unlike its counterpart in Ferrara, this Santa Caterina is simple and unadorned, set away from the town center.

Within the week I have an invitation from Reginald to join him in the afternoons, when a small group meets at his home for study and discussion. I am happy to see him so engaged with the life of the spirit and distracted, if only momentarily, from English politics.

"My lady, I am thankful to have you so near. Your presence is a comfort to me and your contributions to our conversation will surely bring us closer to an acceptance of God in our lives."

Joining us every day are Pietro Carnesecchi and Marcantonio Flaminio, both men I know through Fra Bernardino and Juan de Valdés. Pietro and I met when I came to Rome with Caterina Cibo to petition Pope Clement for the Capuchins. He was a secretary to the Holy Father then and met Fra Bernardino when I did. Like Pietro Bembo, he is an avid follower of the monk and traveled from city to city to hear him preach. Because of Fra Bernardino, our paths crossed frequently over the years and our common beliefs are a bond.

Marcantonio Flaminio I know less well. He is a disciple of Juan de Valdés, but joined his circle after I left Napoli. As intense a visionary as Juan, Marcantonio takes our discussions to a piercing lucidity, spinning out his thoughts on Scripture and God's grace with energy and power.

We call ourselves the "Spirituali." Our group swells and contracts now and then as others on the same spiritual journey come to Viterbo to share in our study, including Cardinals Gasparo Contarini and Jacopo Sadoleto. I am the only woman.

It is exhilarating and provocative to seize upon a passage of Scripture and unravel its meaning. It is also deeply satisfying to immerse ourselves in a passionate exploration of the question of justification by faith—a topic driving all of Christianity during this turbulent time since Martin Luther proposed that salvation was a gift from God earned not by good works, but by faith.

These afternoons are a heady experience. Reginald one day describes our explorations as a spiritual meal, nourishing us with a "meat that does not perish."

I didn't comprehend how hungry I was.

In the evenings, however, when I return to the convent and my solitude, my thoughts retreat to Michelangelo and the fear that drove me away from him.

As I did in Ferrara and again in Orvieto, I want to share with him what I'm discovering. I come away from every impassioned conversation churning with new insights that are both a consolation and an impetus to learn more. I have encountered Michelangelo in the depths of his own doubts. With intense clarity, I grasp that what I'm absorbing in Viterbo can only ease his agitation and feed his longing to know God.

And yet…. The meal that is satisfying my spiritual hunger seems incompatible with the emotional and physical hunger I feel for Michelangelo. I told him I needed to leave to pursue answers to the dilemma that torments me. I am struggling to reconcile Vittoria, the seeker after God, with Vittoria, the woman who loves Michelangelo. What I desperately long to do is knit together these divergent "selves" who seem to be on very separate paths.

At night I pray; I cry; I rail against my own contradictions. In the mornings I walk along the city walls high above the valley and breathe in the immense beauty of God's creation. Nothing helps.

Without Michelangelo, and questioning God's purpose in my divided identity, I catch myself falling back into old afflictions. I feel I should nourish myself with meditation and contemplation instead of bread and meat. Reginald assumes I am eating at the convent and the sisters think I am eating at the Cardinal's house, so my misguided fasting goes unnoticed. I am punishing myself and I do it knowingly. I have been in this situation before, but I stubbornly resist the memory of my destructiveness. Didn't such deprivation fuel my poetry? Doesn't my physical denial offer me new insights?

I fast from Michelangelo as well as from food. I stop writing to him and leave his letters to me unopened.

Flinging myself into the afternoon discussions at Reginald's house with unbridled zeal, I submerge myself in the language as if submitting to John the Baptist in the river Jordan. But even drenched in these waters, I cannot find harmony. Despite what I expected, the Spirituali do not provide me with all the sustenance I need.

The morning hours are difficult for me to fill. Normally I would have spent them writing, but my descent into abstinence also encompasses my poetry. I am empty of everything.

At one in the afternoon I leave the convent for the brief walk to Reginald's house. The fountain in the little piazza facing the convent trickles lazily, a thin stream of water spilling over the spout into the pool below. Cicadas hum in the distance. I am enveloped by the heat and light and sound of an August afternoon and I don't notice the man on the opposite side of the fountain until he steps into my path.

"Vittoria."

I stop abruptly, surprised to hear my name spoken by an all-too-familiar voice.

"Michelangelo!"

"What has happened to you? You are a cipher! Are you ill? Or have you done this to yourself?"

I see reflected in his eyes my own hollow expression as he holds himself at a distance from me. His hands remain at his sides, fingers clenched. Neither of us moves from the spot where he first called out to me. And then I sink to the ground, my skirt billowing out around my fragile frame. I am lost.

He kneels in front of me and supports me with his arm.

"When was the last time you ate?"

"Communion this morning."

He lifts me from the dusty piazza and leads me to an inn across the way. There he orders broth, and when it comes he feeds me small bits of bread soaked in the steaming, fragrant liquid. He says little until I eat at least a few morsels.

"How long have you been starving yourself?"

"I am fasting," I whisper.

"It's not Lent. And you are hardly a sinner. Has Cardinal Pole advised you to punish yourself so severely?" His anger hovers in the air, seeking a target.

I shake my head. I can scarcely speak to him, as if I suffered some affliction in my throat that holds the words there, captive. All my efforts to abstain from him have not diminished the love I feel for him or the intense joy I experience in his presence, even with his anger.

Surely God does not mean for me to put him out of my life.

"Am I the reason you're suffering?" he asks. I can hear his own suffering in his question, and I cannot bear for him to be troubled because of me. I reach into myself and find my voice to answer him.

"I alone am the cause, not you. I have allowed myself to flounder in a pool of despair. Forgive me!"

"Is this how you've sought to discern the place of our love in your life? By denying yourself everything—not only me, but food, comfort, even my letters? I knew something was terribly wrong when you stopped writing. Your letters at first were full of excitement. I, too, experienced the wonder and mystery as you recounted your conversations. I thought, Vittoria made a good decision to go away, to see with fresh eyes, because we were both gaining from this retreat. But then, without preface or explanation, you extinguished the light that had been guiding us both. When you didn't respond to my letters, I knew I had to come."

"What about your work? The wall?"

"It can wait. Besides, I can't work when I'm so worried about you." He pauses for a moment. "I was right to worry. You need a physician."

"What ails me is not anything a physician can cure."

"Perhaps not a physician who can set bones and relieve fevers like Baccio, but a physician of the mind who can restore balance to your health. Have none of your friends here, especially the illustrious cardinal, seen what has become of you?"

"I've kept my struggles to myself. I don't think anyone here can conceive of what I'm going through."

"*I* do."

All this time, since he found me in the piazza, he has not touched me except to lift me to my feet when I collapsed. He seems especially careful not to overwhelm me or coerce me in any way. On the contrary, I feel that whatever I say to him he will affirm. As much as I sense his longing for me and his desire to heal my suffering, I know he will allow me to accept or reject both his help and his love.

"I know you understand. You are my constant, the immovable block of rough-hewn marble in the middle of my garden, ready to offer me stability in the midst of turbulence."

My metaphor makes him smile.

"Am I so unyielding?"

"You are unyielding in your steadfast loyalty to me. You will not allow me to push you away, no matter how determined I am to convince you that I am not worthy of you."

"I will never believe you are unworthy of me. But you're right, I will always be your bulwark. I want to protect you, Vittoria. I want to do more for you than anyone I have ever known in this world. Let me."

"I would if I understood how."

"Come back to Rome with me. Whatever good Viterbo gave you in the beginning seems lost now."

"I fear I want too much. I want heaven and I want you."

"Are we incompatible, heaven and I?"

He asks me with such vulnerability and simplicity. How can he be at odds with heaven when all he has ever done for me is bring me happiness? Is he part of the grace of God that I long to be open to, that I long to receive?

"We seem to have changed places," he says. "When I was turning away from life, you entreated me to allow you to love me. Now I'm begging you. Let me lead you out of this vale of despair that has entrapped you. Let me love *you*."

I look into his eyes, as I have so many times over the years, and I cannot deny him.

"Yes," I say, and grip his hand. "Take me home."

We leave for Rome the next day, but first I go to Reginald to say my good-byes. I offer the state of my health as an explanation for my sudden departure, which is no lie.

"I'm devastated that you need to leave us, but wish you a speedy recovery. You've become such a part of our circle, my lady. We shall miss your insights and your ability to express our ideas in language that sharpens their clarity."

"I have gained so much, Reginald, from my inclusion and from our friendship."

"As have I. You have eased a most difficult time for me and I am grateful."

He is gracious, but he also seems oblivious to how my private suffering ravages me. I admit that my tendency to mask my inner thoughts and give others what they ask of me has something to do with his blindness. But as much as I respect Reginald and admire him for his piety and his spiritual leadership, I'm not willing to reveal my deepest concerns to him. I can't imagine that he comprehends the ambiguity I confront.

Marcantonio has other concerns when I tell him I'm returning to Rome.

"My book cries out for your guidance and literary genius, my lady. May I call upon you again for help in shaping it?"

"Of course, Marcantonio. When I'm well, I will be honored to be a midwife to your creation."

And so I set off down the mountain at Michelangelo's side, trailed by a mule carrying my belongings. At first we ride in companionable silence as we often have in the past. But about an hour into the journey he breaks into song. Even the horses seem to appreciate his robust joy as they prick up their ears and quicken their pace. And for the first time since I've been away, I laugh.

My arrival at San Silvestro causes a stir. I'm unexpected; my appearance conveys an unsparing revelation of my misguided behavior. The devastating changes, unrecognized until I saw my reflection in Michelangelo's eyes, are confirmed when Suora Francesca greets me.

"My lady! What has become of you!" The concern and dismay on her face is another jolt, awakening me to how unaware I've been of the severity of my condition.

She immediately gives orders for my rooms to be prepared and a nourishing meal to be brought to her quarters, where she takes me, her arm wrapped protectively around my frail bones.

She seats me in her most comfortable chair—one I know she keeps for visiting cardinals and benefactors. She clasps my fingers and prays with me. Her touch is gentle, her words a balm.

"I didn't mean to cause you worry, Francesca. I was lost, for so many reasons. But Michelangelo found me, fed me and brought me home." I smile and gesture to the walls around us.

"You will always have a home here," she reassures me.

I spend the first weeks sleeping, eating the small but frequent meals Francesca sends to my rooms, and sitting in the garden. Summer is fading to a burnished copper. Michelangelo goes back to his wall, but sends Urbino every day with a gift—a sonnet, a drawing, a small crucifix he designed, strung on a slender ribbon to wear around my neck. It is nothing like the diamond cross Ferrante gave me on our wedding day. But the beauty of Michelangelo's cross crucifies me, and I write back to him in thanks. In capturing Christ's suffering so profoundly, he is helping me unravel my own.

Michelangelo himself comes at least once a week to sit with me in the garden. We talk; he sketches; I tease him now and then as we regain our pleasure in each other.

His hand moves across the page as if in a caress. But rather than stroking my face, he is sketching it. The late-afternoon sun in the garden illuminates not only his reluctant subject, but allows me to study him as he works.

The hand holding his red chalk is scarred and stained, the pigments from the *Last Judgment* imbedded in the deep lines of his palm. The hand has neither the elegant proportions of his David nor the evocative power of his Adam on the Sistine ceiling. But it is a robust and beautiful hand to me, a hand that clasps mine and lifts me up. A hand that encircles my own and fills its emptiness.

A light smile plays on his lips and I find myself reflecting it back to him.

"I don't know why you're doing this when you have much more important work that begs for your attention."

"I do this because I can give both of us long life by depicting these faces of ours."

"You intend to make us immortal?"

"A thousand years from now, people will see how lovely you were and how wretched I was. But more than that, they'll see how, in loving you, I was no fool."

I shake my head. "But you *are* a fool. What do you know of me to love me like this?"

"I know enough. When others looked at me, they saw only a rough-hewn block of hardened stone, an impassive shell. But you, like a sculptor, carved away at me until you found the soul within."

I receive a letter from Reginald, abject with dismay that he didn't recognize my despair. I suspect that someone has written to him. Probably Francesca, because she and Michelangelo are the only ones aware of how far I have fallen. I cannot imagine Michelangelo writing to the man he blames for being oblivious to my misery.

"Forgive me for my blindness," Reginald writes. "I heard only your impassioned engagement in our spiritual inquiries and didn't see the personal questions for which you also were seeking answers. I wish I was there with you to guide you back to the health I know God wants for you. Take a small step every day—even if it is one more morsel of food or one less thought of desolation. Believe that God's grace will come to you."

I write back to him and find that in doing so that I am regaining my lost self.

"There is no need to ask for forgiveness. We each see what we wish to see. The last thing you needed at that moment in your life was another suffering mother, so I kept my agonies hidden from you. Be assured that I will follow the path you have suggested to me."

The weeks of my recuperation turn into months, and as the feast of All Saints approaches, I experience a resurgence of energy and a desire to be out in the world again. Michelangelo has finished the *Last Judgment*. It is to be unveiled on the Eve of All Saints and I want nothing more than to be there in the chapel with him.

During the fall I work in secret with Innocenza on a gift for Michelangelo—a bound collection of my poems, each one selected with love and care and placed in an order that had special meaning for us, rather than the order in which I'd written them. Innocenza spends painstaking hours copying them in her beautiful hand, because I have no intention of placing the work with a printer. This collection is for Michelangelo alone, and I guard it with my heart. Every evening after the pages are dry I read them, my fingers tracing the words as if I were writing them anew. Captured within the strokes and flourishes of Innocenza's pen are my questioning and doubt and discovery and revelation. Our own humanity and frailty, Michelangelo's and mine, reflected in Christ's journey. Our search for transcendence as we contemplate His sacrifice. The triumph of His crucifixion as the ultimate act of love. I put the sheets away in my chest as they accumulate and then wipe the tears from my eyes.

In the last week of October Innocenza finishes.

"My lady, I thought I knew your poems. But in copying them this time, I found a new message. I feel as if God spoke to me through your words."

"Oh, Innocenza, your reaction honors and humbles me. Thank you, dearest, for telling me."

"I have more to tell, my lady. I am about to make a decision that I have been considering for some time. Working with your poetry has helped me clarify where my life's journey is taking me."

I wait, curious to know what momentous declaration my young charge is about to make. I love her as a daughter, deeply grateful that my secretary, Carlo Gualteruzzi, entrusted her to me for her education. With Innocenza I feel I was given the opportunity to pass on what Costanza imparted to me—curiosity, fierce confidence in my own intellect and joy in learning. She embraces everything with a quiet zeal. What will she do now with what she's learned?

"I'm going to take the veil. I've spoken to the Madre and she believes I am ready." Innocenza is beaming.

Her announcement is not what I anticipated, but I conceal my surprise in a warm embrace so that she cannot see my face. I do not want Innocenza to hide herself away from the world when she has so much to offer it. Perhaps my choice to live in a convent has colored her decision. But my living at San Silvestro as a guest is for the protection of my reputation and the peace it gives me to write. I would no more have chosen to profess vows than I would have to marry again. My freedom and independence are always paramount for me. As intent as I am to find the divine, I do it on my own terms.

A part of me grieves for Innocenza as I kiss and bless her. Grief for what I'm losing in her companionship, but also grief for what she's losing in locking herself away.

My book of poems is bound and ready by the Eve of All Saints. No longer a pile of loose pages but an object whose artistry extends beyond Innocenza's flowing script, I hold it in my hands, feeling its heft and pleased that the bookbinder heeded my instructions for simplicity. This is no jeweled and ornamented piece of work; its ornamentation lies within. I wrap both the book and myself carefully that day. I have gained back some of the weight I lost in Viterbo, but Salviata still has to make alterations to my gown. I choose one I wore during the emperor's visit to Rome, the green velvet rather than the black brocade. The occasion is to be one of celebration and triumph, not mourning, just as the message of the *Last Judgment* conveys.

In place of a necklace, I wear Michelangelo's crucifix.

The Vatican is even more abuzz than usual as invited guests gather in the chapel's anteroom. The chapel was closed for several days as the scaffolding was dismantled, the floor scrubbed and the paint on the final figures dried. I search the room for Michelangelo and find him in a far corner surveying the assembled crowd. I note with a smile that he has taken as much care with his dress as I have with mine. His jacket fits his lean frame well and his boots are tall and polished. His beard is trimmed and still without a strand of gray. It's hard to believe that he's sixty-six, although he often grumbles about the indignities of old age. Surrounding him are much younger men, overindulgent, dissolute cardinals and ambassadors with soft faces and soft bellies.

I catch Michelangelo's eye across the room and he nods with a grin and a shrug, as if to say, "It's done. Too late now to be troubled about how people will judge it." But I know he cares deeply.

We do not move toward each other. The room is too crowded and we have long become accustomed to maintaining our distance at gatherings like this, where everyone's movements and conversations are fodder for gossip. The pope is hosting a meal after Mass. We will see each other then.

A hush comes over the assembly as the pope enters the chamber. The Swiss Guards stride across the room to the chapel doors and fling them open as the choir begins to sing. The pope leads, followed by the cardinals and bishops, then Michelangelo and the other guests. I am near the end of the procession. I have no need to rush to see the wall because I've been a witness to its creation. I can hear the murmurs and gasps of those up ahead as the full impact of Michelangelo's vision becomes known.

I take my place near the rear of the chapel and have a vantage point of both the wall and the congregation. Few are attending to the pope reciting the opening prayers of the Mass; most are staring gape-mouthed at the figures rising or falling on the wall, pulled up by angels to the welcoming Christ or thrown down to the ravages of hell. In addition to the sacred figures, the angels and saints, Michelangelo has included references to his beloved Dante's *Inferno*. Charon, the gatekeeper of the river Styx, and Minos, the king of Hell, reflect Michelangelo's vision of the horrors awaiting the damned.

Around me heads shake or bend to neighbors in whispers. The fresco is unlike any depiction of the *Last Judgment* before it.

Michelangelo is no stranger to controversy, but this masterpiece seems to be eliciting far more than usual. Behind me someone mutters that the painting is more appropriate for a brothel than a sacred space. I do not turn around, but recognize the voice of Biagio da Cesena, the pope's Master of Ceremonies. He and many others see only the nudity and stark passion of Michelangelo's magnificent figures, ignoring entirely the theology they represent. I remember my long-ago conversation with Michelangelo about the nature of sacred art. Clearly there are those in the chapel who disagree with us.

I don't know how much of this Michelangelo hears. I can't see him during the Mass, and when I arrive at the pope's apartment for the meal, he is nowhere to be found. I suspect he left quietly, unwilling to listen to any more boorish criticism from those who don't appreciate his art.

I endure the meal unhappily, not only because Michelangelo is absent. It is excessive both in the lavish display of food on which the guests gorge themselves and in the unrestrained and even ignorant comments about the painting. I keep my own counsel. I have been too involved in the conception, if not the implementation itself, to be an objective participant in the conversation. I am also afraid I would defend Michelangelo too fiercely, probably to knowing smiles around the table.

Refraining from speaking, I listen, and hear something far more chilling than a concern with Michelangelo's naked saints. The conversation drifts to reflect an undercurrent of fear about the very topics that consume the Spirituali in Viterbo. Cardinal Carafa, in particular, speaks in threatening tones about the need to silence the voices of those who encourage the direct relationship with God through Scripture, which has been the foundation of Fra Bernardino's preaching and Juan de Valdés's teaching.

I excuse myself early, my fatigue evident to the Holy Father, and return to the convent. Although exhausted, I can't retire without seeing Michelangelo and send Nicolo to his house to invite him to visit me.

I do not have to wait long. He comes to me in the garden as the sun is setting, lighting his features with a fire that might have illuminated one of his paintings.

In greeting me he gently lifts the cross that hangs around my neck. "I saw this morning that you wore it. Thank you."

"I always wear it."

"If you have called me to discuss the reactions to the wall, I don't want to listen."

I read in his words and on his face his desire to push away the murmurs and misinterpretations of the morning's crowd.

"That's not why I wanted to see you," I assure him. "I have something for you that has nothing to do with the wall, but everything to do with us."

I hold out the wrapped book to him and he takes it.

"Open it."

He sits then and unwinds the cord. When he lifts the book out and opens it, a tender smile eases across his face, erasing the dark mood with which he'd arrived.

He turns the pages slowly, stopping to read a poem or run his finger over Innocenza's beautiful lettering, as I'd done. Then he looks up.

"I do not know how to thank you or repay you."

"There is no need. I give it without any expectation of reciprocation. I give it purely out of love."

"I know this book will bring me hours of happiness, not only because of your beautiful words but also because of your desire to do this for me. It's a sign to me that you're healing, that you are less afraid."

"I began to be less afraid the moment you came to me in Viterbo. I could no more cut you out of my life than cut out my heart. I have accepted God's gift of you to me. That is what you are—a gift."

"As you are to me."

CHAPTER FORTY

Inquisition

Vittoria
1542 – 1547
Rome

The strength of my friendship with Michelangelo more than sustains me as the world beyond us once again begins to unravel.

I write to Reginald Pole after attending the pope's dinner, alarmed by the perceptions at the table that the ideas of Fra Bernardino and our spiritual circle are a danger to the Church.

"Do they not recognize that what we seek, and what we encourage in others, is personal renewal with Christ? I know Pope Paul is an advocate of reform, as we are. But he seems to be listening to voices who see reform leading to schism, not reinvigoration. I am worried that our ideas have been misunderstood."

My worries are not unfounded. Although it takes several months, the fear in Rome festers. The loudest voice in the pope's ear is Cardinal Carafa's, an extremist who suspects heresy everywhere.

In July, Reginald sends me a warning.

"You were prescient in your estimation of the danger we face. I have heard through sympathetic colleagues in the Vatican that Paul has established a Holy Office of Inquisition on the advice of Cardinal Carafa. Fra Bernardino has been called to Rome to answer questions. My advice to you, difficult as it must be for you to hear, is to distance yourself from Bernardino."

Fra Bernardino does not go to Rome. Instead, he flees Italy when his friends see no possibility that he will be received safely in Rome. Caterina Cibo is among those who aid him in his escape across the Alps, and for that she is suspected and harassed by the Inquisition. To my great surprise, Ascanio is also involved. He tells me this when he makes a quiet visit to me at the home of friends outside of Rome.

"I know you followed Bernardino avidly, and I thought you'd want to know that he made it safely to Geneva."

"How did you find out?"

"I'm the one who provided him with horses and men for the journey. My men returned with the news."

"You! Why? I didn't realize you were even aware of him."

"Despite your opinion of me, dear sister, I do occasionally exhibit noble qualities. I came into contact with his teachings when I was in exile in Napoli and was moved to embrace them. I've also read some of your own work, inspired by the Spirituali."

"You surprise me, Ascanio. You took a great risk in helping him."

"I decided I was already known as the pope's enemy. I've lost everything. The risk for me was much lower than for others."

"Please take great care. There is still much the Inquisition could do to destroy you."

"Right now they're going after the thinkers, not someone like me they consider an outlaw in the mountains, spiriting away their supposed enemies. You're the one who should take care. They're watching you."

He leaves me, a changed man. He is correct about the Church's targets. In horror, I watch as one by one, my spiritual friends come under condemnation for their ideas. I believe I escaped being called before the Inquisition in those early years because of my position with Pope Paul. He is not above entreating me when he wants me to use my influence with others. Also, unlike Fra Bernardino, who renounced the Church and declared himself a Protestant when he arrived in Geneva, I still believe reform is possible from within.

Reginald remains on that path as well and urges Paul to send him to the Council of Trent to address the possibility of reconciliation and reform. However, Cardinal Carafa continues to prevail, and any compromise with the north seems truly out of reach.

But for me, the tempestuous and precarious state of the Church pales in comparison to the pain inflicted upon my personal life.

Over the years I return occasionally to Viterbo to spend time with the Spirituali and to escape the heat and miasmic air of Roman summers. As I promised Marcantonio Flaminio, I assist him with the final preparations for the book he is editing, the *Beneficio di Cristo*, the *Benefit of Christ's Death*. The book reflects the message we hold to be the salvation of the Church. As soon as it is printed, its powerful meaning resonates with all who read it. It becomes a phenomenon, passing the light of Christ's sacrifice from hand to hand like a flame spreading through a forest. It should have been no surprise to us that its popularity enrages the Inquisition. The book is placed on the Index of Forbidden Books, but not before forty thousand copies had spread to all the corners of Italy.

But even when I'm separated from Michelangelo by my work with the Spirituali, I always remain in close touch with him. Viterbo's proximity to Rome makes it possible for me never to be more than two days from him. My ability to travel comfortably comes to an abrupt halt, however, in 1544. I become seriously ill during one of my stays in Viterbo and am forced to acknowledge that as a woman in her fifties, I no longer have the resilience to overcome sickness easily. When I decide to return to Rome, there are many objections in Viterbo—from Reginald, from my physician and from the sisters at Santa Caterina. They do not comprehend that the pain of travel is dwarfed by the pain of separation from Michelangelo when I need him most. I prevail, but not without considerable persistence on my part. I write to Michelangelo.

"I am coming back to Rome as soon as I can arrange a carriage. I am too ill to ride. I fear that a full recovery is not possible and I have no desire to stay here apart from you."

When I arrive in Rome I move to the Convent of Sant'Anna de Funari, where the sisters can nurse me. It is also closer to Michelangelo's house. Awaiting me in my room is a vase exploding with sunflowers, which grow in Michelangelo's garden. I fall asleep, exhausted by the journey but comforted by the warmth of both the brilliant yellow of the blooms and the gesture of love they represent.

When I awaken, Michelangelo is sitting by the window sketching.

"You haven't been drawing me in my sleep, have you?"

"Your face in repose is beautiful, even now when ravaged by illness. But no, I'm sketching a building, not a body. Against my vehement wishes, Pope Paul wants to 'honor' me by appointing me the superintendent of St. Peter's building work."

"And you don't want it."

"I am done. I am old. I have no wish to be at the service of others, except for you."

"And yet, you sit here making drawings of a basilica."

"Only to pass the time until you woke."

"You know you'll do this, don't you? You won't be able to abide it if the building isn't perfect—and it won't be perfect if you don't supervise it."

I smile. This conversation, so familiar to me in its intimacy, affirms my decision to spend whatever time remains to me with Michelangelo. God smiles on me, however. I do not succumb, despite how gravely ill I am. The nuns of Sant'Anna call the priest to administer Last Rites. But I am all too aware of the odor of the candles, the rough thumb of the padre making the cross on my forehead and the low murmur of his prayers. A few hours after he leaves, I sit up and ask for wine. Stunned, the suora at my bedside gives me a few sips and then runs to alert the rest of the house that I am not ready to die.

Although never completely restored to my former health, I recover enough to leave my bed and resume a simple life.

"Don't even contemplate returning to Viterbo," Michelangelo lectures me when I am well enough to be out in the garden.

"Of course not. I intend to remain at your side as long as God allows and we can bear each other."

"I will never tire of you."

God gives us a few more years together, years of excruciating personal despair that I survive because of Michelangelo.

The first blow is a devastating loss on the battlefield of Ceresole in April of 1544. Alfonso, my brilliant son, whose life until this moment has been without blemish, leads his army into a catastrophic confrontation with the French. Twelve thousand of his men perish; three thousand are taken prisoner. He himself is gravely wounded, not only in shattered limbs but also in spirit. The devastation of the loss prompts Charles V to relieve Alfonso of his military duties and my son is disgraced. The echoes of Ferrante's descent haunt me. Maria, desperate to heal the suffering of her damaged husband, writes to me in anguish.

"I do not know what to do for him. I have tried to lift him from his melancholy with the discussions of history and spirituality that once were our lifeblood; I read to him from his poetic guideposts, Petrarch and Dante; I have even invited the women of my court to entertain him with games, dances and conversation. He turns his head to the wall and will not speak. Pray for him."

When I receive the news of his death, it is Michelangelo who catches me as I collapse. For all the battles Alfonso fought, all the wounds that tore his body, it is a simple fever that takes him. But more deadly than any physical ailment, his killer is the festering torment of dishonor.

Michelangelo holds me until my rage is spent.

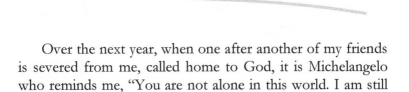

Over the next year, when one after another of my friends is severed from me, called home to God, it is Michelangelo who reminds me, "You are not alone in this world. I am still with you and I love you."

And when I can no longer fight the enemy gnawing at me from within, it is Michelangelo who moves me to a room in the Cesarini Palace overlooking its garden and who sits with me, his gnarled and stained fingers entwined with mine.

"I am here," he whispers. "You are safe with me."

I close my eyes, knowing I am loved.

EPILOGUE

Without Her Spark

Michelangelo
1547
Rome

The Cesarini garden is blue-gray in the winter dusk. *Un campo azzurro*, he reflects, like the note he'd written to her long ago on paper the color of the raised flower beds below her window. He remembers her smile at his little jokes, her laughter when he sang coming down from the mountain that day he brought her home from Viterbo.

He turns from the window and adds a log to the fire. The room is cold; her lips will turn as blue as the garden if he does not work quickly.

There was a time when she didn't need the fire because she *was* the fire—a radiant blaze that burned and nourished him.

Behind him she sleeps. The priest had been there earlier with incense and chrism and candle flame; she can no longer swallow and so didn't take communion. Out in the corridor a nun prays a novena. Another will relieve her in an hour.

He has no prayers left, but he stays. He will allow no one to take his place.

The wood catches and he adds another log as flames creep along the edge of the blackening timber. Despite the heat emanating from the hearth, he feels his own fire dwindling to ash.

Without her as his spark, he grows cold.

ACKNOWLEDGMENTS

Love That Moves the Sun is a significant departure for me as a writer. Until I ventured into the sixteenth century, my stories, although firmly rooted in history, were set in the twentieth and twenty-first centuries. Given the unfamiliar terrain, I am especially grateful to those who guided me along the way.

My first note of thanks goes to my agent, Maura Key-Casella, who first encouraged me to explore historical fiction as a genre and who kept sending me back to hone the story. I also extend my appreciation to the enthusiastic librarians at the Richard Salter Storrs Library, Barbara Fitzgerald and Freya Wolk, whose delight in unearthing obscure articles was infectious and sustained me through the long haul of research. I'm also indebted to Nancy Corbino, my tireless and knowledgeable guide on the island of Ischia, who led me in Vittoria Colonna's footsteps at the Castello Aragonese.

Once my words were on the page, I turned to my first readers for their insights. Many thanks to Bethe Moulton, Andrea Taupier and Karen Gladwin for offering their reactions to the earliest draft of the novel. Their astute observations helped to shape the next version. A special thank you to Daisy Miller, whose perceptive and learned review shed new light on the book. To literary scholar Ann Brian Murphy, my sincere gratitude for her penetrating grasp of the story and wise advice as I reached the final stages.

My editor, Paula Eykelhof, has always made my stories better, and this book was no exception. From her understanding of the grand sweep of Vittoria's life and her relationship with Michelangelo to the minutiae of how many times I used my favorite words, Paula guided me with skill and understanding. I am deeply grateful for her continued support of my work.

My thanks also to Beth Landi, whose sharp eyes proofread this lengthy and complex manuscript with grace and curiosity.

Special accolades to artist Eliza Moser, whose training in Renaissance art techniques came to fruition in her masterful creation of the cover. It is everything I hoped, conveying both the hidden depth of Vittoria and the reference to Michelangelo's drawings.

A work of this magnitude takes many years to complete. My thanks and love to my husband, whose enthusiasm and support never waned.

SELECTED BIBLIOGRAPHY

Arnold, Thomas F. *The Renaissance at War*. New York: Harper Collins Publishers/Smithsonian Books, 2006

Barolini, Teodolinda, trans. "Paradiso 33: Invisible Ink." Commento Baroliniano, Digital Dante. New York: Columbia University Libraries, 2014

Bartlett, Kenneth R. *A Short History of the Renaissance*. Toronto: University of Toronto Press, 2016

Brundin, Abigail. *Vittoria Colonna and the Spiritual Poetics of the Italian Reformation*. Surrey, UK: Ashgate Publishing Company, 2008

Colonna, Vittoria. *Sonnets for Michelangelo*. Chicago: The University of Chicago Press, 2005

Gayford, Martin. *Michelangelo: His Epic Life*. London: Fig Tree, Penguin Random House UK, 2013

Giovio, Paolo. *Notable Men and Women of Our Time*. Cambridge, Massachusetts: Harvard University Press, The I Tatti Renaissance Library, 2013

Holroyd, Charles. *Michael Angelo Buonarroti, with Translations of the Life of the Master by His Scholar, Ascanio Condivi, and Three Dialogues from the Portuguese by Francisco d'Ollanda* . London: Duckworth and Company, 1903

Jaffe, Irma B. and Gernando Colombardo. *Shining Eyes, Cruel Fortune: The Lives and Loves of Italian Renaissance Women Poets*. New York: Fordham University Press, 2002

Jerrold, Maud F. *Vittoria Colonna: With Some Account of Her Friends and Her Times*. London: J.M. Dent & Co., 1906

Nicholson, Elizabeth S.G., ed. *Italian Women Artists from Renaissance to Baroque*. Milan: Skira Editore S.p.A., 2007

Panizza, Letizia and Sharon Wood, eds. *A History of Women's Writing in Italy*. Cambridge: Cambridge University Press, 2000

Robin, Diana. *Publishing Women: Salons, the Presses, and the Counter-Reformation in Sixteenth-Century Italy*. Chicago: The University of Chicago Press, 2007

Robin, Diana; Anne R. Larsen and Carole Levin, eds. *Encyclopedia of Women in the Renaissance*. Santa Barbara, California: ABC-CLIO, Inc., 2007

Stone, Irving and Jean Stone, eds. *I, Michelangelo, Sculptor: An Autobiography through Letters*. Garden City, NY: Doubleday & Company, Inc., 1962

Zimmermann, T.C. Price. *Paolo Giovio: The Historian and the Crisis of Sixteenth-Century Italy*. Princeton: Princeton University Press, 1995

ABOUT THE AUTHOR

Linda Cardillo is an award-winning author who writes about the old country and the new, the tangle and embrace of family, and finding courage in the midst of loss. Hailed by *Publishers Weekly* as a "Fresh Face," Linda has built a loyal following with her works of fiction—the novels *Dancing on Sunday Afternoons* (2007, 2016), *Across the Table* (2010), *The Boat House Café* (2014), *The Uneven Road* (2016), and *Island Legacy* (2017), as well as novellas in the anthologies *The Valentine Gift* and *A Mother's Heart* and the illustrated children's book *The Smallest Christmas Tree*.

Visit Linda's website at http://lindacardillo.com/; follow her on Facebook at Linda Cardillo, Author; or write to her at linda@lindacardillo.com.

CPSIA information can be obtained
at www.ICGtesting.com
Printed in the USA
JSHW020358051019
1822JS00002B/11